Early American
Detective Stories

Early American Detective Stories

An Anthology

Edited by LeRoy Lad Panek *and*
Mary M. Bendel-Simso

McFarland & Company, Inc., Publishers
Jefferson, North Carolina

ALSO BY LEROY LAD PANEK

Before Sherlock Holmes: How Magazines and Newspapers Invented the Detective Story (2011)

The Origins of the American Detective Story (2006)

Reading Early Hammett: A Critical Study of the Fiction Prior to The Maltese Falcon (2004)

The American Police Novel: A History (2003)

The present work is a reprint of the library bound edition of Early American Detective Stories: An Anthology, *first published in 2008 by McFarland.*

LIBRARY OF CONGRESS CATALOGUING-IN-PUBLICATION DATA

Early american detective stories : an anthology / edited by
LeRoy Lad Panek and Mary M. Bendel-Simso.
      p.   cm.
      Includes bibliographical references and index.

      ISBN 978-0-7864-9560-3 (softcover : acid free paper) ∞
      ISBN 978-1-4766-1017-7 (ebook)

      1. Detective and mystery stories, American.   2. American
fiction—19th century.   I. Panek, LeRoy.   II. Bendel-Simso,
Mary M., 1965–
PS648.D4E25 2014
813'.08720804—dc22   2008001849

BRITISH LIBRARY CATALOGUING DATA ARE AVAILABLE

Cover image © iStock/Thinkstock

Manufactured in the United States of America

McFarland & Company, Inc., Publishers
   Box 611, Jefferson, North Carolina 28640
      www.mcfarlandpub.com

For Rick and Kay Bendel,
partners in crime for over 50 years

Contents

Preface

Joseph M. Stoddart and S.S. McClure probably thought the Sherlock Holmes stories made pretty good reading when they bought the rights to publish *The Sign of the Four* and then the stories that began with "A Scandal in Bohemia" in the United States. But those Yankee businessmen didn't shell out cold, hard cash just because they liked the stories. They bought the rights to Arthur Conan Doyle's creations because they knew that detective stories were hot stuff back home. McClure, in fact, had been buying and syndicating them well before he came across Holmes and Watson. Practically ever since Edgar Allan Poe created the detective story in the early 1840s, in fact, the country had been awash in detective fiction.

This fact has not worked its way into the standard view of the history of detective fiction. Most historians, critics, and readers have accepted Howard Haycraft's notion that after Poe created the detective story in Philadelphia in the early 1840s the form fled to France and Great Britain, and that "it cannot be pretended that the American detective story revealed anything like the quantity of its English counterparts in the years up to the first world conflagration." Except for dime novels—avid collectors and cataloguers have ensured the place of the colorful and fanciful adventures of detectives like Cap Collier and the Sleuths, young and old, in the history of the genre. Of course after Poe those other countries did produce the big three second-generation founders of the form—Charles Dickens, Wilkie Collins, and Émile Gaboriau. And given the limits of then available bibliographic resources, it used to look like—other than Anna Katharine Green and a few others—Americans had other things to do than read detective stories. Up until now. Up until now nobody has looked much at magazine fiction and, more importantly, newspaper fiction has been totally ignored. And that's precisely where most detective stories were published in America from Poe all the way through to Conan Doyle's arrival in the New World—the Sherlock Holmes stories, remember, also first appeared in newspapers in this country. And by newspapers we do not only mean family story papers like the *New York Ledger* or *The Fireside Companion*. While they certainly played a role in nurturing the detective story in America, from major cities to one-horse burgs in the middle of nowhere, from the mid–1800s into the beginning of the next century, most Americans read their detective stories in papers like *The New York Sun*, or *The New Orleans Picayune*, or *The Morning Oregonian*, or *The Hagerstown* [MD] *Mail*, or *The Daily Sanduskian*, or *The Allen County* [OH] *Democrat*, or *The Decatur* [IL] *Daily Republican*, or *The Bangor* [ME] *Whig and Courier*.

While there may be veins of undiscovered detective fiction in British and French magazines and newspapers of the period, in the pages that follow we offer readers a miniscule sample of the hundreds of detective stories published in those media in the United States. With two notable exceptions (the Freeman and Chamberlin and the Matthews stories in the final section) we have included only stories published before 1891, before the Sherlock Holmes stories appeared in America. Making these texts available has not been without its own set of challenges—beyond finding them in the first place. One of these has been the condition of some of the original texts—the print in newspapers more than a hundred years old is not always as legible as we could have wished and we have very, very occasionally had to make educated guesses about words or clusters of words. These are marked in the following stories. Additionally, texts from small town, daily newspapers which were originally proofread (if at all) on the fly, often present spelling, punctuation, and grammatical anomalies. We have modernized spelling and punctuation, but have not altered grammar to make it conform to contemporary usage—then or now. And when it comes to authenticity, difficulties abound. Plagiarism during the nineteenth century was epidemic, and because of their popularity detective stories were particularly susceptible to piracy. The same stories pop up in newspapers in places from Maryland to California, usually without the name of an author or acknowledgement that anyone holds a copyright— because for much of the nineteenth century American publishers viewed copyright with cavalier abandon. Indeed, sometimes the same story will appear under different titles—for example, *The Cambridge Jeffersonian's* "How to Prove an Alibi" in 1871 was "An Evening with a Detective" in *Ballou's Monthly* the year before. As will be seen below with the New York

Detective stories, sometimes different authors' names are attached to the exploits of the same character. And some stories exist in versions of plus or minus a thousand or more words. While a very small number of stories we have found do acknowledge the names of authors and sources (e.g. *Chambers' Edinburgh Journal*, *New York Sun*, *Flag of Our Union* etc.) most do not. We, nevertheless, have attempted to base the following pieces on the best and fullest originals available.

We have organized the following fiction in categories that seemed natural, convenient, informative, and representative. Because of space limitations, however, we have not been able to include any examples of serial novels which began to become the norm in detective fiction in newspapers in the later decades of the century. Although we have been able to present here only a very, very small fraction of the detective fiction that appeared in this country in the nineteenth century, we hope that it will provide readers with interesting, occasionally pleasurable, and sometimes even amusing reading—as well as new insights into the history of the detective story, a history that began long before Dr. John Watson returned from the wars and began his search for a roommate.

This collection would not have been possible without the help and support of our families, colleagues, and friends. Among those, the librarians at McDaniel College's Hoover Library—Sally Jones, Lisa Russell, and Rhonda Stricklett—deserve our special thanks. Paul Bendel-Simso and Christine Mathews, as always, have served above and beyond the call, and, in their own inimitable ways, so have Flannery and Isabel.

MMB • LLP • Westminster, Maryland

Introduction

Which came first, detectives or detective stories? While today the answer seems pretty obvious, in the nineteenth century the answer depended on where one lived. Quite literally millions of Americans who read about detectives in books, magazines, and newspapers had never seen a detective—indeed, it wasn't just detectives; most people who read about them lived in communities in which there were hardly police and police were hardly needed.

Police and Detectives

As a social institution, the police were a nineteenth-century innovation—an innovation made necessary by the rise of great cities, the explosion and disproportionate distribution of wealth, a new emphasis on the observation and application of the rule of law, and many, many other complex social, economic, technological, and even psychological factors. The first movement toward modern policing began in France, where in 1812 Eugène François Vidocq talked his way into founding the *Brigade de Sureté* (Brigade of Security). Based on the secret police model inherited from Napoleonic times and predicated on knowing what had or was going to happen among people inclined to do bad things, Vidocq aimed to provide public safety through undercover work, and by 1820 his force of thirty detectives—most of whom, like Vidocq, were reformed felons— claimed to have decreased the crime rate in Paris by forty percent. The next step in French policing came in 1829 when uniformed policemen, *sergents de ville*, began to patrol Paris and other French cities. In the same year Sir Robert Peel's Metropolitan Police took to the streets of the English capital. Unlike the French model, however, the British force was originally to be solely a force of preventive police—their uniformed presence serving as a warning to would-be lawbreakers. Twenty years later, in 1849, the Metropolitan Police had an authorized strength of 5,493 men, but by that time not all of them were uniformed patrolmen. In 1842 (the year after Poe wrote "Murders in the Rue Morgue") Parliament, acknowledging that preventive police could not altogether prevent crime, authorized the formation of a detective department in London. While they were permitted to operate in civilian clothes, department rules made it clear that plainclothes officers were to distinctly identify themselves as police when investigating. In less than a decade the new detectives had inspired enough public confidence that Charles Dickens took up their cause by chronicling the exploits of detectives in a series of articles about detectives, culminating in "On Duty with Inspector Field" (*Household Words* June 14, 1851).

Coming to the realization that police were necessary adjuncts to modern urban society, around the middle of the nineteenth century politicians, public-minded individuals, and newspaper publishers in cities across the United States began to think and talk about whether and how to create police forces to replace the essentially medieval institutions of the watch and elected constables that were the only guarantors of public safety in the first half of the century. Part of this public discussion, one that is reflected in fiction as well, centered on a debate over the respective merits of the British and French systems of policing. In the popular view, established both by Dickens and by the police "Recollections" pieces from *Chambers' Edinburgh Journal*, the British detective demonstrated independence, humaneness, and intellectual flexibility. On the other hand, in spite of their penchant for adventure, French detectives, until they were intellectualized by Gaboriau in the 1870s, represented sinister central authority, particularized in the fate of Edmond Dantes in *The Count of Monte Cristo* (1845) and articulated in *Putnam's Monthly's* April 1853 article, "How they Manage in Europe":

> Of course, it is necessary for the European powers in maintaining this watchful guardianship over every interest and motion of society, to keep in operation a most comprehensive, rigid, and unrelenting system of police, whose agents are to be found in every city and village, and almost in every house. They are more plentiful than the frogs which came upon Egypt, as one of the plagues, and like the frogs, too, they hop and croak through the very kneading-troughs. But they are unlike in one respect,

which gives them an immeasurable superiority, as a means of malignant annoyance and abuse; in that they are the most thoroughly organized body in the world,—more compact than the church, and more controllable than the army.

While fictional British and French detectives continued to vie for the attention of the reading public from the 1850s to the end of the century, in the real world neither model came out on top. Instead American politicians cobbled together systems that fit their own (as often opposed to their communities') particular reality. At mid-century, then, these "new" police forces began to pop up in major cities across the country—in Boston in 1838, in New York in 1845, in San Francisco in 1849, in Baltimore in 1853, in Philadelphia in 1854, and in Chicago in 1855. Although none of these departments had official detective divisions at their founding, it is clear that most of them soon had *de facto* detectives—indeed, Allan Pinkerton was a paid detective in Chicago as early as 1850, and the New York department from its inception used undercover officers as "shadows." Boston, however, was the first municipality to create an official detective branch— founded in 1846. It took Chicago until 1861 and New York until 1882 before detectives became recognized, organized, and sanctioned parts of those cities' police forces.

While all of this activity meant that by the time of the Civil War major American cities had abandoned the creaky and unworkable old watch-and-constable system of protecting the public and adopted a new police model, the millennium had scarcely arrived. In most jurisdictions squabbles almost immediately began over who controlled the police. At one time New York City had two police forces, one appointed by the city and one by the New York State legislature. In Denver President Cleveland had to send federal troops to keep a dispute between the governor and the city's police board from erupting in violence. Political spoils almost universally determined who was hired and promoted in American police departments; they also sometimes determined who was arrested and who was not. By the end of the century graft infected most big city police departments in the nation—highlighted by the 1892 Lexow Investigation in New York City which revealed deep-seated, institutionalized police corruption. And, of course, there was violence and officially subverted justice. The best known spokesman for both of these was the New York Police Department's Alexander "Clubber" Williams, renowned for his adage that "There is more law at the end of the policeman's nightstick than in all the decisions of the Supreme Court."

Private Eyes

While cities across the country struggled with establishing and organizing police departments and detective bureaus in those departments, a parallel growth of private detectives began. Private detectives were another French innovation: when political pressure forced Vidocq out of public office he established his own *Bureau de Renseignements* (Office of Intelligence) and offered his services to everyone—for a fee. Possessing the same skills as a detective—and the same instinct for self-promotion—in 1852 Allan Pinkerton left the employ of the city of Chicago and, with lawyer Edward L. Rucker, opened Pinkerton's Detective Agency. After Pinkerton set up shop, others across the country followed—apparently in droves. They supplied services that understaffed, overwhelmed, and sometimes indifferent or corrupt police departments could not offer—services from background checks on employees to divorce investigations; from body guarding to bounty hunting. Indeed, there was scarcely a high profile trial during the last quarter of the century in which private detectives did not play a role. And all too often that role was one which involved the violation of individuals' rights and broke the law: intimidation, brutality, and even kidnapping were included in the repertoire of too many nineteenth-century private detectives. This was the reality which led state legislatures across the United States at the beginning of the twentieth century to pass laws requiring private detectives to be licensed.

Law

Just as Western societies struggled with how to ensure public safety in their crowded urban environments, Anglo-American courts also faced the problem of reconciling a thousand-year-old system of law with the advances nineteenth-century science and technology were producing. A significant part of the legal history of the century turned on the sometimes lengthy process of courts gradually accepting the proofs offered by new tools provided by science and technology—photographs, fingerprints, ballistics, blood typing etc.—as legitimate evidence. In the nineteenth century Anglo-American jurisprudence for the first time witnessed the birth and burgeoning of expert testimony and expert witnesses. The first overt sign of this was Alfred Swaine Taylor's efforts to categorize and explain contemporary medical and the legal aspects of physical evidence in his *Medical Jurisprudence* (1843). This became a standard reference work, beginning a new era of scientific examination of evidence, establishing new standards for scientific testimony, and also inspiring a robust medical jurisprudence movement in Britain and America. And those newly accredited scientific experts played important roles in two nineteenth-century landmark trials, one British and one American. The first was the trial of Daniel McNaughton in 1843. McNaughton was tried for the murder of Edward Drummond whom he shot by mistake—he was aiming for Prime Minister Robert Peel and killed his secretary, Drummond, instead. Medical witnesses summoned by both the defense and the prosecution all agreed that McNaughton was insane, and the jury returned a special verdict that sent McNaughton not to the gallows but to an asylum. This gave rise in both British and American jurisprudence to the adoption of what came to be called the McNaughton Rule, viz. the principle that a person is legally sane unless it can be proved that "at the time of committing the act, the accused was laboring under such a defect of reason, from disease of the mind, as not to know the nature and quality of the act he was doing or, if he did know it, that he did not know what he was doing was wrong." It acknowledged, in other words, both the validity of scientific testimony and that criminal acts cannot always be simply linked to right and wrong, good and evil. The second trial was the 1850 trial of Harvard Professor Dr. John Webster. The State accused Webster of murdering Dr. George Parkman, but could not produce proof in the form of identifiable parts of Parkham's body—holding that Webster had cut up and disposed of most of Parkman's remains. In its guilty verdict, however, Webster's trial produced one of the first murder convictions in America based solely on medical evidence and established the standard of "beyond a reasonable doubt" for conviction. In both cases, moreover, public interest went far beyond those who could crowd into Old Bailey or the Cambridge courthouse. The Webster trial, especially, was followed with interest by newspapers, and not just the big city papers, but dailies like *The Zanesville* [OH] *Courier* and *The Sheboygan* [WI] *Mercury*. Everybody, it seems, was interested in crime.

In the middle of the nineteenth century, Americans could find plenty of news and opinion about crime and detectives. But they could also find an awful lot about detectives in books, magazines, story papers, and newspapers. And, increasingly, the majority of it was fiction.

Books

Significant books supposedly about real detectives began in America with a British import, *The Recollections of a Policeman* (1852) by "Thomas Waters" (the pseudonym of William Russell). *Recollections* comprised, in part, fabricated pieces that Russell had churned out for *Chambers' Edinburgh Journal*, some of which were reprinted in American newspapers and magazines before the publication of *Recollections*: for instance, "Guilty or Not Guilty" from *Chambers'* appeared in *The Milwaukee Sentinel and Gazette* (November 1, 1849), and "Mary Kingsford: From the Recollections of a Police Officer" came out in *The International Magazine* (June 1, 1851). Far from having been a detective, Russell was a prolific commercial writer who possessed the literary ethics of a felon. Thus, as Nadya Aisenberg notes in *London Crimes*, his *Recollections of a Policeman* included not only Russell's pieces from *Chambers,'* but also three stories lifted directly from Dickens' articles on London's new detective force in *Household Words* ("Modern Science of Thief Taking," "The Detective Police Party," and "Three 'Detective' Anecdotes") and passed off as being part of "Tom Waters'" memoirs. Pirated or not, *Recollections* quickly became popular in the United States and went through a number of editions published in both New York and Boston, including printings in 1852, 1853, 1856, 1859, 1860, 1880, and 1887. In addition to *Recollections*, Russell wrote a succession of other pseudo-autobiographical detective works, including *Recollections of a Detective Police-Officer* (1856), *Recollections of a Sheriff's Officer* (1860), *Experiences of a French Detective Officer* (1861), *Experiences of a Real Detective* (1862), and *Autobiography of a London Detective* (1864). His name has also been attached to the first American series of detective "recollections," published as *Strange Stories of a Detective, or the Curiosities of Crime* (1863), by "A Retired Member of the Detective Police." Witnessed by "The Torn Glove" included below, however, *Strange Stories* is one hundred percent American and even attaches a brief survey of the history of policing in New York to what is actually a collection of short detective stories.

Following *Strange Stories* by two years came "Dr. John Williams'" pseudo-memoir titled *Leaves from the Note-book of a New York Detective* (1865). In spite of its title, however, *Leaves* is an assortment of stories about Detective James Brampton originally printed in *Ballou's Dollar Magazine* and an assortment of newspapers, filled out to book length with a handful of admittedly non-detective stories and then hastily thrown together with only the thinnest pretense of being in any way connected. It is note-worthy that the book's publisher, Dick and Fitzgerald of New York, was an avowed purveyor of "cheap publications," and that they not only published *Leaves from the Note-Book*, but also the aforementioned *Strange Stories* and many of William Russell's "Waters" books.

The pseudo-biographies were followed by the series of works more connected to reality, written by real detectives. First there was Edward H. Savage's *A Chronological History of the Boston Watch and Police, from 1631 to 1865 together with the Recollections of a Boston Police Officer, or, Boston by Daylight and Gaslight, from the Diary of an Officer Fifteen Years in the Service* (1865). Then, in 1871, came George McWatters' widely advertised *Knots Untied: Ways and By-Ways in the Hidden Life of American Detectives*. Hardly the exposé suggested by the title, the book begins with accounts of McWatter's emigration to the United States and gravitation to police work followed by short narratives of encounters with con men and other denizens of the underworld. Finally, the most well-known detective of the age turned to publishing as another facet of his personal and corporate self-promotion. Anticipated by two self-congratulatory pieces connected to the Civil War (*Allan Pinkerton's Unpublished Story of the First Attempt on the Life of Abraham Lincoln* [1866] and *History and Evidence of the Passage of Abraham Lincoln from Harrisburg, Pa., to Washington, D.C., on the Twenty-second and Twenty-third of February, 1861* [1868]), Allan Pinkerton attached his name to ghostwritten books that chronicled the adventures, successes, and services to clients of the great man and his operatives. Beginning with *The Expressman and the Detective* in 1874, a new book recounting the exploits of the Pinkertons appeared every year until Pinkerton's death in 1884.

Like the authors of notebook fiction, Pinkerton claimed to provide firsthand insight into the experience of real detectives. That is as may be. But, in varying degrees, each of the authors answered the siren call of storytelling, with *Recollections of a Policeman*, *Strange Stories* and *Leaves from a Note-book* pretty transparently inhabiting the fiction end of the spectrum, and Savage, McWatters, and the corporate Pinkerton publicity apparatus residing closer to the non-fiction end. Stories from the so-called notebook writers, however, didn't remain long between hard covers but many of them quickly appeared as separate stories in magazines and newspapers across the country, thereby losing their biographical trappings and entering more fully into the world of fiction.

Shortly after the Civil War a smattering of genuine book-length fiction about detectives was published in the U.S. In 1866 Metta Fuller Victor wrote *The Dead Letter* for the dime novel house of Beadle & Company. Under the pseudonym of Lawrence Lynch, Emma Murdoch Van Deventer wrote a number of detective novels beginning with *Shadowed by Three* in 1879. And Anna Katherine Green came to be celebrated as the nation's foremost (if not its first) mystery writer after the success of *The Leavenworth Case* in 1878. But other than the stir caused by Green's occasional book, hardback detective fiction was scarcely a hot item. Detective fiction did better as short stories and short stories did better in magazines.

Magazines

The first detective stories, anywhere, appeared in American magazines: "Murders in the Rue Morgue" came out in *Graham's Magazine* in 1841, *Snowden's Ladies' Companion* ran "The Mystery of Marie Roget" in 1842, and "The Purloined Letter" came out in *The Gift: A Christmas, New Year and Birthday Present* in 1844. Edited by Poe, *Graham's* was perhaps a bit snootier and less directed to female readers than the others; however, they all viewed themselves as "literary magazines" and featured poetry, essays, and fiction—with *Snowden's* and *Godey's Ladies' Book* (in which Poe published his amateur detective story "Thou Art the Man") adding drawings, music, and even fashion and needlework patterns. As Poe found out, however, literary magazines didn't pay writers or editors very much and for most of them it was a struggle just to stay in business. It was another decade before most permanent and substantial American literary magazines came on the scene. Their aims were the same as all of their struggling high-minded predecessors: to bring literature and the arts to cultivated readers. But even though they didn't pay their writers very well either, they did have more money and prestige: they had money because *Harper's, Putnam's* and *Scribner's* magazines, all founded at mid-century, belonged to established book publishers, and they had prestige because of connections with famous and influential people—Ralph Waldo Emerson, Henry Wadsworth Longfellow, James Russell Lowell, and Oliver Wendell Holmes were the founders of *Atlantic Monthly*.

The new mid-century magazines also aimed to provide a medium in which their readers could experience both accomplished American writers and a broader literary culture, an international culture—which largely meant British culture. We can see this in the following mission statement from 1850:

> The INTERNATIONAL WEEKLY MISCELLANY will be a result of efforts to satisfy a plain necessity of the times. It will combine the excellencies of all contemporary periodicals, with features that will be peculiar to itself.
>
> 1. A leading object will be to present the public, with the utmost rapidity and at the cheapest possible rate the best of those works in Popular Literature which are appearing abroad in serials, or in separate chapters.

There were American writers represented in the new magazines to be sure, but the pages of *Harper's New Monthly Magazine*, and *Putnam's*, and *Scribner's* were dotted with pieces by or about William Makepeace Thackeray, Wilkie Collins, Bulwer Lytton, and William Harrison Ainsworth. And among those works appearing from abroad were pieces about the Old World's fascination with the nature and character of the detective police and the detective. Thus we can find articles like "Vidocq in London" in *The Living Age* (August 9, 1845), stories cribbed from *Chambers' Edinburgh Journal* ("Villainy Outwitted" [November 1850] and "Mary Kingsford" [July 1851] both in *Harper's*), and articles borrowed from *Household Words* ("Old Brank, The Forger" in *The International Magazine* November, 1850 and "The Metropolitan Protectives," in *The Living Age* July 12, 1851).

Household Words, of course, was Dickens' magazine, and in the 1850s, when the American public thought about big names in British literature, the first to come to mind was that of Charles Dickens. He is mentioned everywhere in the new literary magazines of the 1850s. Significantly for the development of the form, a detective plays a significant role in Dickens' big book of the decade, and in April 1852 *Harper's* ran the first installment of that big book, *Bleak House*. After *Bleak House*, *Harper's*, and, to a lesser extent, other literary magazines, occasionally ran detective stories. Anticipated by "The Costly Kiss" (April 1859), included below, in the early 1860s *Harper's* ran pieces like "My Mysterious Foe" by Mary Mapes Dodge (April 1863), C. Davis' "The Pigot Murder" (December 1864), and Harriet E. Prescott [Spofford's] "Mr. Furbush" (April 1865). Indeed, detective stories sporadically appeared in *Harper's* and a few other mainline literary magazines until the big illustrated magazine boom of the 1880s which gave the English speaking world *The Strand Magazine* as well as *McClure's* and *Collier's*. But literary magazines were hardly the principal outlet for detective fiction in the United States in the middle of the nineteenth century. A lot more readers could find a lot more detective stories for a lot less in family story papers.

Family Story Papers

Begun in the 1830s with the inexpensive weeklies *Brother Jonathan*, *New World*, and *Notion*, family story papers were tabloid-sized publications, ranging from four to eight pages, containing miscellaneous fiction and verse aimed at the whole family. The first of these was published in Boston, and in its early days the *Flag of Our Union*, founded in 1846, was notable for publishing Poe's poem "For Annie." In 1851 the center of family story publishing shifted from Boston to New York when Barnumesque Robert Bonner took over *The New York Ledger* and even more emphatically when George Munro became editor of *The Fireside Companion* in 1867. Neither of these publishers had scruples about piracy and—as had been standard family story practice—ran British works with apparent abandon in their papers. In the detective realm, for instance, Munro ran Collins' *The Woman in White* as a serial, offered Mrs. Henry Wood's *East Lynne* as a premium for new subscribers, and borrowed the hero from Tom Tyler's play, *The Ticket of Leave Man* by running a piece titled "Quick Work. The Diary of Hardshaw the Detective" in *The Fireside Companion*. Counterbalancing this kind of thievery, both Bonner and Munro were willing to pay big-name writers top dollar for their work: thus Bonner paid Boston Brahman Edward Everett $10,000 for a year's worth of columns. What set both Bonner and Munro apart not only from other family story papers but from all other contemporary publishers was the immense amount of money and ingenuity they expended in advertising. Bonner routinely took full-page advertisements in New York daily papers trumpeting coming attractions in *The Ledger* and from the late 1850s well into the 1870s he supplied daily newspapers across the country with teasers—the first installment of serial novels—with the notice that the succeeding chapters could be found only in *The Ledger*. In the 1880s Munro claimed he spent $200,000 a year on advertising—and the notoriety caused by Anthony Comstock's arrest of Munro in 1872 for publishing stories (including detective stories) that incited youths to vice and crime ironically didn't hurt either. The result of all the money and publicity was that by the late 1870s both *The New York*

Ledger and *The Fireside Companion* could claim over a half million readers apiece.

Of the family story paper editors Maturin M. Ballou manifested the earliest and most committed interest in detective stories. Thus in 1859 he published both "My Mysterious Neighbors" by Mrs. M.A. Denison and "The Robbery of Plate" by Harry Harewood in the *Flag of Our Union*, and in the mid–1860s he began running M'Cabe's stories about French detective Laromie in the *Flag*. He carried his interest in detectives over to his magazine, *Ballou's Dollar Magazine*, where, beginning in 1862, Ballou began running the Brampton New York Detective stories. Perhaps because of this, Munro began publishing detective stories in his family story paper, *The Fireside Companion*, beginning with "My First Case" ("I had not been in the detective service long when a singular case came to my notice") by Frank Dumont in June of 1868: two years later Munro moved from the short story to the detective serial with Kenward Philips' *The Bowery Detective* (1870). After 1870 *The Fireside Companion* made detective stories one of the features of the paper, and the flamboyant Munro even went to the extreme of attaching popular actor and theatrical impresario Tony Pastor's name to detective serials in the early 1870s. Indeed in that decade, detective stories became standard features of most family story papers and appeared with regularity even in publications which targeted female readers like *New York Weekly Story Teller. A Story Paper Devoted to Young Female Readers*.

Detective stories moved out of the family story paper into the world of the dime novel beginning in 1872 when Munro published the first Old Sleuth story in *The Fireside Companion*. Perhaps inspired by his brother Norman's creation of a dime novel library (essentially a weekly and then semi-monthly magazine containing a novella about a continuing hero) about detective Cap Collier in 1883, Munro created The Old Sleuth Library in 1885, and by the 1890s all of the dime novel houses, Beadle and Adams, Smith and Street, and Tousey, had their own detective (or dime novel) libraries.

Newspapers

It is hardly surprising that so much detective fiction flourished in mid-nineteenth-century newspapers: changes in publishing, copyright law, and postal regulations, as well as writers and eager readers, all worked together to make it happen. That, and in the real world detectives were sometimes in news stories on front pages.

During the mid-nineteenth century daily and weekly newspapers became remarkably accessible. By mid-century, railroads and steamboats allowed the timely distribution of newspapers across the country, and this had more than a bit to do with the meteoric rise in the number of papers in the U.S. In 1850, there were 254 daily papers and 1,902 weekly papers in the country; by 1899 that number had risen to 2,226 daily papers and nearly 12,979 weekly papers and another 3,500 published less frequently — which means that a whopping 18,793 individual newspapers were published in America at the turn of the century. Readers in large cities could choose from a long list of papers, with New York boasting fifty-some dailies. And every small community, especially in the North, had its own paper or even competing papers. Thus there were titles like the *McKean County* [PA] *Miner*, the *Bucks County* [PA] *Gazette*, the *Marion* [OH] *Weekly Star*, the *Hamilton* [OH] *Daily Democrat*, the *Elyria* [OH] *Republican*, the *Coshocton* [OH] *Daily Times*, the *Badger Workman* [Neillsville WI], the *Monroe* [WI] *Semi Weekly Times*, the *Stevens Point* [WI] *Daily Journal*, the *Freeborn County* [MN] *Standard*, and the *Cedar Rapids* [IA] *Republican*.

And they were cheap. For one thing, the postage on these papers was minimal. Since the Revolution, politicians and the American elite had promoted newspapers as ways to spread information and educate the masses, and they had supported their publication through generous subsidies of the mails. In 1845 an act of Congress provided for the free distribution of 4-page newspapers (or those less than 1900 square inches) within 30 miles of their printing; in 1851 weekly papers of less than 3 ounces could be delivered free within the county in which they were printed. For greater distances, Congress set up the delivery charge at less than a cent a copy; for delivery of smaller papers (those of 300 square inches or less) the cost was set at one quarter the rate. Subscribers were required to pre-pay for this delivery; however, as few did, those who complied were offered a fifty percent discount. The biggest boon to newspaper subscribers came in 1874, when Congress reduced the postal rate on papers published weekly or oftener and assessed this charge to the publishers rather than to the subscribers. Thus, by 1880, 2,067,848,209 copies of newspapers were printed annually in the U.S. and of these, 852,180,792 were delivered by the post office. So the residents of Winnebego County, Wisconsin could receive any of the four Oshkosh papers free of delivery charge and the delivery charge for the over 27 other Wisconsin papers would be assessed to the publisher. And the papers themselves were also affordable for everyone. After the Civil War, prices per copy ranged from 1 to 5 cents per copy, although penny papers remained common until after World War I, and in 1880 the annual subscription rates were from $6 to $10 a year. While *The New York Times* sold for 4 cents per copy (this went down to 3 cents and then was further reduced to 1 cent in 1898), papers in rural areas were even cheaper; most weekly papers sold for less than $2.00 per year.

But these papers weren't only about news. Indeed, most mid-nineteenth century papers saw that their obligation to the public included more than reporting on politics: thus the *Maryville* [OH] *Tribune* identified itself as "A Family Newspaper: Devoted to Politics, Literature, the Arts, Sciences, and Interests of Union County." In 1875 the *Chicago Daily News* promised a daily short story of "intense dramatic interest," but also one that was "instructive as well as entertaining." More and more, mid-century readers looked to their newspapers for entertainment, and they found poems, fiction, memoirs, speeches, correspondence, sermons—and advertisements, lots of advertisements. Fiction was usually located in the upper-left-hand corner of the page (in the 1860s often page one) just after a poem, which was often preceded by the large-print heading "Select Poetry." Even before the Civil War, across America those literary pieces in the papers regularly began to be stories that editors, writers, and readers consciously identified as "detective stories." So detective stories and poems went together, as they did in the November 11, 1873 edition of the *Ohio Democrat* with the poem "The Rising of William Allen" by Thomas Hubbard preceding "The Murder of the Miser," or on July 26, 1877, in the *Allen County* [OH] *Democrat*, where the poem "In the Conservatory" by Karl Marble precedes "The Girl Detective." And the impulse to adopt detective fiction as a staple of the newspaper business as well as the stories themselves eventually spread across the nation like a prairie fire.

The growth of detective stories in newspapers began slowly in the late 1850s with the publication of imported stories like "Vidocq's Last Exploit" in *Western Fireside* in 1857, pirated pieces from *Chambers' Edinburgh Journal* about Britain's new detective police, and material filched from Dickens (thus the two "detective" anecdotes published in the *Watertown* [WI]

Chronicle in April of 1851 came from Dickens' "Three Detective Anecdotes" published in *Household Words* in 1850): to the dismay of Europeans, Americans did not consistently observe international copyright until the Chace Act of 1891. But by the early years of the Civil War there began what could be described as a detective story boom in the nation's magazines and newspapers. Imported fiction couldn't meet the demand and detective pieces by American writers quickly took over from the trickle of imports. From coast to coast stories about detectives in New York, Chicago, Sacramento, Boston, and dozens of no-name burgs joined the imported stories about sleuths in London and Paris.

Some of them, however, were not quite as original as they pretended to be. Since few papers other than those in big cities could generate enough new material to fill a daily or even weekly issue, many editors relied on the "scissors and the paste pot" method for much of their copy: they snipped it from whatever papers or magazines they could find. Detective stories were particularly susceptible: thus, for example, the gender-bender detective sketch that ran as "A Detective's Ruse" in the *Chester* [PA] *Daily Times* on August 8, 1880, popped up as "A Good Detective Story" in the *Manitoba* [Canada] *Daily Free Press* on August 28 and as "A Detective Story" in the *Indiana Weekly Messenger* and the *Racine* [WI] *Daily Argus* on September 15 and October 11, respectively, and as "Trapped" in the *Palo Alto* [Emmetsburg, IA] *Reporter* on January 22, 1881. Rather than piracy or theft, however, editors saw the practice as "exchange." Because of their often dubious provenance, moreover, author's names were rarely attached to most newspaper detective stories or editors supplied generic bylines like "a New York Detective" to their stories.

Fiction recurring in paper after paper with different titles and no identified author, however, wasn't always the product of brigandage. After the mid-century, publishers' and editors' and readers' appetites for fiction—particularly detective fiction—were fed by several significant innovations in the publishing industry: patent insides, ready-print type, and syndication. In 1861, after his printer enlisted to serve in the Civil War, Ansel Nash Kellogg lacked the manpower to continue printing his *Baraboo* [WI] *Republic*. So he asked the publishers of the *Wisconsin State Journal* to print war news on sheets he could insert in his paper, and later he requested that they print news on the insides (e.g. pages 2 and 3) of folio sheets and send them to him so that he could typeset local news on pages 1 and 4. A decade later Kellogg improved a process invented in 1871 by B.B. Blackwell by which type could be cheaply set on celluloid plates, locked and transported. Kellogg sold these preset celluloid plates and even offered specialist services to local papers—including providing serial fiction: "Parties can order a certain number of columns of Story Department, or Miscellany, or Agricultural, or Children's Reading, as may suit their own tastes.... Special care will be taken, by a complete record, to avoid sending any matter which would interfere with, or duplicate, that furnished to other parties in the vicinity."

Alongside these technical innovations literary syndicates were developed and also made their mark. Syndicating fiction had been successful in France since the 1830s. The *feuilleton*—a part of a newspaper reserved for short literary compositions or installments of longer works that are sent to the provinces for printing—had originated in 1836, and with the *roman policier* played a role in the history of detective fiction. In the 1870s, British publisher William Frederic Tillotson brought syndication to the English-speaking public when he founded Tillotson's Newspaper Fiction Bureau, which sold serial novels and stories first to British newspapers—and then to newspapers throughout the United Kingdom, Europe, and America. This innovation further affected the publication of fiction in newspapers in America in 1883 when Irving Bacheller began the first successful American newspaper syndicate furnishing features for daily newspapers and their Sunday supplements. Kellogg soon made an alliance with Bacheller, and thereby provided the material generated by the Bacheller syndicates to rural daily and weekly papers. While a great deal of research remains to be done to determine which of the myriad detective stories in American newspapers were connected to these innovations, it is clear that Kellogg, Bacheller, and then McClure all had an immense impact on what Americans read in the last quarter of the nineteenth century. And it also is clear that they made signal contributions to the history of the detective story. Among the achievements of the Bacheller syndicate was the contest which produced Mary E. Wilkins Freeman and Joseph Edgar Chamberlin's "The Long Arm," included below. And to McClure goes the credit for introducing the American public to Sherlock Holmes, but he had been interested in detective stories before he met Holmes, as witnessed by his syndication of Malcolm Bell's serial *The Strange Footprint*, featuring Private Inquiry Agent Joshua Padger in 1889, two years before he bought the rights to syndicate the stories that comprise *The Adventures of Sherlock Holmes*.

In the 1860s and 1870s the principal vehicle for newspaper detective fiction was the short, short story: very few pieces ran to more than four thousand words and the average length was between two and three thousand words. But *The Milwaukee Daily Sentinel* began experimenting with serials by publishing Dickens' *Bleak House* in the spring of 1852. Papers ran detective serials sporadically during the next two decades—*The Milwaukee Daily Sentinel*, for instance, ran *The Legend of the Fatal Ring* in 1860 and a number of papers ran as a serial a plagiarized version of Gaboriau's *L'Affaire Lerouge* titled *The Parisian Detective.* By the 1880s, however, a number of phenomena changed detective fiction in newspapers from the short story into the serial novel. The first of these was that detective novels began to be written—beginning in the U.S. with Metta Fuller Victor's *The Dead Letter* published by Beadle in 1864, with Collins' *The Moonstone* serialized in *Harper's Weekly* in 1868, with Munro's introduction of serial detective novels in *The Fireside Companion* in 1870 coupled with the emergence of dime novel "detective libraries," and finally with Anna Katharine Green's *The Leavenworth Case* in 1878. Corresponding with this was the development of Sunday supplements in metropolitan newspapers which blurred the line separating newspapers and magazines; newspaper magazine supplements contained literary miscellany and other features that made them almost indistinguishable from the weekly and monthly magazines. By the mid–1880s, then, competition between magazines, book publishers, and newspapers brought the serial detective novel to Sunday papers, serials like Metta Victor's *Who Owned the Jewels* (1870), Erskine Boyd's *Written in Blood* (1884), Joseph Hatton's *Needham's Failure* (1886), Fergus Hume's *Mystery of the Hansom Cab* (1888), B.L. Farjeon's *Richard Pardon's Peril* (1889), Malcolm Bell's *The Strange Footprint* (1889), Barclay North's *The Diamond Button* (1890), Hume's *The Piccadilly Puzzle* (1890), and Barclay North's *The Man with the Thumb* (1891). Here American publishers simply followed British and French examples of using serials and cliff-hanger endings to boost circulation. But contests were a means of attracting readers, too. When Tillotson, Bacheller, McClure, and other literary syndicates signed contracts with newspapers to provide fiction on a daily or weekly basis, they suddenly needed that fiction—and lots of it. Often, to supply it, syndicates ran contests offering prizes for the best story of a particular genre—including detective stories. A "Prize Story" appeared in Tillotson's *Bolton Weekly Journal* as early as 1878; and a writers' contest run by McClure received upwards of a 1,000 entries. These contests not only generated publicity and a prize-winning story, but also a pool of publishable fiction from the also-rans: thus "other stories submitted for the prize, if of sufficient merit, will be purchased at the regular rate." About a particularly important detective-story-writing contest run by Bacheller more will be said below. But there was another type of contest run for promotional purposes by a number of big city newspapers—the find-the-solution contest. Thus, from the early 1890s newspapers from the *Boston Globe* to *The Philadelphia Inquirer* ran contests offering readers prizes if they could guess, deduce, or otherwise figure out the solution to a detective serial before the paper ran the last installment. And both the popularity of the serial novel and the contests for readers brought a fundamental change to the genre—they changed the story about the detective back into the kind of detective story that Poe invented in 1841.

Fact or Fiction?

With the detective story, the history of the relationship between fact and fiction is quaint and curious. It started with Poe. There was, of course, his offhand use of standard nineteenth-century conventions of coy verisimilitude—things like pretending that the narrator knows the real name of Minister D— but can't reveal it. But in the second Dupin story Poe goes much further and indeed stepped seriously into genre-bending when he took what he believed to be the facts associated with the death of Mary Rogers as well as actual newspaper reports of her death and converted them into fiction as "The Mystery of Marie Roget." A decade later when the real detective story boom began in the U.S. the same thing happened, only the other way around. The books that led off that explosion were not facts dressed as fiction but fiction dressed as facts: *The Recollections of a Policeman* was not, in reality, comprised of the recollections of officer Thomas Waters but was made up of the imaginings of Grub Street writer William Russell or purloined from *Household Words*. And the same held true for a number of the other so-called notebook writers. From these beginnings, a double perspective became attached to detective fiction which lasted well into the 1890s when a few writers and publishers began to recognize the game potential that Poe intended when he invented the detective story and moved toward creating a new imaginary realm for the detective story to inhabit. At mid-century detective stories carried with them clear indications that they were fiction. Newspapers often placed them in what amounted to literary sections coupled with poetry and labeled as "Select Stories." Reviewers by the 1870s acknowledged the existence of the genre of the detective story. Furthermore, narrators frequently used the terms "tale" and "adventure" to describe what listeners and readers were about to experience. At the same time, writers turned to the traditional toolbox of superficial realism. Thus, as in the following, a number of detective stories began by citing dates in the past:

> Many of our readers will doubtless remember the mysterious murder committed in Grand Street, Williamsburg, in the year 1836 ["The Porcelain Button," *The Fox Lake* (WI) *Gazette*, May 12, 1859].

> The occurrence I was about to narrate, took place in the year 1849, when I had been in the work only about two years ["A Detective's Story," *Flag of Our Union*, June 1, 1867].

> Early in the spring of 1872 the boarders at Mrs. Frelinghuysen's house, on West Adams street, felt themselves constrained to discuss and decide a very delicate question ["The Stolen Laces," *The* (Warren, PA) *Ledger*. December 7, 1888].

But more than these small accoutrements, the credentials of the people who tell the stories suggest that they are fact and not fiction. The most frequent title of the era was "A Detective's Story": we have catalogued sixteen instances of different stories titled "A Detective's Story" from 1863 to 1887 appearing in papers as far flung as *The New Hampshire Sentinel, The Gettysburg* [PA] *Compiler*, and *The Iowa State Reporter* and six others from similar papers from the same period labeled "The Detective's Story." Generally told in the first person, the favored narrator in the mid-nineteenth century was the detective himself ("I had been some years connected with the Detective Bureau..." ["A Curious Stratagem," *Ballou's Dollar Magazine*, April 1859]; and "I had been eight years on the special detective force..." ["The Pigot Murder, *Harper's Monthly*, December 1864]), followed by the reporter: thus the stories "Blown Upon: or The Sagacious Reporter," in *Life* February 15, 1883 or "A Reporter's Romance" in *Harper's* in January 1879. Indeed, so close was the connection between the detective story and first-person narration that on July 28, 1887, *The Iowa State Reporter* saw fit to add to "Ribaud, The Miser," a straightforward, conventional story, the subtitle "A Thrilling French Detective Story Told in an Attractive Way" because it was not told in the first person but the third.

The Unblinking Eye

Adding to the genre confusion were the mixed objectives of writers and publishers. One thread of mid-century detective fiction was connected to contemporary sensation fiction and the older murder-will-out tradition of crime literature. Thus a number of stories use the detective story format to demonstrate that, inevitably, bad things will happen to people who do bad things. In "A Double Crime" in *The Marion* [OH] *Daily Star* (May 9, 1881), for example, the result of the detective's investigation is that

> Pembroke Sharon was generously recompensed by his employer for his heroic attempt to prevent the robbery, and promoted to a responsible position in the store, which he filled with credit both to himself and his grateful employer.
> Yerkes lived a year or so after his confinement, and died a raving maniac, a terrible retribution for his attempt to fasten a crime on an innocent person and thus rob him of both his reputation and life at one fell blow.

Mid-century fiction, however, began to shift away from the focus of the detective story as a means of demonstrating providential justice and toward fascination with a new category of hero. A significant part of the allure of the detective story to nineteenth-century readers was that, with the novelty of the profession and detectives' increasing presence in the news, they wanted to know what detectives did and how they did it. So, first of all, many contemporary stories touch on nascent judicial and police procedure: there are cameos of surgeons and coroners looking at bodies, chiefs assigning cases, brief accounts of trials to assign guilt and accredit the detective's accomplishment, and even bits of jargon—"working up cases," and "shadowing" suspects. Interest in the profession also connects to those detective stories that take baby steps into the world of forensic science— stories in which the detective uses photography or finger-marks to find the culprit.

In the main, however, nineteenth-century detective heroes rely upon their legs, their eyes, and their wits. Literally tracking one's quarry became a frequent theme in period detective fiction with heroes traveling by foot, by stagecoach, by boat, and especially by train, in the streets and alleys of big cities, from state to state, and even across to Canada in order to make an arrest. But persistence alone does not make the detective. It was not whimsy that made Pinkerton adopt the all-seeing eye as his corporate logo—it was the way detectives solved most crimes. And again and again in the fiction the detective hero sees something or someone that no one else sees. Seeing things is a professional attribute:

> There was too much regularity in the uprooting of the flowers and roots, and the shrubbery was broken too systematically not to set this point at rest to the eye of the detective ["The Club Foot," *Ballou's Dollar Monthly Magazine*, August 1862].

> I had one clew, a clew so slight that it had been overlooked by the Russian police, but one which no really first-class detective would have passed unnoticed ["The Twisted Ring," *The* (Monroe, WI) *Daily Independent*, October 2, 1890].

Along with specialized, acute vision, there was something else. Not genius, though; that was a Poe concept and would come back to detective fiction with Sherlock Holmes. First there is nonchalance. Most period detectives act like the hero in "The Alden Murder" (*The Atlanta Constitution*, May 16, 1886):

> He dropped lazily back into this chair and his face resumed his usual impassive expression. "I suspect," he replied coolly, "that I am employed in behalf of Charles Alden's murderer."
> "Then why do you go?"
> "A detective would be nothing without his curiosity," he replied with a quiet laugh, "and I have got my blood up. I am going to find out about it."

But it's not just that detectives are (to use the often repeated word) "cool." They are clever and shrewd. The terms are ubiquitous in period stories, and it is what sets both the hero and the narrative apart from traditional, murder-will-out stories or contemporary sensation fiction involving crime and detectives. Mid-nineteenth century detectives are uniformly clever. For instance:

> It was on the stroke of twelve when I entered the office, and thought at first that Betts had failed me, for no one was there but a ponderous old gentleman with gold glasses and white side-whiskers. I am not used to intrigues and masquerades, and when I recognized Betts in this disguise I could hardly refrain from exclaiming at his cleverness, but his own coolness kept me within bounds, and I sat down beside him and began reading a paper ["My Wife's Maid," *The Stevens Point* (WI) *Journal*, March 28, 1874].

The criminals, as worthy opponents, are clever too, and the narrative which brings detective and criminal together became in many mid-nineteenth century detective stories a contest rather than an example of the triumph of providential justice. Thus in "A Butterfly" the detective figure summarizes the intent of the contemporary detective story when he "entertained the colonel with the most thrilling Scotland Yard narratives, all illustrative of the cleverness of rogues and the superior astuteness of detectives" (*Sandusky* [OH] *Daily Register*, July 8, 1890).

Just Like Us?

The heroes of these "thrilling narratives," moreover, are very much different both from Auguste Dupin, the first great detective, and Sherlock Holmes, the next great detective. A lot of them are, in fact, much more like Inspector Bucket from *Bleak House* in one essential way: they are happily, comfortably married. And mid-century writers made that a marked feature of their detectives' characters:

> That troubled me but little; it was enough that I did succeed; at the end of the eight years had a snug marble-slabbed brick house out on Green Hill, which my wife had as prettily fixed up as any of the old blooded nobs in town. She had a fanciful way of hanging plant baskets about, and matching colors in carpets and the other trumpery, that set off a room somehow; she got up prime little game suppers for our friends, in winter, too; we had the boys at good schools; and altogether, bid fair to settle down early into a comfortable, easy middle age ["The Pigot Murder," *Harper's*, December 1865].

> I was walking one day quietly down Broadway, thinking that I would buy a present for my wife, for the following day was her birthday, and she and I have always kept up the good old fashion of making each other presents on these occasions ["The Lottery Ticket," *Ballou's Dollar Magazine*, October 1862].

> I returned home as usual after the labors of the day. I found my wife seated by a cheering fire, with the tea-urn hissing on the table, on which, too, was placed the tea-service, and the toast racks fastened to the fender, betokened that the evening meal was waiting for me ["The Defrauded Heir," *Ballou's Dollar Magazine*, February 1863].

> I returned home in an irritable state of mind, and my poor wife was soon made aware of the fact, for all the questions she asked me were either not answered at all, or responded to in no very gentle manner.
> My wife, who is a sensible woman, saw there was something wrong, and left me to my own reflections ["The Torn Glove," *Strange Stories of a Detective*, 1865].

If during the last half of the nineteenth century detective stories were not all things to all people, they were many things to an awful lot of people. Among others, they gave their readers interludes of adventure combined with the implicit assurance that there were individuals out there who made their world safe—even if their world was one largely exempt from crime. We hope that the following will, in some measure, provide at least some of the myriad satisfactions that reading can bring, and that it will also assist in developing a fuller understanding of the history of the detective story in America.

Bibliography

Aisenberg, Nadya, ed. *London Crimes*. Boston: Rowan Tree, 1982.

Johanningsmeier, Charles. *Fiction and the American Literary Marketplace: The Role of Newspaper Syndicates, 1860–1900*. Cambridge: Cambridge University Press, 1997.

Lee, Alfred McClung. *The Daily Newspaper in America: The Evolution of a Social Instrument*. New York: Macmillian, 1937. (2 vol. reprinted by Routledge in 2000.)

Mott, Frank Luther. *A History of American Magazines*. Volume IV: 1885–1905. Cambridge, MA: Belknap Press of Harvard University Press, 1957.

Nord, David Paul. *Communities of Journalism: A History of American Newspapers and Their Readers*. Urbanna: University of Illinois Press, 2001.

Tebbel, John, and Mary Ellen Zuckerman. *The Magazine in America 1741–1990*. New York: Oxford University Press, 1991.

1

Series Detectives

The first series of stories with a continuing detective hero we have found includes "A Curious Stratagem," "The Guest-Chamber of the Inn at St. Ives," and "The Mysterious Deaths at Castellane," all originally published by Ballou throughout 1859. They feature a French detective, one M. Guillot, who "had been some years connected with the Detective Bureau ... and had naturally arrived at a great degree of proficiency" ("A Curious Stratagem"). Although the byline became "From the Journal of a Detective" and "From the Records of a French Detective," *Ballou's Dollar Magazine* attaches the names James F. Franklin and James Franklin Fitts to the first of the Guillot pieces. Within the first year of their publication, the Guillot stories appeared in papers from coast to coast: from *The Oconto* [WI] *Pioneer* to the Placerville, California *Mountain Democrat*. By coincidence (or not), the name of the villain's associate in "The Mysterious Deaths" is Dupin.

Perhaps the most ubiquitous of the series heroes between Poe's Dupin and Conan Doyle's Sherlock Holmes was detective James Brampton. In the following story from *Ballou's Dollar Magazine,* the author's name is listed as Percy Garrett; most of the other Brampton stories appearing in magazines and newspapers through the 1870s, however, identify the author only as "A New York Detective." Reflecting the hero's popularity and the fashion for publishing pseudo or real police officers' memoirs (and adding to the bibliographic confusion), in 1865 a collection of twenty-nine stories was printed in both New York and London (the U.S. title was *Leaves from the Note-Book of a New York Detective. The Private Record of J.B.*). The framework of *Leaves* recounts the chance meeting between the detective James Brampton and the narrator/editor, highlighted by the detective's spur of the moment deduction demonstration ("I will wager anything ...

that the young man who has just entered, has, a few minutes ago, robbed his employer's till"). The title page lists the editor/narrator's name as "John B. Williams, M.D." *Leaves from the Note-Book* includes fifteen Brampton stories: "The Silver Pin," "The Mysterious Advertisement," "The Club-Foot," "The Accusing Leaves," "The Struggle for Life," "The Bowie-Knife Sheath," "The Night of Peril," "Stabbed in the Back," "The Masked Robbers," "The Lottery Ticket," "The Coiners" (a.k.a "Five Thousand Dollars Reward"), "The Defrauded Heir," "The Shadow of a Hand," "Mr. Sterling's Confession," and "The Knotted Handkerchief." The rest of the stories do not include Brampton: "The Phantom Face" is a murderer's confession; "The Broken Cent" and "My First Brief" are both subtitled "A Leaf from a Lawyers Note-book"; "An Adventure at an Inn" bears the label "A Leaf from a Physician's Note-book" and "the stories that follow are not details of my own experience ... nor are they strictly of a detective character"; thus "The Walker Street Tragedy," "Buried Alive," "The Mystery of Darewood Hall," "The Artist's Story," "A Churchyard Adventure," "A Terrible Night in Baltimore," "Magnetic Influence," and "A Story of a Pack of Cards." The Brampton pieces highlight the accomplishments of "a man of extraordinary sagacity ... [who] had succeeded in discovering the perpetrators of crime, when to ordinary men all clues appeared to be lost" ("The Knotted Handkerchief").

Harper's Weekly Magazine had an interest in mysteries going back to their serial publication of Dickens' *Bleak House* in 1852. During the next decade stories about detectives became relatively common in its pages. One of *Harper's* most prolific contributors was Harriet E. Prescott who introduced Detective Furbush, "a man of genteel proclivities, fond of fancy parties, and *haut ton*, curious in fine women and aristocratic defaulters and peculators." In "Mr. Furbush" (April 1865) the hero ingeniously solves a high society murder but then, depressed, resigns from the force. Three years later, however, under her married name, Harriet E. Prescott Spofford reintroduced Mr. Furbush as a private investigator in "In the Maguerriwock" (August 1868).

In 1866 Maturin M. Ballou—who by the mid-sixties managed both his *Monthly Magazine* and the *Flag of Our Union*—introduced American readers to another French detective in a series of stories written by James D. M'Cabe, Jr. They included "The Telltale Eye" (January), "An Official Blunder" (April), "Seventy Miles an Hour" (June), and "A Little Affair" (October). Far more insouciant than his Gallic predecessors, M'Cabe's Laromie is also an action detective, who "had passed through some wonderful adventures and been nearer death than most men cared to be. His success in ferreting out and bringing to light crimes of all kinds had won for him the bitter enmity of all of offenders, both political and criminal, in the city. They had repeatedly vowed vengeance against him, for they declared that there was no chance for them while he remained in Paris. Laromie only laughed at their threats, and kept his wits about him. He declared his eagerness to meet them whenever they [chose] provided they gave him fair play" ("The Little Affair").

The Guest-Chamber of the Inn at St. Ives
from the Journal of a Detective
by James Franklin Fitts

"It is strange," said Monsieur Berret, "passing strange. I was never so sorely puzzled in my life."

"It is not possible then, that you are laboring under any misapprehension?"

"Certainly not; have I not facts to deal with? Supposing, M. Guillot, that half-a-dozen dead bodies were to be found in a certain neighborhood in rapid succession, and under very suspicious circumstances—would it not be a fair conclusion that there had been foul play somewhere?"

"I should certainly deem it so."

"Well—and if in addition to this let us suppose that no clue could be obtained which would even give color of guilt to any person, notwithstanding that every effort had been made—would it not have been very strange and mysterious?"

"I must agree with you that it would!"

"And by my life it is—the strangest thing I have ever known! It is not at all wonderful that men die from disease, or from accidents, but when we hear of death without apparent cause, and of which no explanation can be given, I am bound to say that it puzzles me beyond measure."

"But do you mean to say, M. Berret, that there has been no apparent cause for these mysterious deaths?"

"Ah—I forgot. In the back of each was a wound, apparently made by some sharp weapon. This was without doubt the cause of their deaths."

"Such a wound, then, must have been inflicted by human hands—

nothing can be clearer than this conclusion. Now, Monsieur Berret, be so good as to state any particulars which may throw light upon this subject, that I may determine in what manner to act."

The foregoing conversation took place between myself and the sub-agent, in the diligence between St. Malo and St. Ives. I had received a letter from him several days previously, urgently requesting my immediate presence in the latter place, and in the last few leagues of my journey, I was so fortunate as to meet him. Upon my request, he gave a brief history of the strange occurrences in the investigation of which he wished my assistance.

All, however, that he knew of the matter was, that within the compass of a few weeks, a succession of startling murders had been committed at St. Ives, a town within his official guardianship. Bodies had been found in the street, bearing in every instance the wound in the back, of which he had spoken—and thus far suspicion had been entirely baffled and left without a resting place. The excitement consequent upon this alarming state of affairs, had caused the subagent to decide upon a personal investigation of the matter, and when I encountered him, he had already started for St. Ives, so that our destination was the same.

"You entrapped that rascal, Jacques Guichard, so admirably," M. Berret remarked, "that I am led to hope for your success in the present case, dark and doubtful as the matter now looks."

"At all events," was my reply, "I deem it no more than justice to myself, to make a strong effort. I must ask you, however, Monsieur Berret, to give me the entire management and control of this matter, in every particular."

"I will do so, and with pleasure. Frame whatever plans and whatever means you please. I will be guided by you in all things pertaining to this business."

"This will be well. But one thing more, Monsieur Berret. You must be as secret as the grave. Do not, upon any consideration, let it be known in St. Ives that there is a detective officer nearer to them than in Paris; and above all, do not suffer yourself to make an inquiry concerning these murders. Leave me to ask all questions in my peculiar manner."

The subagent promised full compliance with my instructions, and in a few moments we were rolling through the darkness and rain into the village of St. Ives. During these few moments, however, an incident occurred, which necessarily has an important bearing upon my narrative.

Our conversation had been held, as a matter of course, in so low a tone as not to be overheard by the other occupants of the diligence; in fact, I had hardly noticed any of their faces. But now, as I finished speaking for the time with M. Berret, and looked around me, I discovered in the elderly gentleman who sat directly behind us, Monsieur Auguste Lemare, a wealthy wine seller of Bordeaux, and with whom I was quite intimate. Upon recognizing me, he greeted me cordially, and we conversed together upon passing topics for a moment.

"You stop at the Hotel of St. Ives, I suppose?" he said, changing the subject somewhat abruptly. I consulted the subagent, and learning that this was the only place in St. Ives at which he ever stopped, I answered the question in the affirmative.

"Well, I shall stay there also; but it is possible that I shall not see you again, as I intend to leave St. Ives early tomorrow morning. I am now on my way to England, traveling as my business compels me to, in a roundabout way. Contrary to my usual custom, I have neglected to obtain letters of exchange, and have now the sum of five thousand francs with me. Permit me to count this over before you, that in case any unforeseen misfortune should deprive me of it before reaching Calais, you may be able to certify to my creditors as to my possession of the money at this time."

Producing a plethoric pocketbook, the wine merchant counted its contents. The sum was correct, as he had stated—five thousand francs. M. Berret, also, at his request, became a witness to his possession of the money.

The diligence now came to a stop before the inn, and the passengers hastened to leave the one for the other. After we had taken our supper, I accompanied the subagent to his room, where for an hour we talked on the subject of our mission to St. Ives, and the probabilities of success; and then, as the hour was quite late, I bade him goodnight and retired to my own chamber, and soon after to sleep. Nothing unusual occurred during the night—if I may make one exception, which it may be well to notice in this place. I had been sleeping for more than two hours, and was lying in a half-unconscious state, when I was suddenly awakened by a heavy though smothered groan. I was perfectly sure that I had not mistaken the sound, and mentally deciding that it had been occasioned in some manner in the next room, I sat upright and listened intently. But I heard nothing more, although I placed my ear close to the wall. Whatever the strange sound may have been, it was not repeated.

Upon inquiring for the subagent the next morning, I was told that he had risen before me, and left the inn. The idea then occurred to me, that

I might have an opportunity to pass half an hour with Monsieur Lemare; and addressing the landlord, a heavy-browed, ill-featured man, I asked for him. The man elevated his brow in surprise, and declared that the wine seller had not been in his house for a month.

"Perhaps you do not know M. Auguste," I said.

"But I do, monsieur, perfectly," he replied. "You must be mistaken about seeing him here."

"He was certainly here—in this town—last night."

"But not in this house—you are doubtless thinking of some other person."

As I walked away, I noticed that he followed me suspiciously with his eyes. His manner seemed strange to me. It was, in fact, rather anxious and overstrained, as though he wished very much to impress it upon my mind that Monsieur Lemare had in reality not been in the hotel. Upon further reflection, however, I was forced to confess that I really had not seen the wine merchant in the inn. True, he informed me that he intended to stop there, but I concluded that he had changed his mind, and so I dismissed the subject from my thoughts.

Passing into the street, I strolled along in search of the subagent. I had continued my walk for but a few moments, when upon turning a corner, I was brought abruptly upon a singular and terrible scene. A number of persons were crowded in confusion upon the sidewalk—and among them, as it happened, M. Berret. He quickly saw me, and seizing my arm, conducted me forward to the object of common attention. It was, as I had already begun to suspect, another victim of the mysterious assassin of St. Ives—the body of a man lay extended upon the pavement, face downward, the back penetrated by a deep and ghastly wound. But no words can describe my astonishment and horror, when, upon the face of the corpse being exposed, I recognized my aged acquaintance, M. Auguste Lamare! The subagent, too, started back in horrified surprise, and for a moment we both gazed at the body in silence. My habitual caution, however, soon returned, and drawing M. Berret hastily aside, I whispered a few words in his ear.

"Now, Monsieur Berret, if you will follow my instructions, I think I shall be able to solve this mystery in the course of the next twelve hours. Have this body conveyed as quickly as possible, to some place where it can be kept privately, and then search and see whether those five thousand francs can be found upon it. Do this, and rejoin me in half an hour at the inn. I will wait for you there."

I returned immediately to the hotel, and before the expiration of the appointed time, M. Berret entered my room.

"There is," he said, in a voice laboring under great excitement, "no vestige of that money upon the body of this unfortunate man. It has been plundered of everything valuable."

"Ah—I expected it. Now Monsieur Berret, let us sit down and talk calmly of this affair. I think I may be able to tell you that which may surprise you."

"Is it possible that you have gained a clue to the author of these murders? Your words and manner lead me to hope for it."

"You are right. I flatter myself that I have not only obtained a clue, but am able even to lay my finger upon the guilty parties. Would you like to hear of my discoveries?"

"Yes—I am all impatience. Please go on." The subagent drew his chair close to mine and listened eagerly, while I disclosed the significant facts which I had gained since my arrival at St. Ives.

"In the first place, then, Monsieur Berret," I said, "the discovery of this morning renders it certain that we have selected the right theatre for our operations. There can now be no question that these murders have been committed in this town, since we have ourselves seen one of the victims."

The subagent nodded affirmatively, and I continued:

"First, then, it seems rather remarkable that these wounds should all be inflicted in the back. As to the manner of their infliction, I am not prepared to explain; but it seems conclusive to me that these blows must all have been produced by the same hand. In the next place does it not seem singular that every one of these unfortunate men has been a stranger?"

"Now that I think of it, it does, as I live," the subagent thoughtfully replied. "But what do you argue from this fact?"

"I will draw my inference in a moment. You will remember the circumstance of M. Lemare counting his money in the diligence in our presence—this morning, we have seen his dead body lying in the public street, rifled of the money. There is now one question in my mind. Did, or did not, M. Lemare lodge in this hotel last night?"

"The landlord told me that he did not."

"So he told me—but I prefer to investigate for myself. We had it last night from Lemare's own lips, that it was his intention to stay at this inn until morning, and I am inclined to the belief that he *did* put up here last night, notwithstanding that nobody appears to have seen him within the house. It is probable that he retired immediately to his room, and communicated with no one but the innkeeper or one of the servants. Now, Monsieur Berret, let me recur to a circumstance which happened in the diligence, which I think escaped your notice. Just as M. Auguste was replacing his pocketbook, I happened to glance behind me, and then saw an object which instantly attracted my attention. It was a man, bent forward in an eager attitude, his eyes intently fixed upon the operations of M. Auguste. He quickly became aware that I was watching him, and shrank back out of sight, but not before I had observed his face. I have seen it again this morning—it is that of Antoine the hostler!"

"This is truly an important discovery," the subagent observed.

"But this is not all. Last night I heard a groan from the chamber adjoining mine. The discovery of this morning, considered with these others of which I have been telling you, leads me to believe that this was the death groan of M. Auguste Lemare! In any event, you can draw your own inferences. It is a fair conclusion that the unfortunate man retired to bed in this next chamber. Whether or not he ever left it alive, is a question, which in my mind admits of but little doubt."

"Do you, then, really mean to say that your belief is that M. Lemare was murdered under this roof?"

"I am positive of it—and not only he, but each of the other victims. And I am also induced to believe that every one of these midnight assassinations, has been committed in the adjoining chamber."

"I have no doubt that you have arrived at the truth," the subagent replied. "And now, what do you propose to do first? Would it not be better to arrest this innkeeper and his hostler at once?"

"By no means, M. Berret. I think that would be an extremely injudicious step. What I have been telling you are only conjectures of my own, which, though probably true in almost every particular, would, I greatly fear, avail little as proof to charge the villainous innkeeper and his servant (who, beyond all question are the criminals) with these crimes. There is now one decisive step to be taken. I propose to pass the night in this mysterious chamber."

Monsieur Berret heard my quietly spoken words, and looked perfectly aghast with astonishment.

"What, Guillot! Are you mad?" he exclaimed. "Pass the night in that infernal slaughterhouse! Why—are you tired of life? Consider the danger of the thing, and the great loss to the service which your death would occasion!"

The earnest anxiety with which this last remonstrance was uttered was so perfectly ludicrous, that I refrained with difficulty from laughing outright. But I soon succeeded in silencing his objections, if not in satisfying his scruples.

"You have, I believe," I then remarked, "a considerable amount of money with you."

"Yes. *Mon Dieu!* Had this rascally landlord known it last night, I might now be as cold as poor Lemare! Can it answer you any purpose?"

"A very important one. Lend me your pocketbook."

Still holding it in my hand, I descended the stairs, the subagent closely following me. The innkeeper was sitting behind his bar, seemingly half-asleep and half-wake, but the instant that he saw the pocketbook, his dull eyes lighted up with an eager gleam, and he watched my motions with strict attention.

"The amount is correct," I said aloud, to M. Berret. "Two thousand francs—this, then, discharges the debt." Then walking up to the bar, I said to the innkeeper: "The room which you have given me does not suit me in the least—have you not a larger one where I can lodge?"

"Yes, monsieur," the man replied, with remarkable alacrity, "I should have spoken of it myself. There is a large and pleasant chamber next to the one in which you slept last night—do me the favor to occupy it as long as you please."

"You had better decline before it is too late," Berret whispered in my ear. "I fear you will not occupy it for more than one night. If you do, you will accomplish what no person has yet done."

"Show me the room," I calmly replied, paying no attention to the anxious whisper of the subagent.

There seemed nothing remarkable about the room when we had once entered it. It was a trifle larger than the other chambers of the house, and the furniture was of a more antique pattern, especially the high-posted bedstead.

"I think this will answer," I said, after surveying the apartment and its belongings.

"Will you lodge here tonight, then, monsieur?"

"Certainly, the room suits me in every particular."

If the dark-browed host had entertained any suspicions of my intentions, they were certainly by this time entirely dissipated; and he left the room, I have no doubt, gratified in the depths of his black heart that another victim was to fall so easily into his trap.

"You are determined on this step, I perceive," M. Berret remarked, after he had gone. "Well, I will not attempt to dissuade you, since I know you cannot be moved, but I promise you, should you be missing in the morning, I will burn this old rookery to the ground, and hang the villainous innkeeper upon his signpost, as surely as I shall myself live till then!"

"Take whatever steps you please when you find me missing, M. Berret—until then, leave the matter in my hands. But there is one material service which you must not fail to render me. You will, if you please, conceal yourself, with two or three trusty men, in the room next to this, which I occupied last night, and there await my signal. When you hear from me, you will instantly rush in and assist me to secure whoever you may find."

These arrangements were at the proper moment put fully into operation. As evening drew on, I saw that the subagent and his allies were properly secreted, and first enjoining vigilance upon them, I entered the mysterious and fatal guest-chamber. The lamp which I carried served to reveal every part of it, and I quickly became aware that there was nothing unusual about the appearance of the room. It was very much such a bed-chamber as might be met with in almost every village inn. Nevertheless, I resolved to put no faith in appearances, and immediately I commenced a systematic examination. I searched everywhere—under the bed, in the closet and behind the window curtains—but my search revealed nothing. It was certain that no one was concealed anywhere in the room, and there as certainly seemed no place for ingress, save the door. I was beginning to become anxious. I reflected that the danger might come upon me unexpectedly, and from an unexpected source. I sat down, and for half an hour I waited—waited in restless expectancy for the appearance of the assassin, but still I waited in vain. Looking at my watch, I perceived that it was nearly midnight. My unaccustomed vigil had wearied me, and placing my pistols beneath the pillow, I lay down upon the bed without removing my clothes. I was not long in discovering that this bed was of somewhat singular construction—the formation of the top being rather concave than otherwise, and so adjusted that the occupant could not possibly rest in it in any other manner than upon his back, in the middle.

Upon his back! That seemed rather a singular discovery to make just at that moment. Had not every one of the murdered men been stabbed through the back? Yes—and each of them must have received his death-wound while lying in this very bed, just as I—

Click—click—click!

Three sharp, distinct sounds, apparently near at hand, interrupted my reflections. I knew their meaning in an instant—those sounds needed no interpreter! I rose quickly and silently, and grasping my pistol, awaited the next movement of the unseen assassins. Click—click. That noise again, and now like the creaking of a hinge. Next there was a shuffling sound which made me aware that there was a man beneath the bed—and the next instant I saw the blade of a dagger driven up through the thin mattress, in the very place where I had been lying! I gave a low groan, which was answered by a chuckle from beneath the bed.

"An easy death! Now for the spoils," I heard the same voice say. And at the same instant the head and shoulders of the innkeeper were thrust out from behind the bed-hangings. Covering him with the muzzle of one of my pistols, I said:

"Come forth, sir, and deliver yourself up! Your innocent guest is no other than a detective officer! Don't try to escape—I shall certainly fire if you do!"

But he did try, and I speedily sent a pistol ball after him. The report was succeeded by a deep groan, and instantly M. Berret and his assistants rushed in. A hasty search was sufficient to discover the landlord under the bed, weltering in his blood, and the hostler was seized before he had an opportunity to close the secret panel in the wall, through which he endeavored to escape.

This panel, as a short search disclosed to us, opened directly into a hollow partition, which communicated with a lower room. By means of this strange contrivance, the assassins had always been able to enter this particular chamber at any time—and once through the panel without having disturbed the unsuspecting sleeper, their work was easily done. The bed was, as I have said, constructed in such a manner that a sleeper could maintain only one position in it—a hollow had been worn for the passage of the dagger, and a single powerful thrust had been in every instance enough to transfix the heart of the victim. After rifling the body of everything valuable, the murderers were accustomed to carry it out in the darkness of the night and leave it [in] one of the public streets of the town. And so adroitly had this game been played that no shadow of suspicion had attached to the real criminals.

The innkeeper recovered from the wound which I gave him, but it was only, together with his partner in guilt—the hostler—to receive one of a much more serious character from the hands of the public executioner. And when I next came to St. Ives, I occupied the same chamber and the same bed at the inn, with a sense of the most perfect security, undisturbed by any remembrance of my former remarkable adventure.

—*Ballou's Dollar Monthly Magazine*, December 1859

The Knotted Handkerchief by Percy Garrett

About ten years ago I was studying medicine in New York. I had been working very hard, having specially devoted my attention for the last six months to pathology. This is a tedious study, demanding the most determined mental attention. I threw myself into it with all the ardor of youth, and consequently at the end of six months I had completely exhausted my mental energies.

One day I was sitting listlessly in my room endeavoring to master Bayle's "*Recherches Phthisie Pulmonaire*," but I could not comprehend what I was reading; my thoughts unbidden reverted back to my own home, and it rose up in all its neatness and charms before my mental vision. My heart yearned to see my family again, and I knew that two more long years must elapse before my wish could be gratified. A sudden knocking at the door interrupted my reverie. At my summons to "come in," the door opened, and my particular friend Charles Seldon entered the room.

"What! Still poring over your books?" said he.

"Yes," I replied, "I am trying to master Bayle, but I don't make much progress."

"I tell you what it is, my dear fellow," said my friend, good naturedly, "you will make yourself ill. You don't know how pale you look. Now take my advice, throw your books on one side."

"It's all very well talking," I replied; "but I want to perfect myself in pathology, and it is impossible for me to do so without application."

We then entered into a long discussion as to the necessity of an intimate knowledge of pathology to practice medicine, and ended as these discussions usually do, by neither of us being convinced.

"Well, old friend," said he, "the fact is, you must have some relaxation.

I am going home tomorrow for a month. Now I propose you accompany me. You have no idea how delighted my friends will be to see you. We live in a homely style, 'far from the busy haunts of man,' but I am sure the change will do you a world of good. Come, make up your mind and join me."

I reflected a moment—the temptation was too strong for me, and I agreed to accompany him. The next morning we started off. His father was a farmer, and lived in the western part of the state of New York. I shall not dwell on my visit. Suffice it to say that I was received with the greatest kindness, and treated with genuine hospitality, and I passed there four of the happiest weeks of my life. I had been there about a week when I went out one day for a long walk by myself. Seldon had a headache and preferred to stay at home. I walked several miles, and growing tired, I entered a country tavern, and calling for a glass of ale and a cigar, I sat down to rest myself.

While thus engaged a slight cough attracted my attention, and I glanced at the spot from whence it proceeded. Seated at the further end of the barroom was an individual I had not noticed before. He was a man between thirty and forty years of age. There was something very peculiar about his features which immediately arrested my attention. I do not know how to describe it, but it gave me an idea that he possessed a very acute mind. This impression was further increased by his movements. They were quick, and it was evident that he did not allow the slightest circumstance to escape him. I am not naturally inclined to make friends with strangers, but there was something in this man which attracted me to him. I drew my chair nearer his and commenced a conversation.

"A pleasant day," said I.

"You are right, sir," he replied; "it is very pleasant indeed, considering the time of year. One would expect to find it much colder than it is in this part of the state."

"I should judge from your remarks that you do not live in this neighborhood," I ventured to observe.

Before replying he gave me a scrutinizing glance.

"I live in New York," he replied, after a moment's pause. "My name is James Brampton; my profession a detective officer."

I was delighted to meet Mr. Brampton. His name had lately been very prominently brought before the public in more than one instance. He was a man of extraordinary sagacity, and had succeeded in discovering the perpetrators of crime, when to ordinary men all clues appeared to be lost. His faculty in this respect was evidently owing to his keen observation, his acute mental analysis and determined perseverance. No difficulty daunted him, in fact his power seemed to increase in proportion as the case was enveloped in mystery. He was a man of great courage, and what was still better for his profession, extraordinary coolness.

We grew quite familiar, and in the course of conversation I asked him what brought him so far from New York. He told me he was in pursuit of a burglar, and had laid a trap for him and expected to arrest him that very day. Our interview lasted some time, when I arose to go. He then gave me his address in New York, and stated that he should be happy for me to call and see him. After the time for our visit had expired, Charles Seldon and myself both returned to New York together, and I applied myself to studies with renewed energies. It might have been about a month after this, that one morning I took up the *New York Herald*, and the following paragraph caught my attention:

> HORRIBLE MURDER.—The inhabitants of Lispenard Street were yesterday thrown into a terrible state of excitement, by the discovery of one of the most fearful murders it has ever been the lot of humanity to witness. It appears that No. 121 is let out into lodgings. An apartment on the second floor is occupied by a young medical student named George Wilson. It was noticed yesterday that he did not make his appearance as usual. It was supposed that he was sick, and the owner of the house, who occupied the ground floor, went up to his room to see if he had need of anything. When he entered the room a dreadful sight presented itself. The young man was lying before the fireplace quite dead. His throat was cut in a fearful manner. Some of his hair which had evidently been pulled out by the roots, lay scattered about the room. The motives for this horrible deed are entirely unknown. The property of the deceased did not appear to have been disturbed. We are happy to say that the probable murderer has been arrested. We refrain from giving more particulars today, as it might defeat the ends of justice.

I was very much shocked to learn that poor Wilson had met with such a dreadful end. I knew him well, as he was studying at the same college as myself, and although I could not exactly rank him among my friends, still the little intercourse I had had with him had impressed me very favorably as to his general character. I had only spoken to him the very day before in the chemical lecture room, and it seemed so shocking to know that at that moment he was lying dead. I went down to the college as usual, and the first person I met in the hall was Mr. Dolman, the worthy janitor.

"Have you seen poor Wilson's body?" said he, after we had been conversing a few minutes about the murder.

"No," I replied; "I suppose it is a shocking sight."

"It is, indeed—but there is one consolation—the murderer is arrested."

"So the paper said, but it did not give his name—who is it?"

"One you know very well. It's no other than Charles Seldon."

"Seldon!" I exclaimed. "Impossible! Why, he is my dearest friend!"

"I am sorry to hear that, sir, because there can be no doubt about his guilt."

I begged Mr. Dolman to enter into full particulars. His statement, divested of all extraneous matter, amounted to substantially as follows:

George Wilson and Charles Seldon had at one time been great friends. They had been inseparable, and it appeared as if nothing could occur to disturb their friendship. But one day they had a quarrel in the dissecting room about the origin and insertion of some muscles. High words took place, and threats were freely indulged in on both sides. But by the interposition of some friends they were reconciled. After this quarrel they became as firmly attached to each other as ever. They constantly visited at each other's rooms, and were frequently seen together in public.

On the evening of the murder, they had attended the theatre together, and Seldon had returned home with Wilson. The owner of the lodging house testified to their both returning about twelve o'clock at night. He did not know what time Seldon had left. The police immediately proceeded to search Seldon's room. They found the student absent. After a strict search they discovered in one corner of his sleeping apartment, a handkerchief saturated with blood, and a dissecting knife also smeared with blood. In a drawer was a letter containing a challenge to Wilson to fight a duel; this letter had no date to it. This evidence was thought conclusive, and Charles Seldon was immediately arrested, charged with the willful murder of George Wilson.

I must confess when all this was told me, the case appeared a very black one for my friend Seldon. It was proved that on the night of the murder he had accompanied the deceased to his rooms; that it had not been noticed when he left; that the strongest evidences of his guilt were found in his rooms, but still I was not satisfied. I knew Seldon so well that I could not persuade myself he had been guilty of so atrocious a crime. I at once determined to pay my friend a visit in prison, and easily obtained a pass for that purpose. In an hour I was at the prison door. On delivering the pass I was immediately admitted. When I entered the cell, I found my friend sitting on the edge of his iron bed, with his face buried in his hands. As soon he heard my step he looked up.

"My dear fellow," said he, rising, "this is indeed kind of you."

"I should indeed be wanting in friendship," I replied, "if I were not to visit you when in trouble."

"You know about the dreadful crime with which I am charged, but as surely as there is a God in Heaven, I am guiltless of this bloody deed."

The poor fellow could restrain himself no longer, but letting his face fall on my shoulder, he wept and sobbed like a child. I had no doubt whatever of his innocence now.

"Come, come," said I, trying to console him; "Cheer up, Charles. I am perfectly satisfied as to your innocence, and so shall the world be before many days are over!"

"It is not for myself I care," he exclaimed between his sobs, "but my mother—my poor dear mother, it will break her heart when she hears of her son's disgrace."

"My dear fellow," I answered, "you let your fears get the better of you. There can be no disgrace when there is no crime; but come, compose yourself, I want you to tell me a few particulars regarding this matter. Do you suspect anybody of having committed this murder?"

"No, I have not the slightest idea who did it. You well know that poor Wilson and I had settled our quarrel; we were as good friends as ever, and even on the fatal night we went to the theatre together. We returned about midnight, and I accompanied him to his room, where I stayed with him upwards of an hour, smoking a cigar and talking about old times. I let myself out without disturbing anyone and went immediately home. This morning I was arrested on the charge of murder, and this is all I know about the matter, so help me God!"

"Have you employed anyone to look after your interests?"

"Not yet. Everything was so sudden that I appear to be in a dream."

"A sudden thought has struck me. You remember my telling you about meeting with a famous detective officer, named Brampton, when I was on a visit to your house? Now if anybody can find out the truth, he is the man."

"You are right—see him at once, my dear fellow. There is no time to lose."

I agreed with Seldon, that it would be better to see Brampton immediately, and hurriedly bidding him goodbye, I proceeded at once to the address the detective officer had given me, and which, fortunately, I had preserved. I found him at home, and in a few words I explained to him all that had occurred. He appeared I thought to take the matter very coolly, but consented without any hesitation to examine into the affair.

"What are the proofs against the young man?" asked Brampton.

I then told him about the bloody handkerchief, the dissecting knife, and the challenge which had been found in Seldon's room; at the same time I upbraided myself that I had not mentioned anything about the supposed proofs of his guilt to my friend when I visited him in prison.

"The first thing we have to do," said the detective, "is to examine these things; we will then visit the scene of the tragedy."

He put on his hat and we went at once to the police office. The articles were shown us without any hesitation. Mr. Brampton scrutinized the bloody handkerchief, knife, and compromising note very closely.

"If this is all the proof they have got against your friend, it does not amount to much," said he. "With respect to the handkerchief, you see it is only bloody in spots; had it been used in murder it would have been saturated equally through the whole fabric; the blood on the knife is at least two weeks old, and the challenge evidently written two or three months ago—you see the paper looks quite yellow, and has already faded."

I was rejoiced to hear him give this opinion, which, when he pointed out to me the reasons for it, was evidently well founded. We left the police office, and started for Lispenard Street for the house where the murder had been committed. It was the middle of January, and the day was bitter cold. A considerable quantity of snow had fallen, which somewhat impeded our progress. In half an hour's time, however, we reached the house which had been the scene of the assassination.

It was quite a modern building situated in the heart of a populous street. One would suppose it to be the last place in the world where such a deed could be committed without instant detection. We had no difficulty in obtaining admission into the fatal chamber. The room remained exactly in the same state as when first discovered. Wilson's body, however, had been moved into another apartment. Mr. Brampton proceeded to examine the room narrowly, determined if possible to discover some clue to the murderer. I must premise by stating that the apartment was the middle of three on the second floor. The one on the right was occupied by a lawyer's clerk, the one on the left by a clerk in a drugstore.

"The first thing to be observed," said Mr. Brampton, "is that it is very singular how this murder could have been committed without any alarm having been given to the inmates of the other two apartments. The natural inference is that the victim must first of all have been deprived of consciousness—this must have been produced by either ether or chloroform. I should judge it must have been the latter, as it is more rapid in its effects."

I did not agree with the theory of the detective, for it appeared to me that a violent struggle had taken place. The room was in extreme disorder, and the floor was strewn with the murdered man's hair. I mentioned my doubts to Mr. Brampton.

"The very thing you mention only serves to confirm me in my first opinion," said he with a smile, and he picked up a lock of hair from the carpet. "In the first place," he continued, "there is too much study and regularity in this to satisfy me, and look at this lock of hair, you see the ends are all even and stained with blood, evidently showing that it was not torn out by the roots, as would be imagined at first glance. The even ends show that it was cut off with some sharp instrument, and the fact of their being stained with blood proves that the hair was cut off after the murder was committed, and with the same instrument. This instrument must have been very sharp, and I conclude it was either a razor or a scalpel."

Mr. Brampton now proceeded to search every corner of the apartment, and discovered under a heap of bedclothes a pocket handkerchief. He picked it up and found that the two ends were knotted together. He raised it to my nose, and I could distinctly trace the smell of chloroform. It was a large white pocket handkerchief, and evidently belonged to a gentleman. In one corner of it were the initials J.D.

"An important discovery," said the detective, putting it into his pocket.

We next proceeded to view the body. The mortal remains of George Wilson were stretched on a low bed in an empty apartment on the next floor. The first thing that Mr. Brampton pointed out to me was that one of the ears of the deceased was almost black and the other was grazed. On the back of the head the hair was matted and pressed.

The detective pulled the handkerchief he had found in the other room from his pocket, and discovered that it exactly fitted round the head of the deceased, and where the hair was matted the knot had been tied. The pressure had been so great as to stop the circulation of the blood, and this accounted for the peculiar appearance of the ears. Mr. Brampton next proceeded to examine the mouth of the deceased. After separating the lips, we both of us perceived a small piece of white or transparent substance adhering to one of the front teeth. He detached it.

"What is it?" I asked.

"It is a piece of human skin," he replied.

"What do you infer from it?"

"I will tell you directly, but it is necessary first that we should again visit the room where the murder was committed."

We did so, and Brampton walked straight up to a large cupboard which he had neglected to examine before. He threw open the door, and he had no sooner done so than an expression of satisfaction escaped his lips.

"I suspected as much," said he. "Do you see nothing peculiar in that cupboard?" he asked.

"No," I replied. "I only see that it is half full of soiled linen."

"Don't you see that the linen is indented in the middle, evidently showing that someone has been concealed there?"

When he pointed it out to me it was plain enough, and I wondered it had not struck me before.

"I think we are now in a very fair way of discovering the murderer," said he. "Your friend is undoubtedly innocent. The murderer, whose initials are in all probability J.D., concealed himself in this closet. He must have been there during the whole of the interview between Seldon and Wilson. When the latter was left alone, he crept stealthily from his hiding place, and first saturating his handkerchief with chloroform, he applied it to the mouth of his victim. A very slight struggle ensued in which the hand of the murderer was bitten by the deceased. The chloroform, however, soon produced unconsciousness; the deed was then committed; the cutting off of the hair, and the disorder in the room, were effected afterwards, as I before told you."

It was perfectly plain to me after his explanation, that everything must have taken place exactly as he stated, and it appeared such a simple and natural conclusion to arrive at, that I wondered I had not come to the same conclusion myself.

"What is the next lecture at the university medical college?" said he.

"Professor P— lectures at five o'clock this afternoon on Materia Medica," I replied, somewhat surprised at such a question.

"Will you allow me to accompany you?" he asked.

"Certainly," I returned, more and more surprised.

We left the house, and it was decided that I should call for him a quarter before five. He gave me no reason why he wished to attend the lecture. At the hour agreed upon I was at his door, and we both proceeded to the college together. When we entered the lecture room he scrutinized every student present, and then appeared satisfied, for he sat down and listened attentively to the end. When it was over he pointed out a young man to me.

"What is that young man's name?" said he.

"His name is Joseph Davis."

"Do you know him?"

"Yes, I know him very well."

"Do you know where he lives?"

"Yes."

At that moment Davis came up conversing with four or five other students. They stood quite near us, and we could overhear their conversation.

"What's the matter with your hand, Davis?" said a student.

I now noticed for the first time that his hand was tied up in a handkerchief.

"I pricked myself while dissecting," replied Davis.

"You ought to be careful of yourself, such injuries are frequently very dangerous," returned another student.

"What a shocking thing it is about poor Wilson," said another of his companions.

"It is, indeed," returned Davis. "I suppose there is no doubt about Seldon's guilt?"

"Not at all. By-the-by, Davis, it is a good thing the murderer is discovered, for you had an awful row with him yesterday morning."

"I know I had. You know he accused me of cheating at cards, and I could not stand that. I own I used some very harsh language, which I now regret."

The young men now passed on. Mr. Brampton followed them. At last the student who had referred to the difficulty between Davis and Wilson, separated from the rest. The detective officer hurried on and overtook him before he turned the corner of the street.

"What is that young man's name?" he asked of me.

"Herman Doyle," I returned.

"Mr. Doyle," said Brampton, as he came up with the student, "I wish to ask you a question or two. I am a detective officer. You referred just now to a quarrel between Mr. Davis and Mr. Wilson—will you be good enough to give me the particulars?"

The young student appeared to be a good deal astonished at being thus addressed, but replied without any hesitation.

"Yesterday morning, Davis, Wilson and myself were playing poker in my room. There was a dispute between the two persons, Wilson accusing Davis of cheating."

"What followed?" asked Brampton.

"Davis, who is a southerner, was very indignant, and swore he would have Wilson's life."

"I thank you. I am much obliged to you," replied the detective, and wishing the medical student good morning, we walked away.

"Now, then, we must go to Davis's lodgings," said Brampton. "Introduce me as your uncle and ask him to lend you a scalpel."

I did not presume to dispute anything he advised. We had not to walk far before we reached the house in which he boarded. He had only arrived a few minutes before us. We were shown at once into his room, and I introduced Brampton as my uncle as had been agreed upon. When the ceremony of introduction was over, I said:

"Davis, will you be kind enough to lend me a scalpel for a day or two?"

"Help yourself," said he, pointing to a box on the bureau. Brampton took the box as if for the purpose of handing it to me. He opened it and glanced at the contents.

"What is the matter with your hand, Mr. Davis?" said Brampton, looking at him as if he would read his very soul.

Davis began to grow uneasy, and moved restlessly in his chair.

"O, it's nothing," he answered. "I pricked myself while dissecting the other day."

"Will you let me see it?" I asked, "Perhaps I can suggest something for it."

"It is really not worthwhile," he answered. Then he added, after reflecting a moment, "but if it will afford you any gratification, you can see it."

He pulled off the handkerchief and showed us his hand. It was as Brampton had expected—his hand had been severely bitten, and the marks of the teeth were plainly perceptible. We then knew that we stood in the presence of George Wilson's murderer! Brampton suddenly rose from his seat, shut the door, and putting his hand on Davis's shoulder, exclaimed:

"I am a detective officer. Joseph Davis, I arrest you for the murder of George Wilson, and here is the knife with which you committed the deed," he added, taking one of the scalpels from the box—"see, some of the hair of the victim still adheres to it."

This sudden action succeeded. He gazed for a moment wildly around him as if meditating flight, and then fell back speechless in a chair. The assistance of some policemen was immediately obtained and he was removed to the Tombs.

Two days afterwards he committed suicide in prison by opening the femoral artery, leaving behind him a written confession of his guilt. In this confession he acknowledged that he had concealed himself in Wilson's chamber, and attacked him exactly in the manner stated by Brampton. Charles Seldon was of course honorably discharged.

—*Ballou's Dollar Monthly Magazine*, July 1862

Mr. Furbush
by Harriet E. Prescott [Spofford]

It is not very long since the community was startled by the report of an extraordinary murder that occurred at one of our fashionable hotels, under peculiar circumstances and in broad daylight, and without affording, as it appeared, the slightest clew to motive or murderer. Public curiosity, finding that nothing was likely to satisfy it, gradually dropped the matter, and as gradually it died out of the newspapers.

The person who was thus abruptly ushered from this world into the unknown region of the next was a young girl, some twenty summers old, and possessed of great personal charms. She was the heiress to a small fortune, a mere annuity, but had resided since her childhood with her guardian, the wealthy and generous Mr. Denbigh, who had always surrounded her with every luxury and elegance. When Mr. Denbigh married, he and his wife took their ward with them on the foreign tour they made, and the three had but just returned to America, residing temporarily at a hotel till their uptown mansion should be suitably prepared, when the sudden and terrible death of Miss Agatha More threw such a gloom over all their plans that the preparations were for a time abandoned, and Mr. Denbigh's energies were called upon to assist his wife in rallying from the low nervous fever into which she had been thrown and prostrated by this tragedy, when returning with her husband from a drive they had discovered it in all its horror.

Mr. Denbigh was himself greatly afflicted by the death of his ward and the fearful manner of it—she had been strangled in her own handkerchief—for besides the debt of affection he owed her as a child of a dear dead friend, long years of familiarity, her extreme loveliness, and the winning gentleness of her sweet and timid ways, had given her a deep and warm place in his heart. Of late she had been a little out of health, not recovering rapidly from the great exhaustion and weakness of severe seasickness, and he had been unremitting in his endeavors to promote her comfort and happiness; while in making ready their new abode, both he and his wife had paid such heed to the tastes and needs of Agatha, meaning, as Mr. Denbigh said, that it should be felt by her to be as much her own home as theirs, without any sense of obligation, that now the place without her seemed too much a desert ever to enter upon it again.

Mrs. Denbigh, moreover, must have felt sorely, it would seem, the loss of the gentle daily companion of three years; but even more than on her own account she appeared to resent the deed for the sake of her husband to whom she was so passionately devoted, and no sooner was she able to lift her head from its pillow once more than she interested herself with revengeful vigor in the proceedings that had been undertaken. Mr. Denbigh, personally, cared little to discover the perpetrator of the atrocious crime; he felt that no human justice of cord or gibbet could restore Agatha; but his wife, burdened with their bereavement and with her own weight of indignation, would not rest with the mystery unraveled. In the deepest mourning, discarding almost every ornament, impressing so upon them more deeply the emergencies of the case and commanding their sympathies, she was closeted every morning with the detectives of the police, sparing her husband as much of the painful duty as possible, as she would have walked over burning plowshares at a word from him.

It was at first supposed that the deed had been done for plunder, as various valuable jewels, gifts of the Denbighs, and heirlooms from Miss More's own mother, were discovered to be missing; but they afforded in themselves insufficient reason, and were subsequently discovered in a package picked up by one of the police themselves at a crossing of a crowded thoroughfare where they had apparently been purposely dropped. Neither did Miss More's lovers afford any clew to the miscreant; she had had several suitors and attendants, none of whom had Mr. Denbigh favored; and though Mrs. Denbigh had urged Agatha to regard young Elliot with kindness, Mr. Denbigh frowned, Agatha remained indifferent, and young Elliot, having taunted Mr. Denbigh with the assurance that since he countenanced none of Miss More's lovers it could be but from sinister intentions on his part, had withdrawn, vowing vengeance, and declaring that, since he could not have her, nobody else should. Still that was hardly murder. And the poor fellow was found, besides, to be in such a heartbroken state as to disarm suspicion. The only other accusation that could take shape and breath might have been directed toward Agatha's maid; but as she was able to prove that she was down in the laundry, and had remained there uninterruptedly from nine till one, while the occurrence had taken place between the hours of eleven and twelve in the morning, and as she had evidently nothing to gain and much to lose by it, that idea was also dismissed, though both young Elliot and the servant-maid remained under surveillance. Finally, in despair, the Denbighs abandoned the investigation, and departed to spend the winter in Madeira, returning in the spring to their city abode, whose adornment had been left to the tender mercies of the upholsterers, since they had themselves so completely lost interest in it.

Here the general course of the matter rested. One officer alone, Detective Furbush—a man of genteel proclivities, fond of fancy parties and the *haut ton*, curious in fine women and aristocratic defaulters and peculators—who had not at first been detailed upon the case, but had been interested in the reports of it, having become at last much in earnest about it, pursued it still, incidentally, on his own account and in a kind of amateur way. It seemed to him a fatal fascination, a predestination of events that kept his steps nearly always about the purlieus of the Margrand House.

One day that Detective Furbush had happened, in a spare hour, to take his little daughter into a photograph gallery, he lounged about a window while the child was undergoing the awful operation. Along the opposite side of the street from this window ran one end of the Margrand House, with its countless windows and projections. The Margrand House fronted on a square, one end of it running down this street, and always receiving, on its stone facings and adornments, the whole sheet of the noon sun. A thought suddenly occurred to Mr. Furbush. So as soon as the operator was at leisure he attacked him with the inquiry if there were any picture of that fine building, the Margrand House? To which the operator replied affirmatively, and showed him one taken from the square. "However," said the operator, "though it doesn't take in so much, and was only what this one window could do for itself, I call this a prettier picture," and he produced something which, having been taken at such a short focal distance, resembled the photographs of the rich architecture of some Venetian façade. "It was the morning of the Great Walden Celebration," continued the operator.

"What one?" asked Mr. Furbush.

"The Great Walden Celebration."

"Ah yes," responded Mr. Furbush, not letting the rest of his thought reach the air, running as it did, "that was the morning of the More murder."

"And we let one of the boys try his hand at the craft," resumed the operator, "there being nothing doing; and it was such a lively scene in the street below, narrow as it is. And, as was to be expected from him, the crowd and procession turned into dot and line, and the whole of that part of the building opposite came out as if it had sat for its picture."

"Exactly," said Mr. Furbush, as, rubbing his finger over his lips, he looked at the sheet on which the central portion of that side of the hotel, with its quaint windows and lintels and ornamentation were most minutely given. It was in that very portion of the house that Miss Agatha More's room had been situated; nay, so well was it all impressed upon him, that Mr. Furbush could tell the very window of the room in which she had met her cruel fate. Never was there such a coincidence, to Mr. Furbush's mind, before or since, never such an interposition of Providence; the day that an unknown hand had brought Agatha More to her doom, perhaps the very hour, the sun had made a revelation of that room's interior upon this sheet of sensitized paper, his Ithuriel's spear had touched this shapeless darkness and turned it into form and truth. The Walden Celebration had defiled through the street and into the square, at a somewhat earlier hour than the supposed hour of the murder, since it was to see the procession from a more advantageous point of view that Mr. and Mrs. Denbigh had driven out, and while they were gone the terrible action was thought to have been committed. Still the window might have a secret of its own to tell even concerning that.

Straightway Mr. Furbush made a prize of the operator; and procuring, through channels always open to him, the strongest glasses and most accurate instruments, had the one chosen window in the picture magnified and photographed, remagnified and rephotographed, till under their powerful, careful, prolonged, and patient labor, a speck came into sight that would perhaps well reward them. Mr. Furbush strained his eyes over it; to him it was a spot of greater possibilities than the nebula in Orion. This little white unresolved cloud, again and again they subjected to the same process, and once more, as if a ghost had made apparition, it opened itself into an outline—into a substance—and they saw the fingers of a hand, a white hand, doubled, but pliant, strong, and shapely; a left hand, on its third finger wearing rings, one of which seemed at first a mere blot of light, but, gradually, as the rest, answering the spell of the camera, showed itself a central stone set with five points, each point consisting of smaller stones: the color of course could not be told; the form was that of a star. Held in the tight, fierce fingers of that clenched hand, between the pointed thumb and waxy knuckles, and one edge visible along the tips deep dinted into the thumb's side, was grasped an end of a laced handkerchief. Now the handkerchief of Agatha More, the instrument of her destruction, was always carried folded in the shape of its running knot in Mr. Furbush's great wallet, a large, laced, embroidered handkerchief; that this was its photograph he needed but a glance to rest assured. All the rest of the dark deed was hidden beyond the angle of light afforded by the window frame. And whosoever the murderer might be, Mr. Furbush said to himself with the pleasantry of the headsman, it was evident that the owner of this picture had a hand in it. And here he paid the photographer for his labors and bade him adieu.

Mr. Furbush was now, however, not much better off than he had been before. He had the hand that did the deed in his possession, to be sure, but to whose body was he to affix that hand, and how was he to do it? And in what did it differ from any other hand? In nothing but that fetter which made it his prisoner, that five-pointed star, that blot of light upon the third finger, above a wedding ring. A wedding ring—that would seem to prove the hand to be a woman's; the five-pointed glittering ring—that proved the woman to be no pauper. Worn above the wedding ring, it must be its guard, and was probably as inseparable as that. To identify that hand, to certify that ring, became the recreation of Mr. Furbush's days and nights, so much to the detriment of all his other business that he fell into sad disrepute thereby at the Bureau. Mr. Furbush became all at once a gay man, plunged into the dissipations of fashionable life; he had been there before, on similar necessity, and knew how to carry himself. His costume grew singularly correct, he handled his lorgnette at the Opera like a coxcomb of the first milk-and-water; he procured invitations to ball and party, and watched every lady who for the moment daintily ungloved herself; he was as constant at church as the sexton; he made a part of the *beau monde*. It was all in vain. And though Mr. Furbush carried the photograph in his breast pocket, ready at any moment to descend like the hand of the Inquisition upon its victim, he might as well have carried there a pardon to all concerned, for all the good it did him.

But the world goes round.

One starlit night Mr. Furbush, pursuing some scent of other affairs along the princely avenue with its rows of palaces, took in, as was his wont, with every wink, a whole scene to its last details. He saw the beggar on these steps shrink into shadow, the housemaid in that area listening to the beguiling voice of the footman-three-doors-off no longer keeping his distance; he saw, there, the gay scene offered by the bright balcony casement with its rich curtains still unclosed; he saw, yet beyond, the light streaming from between open doors down the shining steps at whose foot the carriage waited, while a gentleman at its door hurried, with a pleasant word, the stately woman who came down to enter it beside him. She came down slowly, Mr. Furbush noted, moving like a person whom organic difficulty of the heart indisposes to quick exertion; she was one of those whom Mr. Furbush called magnificent—great coils of blue-black hair, twisted with diamonds, wreathing her queenly head tiara-wise, her features having the firmness and the pallor of marble, her eyes rivaling the diamonds in their steady splendor. A heavy cloak of ermine wrapped her velvet attire, and she was buttoning a glove as she descended. She paused a moment under the carriage lamp, giving her husband the ungloved hand to help her in. The carriage light flashed upon it, and in that second of its lingering, Mr. Furbush saw, plainly as he saw the stars above him, on the third finger of that left hand, above the wedding ring, the circlet with its five-pointed star whose duplicate he carried.

Mr. Furbush was thunderstruck. Here was what he had sought for thrice a twelvemonth; and unexpectedly blundering upon it turned him into stone. When he recovered himself with an emphatic "Humph!" the carriage had rolled away and the doors were closed.

Mr. Furbush was not the man to lose opportunities. The business in hand might go to the dogs; tomorrow would answer as well for that as tonight; for this there was no time like the present. Fortified with an outside subordinate he demanded entrance into the mansion alone, and announcing his intention to await the arrival home of the master and mistress, made himself agreeable to the footman and butler in the upper hall till hour after hour pealing forth at last struck midnight as if they tolled a knell. The footman was asleep in his chair, the butler heard the mellifluous murmur of the visitor's voice by starts with a singing sensation as if his fingers were in his ears and out again momentarily. The wheels grated on the curb below, the horses hammered the pavement, the doors were flung apart, and the master and mistress of the house returned from the entertainments they had shared. She was a little paler, a little more magnificent, a little more imposing in her height and dignity than before; there was only one emotion, though, apparent through it all—that she valued her beauty and power only for its influence on the man beside her. Mr. Furbush's keen eye saw the quick heave and restless agitation that the heart kept up beneath the velvets, simply in the moment when her husband touched her hand helping her across the threshold, and saw the whole story of her eye as it rested that instant on his. He would have had the entire case at once—if he had not had it before.

"Mr. and Mrs. Denbigh," said he, approaching them then, "may I beg to see you alone for a few moments on a matter of importance?"

And in conformity with his request he was conducted, through other apartments, into a library, a place more secluded than they, a rather somber room, wainscoted all its lofty height in bookcases, and with here and there a glimmering bust. Mr. Denbigh himself turned up the gas and closed the door.

"Your business, Sir?" said he then to Mr. Furbush.

"My business, Sir, is more particularly with Mrs. Denbigh; although I desire your presence. I am a member of the police—"

Mrs. Denbigh, who yet stood with her hand laid passively along the back of a chair, slowly grasped the back till the glove that she wore with a quick crack ripped down the length of the finger, and the five-pointed ring protruded its sparkling face like the vicious head of a serpent.

"I am a member of the police," continued Mr. Furbush, quietly. "I have something in my possession which I desire Mrs. Denbigh to look at and see if it belong to her." Perhaps the woman breathed again. Whether she did or not he proceeded to open his great leathern wallet on the library table beneath the chandelier.

Mrs. Denbigh moved forward with her slow majesty, dragging her velvets heavily, and the cloak dropping from her shoulder.

"Queer subjects—women," thought Mr. Furbush. "Ah! You had more spring in you once. As handsome a thing as a leopard!"

But in spite of that calm deliberate step Mr. Furbush saw her heart fluttering there like a white dove in its nest. She did not speak, but waited a moment beside him. "Will you be so kind," said he, "as to remove your glove?"

She quietly did so. Perhaps wonderingly.

"Excuse me, madame," then continued he, lifting her hand as he spoke, doubling its cold fingers over one end of a running knot that a soiled handkerchief made, a laced embroidered handkerchief he had produced, and, powerless in his grasp, he laid hand and all—a white hand, doubled, but pliant, strong, and shapely, holding in its fingers, between the pointed thumb and waxy knuckles, the laced handkerchief's end, just an edge visible along the tips deep dinted into the thumb's side; and with the five-pointed ring burning its bale-fire above it, laid the hand and all on the table beside the photograph that he spread there.

"Is it yours?" said he.

A detective has perhaps no right to any pity; but for a moment Mr. Furbush would gladly have never heard of the More murder as he saw in the long, slow rise and fall of the bosom this woman's heart swing like a pendulum, a noiseless pendulum that ceases to vibrate. Her eyes wavered a moment between him and the table, then, as if caught and chained by something that compelled their gaze, glared at and protruded over the sight they saw beneath them. Her own hand—her own executioner. A long shudder shook her from head to foot. Iron nerve gave way, the white lips parted, she threw her head back and gasped; with one wild look toward her husband she turned from him as if she would have fled and fell dead upon the floor.

"Hunt's up," said Mr. Furbush to his subordinate, coming out an hour or two later, and the two found some congenial oyster-opener, while the Chief explained how he had gone to get his wife's spoons from the maid who had appropriated them and taken service elsewhere. Mr. Furbush made a night of it; but never soul longed for daylight as he did, he had a notion that he had scarcely less than murdered—himself; and good fellow as he must needs be abroad that night, indoors the next day he put his household in sackcloth and ashes.

You will not find Mr. Furbush's name on the list of detectives now. He has sickened of the business. He says there is too much night work. He has found a patron now—a wealthy one apparently. He has opened one of the largest and most elegant photographing establishments in the city; he was always fond of chemicals, he says. He has still, in an inner drawer, some singular but fast-fading likenesses of a hand, a clenched, murderous hand—among them not the one Mr. Denbigh burned. He has a few secrets appertaining to his profession, which no one else has yet obtained. Meanwhile it has never been exactly explained how the story of the ring found the light.

Perhaps it was in order that Mr. Furbush might never be convicted of compounding a felony!

—Harper's New Monthly Magazine, April 1865

The Telltale Eye
by A Traveller
[James D. M'Cabe, Jr.]

Some years ago, while living in Paris, I met with a French detective who was boarding for a while at the house at which I was sojourning. I confess I was drawn to the man from the first. He was a frank, open-hearted, careless Frenchman, whose only aim seemed to be to enjoy life. I had no idea that he was a detective, but supposed him to be simply a young man of fortune. Together we attended various places of amusement, and I soon found my friendship for Eugene Laromie was cordially reciprocated.

He was a tall, splendidly-formed man with a good-looking careless face, black hair and whiskers. A close observer would have noticed self-reliance and determination in every feature, and the calm, clear eyes told of more than ordinary courage. He was quiet and unobtrusive in his manners, and was decidedly a favorite with all in the house.

One morning as Laromie and I were sitting at breakfast, an old gentleman who had been boarding there for some time (he was there before my arrival) came in and seated himself opposite us. Laromie glanced at him carelessly, but I noticed a quiet smile in the corner of his mouth as he did so. I noticed also that Laromie was longer over his breakfast than usual, and rose only when the old gentleman did. My surprise was soon ended, however; for as the old gentleman turned to leave the dining room, Laromie approached him, and laying his hand on his shoulder, said, quietly:

"Monsieur Du Far, you are my prisoner."

The old man turned deadly pale, and glanced around hurriedly, as if to secure some means of escape. But Laromie's grasp on his shoulder tightened, and he continued coolly:

"Monsieur Du Far, I arrest you in the name of the state, for forgery and counterfeiting."

"Who are you?" faltered the old man.

"Eugene Laromie, one of the secret police of Paris, better known to you as Henri Gaubin."

The old man said not a word, but suffered Laromie to lead him away. I followed in the most complete astonishment. Arriving at the street entrance, we found a cabriolet waiting for someone. Laromie, after telling me that he would see me again during the day and explain the matter, entered the vehicle with his prisoner, and drove off.

I was positively bewildered by what I had seen and heard. Laromie a detective! I could scarcely credit it. I felt not a little uneasy, too. I had been expressing my opinions with regard to the government and condition of affairs to him without reserve, and many of them were not very complimentary to the "powers that be." I could not help fearing that his duty as a government official might require him to get me into trouble; and I was somewhat impatient to see him and have an explanation of the whole matter. I did not meet him again until late in the afternoon.

"Well, *mon ami*," said he, as he entered my room, where I sat smoking, "have you recovered from your surprise? Ha, ha! I don't know which was more amusing, your astonishment or that of old Du Far. The rascal was completely caught, and I do myself the credit to believe it has been one of the neatest affairs yet performed in Paris."

"Laromie," said I, as I pointed to a chair, which he took, "I am afraid I have been very imprudent since I have known you."

"What do you mean?"

"Not knowing your real character," I answered, "I have been perfectly unreserved in the expression of my opinions with regard to your government, and matters in general here."

"You fear, then, that I might have been playing the spy on you, and reported your sayings to the head of the Bureau of Police?" he said, hastily, while his face flushed painfully.

"Exactly," I replied.

He rose abruptly from his seat and went towards the door; but in a moment he came back, laughing.

"Knowing your opinions of our system here," he said, good-naturedly,

"I don't blame you for the suspicion, especially after what you witnessed this morning. But believe me, *mon ami*, it is no part of my duty to sacrifice my honor; and being on such intimate terms with you, I should have warned you had I thought it necessary for you to be cautious. But I am willing for you to hold your opinions, so long as you do not interfere with matters here. You have wronged me greatly, but I forgive you."

I at once offered him my hand, and apologized for my suspicions. He laughed good-naturedly, and assured me that I was forgiven. Then we sealed the forgiveness with a cigar and a bottle of claret.

"Now," said I, "I want you to tell me something of your experience as a detective; for, from what I have seen of you today, I think you must be an uncommonly clever fellow. Suppose you give me the history of the case you have just completed."

"They say at headquarters," said Laromie, "that I do my work well, and I believe the compliment is not undeserved. I give great care to my cases, and am usually employed in those which are considered difficult. But instead of telling you of the case that happened this morning, suppose you let me relate what I consider my most famous exploit."

"By all means. I want to know, also, why you became a detective. Tell me anything you like. I shall be a willing listener."

"I think I must have been born for my profession," said Laromie, brushing the ashes from his cigar; "for in my childhood I was always finding out other persons' secrets. My companions could hide nothing from me, and it seemed to me that events had only to happen for me to know them. Many that I did not seek to learn forced themselves under my very eyes, and frequently to my great annoyance. As I grew up, this talent, for so I consider it, increased. When I came of age, I found myself in possession of an ample fortune which was left by my late father. There was no necessity for me to adopt any profession, or enter any branch of business, for my support was already guaranteed; but in order to give my talents room for legitimate use, I determined to enter the secret service of the government. The chief of the secret police was a friend, and I sought him, and asked admission into his force. At first, he advised me strongly against the course I wished to pursue, giving me many reasons which it is useless to mention here. Some of them were good, others of no consequence; but none of them sufficient to alter my determination. I pressed my application with so much earnestness that the chief at last consented to take me on trial for six months. At first, he gave me only trivial cases; but I soon satisfied him that I was capable of better things than these, and he gave me more responsible duties. I succeeded so well in every-thing, that in less than three months I was promoted to a position of great trust and importance. I have now been in the service nine years, and during that time have made myself valuable to the government; and it has become customary, whenever a case requires unusual talents, to entrust it to me; and I do not remember but one instance in which I have failed to give satisfaction.

"Having told you this, *mon ami*, simply in compliance with your request, I will now relate what I consider my greatest exploit.

"About fifteen months ago I was summoned by the chief, and informed that a murder had been committed in Faubourg St. Antoine, attended by an uncommon amount of mystery. He wished me to visit the spot imme-diately and take charge of the case, which promised to be an interesting one. I at once repaired to the house. I found it in charge of the authori-ties, who had refused to allow anything to be disturbed until I had visited the place. I was told that the murder had been committed on the previous night. The victim was an old woman who had amassed a considerable amount of money, which she always kept hidden in her chamber. It was generally known in the neighborhood that she was very miserly and kept her money by her, being unwilling to trust it out of her sight. Her body was lying on the floor of the chamber, and the room had evidently been plundered by the murderer. The woman's throat had been cut through to the spinal column, and though she lay in an immense puddle of blood, there were no stains on her dress, and no blood marks on the floor of the room. This was singular, and at once convinced me that the deed was done by a practiced hand. The murderer had evidently held the woman in one position with one hand, while he cut her throat with the other with one powerful sweep of the knife. There was no other clue to the assassin. It was of importance to know that the murderer was not a novice, and, from the manner in which the deed was done, I inclined to the opinion that he was not a Parisian, for the method had never been practiced in the city before.

"I returned to the Bureau and informed the chief of the result of my observations, at the same time telling him that I had very little hope of succeeding, the clues to the mystery being so obscure. Nevertheless, I promised to do my best to unravel it. In about three weeks I was sent to examine into another murder. The victim this time was the mistress of a boardinghouse, and was a widow somewhat advanced in years. Her chamber had been entered and robbed, and her throat had been cut to the bone, in precisely the same manner as in the other case. She, too, lay on the floor, weltering in a pool of blood, but nowhere else was a drop of the blood visible, on her person, the floor, or the furniture. Evidently the same man had committed both murders. The only difference in the circumstances of the second affair was that I found on the floor near the body a pocket-handkerchief folded into a three-cornered shape, and showing marks of having been knotted at the ends.

"The thing perplexed me greatly and I felt quite hopeless of dispelling the mystery which surrounded it. The pocket-handkerchief was of no use to me, as it had belonged to the deceased. Nevertheless, I took it with me, hoping that it might be of use some day. I was very anxious to trace the assassin, for I began to see that he was commencing an organized system of murder; and besides this, I felt that my reputation was at stake.

"While pondering over the matter—and it was rarely out of my thoughts—one of my friends, who is a photographer, communicated to me some intelligence that he had gained from his reading and studies. He had seen it stated that the last impression made upon the eye of a dying person would be retained there for a certain time after death. That being the case, he thought it possible to obtain a photographic likeness of that impression, and was very anxious to try the experiment. The matter interested me at once, and I readily promised to give him an opportunity to test it in the next murder case that came within my observation. I saw plainly that the discovery, if successful, would be of immense importance in tracing murderers, and I had a vague hope that it would enable me to find the man I was seeking, as I was confident that he would repeat his performance before long. A month passed away, and then a third murder occurred. This victim was, like the second, the keeper of a boardinghouse, and was killed for her money. She, too, lay weltering in a pool of blood, with her throat cut to the bone, while, as in the other cases, the wound had been inflicted so as to cause no splashing of blood. The handkerchief lay near the corpse, as in the second case, but seemed to have belonged to the assassin this time, instead of being the property of his victim.

"I at once dispatched a messenger to my friend the photographer, who soon arrived, bringing with him instruments of great power and delicacy, which he had procured in anticipation of this event. The eyes of the murdered woman were wide open, and we had no difficulty in fixing her face in a proper position. The day being clear and bright, an excellent negative was taken, and when the impression was transferred to the paper, we found it the profile of a man's face. The upper portion was obscure, but the lower part, from the nose down, was perfect. The features were those of an Italian. This confirmed my supposition that a foreigner had committed the murders. Only the lower part of his face being produced, I was somewhat perplexed. It was too bad to be so near the end I sought, yet to be baffled by an imperfect picture. I was sorry that only the profile was the last thing seen by the dead woman. Had it been the full face, I might have had more to encourage me. Then again, there is something common to all Italians in the lower part of the face, and what resembles one might with reason be said to resemble another in this respect. However, my friend and I were delighted with the result of our experiment. It was a novelty then; now it is a common thing. We decided to say nothing about it until we had made other trials, unless we found it necessary for the development of the case I was engaged upon. I provided myself with a copy of the photograph we had taken, and determined to subject every Italian I met to a rigid inspection. On the whole, the matter was progressing favorably, and although the difficulties in my way were formidable, I could not help feeling encouraged by the events of the day, and I resumed my task with new vigor.

"I at once busied myself with searching for my man among all the Italians that I met. I frequented places mostly patronized by them—the boulevards, the cafes, the theatre, and the opera. Every Italian I met, even down to the organ-grinders, I subjected to a rigid scrutiny, and once or twice came near getting into quarrels with persons who resented my conduct as impertinence. At least two months passed away in this fruitless search, and, in spite of the advantages which I possessed, I began to despair.

"At last, the government having occasion to send me to Switzerland on a secret mission, I found myself in one of the small towns of that country. Having transacted my business, I set out on my return. In the compartment in which I was placed were four persons. One was an old lady, another a young one, the third a priest, and the fourth a man whose features I could not see, as his hat was drawn down over them. I knew at once, from the man's manner, that he was trying to avoid being recognized, and I determined to watch him.

"After we had gotten fairly underway, and had left the town some twenty miles behind us, the man raised his hat, and I could hardly repress a scream of delight. There sat the counterpart of the picture I had in my pocket. I was confident of it from the first, but I knew that it would never do to alarm him at first, and I did not wish to arrest him until I was sure of fastening the charge upon him. Every feature coincided exactly with those of the photograph. Although I felt certain of this, I quietly took out the picture and compared it with the face before me. The examination satisfied me.

"It was necessary to proceed cautiously. As soon as I had entirely recovered my self-control, I caught the fellow's eye.

"'Monsieur is Swiss?' I said, inquiringly.

"'No,' he replied, with an unmistakably Italian accent, 'not Swiss.'

"'Italian?' I said.

"'Yes.'

"'Monsieur is going to Paris?'

"'Yes. Are you?'

"'No. I shall leave the cars at Dijon. Has monsieur ever visited Paris?'

"'Yes, frequently. I was there several months ago.'

"'Ah, then you heard of the terrible murders that took place in the city during your visit?'

"The man started slightly, and looked at me searchingly. I could scarcely repress a smile, but I kept my countenance motionless.

"'What murders?' he asked hurriedly.

"I narrated the incidents of the three murders with apparent careless-ness, but all the while watched him calmly. He was nervous, and, as you Americans say, 'fidgetty.' Everything thus far confirmed my suspicions. I was confident that I had my man, but I determined to try him a little further. Since the last murder I had carried with me, together with the photograph, the handkerchief that I had found near the body of the third victim, and which I suppose had belonged to the assassin. Now I drew it out quietly, and, while pretending to use it, displayed it in such a way that the man could not help noticing it. As his eyes rested upon it his face grew perfectly livid. He glanced at me with a look of terror, but then by a powerful effort regained his self-control, and turned to look out of the window. In a few minutes he turned to me again.

"'Monsieur,' said he, 'that is a singular handkerchief you have. Will you let me see it?'

"I handed it to him and he gazed at it searchingly. I saw his lips close rigidly. After a searching examination he handed it back to me.

"'There is a singular history connected with that handkerchief,' said I. 'The last of the victims of whom I have told you was a distant connection of mine, and I was the first one to discover the murder. I saw this handkerchief lying on the floor near the body. It was folded into a three-cornered shape, and had the appearance of having been knotted. I supposed it had been used in the assassination; but as it was not injured, and as I took a fancy to it, I took possession of it before the officials came. Do you know I have always had an impression that the murderer was, begging your pardon, an Italian?'

"'An Italian?' cried the man, suddenly, showing signs of great excitement. 'Why do you think so?'

"'From the manner in which the throat was cut. I have heard that your countrymen are deucedly clever with the knife in matters of this sort. But it's an ugly, unpleasant subject. Suppose we drop it?'

"'Willingly,' said the Italian.

"With that our conversation ceased. During the remainder of the ride, as I sat silent, with my hat drawn over my eyes, feigning sleep, I watched the Italian closely. He never took his eyes off from me, and I noticed that he glared at me with a look that was not indicative of a very warm friendship. As the train entered the town of Dijon, I quietly prepared my revolver (with which I am always provided when on duty) for use.

"By the way,' said I, taking the photograph from my coat pocket, 'I forgot to tell you of a new discovery which was made in connection with the last murder of which we have spoken. It has been found that the eye of a dead person retains for a certain time the last impression made upon it. This being made known to us, we determined to try it with the hope of discovering the murderer of my relative. We procured an artist who made an excellent photograph of the eye of the murdered woman. To our delight the features of the assassin were revealed distinctly. Here is the picture, if you would like to see it.'

"The train stopped at the depot, and the guard appeared at the door as I handed the photograph to the man. He glanced at it for a moment, and then with a yell sprang to his feet, and moved towards the door. I had anticipated him, and as he turned he saw me standing at the door, covering him with my revolver.

"'One more step and I will fire,' I said. 'In the name of the law, I arrest you upon three distinct charges of murder.'

"In a few minutes I had him handcuffed. I did not get out at Dijon, but kept on to Paris with my prisoner. On the way he confessed everything; and indeed, on searching him, I found a memorandum book with a calendar. Opposite the date of each murder was a black cross, and other dates had a slight mark, with the names of women, and the words 'without husbands.' These, he told me, were murders which he meant to have committed. I also found in a private pocket of his coat a large, pointed, sharp double-edged knife in a paper sheath. The picture which I had shown him had completely cowed him, and had induced him to confess everything to me.

"Well, he was tried, convicted and beheaded, and I was complimented by the chief for the way in which I had conducted the case. I really do think it was done handsomely, if you will allow me to say so."

I thanked Laromie for his story, and we talked for a long time about criminal affairs in France. He promised, now that I knew his true character, to take me with him in some of his rounds, and show me the wonders and mysteries of Paris. I frequently availed myself of this kind offer, and some of these days, when I have leisure, may be tempted to relate my experience for the benefit of my readers.

—*The Indiana* [PA] *Progress*, October 3, 1878
—Originally in *Flag of Our Union*, January 20, 1866
—Reprinted in *Ballou's Monthly Magazine*, September 1875

2
C.S.I.:
Crime Scene Investigation

The nineteenth century experienced not only the much discussed and controversial impact that science had on religion, it also witnessed the impact that science was making on the foundations of Anglo-American law and jurisprudence. That impact had to do with the very nature of evidence. As long as there had been Common Law, proof had depended upon what came to be called direct evidence—the testimony of eyewitnesses, documents, and any other material which did not call upon the jury to make inferences. Everything else carried either much less weight or none at all and was deemed inadmissible. As the nineteenth century progressed, however, science did two things that fundamentally affected concepts of evidence. Science, for the first time, called into question whether people can always understand or competently recall what they have witnessed, and science began to discover techniques and invent machines which could make the unseen world visible.

But science did some decidedly bad things, too. When it came to crime the nineteenth century spawned an awful lot of claptrap: in attempts to explain criminal behavior pseudo-science of the period led to concepts which were at best quaint fallacies and at worst malicious racism or class prejudice. Thus phrenology claimed to be able to predict criminal tendencies from the analysis of head bumps and Caesare Lombroso ticked off the physical "stigmata" which he claimed identified "devolved" individuals and incipient criminals. These concepts along with mesmerism and other varieties of quack science were very much in the air because of the growing desire to believe that science could solve human problems.

At the same time these frauds were practiced, forensic science had its real beginning. Nineteenth-century science, for instance, changed forever the way investigators viewed bodies and crime scenes. When Poe wrote "Murders in the Rue Morgue," for instance, no one could determine, (1) whether any miscellaneous reddish stain was blood, (2) whether it was human or animal blood, or (3) whether it could be connected to any specific individual. By the end of the century two of the three queries could be answered with certainty and scientists were narrowing down the search for certainty in the third with the discovery of blood types. When Poe wrote "Thou Art the Man," only gross size and weight differentiated one rifle ball from another. In 1900 Albert Llewellyn Hall published "The Missile and the Weapon" in the June issue of the *Buffalo Medical Journal* outlining for the first time the ways in which the rifling of the barrels of firearms marks bullets passing through them. When Poe wrote "The Mystery of Marie Roget" the camera was only a savant's plaything. By the time of the 1860s, photographers testified in U.S. courts and by 1886 New York's Inspector Byrnes published *Professional Criminals of America*, a "rogues gallery" containing photos of all the criminals who had the misfortune to encounter him. When Poe wrote "The Gold Bug" (1843), the tips of one's fingers told no tales. By the end of the century the uniqueness of human fingerprints was about to be accepted by courts in the U.S. and Britain. And then there were poisons: by 1836 James Marsh had devised a test to determine the presence of arsenic, and by the end of the century chemists were closing in on ways to detect the presence of vegetable alkaloid poisons like atropine, hyoscine, scopolamine, ephedrine, nicotine, strychnine, and even the thriller's favorite, curare. And on top of all the discoveries in the realm of the natural and physical sciences, the emergence toward the end of the century of the new science, psychology, sent a tremor or two through the absolute certainty that witnesses can correctly process what they see.

What all of this meant was that judges (who decide what evidence is admissible), juries (who decide what evidence carries the most weight), and the public from which those juries were drawn needed to either reject science or to understand new ways of looking at evidence. And one of the results of this was the century's obsession with circumstantial evidence, or indirect evidence which relies on the observer's inferences. A lot of that indirect, circumstantial evidence was susceptible to scientific scrutiny and analysis. It was also something that nineteenth-century courts had to wrestle with—whether, for instance, photographs, or chemical tests, or fingerprints were admissible evidence. And the new approaches to evidence also proved to be fertile ground for stories in which the hero (1) uses superior observation and reasoning to supplant improper interpretations of facts and circumstances, and (2) uses new, interesting methods or devices to bring accurate answers to misinterpreted facts and circumstances. The mid-nineteenth century, then, became fertile ground for stories about detectives who possessed keen eyes, peerless powers of analysis, and openness and even enthusiasm for the aids that science provided. We have included several stories in the previous chapter in which cameras play decisive roles. What follows is a collection of other mid–nineteenth-century C.S.I. stories.

The Left-Handed Thief
Anonymous

"How many young men have been injured and perhaps ruined, by false suspicion," remarked my mercantile friend, as we were conversing upon the subject of the panic a few evenings since. Suspicion is like an assassin in the dark; it stabs its victim and he knows not whence the blow comes. Or it may be more like the keen frost seizing upon the ears, and driving back the lifeblood, and yet the poor man is totally ignorant of his situation till he comes in contact with the heat, and begins to feel the stinging pain. But I believe I never told you of the time that suspicion of evil was fastened upon me. It has nothing to do with the subject under consideration, though it serves to show how merchants lose money.

When I was a mere youth I was placed in the hands of Jacob Wharton, a merchant doing a good business. I was frugal, industrious, and faithful, and at the age of twenty-one I was advanced to the position of bookkeeper with a good salary. I had charge of the books and the safe, and all the money left over banking hours was also in my care. I tried to do my duty faithfully and I think I succeeded. Mr. Wharton was a close methodical man, with a quick eye and ready understanding of business, and as I fancied he was satisfied, I felt much pleased.

I had been a bookkeeper a year, when I thought my employer's manner towards me seemed changed—he began to treat me more coolly and finally I was sure he watched my movements with distrustful glances; I became nervous and uneasy, for I feared I had offended him. But the thing came to a head at length.

One evening when I was alone in the store engaged in making up my cash account, Mr. Wharton came to me with a troubled look and spoke. His voice was tremulous and I could see that he was deeply affected; he said:

"George, I am sorry for the conviction which has been forced upon me; I fear you have not been treating me as you had ought."

I managed in spite of my astonishment to ask him what he meant.

"I fear you are not honest," was his reply.

Had a thunderbolt fallen upon me, I could not have been more startled.

Not honest! And there I had been for years making it my chief aim and study how to serve him faithfully!

I do not remember what I said at first—I only know that tears came to my eyes—that my lips trembled—and that my utterance was almost choked. How long had he held suspicions? I asked him and he told me for two months.

"Heavens! You have suspected me then and still left me in the dark! After serving you so long—after striving for faith and honor that I might win your esteem—to suspect me in secret! To look upon me as a thief and yet not tell me! Oh, I would not have believed it!"

"Let us talk this matter over calmly," said he, his old kind tone returning. He was wavering.

I felt at first like telling him that he should have done this before; but as he seemed ready to reason now, I found no fault.

"You have spent considerable money of late," he began.

"How?" I asked.

"Have you not built a house?"

"Yes, sir—and paid for it, too—and thus have given my dear mother a nice comfortable home."

Mr. Wharton was staggered for a moment by my frank and feeling reply; but pretty soon he asked:

"What did the house cost you?"

"Just fifteen hundred dollars.

"My mother owned the land. And I suppose you would like to know where I got the money. You, sir, learned me how to save it. I have been with you for six years. The first year you paid me fifty dollars and I laid up twenty-five of it.—The second and third years you gave me a hundred dollars, and of that I laid up sixty dollars a year. The fourth year you made me a clerk and gave me five hundred dollars. My mother was able to feed me and as our little cot answered for the time, I got along that year upon an expense of seventy-five dollars. The next year you paid me six hundred on condition that I would help you keep your books. I saved five hundred that year. This last year you have paid me one thousand dollars, and I have spent only the interest of what I had previously invested, so that thousand was not touched.

"Of course my mother has worked, but she chooses to do it. I have paid fifteen hundred dollars for my house and have five hundred dollars in the savings bank. This is a plain statement of affairs."

My employer seemed more puzzled than before.

"Now," said I, "I have given you an account and will you be equally frank and tell me all that has happened to excite this suspicion?"

"I will," said he, taking a seat near me.

"Within the last year I must have lost more than two thousand dollars! It must have been taken from the store. I know the amount of goods that have been sold, and I know how much cash I have received.

"I began to be watchful four months since. Two months ago a man paid me in the afternoon five hundred dollars. I put it in the drawer, and on the next morning before you came in, I looked at your cash account and found only two hundred of that set down. From that time I have been very watchful and have detected a dozen similar cases. I have noted every dollar that came in after the bank account was made and have also taken note of the amount entered into the book, and during that time there has been a leakage of over seven hundred dollars! Now who has access to that drawer and to the safe?"

I was astonished. I could only assure my employer that I knew nothing of it; and as I saw he wanted to believe me, I asked him if he had spoken of this to anyone else.

Not a living soul but me, he replied. I pondered a few moments, and then said:

"Mr. Wharton, could I be made to believe that ignorantly I had wronged you to the value of a dollar, I should not feel the perfect consciousness of honor that I now feel. There must be a thief somewhere. Some of the clerks may find access to the money. But are you willing to let the matter rest a few days? I will strain every nerve to detect the evil doer."

He finally consented to let me try my hand at detecting the thief. He promised not to lisp a word upon the subject to anyone else, and also to leave the matter wholly in my hands for a week. He gave me a warm grasp when we separated, and said he hoped I would succeed.

On the following morning, all my energies of mind entered upon the work before me.

There were four clerks or salesmen, the one a boy, in constant attendance besides myself, and all the money received had to pass through my hands.

Sometimes I made up my cash account at night and sometimes not until the next morning.

In the latter case, I generally put the money drawer into the safe and locked it up. The key to this safe was kept in a small drawer to which there were two keys, one of which I kept, while Mr. Wharton kept the other.

The only other one who ever helped us in the store was Henry Wharton, my employer's only son, a youth of twenty years. He was preparing for college under a private tutor, but found time to help us when business was driving; was a kind-hearted, generous fellow, and a strong mutual attachment had sprung up between us. At first I thought of getting him to help me find the thief, but as Wharton had promised to speak to no one on the subject, I concluded to do the same.

That night I counted the money, but made no entry on the account. There were three hundred and forty odd dollars. I put it in a new calfskin pocketbook—placed that in the money drawer, and locked the whole up in the safe.

On the following morning there were fifty dollars missing. I counted the money over carefully and I was not mistaken. I began to feel unpleasant. My suspicions took an unwelcome turn.

During that day I pondered upon the subject, and finally hit upon the following experiment.

When I locked up the safe for the night, I spread upon the knob of the door and upon the money drawer, some pale red lead, being careful not to get enough on to be easily noticed. I had left the cash account open, to be closed up in the morning. When I next opened the safe all was as I had left it.

The next night I fixed the knob in the same manner, and on the following morning I found forty dollars gone!

Upon the pocketbook were finger-marks of red lead and when I came to open the cashbook, I found the same kind of marks there.

So I learned one thing, the thief knew enough to see whether any account had been made of the money before he took it. I felt more unpleasant than before, for my unwelcome suspicions were being confirmed.

I had gained new light. There was a peculiarity in the red finger-marks which told a sad story. Still I wished to try yet further.

For two nights after this, the safe remained undisturbed, but on the third night I missed seventy-five dollars, and I had now set my trap more carefully. The red pigment was not only used, but a private mark upon every bill in the drawer. The pocketbook and the cashbook were fingered as before, and the marks were clear and distinct.

When the week was up, Mr. Wharton came and asked what I had found.

"Ah!" said he, as he noticed the sorrowful expression on my countenance. "You have failed to discover anything?"

"Alas! I wish I could say so," I replied. "I have discovered too much. In the first place, the money has been taken from the safe, and the key left in the proper drawer, and locked up as usual.—Also the cashbook has been examined each time to see if any entry has been made of the money. There have been one hundred and sixty-five dollars taken in all."

"But how do you know the cashbook has been examined?"

"I will show you," I said, producing the cashbook and the pocket-book: "You see those finger-marks?"

"Yes."

"And now," I continued, "just examine them carefully. Observe how the leaves of the cashbook were turned over, and also see how the strap of the pocketbook was tucked into its place. Do you see anything peculiar about it?"

"Only that the finger-marks are very plain."

"But can you not distinguish thumb-marks from those made by the fingers?"

"Yes."

"Then tell me this," I returned: "which hand did the thief use most dexterously?"

Wharton gazed upon the marks and finally gasped—"The *left!*"

"So he did," I returned, "and all the marks have been made the same. The thief is a left-handed one, and is acquainted with the store and the books and can gain easy access here. But I have yet another mark. The last bills that were taken were all marked with a small red cross upon the numerical in the right-hand and upper corner. You can follow these up, for I have neither the courage nor the heart to do it."

The merchant sank back as pale as death itself. "Henry is the only left-handed person on the premises," he groaned, gazing on me as though he wished I would deny the statement. But I could not. I knew that his son was the guilty party.

"Ask no more," I said, with tears in my eyes, for his agony deeply moved me. "The secret is locked up in my own breast, and neither to you nor to any living being will I ever call the name of the one whom I suspect."

The stricken man grasped my hand, and, with sobs and tears, he begged my pardon for the wrong he had done me, and thanked me for the assistance I had given him.

On the following morning he brought me two different bills both marked with the red cross. "I know all now," he whispered, in broken accents: "Be kind to him, and let this not go to the world."

I kept my promise, and lived to see the old man smile again: for when Henry saw the deep agony of his father, his heart was touched, and he not only acknowledged all his wild sins and humbly begged for pardon, but became a true and good man, and an honor and ornament to society.

—*Fort Atkinson* [WI] *Standard*, November 28, 1861

Excerpts from *Strange Stories of a Detective; or, Curiosities of Crime* *Anonymous*

Introduction

Ah, sir! Things are not now as they were when I was a young man; very different, I assure you. Thirty-five years have not passed away without some changes; and I have seen a thing or two in that time. Why, sir, if I were to tell you all I have been through, it would fill a volume as big as the family Bible. Many's the villain I have brought to the gallows. Yes, sir, I took a pride in it; and if there had been no Jack Ketch, why I would have hung them myself, rather than justice should have been balked.

No feelings? You think a policeman has no feelings, do you? Well, perhaps we do get a little hardened with out-and-out rogues; but let me tell you, sir, there are times when a policeman finds out that he has got a heart, like other men, and often in the right place, too. A man can do his duty, and still be a man. Why, there was that case—. But, no, I'll tell you that some other time. You want to know how I became a policeman. Well, sir, I'll tell you. 'Twas partly luck, partly choice. I think I was born for the thing; cut out for it; one of Nature's policemen—it came quite natural. Why, sir, I was a policeman long before the new police was thought of. When a boy, I was mighty 'cute at finding out things. If I saw anything going on wrong, didn't I follow it up and ferret it out! Many's the nice little game I have spoiled by poking my nose in where I had no business; but I couldn't abear to see anything wrong about. Why, there was Barney: didn't I find out where he stowed away the eggs he took from under the hens early o' mornings, and sold to the shopkeeper in the village? And didn't I find out where Bob stole the clover his rabbits got fat upon? And where Sammy hid the pippins he stole out of master's orchard? And master's daughter, too, didn't she agree to run away with that chap from New York, and didn't I prevent it just in the nick of time, locking up the young lady, and going to the gent who was kicking his heels at the appointed place, and chaffing him till he grew mad with vexation and disappointment, and wanted to thrash me, but I wouldn't let him? If there is such a thing as a nat'ral policeman, I am sure I'm one; and it takes a good deal of natural talent, as well as experience, to be a real detective.

As I was saying, I was always in the way, turning up where a fellow was least expected. I verily believe everybody stood in dread of me, and that all were hearty glad when I left my native village to come up to town to seek my fortune.

Well, after several attempts to gain a settlement in the great city, I at last found myself, as I told you, in a large printing office. I had been there about a month, when one day I was sent for by the head of the firm to his private room. When I went in he addressed me in a friendly way; asked me how I liked my employment, and so forth; till at last he said, "We are going to discharge our private watchman for drunkenness, and we think the place would suit you. How do you feel inclined about taking it?"

"Sir," said I, "that depends upon the wages."

"You will receive as much as you do now for the present, and if we see you get on well we shall give you more."

So I agreed at once, and entered upon my new office the next day. I was timekeeper as well as watchman, from seven at night until six in the morning; and I kept a sharp look out, I can assure you. I could always tell when a fellow was carrying off anything in his pocket, by the cast of the eye he gave me as he passed by the window of my little crib; and when I hailed the culprit he made no resistance, but always came in quietly, and turned his pockets inside out.

The prentice boys gave me the most trouble: they were almost always beset by junk dealers, who encouraged the lads to plunder. I followed up two or three of these rascals, and succeeded in getting them tried at Quarter Sessions; but the amount of property which it could be proved they had received was so small, they did not get the punishment they deserved.

I was very fond of an active life, and after a year or so I grew tired of being boxed up all night, so I tried for a watchman's place out of doors, and soon succeeded in getting what I wanted; and for the next seven years, through summer's heat and winter's cold, in wet and dry, in frost and snow, I trod my beat, and that was in Broadway, up by the Carleton House.

Most of the watchmen were old men. I was the youngest that had been known among them, and they could not make it out how it was that I had taken to that sort of life. The *fast* gents found out to their cost that they had woke up the wrong passenger when they fell foul of me. They had it all their own way with the poor old men; but when they played their pranks on me they found they had "caught a Tartar."

I continued in this until the new police was established. Well, I joined the force, and you have no idea what a difference there was between the new system and the old, or rather, between system and no system. There was a good deal of animosity against us for a long while, and all sorts of opprobrious epithets were bestowed upon us. They called us Mayor's Pups, and dear knows what. I am rather quick-tempered, I must confess, and it required a wonderful deal of resolution to forbear pitching into some of the saucy vagabonds who used to taunt and try to aggravate those very useful public servants, the policemen. People took it into their heads that we were "spies," and that foreign tyranny was being introduced under our blue uniforms. It took some time for the public to become reconciled to us; but they settled down to right notions at last, and I think the excellent discipline and general good conduct of the men have fairly entitled them to the favor they now enjoy from all good citizens.

Ah! Times *are* altered. Why, sir, I can remember when the first omnibus started in New York. There were no cars in those days—nothing but old, dirty, lumbering hackney coaches—regular caravans—very useful at burglaries to carry off the plunder. As for railroads, why they came in before the new police; and we have been getting on faster and faster ever since, so that now my old legs can't keep up with the times at all: it is time for me to retire. What I managed to save keeps me very comfortable, so you will be always welcome to come and listen to one of my yarns; and if you print them, why don't give the names, that's all, for I don't want to hurt anybody's feelings.

Tell everything? Why, of course I can't. Might compromise the innocent. Yes, I know a good many things that people don't suspect. I know, or at least I think I do, who murdered Dr. Burdell, and so do a good many more; but they don't like to tell, nor more do I—it might put some folks to great inconvenience.

Which was the greatest case I ever had? Well, now, that is hard to say, because we think every one the greatest while it is on, and there is no knowing what may turn up before you get to the end of it. If you mean which was the hardest work, why, I reckon running after an absconding debtor—or skating after him, I should say—that was a hard night's work, and no mistake. Collaring those forgers was no easy job either; but, after all, there is not much to choose. When your hand is in, why you go at it tooth and nail, and you pretty soon make a hard job of it.

The Torn Glove

On the 4th of January 18—, a startling rumor prevailed in the city of New York that Mr. Stephen Meredith, a respectable merchant and citizen, had been found assassinated in his bed. His house, which was situated in Canal Street, was immediately surrounded by a curious crowd, and upon inquiry it was found that the news was only too true. The utmost consternation prevailed, and a hundred rumors were afloat, but nothing definite could be learned.

At this period I was engaged as a regular detective officer, and Mr.

Meredith's partner called on me the same afternoon to investigate the matter, as the inquiries of the authorities up to that time had led to no result.

My first proceeding was to make inquiries with respect to Mr. Meredith's past history, and the information I gathered amounted to substantially as follows:

The unfortunate gentleman was English by birth, who, at twenty years of age, emigrated to this country. He immediately obtained a situation as a clerk in a commission house, and soon rendered himself so useful that his employers took him into partnership, and finally he became the head of the firm. His integrity was unimpeachable, and he was universally respected by all who knew him. He had never married, but entertained a good deal of company at his house. His partner, Mr. Johnson (for it was from him I obtained this information), further informed me that he was not aware Mr. Meredith had an enemy in the world.

I next proceeded to visit the scene of the tragedy, and on inquiring at the residence of the deceased in Canal Street, I was immediately admitted.

I found that everything remained in exactly the same state as when the murder was first discovered in the morning. I entered the fatal chamber, and found the deceased lying on the bed. A cursory examination of the body was sufficient to decide how the unfortunate gentleman had come by his death, for on one of his temples was a blue mark, showing where a bullet had penetrated to his brain.

The room in which the deed had been committed was on the third floor, fronting the street, and the door opened into a corridor, which was common to several apartments. The second floor was used as a drawing room and breakfast parlor, and the ground floor was used as a drugstore.

On the very onset of my investigations I was surrounded by a mystery, for the two servant girls, the only inmates of the house besides Mr. Meredith, informed me that the front door was fastened on the inside in the morning when they went downstairs, thus showing to a certainty that no one had entered the house by that means.

They further informed me that the fact of Mr. Meredith not rising at his usual hour had first aroused suspicion that something was wrong. One of them went to his chamber door, and knocked several times without receiving any answer. Very much alarmed, she tried the door, and to her surprise, found it fastened on the inside.

She immediately went down to her fellow servant, and calling in some neighbors, they proceeded to break open the door. They found Mr. Meredith dead in his bed. The unfortunate gentleman appeared to have died without a struggle, for the bedclothes were not in the least deranged, and he lay there as calmly as if asleep.

The difficulty with which I had to contend in the first instance, was not who had committed the murder, but how it was possible for anyone to have done the deed at all.

From the above statement it will be seen that no one had broken into the house, as the doors were all fastened, and even the victim's chamber door was found to be bolted on the inside.

When I first obtained the above particulars, I proceeded to examine narrowly Mr. Meredith's chamber. It was a lofty room at the top of the house, as I have before stated. On walking up to the windows, I found they were surrounded by a balcony common to that house and the one adjoining. Here then was a mode of entrance into the chamber; but the windows to the apartment were both fastened, and I learned that they were thus found when the room was first entered. It is true there was a pane of glass broken, but that had evidently been occasioned by the concussion of the gun or pistol with which the deed had been committed, for the pieces of broken glass were strewn on the balcony.

My next proceeding was to visit the adjoining house, which I found was occupied by Mr. Rignal, the proprietor of the drugstore, a young, unmarried man, against whom there could be no suspicion, as he bore an unimpeachable character for honor and integrity.

In answer to my inquiry, he stated that although his bedroom was only separated from that of the deceased by a thin wall, he had heard no report of a pistol shot during the night. Nor could I learn that anybody in the house or the neighborhood had heard any report.

Here was a new mystery, which served to complicate matters considerably, indeed.

In the midst of my inquiries the coroner arrived, and the jury proceeded to investigate. I need not dwell on this matter, as they discovered no more than I have stated above, and after an hour or two they brought in a verdict that "Mr. Stephen Meredith had come to his death from the effects of a pistol shot from the hands of some person or persons to the jury unknown."

Having thus settled the matter, they all adjourned to a neighboring tavern, to talk the matter over their cups. They invited me to accompany them, but I felt in no mood to do so.

I returned home a good deal crestfallen. This had been the only case where I had been so completely nonplussed as not to have discovered some clue; but in the present case I was utterly in the dark. That evening, while smoking a cigar, I thought over the matter in every possible light, until at last, weary of fruitless endeavor, I retired to bed.

It was quite morning before I fell asleep, for this tragedy still continued to occupy my thoughts. My professional reputation was at stake in the matter, and once or twice I upbraided myself for not having made a more thorough examination of the premises, and almost felt tempted to get up and go to the house again, late as it was; but then when I attempted to individualize where I had been remiss, I could not do it.

I did not awake until late the next morning, and perhaps should even have slept later, had not my wife informed me that Mr. Johnson, the late Mr. Meredith's partner, wished to see me. I got up, and hurriedly putting on my clothes, went downstairs to the parlor, where I found the gentleman who had first introduced the matter to me, pacing up and down the room.

"Well, Barker," said he to me, "the murderer is taken."

"The murderer is taken," I repeated. "Impossible!"

"It is a fact."

"Who is it?"

"Rignal, the proprietor of the store."

"That cannot be; I saw Mr. Rignal yesterday, and am persuaded that he could not have committed the deed."

"Your acumen is at fault for once in your life," he returned; "the evidence is overwhelming."

"What is the nature of it?"

"Why, you know he occupies the next house. The balcony outside the windows runs along both houses. It appears that in the night he entered Mr. Meredith's room by the balcony, and shot the poor old gentleman with a revolver."

"And who has discovered the mare's nest?" I asked.

"Sullivan and O'Kief, who have been investigating the matter all night," he said.

These were the names of two rival detective officers, and should it prove true that they had been successful when I had failed, I knew that my prestige was lost, and that I should have to seek for some other means of livelihood.

"Mr. Johnson, they must be mistaken; the windows were all fastened down when the body was discovered."

"Yes, but there was a pane of glass broken next to the fastening. Besides, they have discovered the pistol with which the fatal shot was fired in Rignal's possession; his hand, too, is badly cut with the broken glass."

"But what was the motive?"

"Revenge, it seems; Mr. Meredith and the druggist had a violent quarrel the evening before."

I must confess that I was staggered;—but still I felt this man Rignal could not have committed the deed. When I conversed with him the day before, the impression he made on my mind was so favorable that I had not entertained the slightest suspicion that he could be the guilty party.

"It is strange, Barker," said Mr. Johnson, "that you did not notice one of the panes of glass broken?"

"I did notice it, but my impression was that it was broken by the concussion of the pistol shot; and even now I cannot understand how it could have broken on the outside, for all the fractured glass was strewn on the balcony; in the other case it ought to have been in the room."

"I am surprised, Barker, that it should not have struck a man of your acuteness and penetration that it was very easy for the assassin to throw all the glass out of the window after the deed was committed, for the very purpose of blinding people, as it seems to have done you," he remarked.

"Why, you ought to have been a detective officer yourself, Mr. Johnson; but we shall see. It is my opinion that Rignal did not commit the deed."

"Well, all I can say is the evidence is most conclusive; but I must go and dress for the funeral: it takes place today. Do you mean to investigate the matter any further?"

"Well, yes. I shall at all events convince myself with respect to this druggist's guilt or innocence."

Mr. Johnson then left me.

I determined the moment that I had taken my breakfast to call and see the accused, and hurried through my meal for that purpose.

I had already opened the front door, when I saw a young lady in the act of ringing the bell. Supposing it was some visitor to my wife, I was about passing on, when she accosted me.

"Can you inform me if Mr. Barker is within?" she asked.

"That is my name, madam," I replied. "Did you wish to speak with me?"

"If you please—on very important business."

I led the way back again into the parlor, and asked my visitor to be seated.—I now had an opportunity of scrutinizing the young lady more closely, and was compelled to acknowledge that she was one of the most beautiful girls I ever beheld. She could not be more than eighteen years of age, and possessed of a purely American face, that type of womanly beauty which claims the notice of all strangers who visit our country. Her face was oval, her eyes black, and shielded by long dark eyelashes; her nose was purely Grecian, and her red, pouting lips, slightly separated, revealed a magnificent set of teeth, white as ivory. Her complexion was very fair, and her cheeks tinged with the hue of health. She was above the middle height, and her form was most gracefully rounded.

"Mr. Barker," she commenced, as soon as she was seated, "I have come to see you on a most painful business. My name is Mary Murdock, and I am cousin to Mr. Rignal who is arrested for the murder of Mr. Meredith. I have just learned from him that you saw him yesterday, and I at once concluded to apply to you in my trouble."

"My dear young lady," I replied, "you may command my services in any way I can be useful."

"In the first place, let me ask you, sir, if you believe my cousin guilty of the foul crime laid to his charge? From what he told me about you, I cannot believe this to be the case; should I, however, be deceived in the matter, my visit will be fruitless."

"I will be candid with you, Miss Murdock. I do not think Mr. Rignal is guilty of the murder. I am a pretty good judge of character, and my interview with Mr. Rignal impressed me so favorably yesterday, that I cannot think my judgment has deceived me."

"God bless you for saying that," replied the poor girl, clasping her hands together. "You are right, sir—indeed you are. James Rignal is as innocent as I am. Forgive my emotion, sir, but if you knew how heavily my heart is oppressed, you would make some allowance for me. I will disguise nothing from you—Mr. Rignal and myself have been engaged to each other for more than two years, and we were to have been married next week. And now this terrible charge has wrecked all our hopes."

The poor young lady could not go on, but burying her face in her hands, the pearly tears trickled slowly through her fingers.

"Cheer up, my dear young lady," I replied, trying to comfort her. "I will use every endeavor to prove his innocence, and I have but little doubt I shall be successful. I was about visiting him when you came here. After I have had an interview with him, I shall see my way clearer before me. Call on me tomorrow, and I hope to be able to give you some good news."

She dried her eyes, and pouring out a flood of heartfelt thanks, bade me good morning.

I immediately directed my steps to the Tombs, and had no difficulty in obtaining an interview with the prisoner. I found him in a bare cell, with nothing but a couch on which to sit. He was a fine young man, about twenty-five years of age, his face decidedly intellectual, and its clear, open expression was certainly strong moral evidence against him having committed the deed with which he was now charged.

His eyes lighten up when he saw me, and he pressed my hand with much emotion.

"I little thought, Mr. Barker," said he, "that when I saw you yesterday, I should stand charged with this horrible crime."

"Be of good cheer, Mr. Rignal. I am persuaded of your innocence, and have but little doubt I shall discover something in a day or two which will prove it to the world. I want to ask you a few questions."

"I am ready to answer anything you may ask me."

"It appears that, on examining your rooms, a revolver was found with one of the barrels discharged?"

"That is true; the revolver belongs to me, and I fired off a barrel at a cat in the yard a day or two since," he answered.

"It is also said that your hand is cut with glass?"

"That is also true. Just before closing my store yesterday, I broke a gallon bottle, and cut my hand severely," was his reply.

"Did anyone see your hand cut before retiring to bed last night?" I again asked.

"No, it was late; and I tied my handkerchief round my hand, and went to bed immediately."

"That's unfortunate; but never mind. I believe all you have told me, Mr. Rignal, and have but little doubt I shall be able to ferret out the real criminal. By-the-by, a young lady called to see me this morning."

"It was Mary Murdock, I am certain," said he, his eyes lighting up with joy; "dear, dear girl. I assure you, Mr. Barker, I feel the humiliation of my present situation more on her account than my own, and yet

I know her heart too well to think for a moment that she believes me guilty."

"Have no fear on that head; she is as thoroughly convinced of your innocence as I am."

We continued to converse for some time longer. I did all I could to soothe the poor young man, and really made lighter of the charge than circumstances warranted; for the fact is, the evidence was fearfully strong against Rignal. The broken pane of glass, the cut hand, the discharged pistol, were all important links in the chain.

"By-the-by, Mr. Rignal," I said, taking up my hat to leave, "it is reported that you had a violent quarrel with the deceased the evening before the murder—is it true?"

"It was not a violent quarrel; it is true we had some words. The fact is, Mr. Meredith was a very exacting man. He came into my store and complained about the hydrant in the yard being out of repair, and contended that as I occupied the ground floor, it was my duty to repair it. I contended that the expense ought to be shared between us, especially as he used the hydrant more than I did. One thing led to another, and some sharp—but not violent—words passed between us."

"The difficulty has been a good deal magnified. Did anyone hear this quarrel?"

"There were two or three people in the store."

"That's rather unfortunate; but I must leave you now, for I have a good deal to do. Good-by. You shall hear from me in a day."

Shaking him cordially by the hand, I left the prison. When I arrived in the street I paused for a moment to collect my thoughts, and to decide on the best step for me to take.

While plunged in a brown study, I felt someone tap me on the shoulder. I turned hastily round, and found it to be no other than Mr. Sullivan, my rival detective friend.

A smile of joy illuminated his features, and he could scarcely conceal his satisfaction at having, as he thought, outgeneraled me.

"How are you Barker?" said he. "You don't appear to feel this cold weather, if I may judge from the quiet way in which you stand on the corner of the street. One would suppose that some weighty matter occupied your mind."

"You are right," I returned. "A very weighty matter does occupy my mind—nothing less, in fact, than the way to prove that Rignal is innocent."

"I guess you'll have a difficult matter to do that," he replied with a chuckle. "We've got you in a tight place, I reckon, Barker."

"Let those laugh who win," I returned. "Rignal isn't committed yet. Don't crow too soon."

"Well, Barker, don't get out of temper—good-by. Just sleep two or three nights on it, and then, perhaps, you may come to some satisfactory conclusion."

I bade him good morning, and he went away, his whole face lighted up with a real joy. I confess I felt annoyed at the fellow's triumph, and what was the worst of it, I saw no way of proving the innocence of the accused; but still I was perfectly convinced that he was innocent, and I determined that I would not rest day or night until I had found out the truth. I returned home in an irritable state of mind, and my poor wife was soon made aware of the fact, for all the questions she asked me were either not answered at all, or responded to in no very gentle manner.

My wife, who is a sensible woman, saw there was something wrong, and left me to my own reflections.

A week elapsed without my being able to advance a single step in the task I had set for myself. I have generally plenty of hope in my nature, but I began to grow discouraged. My health, too, began to suffer, for I could not sleep much at night.

One day I was walking down Broadway, and by chance cast my eyes into a store window near Barclay Street. On a card, hanging over what appeared to be a large walking-stick, were printed the words "Air Gun."

I do not know what it was that caused me to stop and examine it. The fact is, I had never heard of such a weapon, and I suppose it was simply curiosity which actuated me.

At last I entered the store, and found a gentlemanly-looking young man behind the counter.

"You've got something new in the window," said I.

"Yes; we received them only a week ago from Europe. They are called air guns; they don't seem to sell very well, though."

"What do they propose to do?" I inquired.

"Well, they fire a ball by means of air compressed, thus doing away with the necessity of loading with gunpowder," he replied.

"A very strange kind of weapon," I ejaculated.

"Yes, and a dangerous one in the hands of bad men."

"How so?"

"When they are discharged, they make no report."

These last words struck me forcibly—for it will be remembered by the reader that not a soul had heard any report of a pistol on the night of the murder of Mr. Meredith. The idea entered my mind that this was the weapon used to effect his death.

"You say they don't sell well?" I carelessly asked.

"No, indeed: we've had them over one week, and have only sold one," he replied.

"I suppose they are very expensive—are they not?"

"Yes, that's the difficulty, very few persons can afford to buy them. Even the gentleman who bought the one we sold got tired of his bargain and wanted us to take it back again the other day—but," he continued, "we never take articles back."

"I suppose he'd be willing to sell it cheap now?"

"I reckon he would take half the price for it. But why do you ask? Do you want to buy one?"

"Well, I wouldn't mind possessing one as a curiosity if I could get it cheap. Do you know the name of the gentleman who bought it?"

"I do not—but he lives somewhere uptown."

"I know a great many persons uptown—can you describe him? Perhaps I may know him."

"He's a tall man with gray whiskers, dressed in black."

"Thank you, sir. I will see if I can find him."

I left the store with a hundred strange thoughts in my brain. I had a presentiment that the man who purchased that air gun was Mr. Meredith's murderer.

The next thing for me to do was to find out who had purchased the gun. The clerk's description, "a tall man with gray whiskers, dressed in black," was altogether too vague to be reliable. I determined first, however, I would again visit the premises; for even after I had found the purchaser, I must prove how he used the weapon.

I immediately turned up Broadway again, and directed my steps to the late Mr. Meredith's residence in Canal Street. Things remained in much the same position as when I first visited the dwelling. I again visited the bed chamber of the deceased and made even a more searching scrutiny than at first.

I really thought it was to be attended with the same result, when happening to cast my eyes up to the ceiling, I noticed for the first time that instead of its being a level surface, without any indentation or inequality, there was something that appeared like a trapdoor on one side of it, but it fitted so closely, that had not the sun at that moment been shining upon it, I am certain I should not have seen it. I called one of the servants into the apartment.

"Where does that opening lead to?" I asked, pointing to the trapdoor in the ceiling.

"Sure, an' it leads to the top of the house, sir," replied Bridget, evidently a recent importation.

"Is it ever used?"

"Niver to my knowledge; but I heard the poor dead gentleman say one day that it was a good place to see the stars up there."

I procured a ladder and found that the trapdoor was easily moved. It opened into a small space between the roof and the ceiling, from which space a short flight of stairs led out to the roof. While searching here very closely, I found a piece of woolen material adhering to a nail which projected from the steps, owing to a piece of wood having been broken away. I immediately recognized this piece of stuff to be a portion of a glove. It was evident that someone while descending the ladder had caught his glove in the nail, and on withdrawing his hand, a piece of the glove had remained behind. The circumstances convinced me that the place had been recently visited.

I also discovered another important fact—the opening made by the removal of the trapdoor, gave a person a perfect command over the bed, and nothing was more easy than to shoot a person reclining there from that situation. I had no doubt in my mind but it was from this spot that the murder had been committed.

I had now decided two facts—the weapon and the place—another followed from this—whoever had committed the deed, must have known the premises thoroughly. But there was still another important point to be settled. How did the murderer reach the trapdoor? It was evident it could not have been through the deceased's chamber.

It seemed to me that the most feasible way of discovering this was to endeavor to find an outlet by means of the roof. I had no difficulty in walking along it, as it was flat, and connected with several other houses which were all built exactly alike. I walked along the roof of four houses without finding any outlet; but when I came to the fifth I found a trapdoor which fastened on the inside. This I knew was the top of a tavern or second-rate hotel called "The Retreat," which I had often patronized with my friends, as it was a noted place for good oysters.

I retraced my way back to the point from which I started, and again descending into the chamber of the deceased, I hurriedly left the house for the purpose of visiting the tavern.

I found the proprietor of the place in the barroom. He knew me well, and advanced and shook hands.

After some desultory conversation, I said to him, "Jones, do you remember the evening of the 3rd of this month?"

"Certainly I do—the night Mr. Meredith was murdered."

"Had you any stranger staying with you that night?"

"Yes, to be sure; there was a gentleman staying with us that night. I remember him very well because he carried a curious-looking cane with him, and he insisted in sleeping in one particular room, and that, too, at the top of the house."

"Would you be kind enough to let me see that chamber?"

"Certainly; come this way."

He led me to the room occupied by the stranger. It was as I expected; in the ceiling was the same species of trapdoor as that in Mr. Meredith's room.

I now felt certain that I was on the right clue.

"What kind of looking man is he?" I asked.

"He was quite a gentlemanly-looking man, tall, well-dressed, and if I remember right, had gray whiskers. But why do you ask all these questions?—You don't imagine he had anything to do with the murder, do you? If you fancy so, I can tell you, you are on the wrong scent. I can swear that he never left the house during the night."

"I am much obliged to you for your information. I may turn it to use or not, according to circumstances. Good morning."

I shook the worthy host by the hand and returned home in high glee.—Nothing inspirits a detective officer more than finding a clue; the first link of the chain found, he is generally able to follow it up very rapidly.

The same evening Mary Murdock paid me a visit, and it gave me great pleasure to be able to whisper words of encouragement in her ear, for the poor girl was becoming discouraged and more anxious every day. It gave me intense satisfaction to see her go away with a load of anxiety removed from her heart. The same night I caused the following advertisement to be put into the morning *Herald*:

"Anyone possessing a second-hand air gun, and may wish to dispose of it, may hear of a purchaser by addressing X.Y.Z., Broadway P.O."

I received no answer for two days. The third morning, however, I got one, and smiled with self-satisfaction when I placed it in my pocket after perusing it. The next afternoon I visited Mr. Johnson, and found him at his office.

"How are you Barker?" said he, as soon as he saw me, "anything new stirring?"

"Nothing particular," I replied; "I thought I would come over to see you, and let you know how I am getting along."

"Well, how do you get along? I suppose you are now convinced that Rignal is the guilty party?"

"By no means," I returned. "I am more satisfied than ever that he did not commit the deed."

"Well, I don't blame you for sticking to your opinion, especially as Sullivan and O'Kief have stolen such a march on you. But I can tell you it will be a very hard matter to persuade a jury to be of your opinion."

"Perhaps not as hard as you imagine," I replied. "The fact is, I have discovered the real murderer."

"Discovered the real murderer, and not Rignal!" he exclaimed. "You are surely joking."

"I was never more serious in my life," I replied.

"And who may he be?" asked Mr. Johnson, in a careless air.

"*You*, sir!" said I, laying my hand on his shoulder, and giving a whistle that was responded to by the entrance of two police officers who had been waiting outside. "Mr. Johnson," I continued, "I arrest you for the murder of your late partner, Mr. Meredith!"

The effect of this speech on Mr. Johnson was terrible to behold. He turned white and red by turns, he trembled in every limb, and gasped for breath.

I thought at first he would have fainted, but after a fearful struggle he recovered himself.

"This is a joke of yours, Barker," said he. "You must either be a madman or a fool."

"Neither one nor the other," I returned. "I assure you I never was more in my senses in my life."

"But where is your proof?"

"Well, I don't see any harm in telling you. I have discovered that on the second of January you purchased an air gun at a store on Broadway. On the night of the third, you stayed at a tavern in Canal Street called 'The Retreat.' In the middle of the night you made your way through a trapdoor in the ceiling to the roof of the house. You then pursued your way across the roof until you reached Mr. Meredith's house, you then removed the trapdoor which opened into his room, and shot the poor gentleman while he was asleep in his bed. This done, you returned by the same way that you had come, closing both trapdoors carefully after you."

"How do you know all this—there is no truth in it."

"I know it all by this," I replied, taking from my pocket the piece of torn glove I found hanging to the nail, "and this," I continued, going to his desk and taking up a pair of gloves I saw lying on the top of it, "and this is the pair of gloves to which the piece belongs."

So saying, I opened them, and sure enough there was a piece torn out of one of them, which the portion that I had brought with me exactly fitted.

Johnson, when he saw the proofs accumulate against him, hung his head and was silent for a moment or two. At last a sudden thought seemed to strike him, and he exclaimed:

"You cannot prove I ever possessed an air gun."

"Excuse me, Mr. Johnson," I returned, in the politest manner possible; "you sold it yesterday, and I bought it, and have it now in my possession. Here is your letter," I continued, taking the note I had received from the Broadway post office—"Making the offer to sell to X.Y.Z. I am X.Y.Z., and, disguised as a countryman, received it from your hands. And what is more, the bullet found lodged in the brain of the unfortunate deceased, exactly fitted the barrel of the gun."

"Gentlemen, I am your prisoner," were the only words he uttered.

He was removed to the Tombs; the evidence against him was overwhelming; he was convicted of willful murder three weeks afterwards.

On examination it was discovered that he had used the means of the firm to a large amount in private speculations of his own, which had all failed. He could not have delayed exposure many days longer, and saw no other means of escape but by taking his partner's life.

I cannot express the joy of Mary Murdock and Rignal on his release. I had the satisfaction of seeing them married a few weeks afterwards. Sullivan and O'Kief were so chagrined at my success in this case, that they at once took up their abode in a Southern city; I have never heard or seen anything of them since.

—From *Strange Stories of a Detective; or, Curiosities of Crime, by a retired member of the Detective Police* (New York: Dick & Fitzgerald, 1863).

The First Case
Anonymous

I could not help admiring the "Doctor." He was one of the handsomest men I ever saw—tall, compact, clear-cut, with a mild and amiable face, and a perfect dresser; always looking as though he had—to use a very original phrase—just stepped out of a bandbox. He sat with his legs under my mahogany, or black oak, and sipped Amontillado, and ate broiled woodcock, precisely as though they were his daily fare. The doctor would not, perhaps, have been considered exactly the associate for a man in my position, the head of a first-class commercial house—barring all egotism—but I would have defied anyone, by his looks, to have named his profession.

In two words, the doctor was a professional detective, and, in the line of his business, had just done me a service which the amount of money I had given him did not pay for, and I had extended the civility of an invitation to dinner, at my own house, for several reasons, one being that I thought him a quiet and entertaining gentleman, and another, that he had, by his penetration and good management, unveiled a matter that had troubled me very seriously for some weeks—not so much by the loss of money involved, as from the fear lest the discovery should inculpate some of my confidential employees in the countinghouse, not one of whom, when the affair first occurred, could I look on with suspicion, or think of as guilty, without a feeling of intense pain, all of them having been many years with me and endeared by faithful service. Before I go on with my main narrative, perhaps it would be well to tell how I came to employ the doctor on my own behalf. Although having no connection with the tale, it will show how wise heads—as they think themselves—can be bothered with a simple thing when unused to the business.

From the day that I first came into our house, as a partner, I have always attended to the cash and banking business myself, all moneys, checks, drafts etc., passing through my hands or accounted for to me. In three-and-twenty years' experience, I never had an error but which, on careful revision, could be rectified, nor had any moneys ever been lost or stolen.

You may judge, therefore, of my surprise when, one day—it had been a very heavy cash day—on making up my account, I found myself two thousand three hundred and fifty-seven dollars short. There was no such amount entered in any way that I could possibly have made an error in, and nothing in all my transactions upon which to base my deficit. I had but one place in which to put my money during the day, and that was in a drawer of my desk, a solid, old-fashioned structure, attached to the building, and put up when the office was built forty years before. Had the desk been one of the modern, flimsy affairs, I might have thought that somebody could have spirited the money out in some way, but even the idea of a false key did not harmonize with the old-fashioned lock and solid wood. I always locked the drawer, and carried the key in my pocket, and was rarely out of the office during the day, except half an hour for lunch, and then there were never fewer than three or four persons in the same room. At night, I invariably removed every dollar to the safe, so that any appropriation of funds must be made in the daytime.

This was the state of the case the day that I was two thousand three hundred and fifty-seven dollars short. I went through every pocket and available place on my person, though I knew that I never put any money about me, and then closed my account with the deficit, making up my mind not to speak of it that day, but to consider it until the morrow, before I asked advice. The morrow came, and, utterly discomposed, I admitted to myself my inability to straighten it, and called in for advice Mr. Conway, our old and confidential bookkeeper, in whose judgment I had great reliance. Mr. Conway did not, like the famous Dutch squire, weigh the two accounts, and give judgment in favor of the heaviest, but he did almost as well. He footed up the column of figures three or four times, counted my cash balance as often, looked at me over his spectacles, and told me the account was wrong—two thousand three hundred and fifty seven dollars short. That's all the satisfaction there was from Mr. Conway. After this, pledging him to secrecy, I thought it better to consult nobody else, but watchfully await events, charging the amount, as I was bound to do, to myself personally.

How much, for days, this matter troubled me, I cannot relate; but, like all things else, after two weeks had gone by and no elucidation had come to me, it began to wear away, when one day I was amazed and horrified to find another deficit of nine hundred and eighty-four dollars. This time, I remembered some of the very missing bills, and knew that they had been taken from my drawer and yet I had not left the key in it one moment while I was absent from the room, and all day there had been present at least two persons besides myself; and there had been also people coming and going all the time, but these were separated from me and the clerks by a railing, so that it was impossible for any person calling on business to approach nearer to my desk than fifteen feet. This time I consulted with my partners, and, after numerous theories—all of which fell to the ground—we concluded to call in the aid of some reputed, able detective officer; and, having applied in the proper quarters for such a person, we were recommended to Mr. Peter Schlidorg, a gentleman, who, by the wink he gave me after I had told him the whole story, and the assertion that "We'll fix this job up in half an hour," convinced me that he would achieve nothing. Mr. Schlidorg commenced his operations by glowering upon my employees, one by one, and looking into my money-drawer, and handling the money lovingly, so that I somewhat feared that he meant to confiscate it as part of the evidence; and ended by settling upon poor old Conway, who, he mysteriously informed me was the guilty man, but could give me no reason for it save that Mr. Conway could not look him in the eye; for which I did not blame Conway, for a more rascally, unpleasant eye I never beheld in a mortal man. I had some trouble in getting rid of Mr. Schlidorg, which was only accomplished by bribing him off, and submitting to his hints that there must be something wrong in myself, inasmuch as I was not willing that the investigation should proceed.

I then thought I would play my own detective, and, having put my money in the drawer, as I always did, watched the movements of everyone with the closest circumspection, although appearing not so careful as usual. Before going to lunch, each day I counted the money and again when I returned; but no result, until one day, on making up my daily accounts a little before three o'clock, I found myself one thousand one hundred and thirty-two dollars short. I almost jumped in astonishment from my seat, for the abstraction must have occurred within three-quarters of an hour, and with myself in the room all the time. This was staggering and serious, and I at once lost faith in myself. Here were four thousand four hundred and seventy-three dollars gone, and not the shadow of a clew. After another consultation with my partners, it flashed across my mind to hunt up one B—, who in his day had been celebrated as a detective, but of whom I had not heard for years, and if he were still alive, to submit the matter to his judgment. The directory gave me his address, and in an hour I was with him. B— was interested, but he had retired from business; rheumatism was the only thing he detected, and that to his sorrow. He, however, would recommend me to a gentleman who, if he would take the job, could unravel it, if it were to be unraveled by human skill, and he gave me a letter to the doctor, or Robert Blaisdell, M.D., as he strangely directed the envelope. Before I went to bed that night, I found Blaisdell, and not only engaged him, but, as I could see, interested him, and he agreed to meet me the next morning at the office, and so conduct himself that there would be no suspicion of his business.

He was there promptly, and opened matters in the hearing of the clerks by talking coffee, and proposing to sell a cargo of Rio to arrive. He never appeared to look at any of my people, but, with his pencil, as he was supposed to be computing quantity and price, asked several questions, and in a few moments communicated to me his belief that the clerks were all right. That was a relief. I opened the drawer, freely handling the money, and giving him every opportunity to see its working. He was bothered. I saw that by his face. He asked me if the clerks could be sent out and we could be alone for half an hour. Yes, at lunchtime, in an hour, all would go but Mr. Conway, and I would contrive an errand for him. Blaisdell went away, and returned at that time, and we were alone.

"This thing is done by somebody outside of your clerks, sir, but by whom or how puzzles me. Let me examine that drawer," said Blaisdell. "Have you any mice about?"

There had been a stray one seen once in a while.

"Because you know such things have been as mice using the soft paper of banknotes to make their nests. No," he continued, after close examination of the drawer—"no mice," and he drew the drawer completely out, and peered back into the opening. "It seems to go chock up against the wall, and to fit too close for even a mouse to get in."

I examined, and found he was right; but in a moment I saw his face lighten up, though I could not see at what. Again he peered into the depth that the drawer was taken from, and slipped it back quietly to its place. Then he got up absently, took a survey of the room, looked out of the window, and, saying, "I will be back in a few minutes," walked into the street, and, returning in less than five, said:

"You had better go on today the same as usual, and, after business hours, I shall want to come in here, with a friend of mine, and be entirely alone with him for a couple of hours."

This, of course, I agreed to, and went on using my drawer the rest of the day, but all came right. At five o'clock I myself admitted Blaisdell and his friend, who looked to me like a locksmith, and left them. The next morning, at ten o'clock, Blaisdell handed me the key of my drawer, which I had left with him the night before, and, opening the drawer, said, pointing to a piece of white paper pasted in the bottom:

"You will please not disturb or touch that, but lay your money carefully upon it. I shall be in and out here every half hour or so, to see how the thing comes out."

"How the thing comes out," rather puzzled me, but, as I was in the doctor's hands, I obeyed orders and said nothing.

Blaisdell came in and out, and talked coffee closely and knowingly, and I had some trouble, once or twice, to persuade myself that I was only going through the motions, and not really buying a cargo of Rio of him. All was quiet, and my accounts right, Blaisdell declining to lunch with me, saying, in an offhand way, that he would foot-up his freight-accounts, in my absence, if I would permit him to sit at my desk. In half an hour I was back, and the moment I entered saw a peculiar expression on Blaisdell's face, an expression of intense listening. He did not get up from my chair, but put his finger on his lip. The office was perfectly silent, with the exception of the scratching of Conway's pen—he always would use quills—when, suddenly, there was sharp noise and a struggling within my desk. Blaisdell jumped to his feet, excitedly, and called:

"The key! Quick! Quick! By George, we've got him!"

I handed him the key in an instant, completely astounded, as was old Conway, for he tumbled right off his stool, and Blaisdell unlocked the drawer. It was not so easy to open it, for it took our combined strength. The first sight that met my eye, when that was done, was a human hand, which Blaisdell seized with a grip like a vice, and in an instant had a handcuff on it. I saw, at a glance, it was a hand without a thumb, and, at the same time, heard Blaisdell say:

"Why, it's Thumby! I thought he was up the river."

I was so dazed that I could hardly understand the thing, and stood looking like an idiot, while Blaisdell took up a heavy poker, clasped the other handcuff on it, and, placing it across the drawer, said, composedly:

"There's your man, sir—Thumby Dick, one of the most accomplished burglars in this country. Shall we go round and see him?"

We went round and saw him, and, the moment I laid eyes on his face, I recognized him as a man who had been several times to see me in reference to a schooner, with fruit, we expected from the West Indies, professing that he wished to buy all the pineapples. This was the greeting between the doctor and Thumby Dick:

"This was a well-put-up job, Dick," says the doctor; "but it's played."

"If I'd known you was on it, doc, I'd 'av struck the heap, and gone."

"Yes," scratching his chin; "but you didn't want to kill the goose that laid the golden eggs, eh?"

"Come, take us out of this, doc; I've got nothing to say."

And so Mr. Thumby Dick was taken out, and accommodated with his bracelets on the same side of the house, and told us the whole story. He had noticed the money-drawer when he first came to see me, his intention at that time being to tap the safe some pleasant evening. He knew the next building well; it was a small drinking place in front, with a back room, and offices upstairs. This back room he managed to hire, and with the nice eye of a mechanic—for the job showed skill—through the wall he went, right behind my desk. At night he had skillfully removed the rear of my money-drawer, and refitted it with four wooden pegs (which was Blaisdell's first clew, as he was examining the drawer), and so could noiselessly help himself during the day; for, even though I might open the drawer when he was in the act, I could not have detected him, unless I bent down and looked back to see the rear part out. Blaisdell and his friend, the locksmith-looking man, had skillfully fitted a spring trap at the bottom of the drawer, under the white paper, so that the crowding of the hand, in the act of grasping the money, sprung the trap, and took Mr. Thumby prisoner—a mishap that he is now expiating at his old residence on the Hudson.

And this is the way I came to be dining with the doctor, all of which has nothing to do with my story.

So now, after telling (egotistically putting myself first) the affair of the money-drawer, I will let the doctor talk:

"Yes, sir; that's true—we do have odd things occur in our line. It has always been my rule not to work in a case with anyone else. I did not begin

so; but I had so many mishaps through stupid people, who thought themselves smart, that I concluded I would rather take the chances of working
everything out by myself. You can make some count on a knave; but a
fool—you never know where to have him."

"And how did you come to enter upon this business?" I queried.

"Ah! That was rather curious in itself. It arose from an accident, and,
if you would like to hear it, I will tell you."

"Of course, I would," and, passing him the sherry, settled myself into
a listening condition.

"Twelve years ago, I was in Boston. I had just graduated, and was
endeavoring, in my effort to establish a practice, to see how near a man
could come to starvation, and still keep alive. I had got as far away from
home as possible, because I did not want any of my own people to see or
know of my struggles, being content to fight patiently on until I had made
a success, and then let them know how I had made it.

"I had but one relative, I may say only one friend, in all Boston;
and that was Charley Drake. Charley was my cousin, and a clerk in a
drugstore—a retail store—where he had plenty of close work, and very
small pay. For him there was no such thing as rest. He slept in the
store, and was liable to be called at any hour of the night, to make up a
prescription, or retail a dose of castor oil. This may seem a trifle to
some; but, to a man who has been going through the petty drudgery of
a retail store from six in the morning until eleven at night, it is no small
matter to be waked from his first sleep to mix and pound, and spread, and
tie up a prescription—a task that requires quietness of head and repose of
body.

"One morning, quite early, I stopped in his store, as it was my almost
daily habit to do, to get some small matter I wanted. The proprietor came
out, with a look of anxiety on his face, and greeted me with—

"'Did you know that Charley is in trouble?'

"'Trouble? No,' I said, 'What trouble?'

"'A wrong prescription he put up has killed a woman. I wish he'd killed
himself, before it had happened in my shop. It will ruin me.'

"I looked contemptuously on the fellow, who only thought of his shop
and his pocket, and made further inquires.

"'Oh, it happened last night, about shutting-up time. The woman
died within on hour; and Charley is under arrest, awaiting the verdict of
the coroner's jury.'

"I felt an utter disgust for this fellow; but I thought I would give him a parting shot before I left him. So I said:

"'But why don't they arrest you? They must look to you as principal.'

"It was almost amusing to see his expression of fright.

"'Arrest me! What had I got to do with it! Why, I wasn't even in the store when it occurred.'

"No—the sneak—he was asleep in his bed, while he put all the work and responsibility off on poor Charley. However, I contented myself with asking a few questions as to who the person was that had died, and when Charley had been arrested; and then I started to see him. I found him, in a very little time, in the custody of one of the coroner's officers, awaiting the holding of the inquest, which would come off in an hour. As a matter of course, Charley was in intense mental agony, and it was only with difficulty I could get him to speak to the point. His mind wandered, and he was in a high fever. I got hold of his hand, and tried to calm him.

"'Now, my boy,' I said, 'this is no time for despairing. You must pluck up courage, and look the thing squarely in the face. All is not lost, as long as life is left. Tell me the whole story.'

"'Well, it was about one o'clock, this morning, and I was wakened out of a sound sleep to put up a prescription, and I put it up wrong. I was so sleepy, and had been so tired, when I went to bed! Oh, poor Nellie! What will she say to this?'

"'No matter about Nellie now,' I answered. 'If she's the little woman I think she is, she'll bear it nobly, and, no matter what the result, she won't think less of you. Now, then, what was the nature of your mistake?'

"'Oh, dear Cousin Rob, a very bad one! I put in three grains of atropia for three grains of assafœtida, and you know that one-sixth of a grain of atropia is a large dose. I knew it was a strange prescription; but, as it came from Dr. Barton Brewster, who knows what he's about, and is a regular customer of our shop, I put it up, and gave it to the messenger. I was so glad to get to bed again, that I didn't think about anything until about half an hour afterward, when the doctor himself waked me up, and asked to see the prescription. I hadn't put it in the book yet, so I handed it to him. He took it to the night-lamp, read it, and handed it back, saying, very harshly:

"'"Young man, just read that prescription again."'

"'I did as he bade me, thoroughly awake by this time, and, to my horror, read three grains of assafœtida, instead of three grains of atropia.

"'Dr. Brewster looked fiercely at me for a moment, and went off leaving me with the prescription in my hand, and saying: "You've killed a woman by your carelessness; you'll have to settle it with the coroner in the morning.""

"'Well; and they arrested you this morning?'

"'Yes; about seven o'clock. The officer says it was good in Dr. Brewster not to give information against me until after daylight, since I might have got away in the meantime, if I had been of a mind to do so; which, no doubt, was the doctor's idea. But, bless you, Cousin Rob! I didn't think of running away. I couldn't run away, if it was only for Nellie's sake.'

"Nellie was a dear little girl, to whom Charley had been engaged for a year or two, and was likely to be for a few years more, as he was waiting, until he could get into business for himself, to marry her.

"I cast over the whole thing in my mind, and the first idea which struck me was, that Charley ought to have a lawyer present to watch the proceedings, and see that he had at least legal rights, where all would be prejudiced against him. No sooner thought, than I remembered that I had been able to do considerable professional service in the family of a young lawyer by the name of Sanford; in fact, I had been fortunate enough to snatch a favorite child of his almost out of the gripe of death. Sanford was, like myself, unable to make both ends meet, and, in telling me his inability to pay me then, hoped that I, or some of my friends, would endeavor to make professional use of him. This was just the time, and, before the inquest opened, I had Sanford on the spot, anxious to be of use.

"The evidence was very simple: The deceased boarded in the house where she died. Was a young girl, about nineteen. Had no relatives, and only one or two friends, in Boston. Nobody visited her but her physician, Dr. Brewster. She had not been very well for a day or two, and Dr. Brewster had prescribed, late the night before, and sent a boy to Marcelin's drugstore for prescription. Prescription book produced by Marcelin, the proprietor of drugstore. Prescription read:

"'R. Hydrarg. chloromite,
    Ext. rhei aa ½ scruple,
    Assafœt. gr. iii,
    Pillules vi'

"It was written with a hard lead pencil, on an ordinary bit of white, unruled writing paper.

"Then came Brewster's evidence. He identified the prescription. When he found there was something wrong with Miss Selby, the deceased, he went to Marcelin's, and saw Drake, who admitted to having put three grains of atropia in the prescription, instead of the same quantity of assafœtida.

"Then came medical evidence as to the effects of atropia, and the amount that should be given in a dose which made half a grain to each pill, when one-sixth of a grain should be enough.

"It all looked very bad for poor Charley, and I saw plainly that, in the present state of the case, Sanford could not help him any. There was only one question he asked Dr. Brewster, which seemed rather to bother the doctor, and was suggestive to me:

"'Doctor,' he said, 'how was it that, when you suspected something wrong with Miss Selby, you left her for nearly half an hour with the ignorant people of this house, and went yourself down to Marcelin's, instead of trying something to relieve the deceased, and sending a messenger to Marcelin's?'

"Dr. Brewster said he wanted to be personally satisfied.

"'And how was it, doctor, that, when you were personally satisfied, you contented yourself with using only simple remedies, such as sulphate of zinc, and did not call in other aid until Miss Selby was past all hope?'

"Dr. Brewster answered that be had acted to the best of his judgment, and he was not responsible to anybody, even if he had erred, which he did not. And so closed the inquest, and Charley was committed to stand his trial for manslaughter, his bail having been placed at ten thousand dollars. Of course, bail was impossible, and Charley was sent to prison, cheered into a little hope by Sanford and myself, but still nearly heartbroken. There either little Nellie Wilson, Sanford, or myself, visited him daily, and did our best to cheer him; but the prospect was dark, and the State Prison loomed up before. The day of his trial was approaching, and there was not a bit of evidence to submit in defense, save good character, and recommendations from former employers and from Marcelin, all of which was poor hope.

"One day business led me past the house where Miss Selby had died, and I do not know what induced the idea, but I thought I would go in. The only idea I had, in effect, was to see the messenger who took the prescription, and talk with him, though I knew him to be only an ignorant boy. I saw the landlady—it was a boardinghouse—who was a kind, motherly sort of a woman, and, after a little gossip with her, I got her interested in

Charley's case, as an orphan, and without a friend in the world but myself. Then I found that the old lady was troubled with a dyspeptic pain, which I undertook to cure, sending out for medicine on the spot, without letting it cost her anything, and finally won upon Mrs. Bramble so, that, as I was going away, she said: 'Now, doctor, why don't ye come and take my little front reception room, and put up a sign here? There ain't no doctor any whars around this neighborhood, and I'll board ye very cheap, jist to have ye in the house on 'casion.'

"I laughed at the old lady's proposition, and told her that I would think it over by next day; I did so, and saw that Mrs. Bramble's house was much superior in appearance and location to the one I inhabited. The result was, I struck a bargain with the old lady, and moved immediately to her domicile. I hadn't been there three days, when, one morning, Mrs. Bramble, who was very fond of gossiping in my room, said: 'Doctor, I can't help thinking all the time about that poor girl that was pisened upstairs. I haven't had that room opened since the morning after she died. Seems to me as if't might be haunted.'

"'Yes!' I responded.

"'There war something strange, too, about her; and that doctor-man that came to see her so much.'

"'Yes!' I said again, pricking up my ears, and looking inquiringly at her.

"'Thar was so much sneaking in and out, and coming at all kinds of queer times; and then they'd quarl, and, when he went away, she'd fret and cry so, that she'd be e'en a'most sick.'

"'Hallo!' I said to myself, 'Here's a new shape to this matter.' And then I said to Mrs. Bramble, 'Where did Miss Selby come from?'

"'Well, that's the strangest thing of all, doctor. She never would tell where she came from; and the most that she ever dropped was, that she was from New Hampshire; but then her name never was Selby in this world.'

"'How do you know that, Mrs. Bramble?'

"'Because every bit of her underclothes had another name rubbed out on 'em; and one day there came a man here, and asked for Miss Goodwin, and, when he was told that no sich person lived here, he insisted, and said he'd seed her come in here. Then, when this was talked of at tea-table, before Miss Selby, she get dreadful excited about it, though nobody said a word about her being the one that just come in before the man asked for Miss Goodwin.'

"The old lady was making some revelations here that stirred my curiosity; but I could not see how they could help Charley's case, except that, if there was anything mysterious between the dead woman and the doctor, I might sift it out, and use it to soften his evidence against Charley, or, perhaps, force his interest to help the poor boy. 'All's fair in love and war,' and so I took hold of the slender clew to trace out who Miss Selby, or Goodwin, might be. The last, I thought, was the true name, and, although it seemed absurd to enter upon the search, in such a way, I concluded to write to every postmaster in New Hampshire. I framed a letter, saying that there was something of great importance pending to a family by the name of Goodwin, somewhere in that State, and requested each postmaster, if the name existed in his locality, to please to send me a list of members or the family, present and absent, especially the latter, and that, if the necessary information proved to be elicited through him, he should be well rewarded.

"This letter brought eleven responses, one of which was from a member of the Goodwin family, into whose hands the postmaster of the town of M— had put my letter. I had no sooner read this letter of Mrs. Sarah Goodwin, than I cried 'Eureka!' The very tone of it showed a mother seeking for her lost child, from the expression she put upon my asking for the names of the absent. She sought a daughter who had left her a year before, and the description, which I read to Mrs. Bramble, was recognized in a moment. Of course, Mrs. Goodwin must be sent for. Her daughter's effects were still in the locked-up room, and they troubled poor Mrs. Bramble almost as badly as if they had been a ghost. I therefore wrote to Mrs. Goodwin that, if she would come to Boston, I could give her intelligence of her lost daughter. It was a sad pilgrimage to bring the mother on, but it was better than to have her child lost, without track, forever. In a few days Mrs. Goodwin arrived, and, in my room, I told her the sad fate of her child, and pleaded with her to tell me all she knew of Brewster. She did not know Brewster, had never heard the name; but, after urgent pleading, confessed that her daughter had left home with a man named Selby, that she had written to her declaring that she was married to Selby, and this was the last she had heard of her. I described the appearance of Selby, and the mother recognized it instantly. It was that of Brewster.

"Light seemed breaking on this affair in a new way. What if this Brewster, who was a legitimately married man, had found himself hampered with Miss Goodwin, perhaps, illegally, married to her, and consequently had taken advantage of Charley's mistake—for it was clear that he had discovered it in time to save her if he had tried, or at least that was the conclusion Sanford and I had come to! This, indeed, was the defense we had designed to offer on the trial, bringing in medical evidence to support it. What if this were so, and we could bring it against Brewster on the trial, or, better still, get him to abscond for fear of the revelation! 'All's fair etc.,' as I said before.

"Mrs. Goodwin went to the room of the poor, dead girl, which was opened for the first time since her death. There was no mistake. Everything was recognized; and the poor, brokenhearted mother was in agony. I had sent for Sanford, and he had arrived, and was shown directly to the room. Mrs. Bramble took the mother away to comfort her, and the lawyer and I discussed the situation. In the center of the room was a table, one of those old-fashioned, wax-polished, mahogany tables, seen only once in a while. On the farther side of this sat Sanford, between myself and the window. While I was talking I glanced at the table, and presently my eye rested upon some scratches. Why I noticed them, indistinct as they were, I cannot tell; but my eyes would not leave them until at last I bent down close, and saw that they were the marks made by the sharp point of a hard pencil, through thin paper, and the very marks made by Brewster's prescription on the night of Miss Goodwin's death. The wax-rubbed table had taken the impression plainly; and there I read, while Sanford looked at me wonderingly, not only the prescription, now in the hands of the law, but the impression of another, almost identical, only substituting the word atropia for assafœtida. I was thunderstruck, and called Sanford round to my side of the table. He read it, and we looked in each other's faces. The whole thing was as clear to me as day.

"I called up Mrs. Bramble and Mrs. Goodwin, and both read the marks. Quick work should now be made of the whole thing. The room was closed, but not until I had made most accurate copies of both prescriptions. Sanford went to police headquarters, and brought one of their principal men, while Mrs. Bramble, in her own name, sent off for Brewster to come directly to her on a matter of importance. He arrived just before Sanford's return with the minister of the law, and seemed very much taken aback by meeting me, whom he remembered, at the inquest, as a friend of Charley's. I said to him: 'Doctor, there are some matters connected with the death of that lady upstairs, which I want cleared up, and I induced Mrs. Bramble to send for you, satisfied that you could enlighten me.'

"'Enlighten you!' he sneered. 'What have you to do with it at all?'

"'Oh!' I said, carelessly, 'I have taken an interest in Miss Goodwin's death, as I have in Mr. Drake's life.'

"The name of Goodwin staggered him, and he turned livid.

"'Goodwin!' he muttered. 'I don't know any Miss Goodwin.'

"'Perhaps you would not know her mother,' I said, as that lady entered the room, with Mrs. Bramble. Brewster staggered toward the window; I jumped between him and it, for I thought he intended to throw himself out.

"'Perhaps, doctor, you don't recognize these two prescriptions.' I continued, showing the copies I had made. 'Here is the one calling for atropia, which you exchanged for the other, when you called at the drugstore of Marcelin, and asked Drake to show you the original. The very same, doctor.'

"'That's a lie!' he hissed. 'I destroyed that.'

"'Oh! Did you? Well, you see it has come to life again. However, I am glad you've confessed that you tried to destroy it. And now, doctor, my advice to you is to make a clean breast of this thing, and throw yourself on my mercy.'

"He caught at this like a cowardly wretch, and, as Sanford came in, he knew him, but did not know the man with him. He told the whole story. He had beguiled Miss Goodwin with marriage, which, of course, was bigamy, and was in daily dread of detection. He had plotted her death, and this plan had occurred to him the very evening of its execution. He knew the working of Marcelin's store, and that, by changing the prescription, Charley could be made the victim, and himself exonerated. And then, as he finished, he said:

"'And now, gentlemen, I have done; what do you intend to do with me?'

"'Have you hanged,' I said, calmly.

"'Is that your mercy I threw myself on?'

"'That's too much mercy for a villain like you.—There's your man, officer. We'll go with you till we see him safe under lock. We don't want to take any chances on that fellow.'

"And that was my first case, and my first arrest. The next morning I was sent for by the authorities, and coolly informed that Brewster had hanged himself the night before in his cell, so you see I only erred by pronouncing who should hang him. As to Charley, the district attorney arranged his business in a few hours, and he was a free man. Marcelin was very anxious to have him back; but I obtained for him a better place, in a larger store, with less work, more sleep, and larger pay.

"As to myself, a few days afterward I was sent for by the president of the B— Bank, who, having apologized for his strange proposal, told me that he had heard from Sanford the whole story of my amateur detective business, and he felt satisfied that if I would take in hand the matter of the robbery of their bank—it had lost eighty thousand dollars some weeks before—which the regular detectives could do nothing with, he was satisfied I could make something out of it. At all events, on his recommendation, the board of directors had told him to offer me five hundred dollars to try, whether I succeeded or not, and fifteen percent on all the money I recovered, if I succeeded. I laughed at the idea, and listened. Five hundred dollars was a great deal of money to begin on. It would be a long time before I would get such a sum as a medical fee. I was interested in the story of the robbery, and I took the job professionally. Two months later I closed it up, having recovered seventy-two thousand dollars of the money, and received my fifteen percent, ten thousand eight hundred dollars, less the five hundred dollars already paid. Out of this money I set Charley Drake up, elegantly, in business, and married him to Nellie; and put Sanford in the way of getting up, sending him since a large practice. I'm done, sir; hope I haven't bored you with the account of my first case?"

—*Appleton's Journal of Literature, Science and Art*, October 2, 1869

The Hob-Nailed Shoes
Anonymous

Many years ago, when Western railroad traveling was not the easiest in the world, and when all the moneys due from the East in payment for western produce, had to be sent in cash by the mails, there occurred, not far from Chicago, each time several accidents in consequence of trains being thrown off the track, during which mail cars are broken open, and the bags robbed of a very large amount. The first of these accidents happened within six miles of the "Garden City," and was caused by the Michigan Southern running into the Illinois Central mail train, if I remember rightly, striking it at right angles, and not only cutting it into two parts, but making a complete wreck of both trains.

The loss was in every way large, and the conductor and engineer were killed on the spot—the former lying with his face upwards close to the mail car—which it was afterwards discovered had been forced open, and the gold and silver it contained, carried off. Mr. Pinkerton, the great western detective, who was then beginning one of the most remarkable and successful careers known to police history, was sent for to investigate the robbery, and he discovered upon the face of the dead conductor of the train, the imprint of a nail head, such as was usually worn by English laborers in the soles of their heavy boots. He then examined the ground, and was lucky enough to find a complete imprint of the sole of the left boot, containing a double row of nails, all of which were exactly like that on the conductor's face. He made also another important discovery—that there were three nails wanting in the impress on the earth, showing that three were also wanting on the sole of the boot that made it.

Mr. Pinkerton's theory so far was this, that the robber was in so great a hurry to force open the mail car that he set his left foot upon the face of the dead man without knowing it, and thinking no doubt that it rested on the earth; and that one of the nails—"hob-nails" he called them—having started from the leather, was more prominent than the rest, and so left its mark behind it, and with it a secret clue for the detective. Unfortunately, before Pinkerton came on the ground, there had been so many people about, that the earth was trodden down hard in the neighborhood of the calamity, and he had no chance of tracing the hob-nailed boot and discovering its owner.

He had made some important discoveries, however, during this difficult investigation. He had found out that the robber, whoever he was, wore boots nailed with hob-nails in a peculiar form round the soles, with three nails missing; and that the boots were of English make, and the wearer of them therefore, was probably an Englishman, and that the left boot had made an impression of the face of the dead conductor, and on the ground. This was all the clue he had to the robber; but meager as it was, he did not despair of hunting down his quarry. He did not believe, however, that the collision of the trains was purposely caused, but that it was an accident, and that the robbery was a sudden inspiration on the part of the robber.

Eighteen months passed away, and Pinkerton, although more or less on the watch, had well-nigh forgotten the hob-nailed boots, when one fine morning he received a telegraphic dispatch, which summoned him to another accident, which had just happened on the same railroad, within twelve miles of the city of Chicago. On his arrival, he found a great concourse of persons, officers and men and passengers about the wreck, and he immediately ordered a rope to be payed out and guarded by the company's servants, while he made an examination of the grounds, and search for the hob-nailed boots, if, by any chance, they might figure upon this scene also. He first examined the locality where the obstruction was placed that overthrew the train, and, in his great joy and surprise, there was the old boot mark with the many hob-nails; and a full impression also of the right boot. Of course he said nothing, but began to make detours in all directions to see if he could pick up the retreating trail.

He thought it most likely that the man would go boldly to the village, after he had laid his trap, and so he hastened on till he came to a bit of grass leading to the main road, on the heights above. Here he stumbled upon the footmarks once more, and proceeding right and left upon a line with the discovery, he found the advancing foot, too. The grass, however, threw him off all further trail, but he had proved that the same man who had a hand in the previous robbery, had planned the present disaster also; and better still, that he came from, and returned to the village. Owing to some accident elsewhere, this train was late by several hours. It was an early morning train, and the design clearly was to throw it off the lines and rob the mails, but it was defeated.

Mr. Pinkerton remained privately in the village, putting up at the chief hotel, and passing for a salesman of dry goods, for several weeks, making observations and notes. He soon knew everybody in the place, and had not been there a week before he began to suspect a man who was then absent, but who, when in town, stopped at the hotel where he then lodged. A short time afterwards he returned, and Pinkerton found that he was an Englishman, and began to look for his cloven foot. But he did not wear it at the time he was introduced to him, and Pinkerton reasoned that such boots as those hob-nailed ones could only be in requisition in wet or dirty weather, and he began to pray that it might rain. He kept a severe and close watch upon the Englishman, and followed him always when he could do so without detection.

A fortnight passed away, and the Englishman began to exhibit signs of great uneasiness and unrest. He was always going out at night, and

Pinkerton was always following him, and his face was always turned toward the railroad, upon which he was seen to descend, and make examinations of the road about a mile and a half on both sides of the village. One day he had received some letters from New York, and Pinkerton watched him more closely than usual. About a quarter of a mile from the village was the graveyard, on a hill which commanded the railroad, and at dark the Englishman set out toward this wild and romantic spot, and Pinkerton after him. The night was cloudy, but every now and then the moon broke out and lighted up the lovely scenery. To Pinkerton's amazement, he climbed the fence of the graveyard, and sat there looking toward the village, so that his "shadow" had to hide himself. Presently he jumped on a grave, and strode along toward the middle of the cemetery, with Pinkerton still after him, but dodging behind the trees and gravestones.

He could hear him muttering to himself, and occasionally talking aloud, and he stole up to him as near as he dared, and managed at last to creep into a vaulted grave close to him, one of the side slabs of which had fallen down. The dew was heavy, and the grass was so surcharged with it that he was wet through, but he kept on listening, and finally made out that he was reciting a soliloquy from Lord Byron's "Manfred," and occasionally gesticulating wildly to the moon. Was this man mad? What remorse had brought him here to vent itself in the terrible and dreadful lines of "Manfred"? At length he drew out his watch and tried to make out the time.

Then he jumped over the fence and ran down to the railroad. He was evidently waiting for somebody. For whom? Time would show, perhaps, for Pinkerton still followed him. Once he lost sight of him. Then he fancied he heard voices and hurried in the direction from whence the sounds proceeded—and as he gained upon them, he found that his man was returning. So he skulked again, and the man went over to the churchyard. He stopped several times and listened. What had he been doing? Had he laid another trap for the overthrow of another train? It was a dreadful thought: and as it struck him the due train was heard in the distance. On it came and no one to warn the engineer of the possible danger. In another moment, it rushed past them, and went thundering on in the darkness. Then, with all his soul in his ears, did the detective listen, expecting a crash every moment. But it was not to be.

The man watched it as it fled past, and then turned toward the village, and Pinkerton followed him back to the hotel. He was all this time in secret conference with the superintendent of the railroad, who lived hard by. The next day, when Pinkerton called on him, he showed him a letter which he had received from someone who said he knew the gang that had thrown the last train over, and that they wanted to get him to join them, their object being to cause more "accidents" before long. He offered for a consideration to join them and become a spy on their actions for the company. Pinkerton advised the superintendent to employ the man, stipulating that he should be allowed to come to the office while the conference took place, in order that he might see and thus be able to identify him hereafter.

He had no doubt in his own mind who the man was. He felt sure that he was the same person whom he had followed so often and so long, up hill and down dale, and into the very jaws of death. And so it turned out. The man was engaged by the superintendent, and was in correspondence with a clerk in the post office in New York, who informed him, whenever large sums were sent from that office, west. This is a fact, however, which transpired subsequently, when all was over with this very smart man who was so fond of playing the spy.

Mr. Pinkerton found that there was another man also in league with the "spy," and that his work kept him chiefly in New York. Pinkerton now expected every day that there would be a "smash up"—but under the pretense that the company called him to New York, the "spy" left the West, and was gone so long that Pinkerton returned to Chicago.

About three weeks afterward he received another dispatch to go immediately to the old station, his expectation being realized in another overthrow and robbery of the mail train. On his arrival he found the same boot marks as in former cases, and was now satisfied that he had got the real criminal—for behold! he had returned to the hotel two days before the "accident" occurred, but he had the cunning to be in bed with some other person all that night, that he might be able to establish an alibi in case he was suspected. But still there was no legal proof against him. The boots never showed themselves upon his legs, and Pinkerton even overhauled his room in search of them, but without effect. He found out, however, that he had a pair of strong and black-green boots which he wore on rainy days, and Pinkerton resolved to lay a trap for him on the next wet day, which happened during the same week the "accident" took place.

His trap was this. He persuaded the superintendent to lay down fine, red sand all over the paths to the office, and then to send for his spy, hoping that he would come in his hob-nails. They had not long to wait, for, expecting a payment of moneys due him for services not rendered, he came wrapped up in a big coat, and having on those very boots that had been so long a mystery to the detective. This time there was no mistake. The red sand was pitted all over with the small pox of those tell-tale boots, and now the reader will think there was nothing to do but arrest the man. But what proof was there against him? Vivid circumstantial proof in abundance—legal proof none at all. Pinkerton had taken the precaution to make perfect casts and drawings of the impressions in the earth; if he could get those boots into his possession, he might manage to scare the owner into a confession. However, he resolved to get him over to Chicago, under the pretense of setting him on the persons suspected of having a share in the late smash-up.

In this he was successful through the cooperation of the superintendent; and strange to say, he carried his boots with him on the train. Pinkerton now made up his mind that he would have them by hook or crook. So at a railway station he got the conductor, who knew the "spy," to invite him to take a drink with him; and when they were out together, those boots, in some quiet way, found their place under Pinkerton's carriage seat. On the arrival of the train at Chicago, Pinkerton followed his man until they got into a quiet street, and then arrested him, charging him point blank with throwing over the two trains in question, and also with the robbery of the Michigan Southern train some two years before. He shook in every limb, turned ghastly pale, and in half an hour, had made a full confession of his crimes. He owned that he and a friend robbed the mail at the collision between the Illinois Central and Michigan Southern, and said that they went to Europe and spent the money in eighteen months, when they returned, designing to make a regular trade of throwing trains off the track and robbing the mails. He was tried and convicted, and sentenced to the Jacksonville penitentiary for life, where he died after an imprisonment of ten years.

Such, as near as I can remember the facts, is the story of these infamous transactions. There is not a word exaggerated, although I am pretty sure that I may be inexact in some of the minor details. And who was the criminal? What was the name of the wretch who could thus harden his heart to destroy his fellow creatures wholesale for the sake of a few thousand dollars? Reader, he was a natural son of Lord Byron, and called himself George Gordon Augustus Byron. His mother is said to have been a

Scotch lady, living in Edinburg at the time of his birth, and a Stewart by name. His accomplice was a nephew of Charles Kepler. There is no doubt about the truth of the story. Mr. Pinkerton is well known over this continent, and in the capitals of Europe, as a sort of Police Napoleon, who never lost any great case he undertook, and whose talents are only equaled by his integrity. It was he who has always recovered the money stolen from the Adams Express Company, and who saved President Lincoln's life during his memorable journey to Washington, and it was the same great detective who, when yet a young man, worked up this Byron case.—*N.Y. Evening Post.*

—*The Fitchburg* [MA] *Sentinel*, September 2, 1871

The Mute Witness
Anonymous

One cold, raw morning in February, Byrd Du Peyster, a detective, received the intelligence of a fearful deed of crime which had been committed during the silent hours of the night just departed. The account of the deed was read by a boarder while the detective quietly sipped his coffee, and the man remarked as he put the paper on the chair beside him:

"There's another entry for the book of mysteries. I am willing to bet one hundred dollars that the proverbial acumen of our best detectives will fail to discover the perpetrator of the crime on Cherry Street. Gentlemen," and the speaker fixed his eyes on Du Peyster, "gentlemen, just think of it! A villain enters the abode of a poor sewing woman, whose only child is a mute, five years old. He comes to do a bloody deed, and his struggles with the widow evidently frightens the child, who runs away, and is found in the attic among a lot of rags. The murder committed, the man takes his departure. The widow's meager savings are untouched, her bureau and stands unrifled. Nothing has been taken save life. That man, whoever he is, laughs at the detectives, and dares them to hunt him down and tell why he took the life of a poor sewing woman. I declare, gentlemen, the murder in this case will not out."

The man's words, directed at Du Peyster, did not elicit a sentence in reply. The detective continued to sip his coffee with an air that seemed to say to the man, "You can't make me deliver an opinion."

The other boarders, more communicative than the manhunter, discussed the case until a general conclusion was reached, to wit: That the murderer of the needle-woman would forever remain undiscovered. The first speaker felt proud of the conclusion reached, and passed the cigars around before the company left the table.

"I would suggest that we watch the developments in this case," he said to the company at large. "It will suffice to amuse our curiosity, as well as stimulate research into the mysterious."

Byrd Du Peyster walked from the dining room to his little chamber on the second floor, he picked up his hat and cane and immediately left the house.

He walked straight to the unpretentious frame building on Cherry Street, wherein the murder of the night before had been committed. He found a swarm of the denizens of that quarter in front of the house, but two policemen stationed at the door kept them from rushing upstairs to the scene of the tragedy.

The detective, after pushing his way through the crowd, easily obtained admittance, and entered the death chamber, where he found a surgeon, two police captains and a newspaper reporter. The surgeon was examining the victim's wound, which consisted of a knife thrust in the left breast. The keen steel had penetrated the left ventricle of the heart, rendering death instantaneous. But there were evidences of a struggle in the room. A chair which had seemingly been thrown backward was broken and pieces of woman's work lay about the room.

Mrs. Nolan, the victim, was a woman about five and thirty years of age. Her husband had been dead near six years, and her mute son, Henry, was a posthumous child. She was a woman against whose fair name nothing had ever been alleged, and she plied the needle industriously night and day that her little family should not want for the blessings that she, despite her poverty, enjoyed. Her unfortunate son was the love of her life, and all of her motherly affection was centered upon him. A mute from his birth, Mrs. Nolan could not expect to hear him speak her name, and her neighbors said that she longed for the time when he might go to the proper school and learn to write, that they might converse together.

Byrd Du Peyster, the detective, examined the apartment without obtaining any clew to the murderer, and the residence of the denizens of the neighborhood did not enlighten him to a satisfactory degree. A man was seen to enter Mrs. Nolan's house about eleven o'clock on the night of the crime. The witness to this was a man named John Starry, who did not bear a very good reputation for veracity, and his word did not go far with the detective. No one knew of any enemies that the widow possessed, while circumstances of the crime clearly proved that booty was not the murderer's object.

For perhaps the first time in his detective life, the little Huguenot was completely at fault. He returned to his room, and, with a cigar between his teeth, threw himself upon a couch. There he conjectured and built theories, which he destroyed, till he lit a second cigar, and watched the smoke float ceilingward and vanish like his ideas.

For one hour he did not rise, and he looked like a dozing man, for his eyes half shut; but he was far from asleep.

All at once he sprang from the couch.

"It is my only hope!" he cried. "It may take years, but I can do nothing else.—Something tells me that the dumb boy knows his mother's slayer, and he must be educated till he can write. I will do this, or, rather, have it done. The great aim of my life now is the discovery of the murderer of Martha Nolan. The dumb shall speak, and it shall not be my fault if the dumb boy's words do not hang *him*."

Du Peyster left his room somewhat excited, and learned that Mrs. Nolan's son was already the ward of the city.

"I want that boy," the detective said to the commissioner of public charity. "I am interested in his case, and I will furnish him with a teacher who has had twenty years' experience teaching the deaf and dumb. Sir, that boy has a mission to perform, and in my hands only can he perform it."

The commissioner listened with patience to the detective, and the result of the interview was that Henry Nolan was placed under the care of a new guardian.

Having accomplished his object, Du Peyster placed the little mute in the care of a lady who had lately retired from the position as a teacher in the school for the deaf and dumb. This lady was the detective's friend, and she promised to bestow great care upon the boy committed to her charge.

The boy was a bright little fellow for one so unfortunately situated, and took quite readily to his change of life. The detective visited him quite often, and brought him many toys that helped to expand his mind.

After all, Henry Nolan might not be able to throw any light upon his mother's murderer; as he might have been frightened from the room by the murderer's first appearance. Du Peyster thought of this, but did not despair, and told his tutor to prosecute her task with vigor.

By and by it was discovered that the boy possessed a remarkable memory—that he seemed to forget nothing—and the detective, when told this, exclaimed:

"That boy is going to hang the man who killed his mother!"

At the end of a year Henry Nolan had made progress in the, to him, silent language; he had mastered the alphabet and was in the easy words.

With what impatience Du Peyster watched his progress, the reader may imagine, as the detective's whole life seemed centered upon the object already mentioned. Meanwhile he had not abated his search for the murderer; but his hunt had gone unrewarded, and without the boy's advancement he seemed as far from success as he was at the discovery of the crime.

It was late in the fall that the mute's teacher told the detective that he was learning to write. Du Peyster's heart leaped in his bosom, and he could not control his excitement. Naturally he was a calm man, but at certain times, since the murder on Cherry Street, he had acted like another person, and his superiors had noticed a change in him. From the chief and every other member of the force he had scrupulously kept all information concerning the whereabouts of Henry Nolan. If his great undertaking should fail, his associates should not laugh at him; should it succeed, he would laugh at them, for they had long since given over the hunt for the murderer.

That he might talk with his charge, the keen little Huguenot had learned the mute's alphabet, and thus materially helped the teacher in Henry's education. By and by the boy brought him specimens of his first attempts at writing, and Du Peyster brought a magnificent little engine with cars attached, to the house.

One night he entered the house and discovered that Miss Hurley, leaving the boy alone. The present just spoken of had stimulated the mute's ambition, and he showed the detective some fair copies.—Then, with his heart in his throat, Du Peyster began to question him about that one terrible night in his history. At the second question, in which was spelled his mother's name, the boy started, and the detective saw that he was recalling events connected with her. He seemed to be awakening from a dream, but was unable to put his thoughts together, and Du Peyster said:

"I must wait awhile. The boy knows something. It will pay me to wait!"

And so another year rolled away, and Henry Nolan was eight years old.

But when the detective again thought of questioning the boy, a malarious disease interfered and he saw the mute hovering between life and death.

For weeks the boy suffered; and the detective saw that in the end death would gain the victory. The attending physician told him that medical skill could not save his *Protégé*; and he felt his hopes one by one fly away.

It was a dark night in December, and the streets of New York were white with snow. The air was crisp and cold, and the wind rattled those shutters from the Battery to the northmost limits of the city.

In a small room sat Byrd Du Peyster and Nettie Hurley. On a bed at their side lay the pale emaciated form of Henry Nolan. A strange light sparkled in his eyes, and he looked like a person very near the gates of death. And they were not far away; for he knew that he would never see the dawn of another day.

At last his eyes became fastened on the detective, who, seeing the strange stare, rose to his feet and looked down upon the sufferer.

This action seemed to satisfy the mute, and the next moment he was spelling with is fingers:

"I tell you now," his fingers said, and in a hasty voice the detective summoned Nettie to his side.

"It is coming, Nettie—coming at last!" he exclaimed, and then the pair watched the mute's skeleton fingers as they said:

"A tall man did it. I saw him before I run away. He had a red mark over his right eye, like a scar. He turned the light down before he struck mother, and knocked her from her chair. This is all I know."

With the last word falling from his fingers, the mute sank back exhausted, and Du Peyster looked at the teacher.

"Poor boy! He's told enough!" he said. "What he has said is sufficient to hang a certain man in this city."

"What do you mean, Byrd?" cried Nettie Hurley, grasping the detective's arm. "Do you know anything about the man with the scar?"

"Do I know anything about him, Nettie? Indeed I do!"

"What, Byrd? Tell me!"

"Not now, girl. Let us attend to little Silence. See how weak he is. Why, I do not think he is living!"

Henry Nolan did look like a dead child; but he suddenly roused himself, and his fingers began to spell again.

"Good-bye! I am going to hear and talk now!" they said.

Then the head fell back again, and Du Peyster, who lowered is head heard the last throb of the mute's heart.

It was nine o'clock in the morning of the next day when Byrd Du Peyster entered one of the large pharmacies of the city. Approaching a clerk he remarked that he wished to see Turoyal Smiley on private business, and was shown to the elegantly furnished counting room.

The apartment was occupied by one man who was Turoyal Smiley, the head of the well-known firm of Smiley, Bridgeman & Co.

"To who am I indebted for this visit?" asked the lord of the counting room, turning from the *Herald* to survey his visitor from head to foot. "To Byrd Du Peyster, a detective," replied the caller, quietly, dropping unasked into a chair. "Well, Mr. Du Peyster, what can I do for you?" asked the pharmacist, turning slightly pale. "Have my clerks sold poison again?"

"They have not, to my knowledge," was the detective's reply. "Mr. Smiley, I want to know why you entered Martha Nolan's house one night three years ago and basely took her life."

The next moment the paper fell from the druggist's hands, and he was on his feet looking more like a ghost than a man.

"Martha Nolan, did you say?" he gasped.

"Yes sir. You killed her!"

"Who told you?"

"The only witness to the deed—her dumb boy. I want to know why you did it?"

For the space of a minute there was silence in the counting room. At the end of that time the druggist dropped into his chair and said:

"She knew me in Ohio—knew my crime committed there. I was afraid of her—knew that she would not take my money, and so I did the deed that night. I [will] write you my confession."

The druggist wheeled his chair and opened his writing desk.

"I knew it would come to this," he murmured. "I almost had forgotten about her boy!"

Byrd Du Peyster saw him open the desk, but did not watch him closely.

All at once, something touched his arm. He started, and saw the druggist's hand clutching a vial, while his face had assumed a color almost indescribable. The detective sprang to his feet and sounded an alarm.

A moment later several white faced clerks entered the countingroom; and hastened to the head of the firm, from whose nerveless hand the half-empty vial of prussic acid had fallen.

The tragedy was finished, for Turoyal Smiley was dead.

On his desk lay his brief but terrible confession, which startled all who read it in the evening papers.

—*The* [Hagerstown, MD] *Herald and Torch Light*, March 1, 1876

The Secret Cipher
A Detective's Story
Anonymous

"Ozlib:—Nvvy nv hzgfiuzh mrtsg zg 127 Uriv hgivvg.   MVW."

There it was, in italics, halfway down the "personal" column of the *Herald*, conspicuous only for its most aggravating combination of letters and figures, the sole clue to the whereabouts of the game I had been after for over a week, scarcely resting, eating, or sleeping in my anxiety to secure the reward offered in a heavy burglary case—and something else.

That "something else." Ah! My heart sank within me as I flung aside the enigmatical puzzle before me, and leaning back in my chair, gave myself up to the gloomy reveries of the past. Edna Dayton—how I loved her! How fair and beautiful as a Summer's idyl had been the weeks in which I had met her, loved her, and had been told that my affection was returned! How well I remember the bitter parting—a hopeless one, it seemed to me—when I learned my fate from her father's lips, and passed down the brownstone steps of the Dayton mansion, wondering if the inclination of moneyed men toward stone residences was not caused by the existence of a similar hard material in that part of the human anatomy known as the heart.

I was a poor man, he said, and the profession of a detective a precarious one. His daughter loved me—he could not deny that—but she was his only child, and her wealth and position demanded a match with some social equal. He would not break her heart by absolutely refusing to sanction our engagement; but if within a year I could secure a fortune of twenty-five thousand dollars and a lucrative business, and Edna was still of the same mind—well, he would consider it.

Twenty-five thousand dollars! I grew sick at heart at the thought of the condition imposed upon which I was to purchase my future happiness. Friendless, the recipient of a meager salary, and utterly unknown, where was I ever to raise this amount, and what business capacity had I, the son of parents who had given me every luxury, and neglected a practical education, until a crash came that left us homeless and in penury?

Day and night for over a month I had brooded over my sorrows, and then one day I was aroused into renewed life by the reception of a formal but courteous note from Mr. Dayton, requesting my immediate presence at the mansion.

My feet seemed winged as I hastened to the house of my beloved Edna. What did it mean? Had he relented? Was Edna sick, or did business await me at the pleasure of my hard-hearted censor? I was ushered into the library, where I found the old gentleman in an intense state of excitement pacing the floor, the window broken in, papers and boxes scattered about the apartment, and a safe in the corner broken open.

I stared at him in amazement.

"You seem agitated, Mr. Dayton," I ventured to suggest.

"Agitated! Agitated, sir! I am wild! Late last night or early this morning, burglars entered this apartment by means of yonder window and broke open the safe. When I came down this morning I found affairs as they now are, and nearly one hundred thousand dollars in money, bonds, and jewels gone!"

I stared mutely. The immensity of the robbery petrified me.

"You have informed the police?" I asked, when I could find my voice.

"No!" he thundered, coming to a full stop. "I have no confidence in a police force which fails to protect a house from such an audacious burglary and expects one half the booty for its return. Here is the room, and yonder is a list of the stolen property. I believe you are honest, and I leave the entire affair in your hands. Call upon me for whatever money you require in an attempt to recover the property or to detect the thieves. If you succeed within the month I will give you thirty thousand dollars. If you fail I will pay your expenses for the month, and place the case in other hands. Are you satisfied?"

I gasped spasmodically. Thirty thousand dollars! A fortune—more than the price of my happiness! And then the pride of my profession came to my aid, and I told him I should succeed!

I examined the apartment. The burglary had been effected very simply, apparently. Edward, the footman, a tall lank specimen of humanity, had heard a noise in the night in the library, but had paid no attention to it, as Mr. Dayton was in the habit of writing very late, and he thought it was his employer.

What puzzled me most was the means of entrance and egress adopted by the burglar, or burglars. The library was fully fifteen feet from the ground, had a bay window, and, except the broken pane of glass, there was not the slightest sign to show how the window had been gained. A ladder would have done it, but no marks of a ladder, no signs of footsteps, exhibited themselves in the damp ground, wet from recent rains.

I was sorely puzzled. I examined the servants one by one, but could find no clue to justify the remotest suspicion of complicity in the affair on their part. The work had evidently been done by scientific burglars, and they had worked at their leisure.

I inquired into the antecedents of Edward, the footman; but Mr. Dayton averred that he would allow no suspicion to rest on so faithful a servant to the family. I resolved to inquire more in regard to him, however; but I found nothing against the man, and temporarily dismissed him from my mind as having any connection with the case.

"You heard no noise on the night of the robbery?" I inquired of Mr. Dayton.

"None. I slept unusually heavy last night."

I went away thoughtfully, for I had found in the library an empty bottle, which, from the scent, I knew to have contained chloroform, and had I noticed the marks of muddy boots leading from the apartment, while around the window none were to be seen. The glass, too, had been broken by a quick blow, not cut out. Altogether it was a most mysterious piece of business.

I watched all drives frequented by the cracksmen of the city, and worked like a beaver. I could not obtain a clue to the perpetrators of the daring burglary, and after three days of unremitting toil, I was considering if it would be as well to call in professional assistance, when the advertisement in the *Herald* at the head of this story, attracted my attention. Instinctively I divined some connection with the "crooked" business, and, whether it referred to my case or not, I resolved to ascertain its meaning.

I went to the *Herald* office that morning, and introducing myself, attempted to obtain some description of the person who had handed in the advertisement. The clerk stated that it had been received by mail, in a letter inclosing the amount requisite for its insertion in the paper. Could

I see the original copy? He would see; and a message was sent to the composing room. Luckily, the copy had been preserved. It was written in a disguised hand, on a little scrap of paper. I asked leave to retain it, and, permission being granted me, I returned to my room at once.

I poured over the cipher for a long time, and discouraged at my inability to make out one word of it, was finally about to abandon it, when I chanced to look at the reverse side of the paper. There were figures and words on it, and I read "US Bonds, $-0,000," and other memoranda, indicating that it had been a loose wrapper for valuable papers.

Then I knew that the advertisement bore an important relation to the robbery.

And so, until the day upon which the story opens, I was unable to make head or tail of the secret enigma.

So wearied was I that I fell asleep with my head upon my desk, and I did not awaken until noontime. It is wonderful how a brief repose will clear the mind. I took up the paper with renewed energy, and a bright idea flashed over me.

Simple as it was, I had not thought of it before. *The entire message was written on the system of a substitution of letters, based on the reversal of the alphabet.* Thus, instead of writing *a*, the first letter of the alphabet, *z*, the last one, was substituted; instead of *b*, *y* was used—the alphabet reversed was the key to the solution of the puzzle.

I gave utterance to a shout of joy, for, following out the theory, it read:

"LARRY, Meet me Saturday night at 127 Fire Street. NED."

And "Ned" or Edward was the name of Mr. Dayton's footman. I began "to see a very large mice." But Fire Street—there was no such thoroughfare in the city, and I was "floored" again.

Gradually, however, the thought occurred to me, on the basis of reversal and opposites adopted by the sender of the message, why should not "fire," mean "water," its direct reverse?

I dashed down the stairs, and hailing a cab (for I did not forget that it was Saturday, and that that evening was the appointed time for the meeting of the two burglars, if such they were), I soon reached Water Street. Vacant! No. 127 was an empty lot!

I paused, disappointed, and dismissed the vehicle, again having recourse to the puzzling enigma. So near the solution, and yet doomed to be balked at the last, and—

A sudden inspiration of renewed energy, and I had forged the last link in the chain of evidence! There had been reversal in the order of the numbers, from 1 to 10, as the letters of the alphabet, and 127 meant 1094.

I looked at my watch; three o'clock. I went to the nearest local telegraph office, and sent the following dispatch to the chief of police:

"Send to this office three efficient men in citizen's clothes."

I signed my name, lit a cigar, and awaited the arrival of evening and my companion officers.

It was dark when we reached the place for the meeting appointed by the two men. It was a vile groggery kept by a woman, and a resort for the very lowest class of ruffians. I had put on a felt hat and a pair of false whiskers, and I entered the barroom, having first placed my men in advantageous positions on the outside.

Within half an hour there entered an old woman, veiled, bearing some bulky object under her cloak. She made a sign to the woman behind the bar and, went into the next room. I caught sight of her feet as she passed through the door; they were incased, not in shoes, but in men's boots. I went quickly to the bar, and made a sign to the woman.

"Is Larry in there?" I inquired in a loud voice, pointing to the other apartment.

She looked at me sharply, and then replied in the affirmative.

"Keep anybody that comes out," I said, significantly. "We're going to divide the swag."

And I opened the door.

There was no one in the first room, but in the second, by a table, on which lay a large tin box, was my game—Larry, the burglar, and a tall, spare form in female attire, with veil thrown back, and terrified face—the footman, Edward.

"You can drop on my little dodge, gentlemen," I said, quietly whipping out a brace of revolvers. "The house is surrounded, and any resistance will only make it worse for you. Larry, open that door."

He unbolted the rear door under the silent, persuasive eloquence of my revolvers, and the three officers entered.

Need I tell you the rest? Edward, the footman, had admitted his accomplice into the house, and had chloroformed his employer. He had kept the booty hidden in his room, not daring to go out to communicate to his pal, except as has been seen, for fear he was watched.

The property had not been disturbed; but justice was cheated for both the men escaped before conviction, and were never heard of again. As for me, I quietly handed five thousand dollars to the department, resigned, engaged in business, and married Edna.

> —*The Indiana* [PA] *Democrat,* November 28, 1878
> —Published as "Unraveling a Cipher" in *The Defiance* [OH] *Democrat,* October 17, 1878

A Tell-Tale Ink Mark
Anonymous

It Led to the Detection of a Murderer

A few evenings since a St. Paul *Pioneer Press* reporter stepped inside a small retail establishment to make the purchase of a cigar, and after securing the weed, was turning to leave, when the proprietor remarked: "Some time ago I noticed an item in your paper which said that in San Francisco they photographed the thumbs of Chinese, and that there seemed to be a greater difference in their thumb nails than in their faces. Now, that's a wrong impression of the matter. It is the underpart, or sole, of the thumb which is photographed, as the lines and circles in the skin are not the same on any two persons in the universe. This fact is not generally known; but, if I am not mistaken, is taken as a subject of illustration in Mark Twain's *Life on the Mississippi*, in which a murderer is ferreted out, but at the end the wrong man pays the penalty of the crime. For many years I was in the detective business, and, in one case the only clue I had was the imprint of a man's thumb. It is not a very long story, and if you are not in a hurry I will tell you about it." Being requested to relate the incident, he resumed: "At the outbreak of the war, I enlisted from Illinois; and after receiving my discharge from Memphis, I made my way up the Mississippi to a city situated on the river—the name of the place I will omit for various reasons—for the purpose of visiting relatives before returning to New York, my native state, where I had been offered the position as head of a detective agency. The city where I was visiting had a population of perhaps eight or ten thousand inhabitants, and by the time set for my departure I had cultivated quite an extensive acquaintance, among whom was a very eccentric old man living alone with his granddaughter, a young lady just verging into womanhood and between whom there was a strong attachment. Very little was known concerning them, but from the young lady herself I afterward heard a very remarkable history concerning her parents and grandfather. They had formerly lived in Virginia, where the old man had been highly connected. His only child, a daughter, married against his wishes, a shiftless, lazy fellow, and was disowned by her father, her mother having died several years before. This man, finding that he would get none of the fortune which rightfully belonged to his wife, soon tired of her, and before they had been married a year, he kicked her out of the house on a winter night. She returned to her father's house and asked forgiveness, but he was relentless, and in a week's time she died in the almshouse after giving birth to a daughter. When it was too late the old man repented of the manner in which he had treated her and took his little grandchild and left for the West, hiding from the disgrace to which he had subjected himself. Buying a home, he devoted his life to the education of his grandchild. The house in which they lived was situated on a high bluff overlooking the river, and was gained only by a narrow path running up the side of a hill.

This path, I must confess, I had traveled almost daily for some time previous to my intended departure—not for the purpose of viewing the scenery after reaching the summit, but for the pleasure of an hour's chat with the old man's granddaughter. On one of these occasions the young lady told me that one of the peculiarities of her grandfather was that he had for years kept a large sum of money in the house, not trusting the bank for its safe keeping, and that she was always in fear of her life in consequence. This story I had heard from my own relatives, and was not greatly surprised when, on the way to the steamboat landing one morning to secure passage to St. Louis, I heard that during the night someone had broken into the old man's house, murdered him as he lay in bed and made his escape with the money. This news banished all intention of leaving, and I at once hastened to the scene of the tragedy and prevailed upon the young lady to accept the hospitality of my relatives until the matter could be straightened up, which she thankfully accepted. I then set to work to ferret out the murderer. The entrance and exit had been made through a window in the rear of the building, and, while looking for tracks under the window, I noticed a black mark on the sill which had been painted white. Upon close examination it proved to be the imprint of a man's thumb. The manner in which it came there was easily explained. The money which had been stolen had been hidden in a common writing desk in the old man's bedroom, and in a hurried search for the treasure the assassin had overturned a bottle of ink, getting some of it on his hands, and in leaving the house had, by this means, left the mark. This, I soon discovered, was the only clew I had; but, poor as it seemed at first, it afterward proved a good one. I immediately sent word to the agency in New York asking to be released from the engagement, and then settled down to work the case. The first thing I did was to saw out the piece of the windowsill on which was the stain, and I kept the piece of wood secreted in my trunk. The only chance for me to ever find the murderer lay in the hope that he would not leave the city; but if he had gone the probability was that he would never be apprehended. Picking out those whom I suspected, I gained their friendship, and in time would show them the peculiarity of the imprint of a thumb, and after gaining possession of it, would compare it with the one on the block of wood. Things went on in this manner for several months and I began to get discouraged; and as winter came on, I partially lost interest in the work, devoting my time to social enjoyments. While at a social gathering one evening, I became acquainted with the cashier of one of the leading banks of the city, and as he was a bachelor like myself, a warm friendship soon existed between us. As we were parting for the night he invited me to call at his room in the rear of the bank the next evening and we would visit the opera house. I was on hand at the appointed hour, but, as he had a little writing to do, he handed me a cigar, with the request that I should make myself at home for a few minutes. While thus waiting I allowed my mind to wander back over the past few months, and was thinking of the murder when my companion announced he was through with his writing.

For want of anything else, I made the remark that it was rather strange that no trace had ever been found of the murderer of the old man on the hill. As I said this a deadly pallor came over his face and he shook from head to foot as if with a chill. He arose and commenced to arrange his papers on the desk, vainly trying to conceal his agitation, but in doing so partly upset a bottle of ink. Not pretending to notice his discomfiture, I made some jovial remark, and when he brought a cloth to wipe up the ink, I asked him if he had ever noticed the peculiarity of the under part of a person's thumb. He had never heard of it, and entered heartily in the experiment, soon regaining his self-composure. With little trouble I secured one of the pieces of paper on which he had placed his thumb, and we were soon on our way to the theater. I paid little attention to the play, and when it was over rushed home to compare the mark on the piece of paper with that on the block. They were identical; every line and curve was the same. I knew that was proof enough to convict him; and the next day a warrant was sworn out for his arrest. I accompanied an officer to the bank, and the warrant was read to him. He seemed cool and collected now, and requested to be allowed to enter an adjoining room for his hat. He had hardly disappeared before a shot was heard, and, rushing into the room in which he had gone, we found him lying on the floor with a revolver in his hand and the blood streaming from his head. He was conscious, but lived only long enough to make a confession of the crime. He said that gambling was the cause of it all. He had lost heavily of the bank's funds, and, knowing that detection was imminent, he resolved to replace it by robbing the old man, having heard that he kept a large sum of money in the house. The old man had awakened while he was searching for the money and recognized him, and he was forced to commit the murder. The real cause of the suicide was never generally known, the affair having been hushed up as much as possible by his relatives. I was remorseful that I was the cause of his death— although it was far better than for him to have spent the remainder of his life in the penitentiary. I resolved to give up the profession, and marry the old man's granddaughter. I moved to Minnesota. This may seem a very improbable story, but it is nevertheless true."—*St. Paul Pioneer Press.*

—*Iowa State Reporter*, June 17, 1886

3

Help from Abroad

It didn't start with Joseph M. Stoddart and S.S. McClure buying the U.S. rights to Sherlock Holmes stories; half a century earlier American publishers were actively looking abroad for detective stories they could use—with, but often without, the original author's consent or name. At the same time, writers in this country looked to foreign sources for inspiration and for material to use in their own stories about detectives.

From the very beginning much of the imported material came from France and, significantly, it fused fact and fancy. Indeed, Vidocq's *Memoirs* to which Poe refers in "Murders in the Rue Morgue" were not simply a record of the world's first official detective's acts and monuments, they were ghost written by L'Héritier, whose imagination may have gotten so far away from reality that Vidocq refused to authorize the final two volumes of the four volume set. Whether fact or fiction, Vidocq's exploits not only influenced Poe in the creation of the first detective stories in the 1840s, but accounts of his adventures continued to attract publishers and readers well into the 1890s—thus American editions of Vidocq's *Memoirs* were published in Boston, New York, Philadelphia, and New Orleans in 1834, 1844, 1858, 1859, and 1891, and Vidocq tales appeared in newspapers across America well into the 1890s. In addition to Vidocq, Frenchman Émile Gaboriau, loomed large in American detective fiction during the last quarter of the nineteenth century—although not always under his own name. Thus the serial "The Parisian Detective: or a Desperate Deed" by "Erskine Boyd," widely reprinted in newspapers in the 1870s, was in fact a literal translation of Gaboriau's *L'Affaire Lerouge* (1866). But it wasn't just Vidocq and Gaboriau—in addition to the nineteenth-century detective stories published in America directly or indirectly based on French originals, some American writers believed that being French granted the imprimatur of detective expertise. So they created their own French detectives and told their stories against the background of the exotic place that American readers had come to identify with detectives and fashionable intrigue: Paris.

But British detectives—imagined and perhaps real—were very much in evidence in nineteenth-century America, too. Part of that can be traced to Dickens' *Bleak House* with its murder mystery solved by Inspector Bucket as well as Dickens' *The Mystery of Edwin Drood*. In addition, the pieces Dickens wrote for *Household Words* ("A Detective Police Party," "Three Detective Anecdotes," "On Duty with Inspector Field," and "Metropolitan Protectives") appeared both in American periodicals and newspapers and in Russell's *Recollections of a Policeman* soon after their British publication—much to Dickens' dismay. But Dickens' pieces were hardly the only British detective imports. There was Tom Taylor's play *The Ticket of Leave Man* (the drama that introduced Hawkshaw the detective to Anglo-American audiences) which ran non-stop for a decade in New York after its introduction in 1863 and was performed in places like Helena, Montana, and Albert Lea, Minnesota, as late as the mid–1880s. There was also the serial publication of Fergus Hume's novel *The Mystery of the Hansom Cab* in a variety of American papers in the late 1880s, and Hume's *The Piccadilly Puzzle* was serialized in the papers in 1890. Most important, too, were the imports from Scotland. In Scotland the Chambers brothers maintained a robust interest in highlighting (or creating) the romance they associated with the work of the fledgling British detective force, and regularly included stories about detectives—fiction thinly disguised as autobiography or reporting—in their *Chambers' Edinburgh Journal*—a publication readily available to the youthful Arthur Conan Doyle. American magazines and papers quickly scooped up *Chambers'* superficially real stories about detectives and reprinted them all the way from 1849 ("Police-Office Reflections: Guilty or not Guilty!" was printed in such diverse papers as *The Daily Sanduskian* and *The Oshkosh* [WI] *True Democrat*) to 1880 ("Hunting Rogues" appeared in the Burlington Iowa *Hawk-Eye*).

Besides Britain and France, other countries' detectives appeared in American newspapers and magazines in the nineteenth century with regularity. Several mid-century detective stories take place in Australia ("In the Cellar" in *Flag of Our Union* in 1868, and "Murder Will Out: A Gold Digger's Adventure" in the *New York Star* in 1877). A few detectives travel to help solve crimes in Russia ("The Twisted Ring" included in this chapter, and "The Red Chest: An Experience in the Life of a Russian Detective," printed respectively in *Hornellsville* [NY] *Weekly Tribune* and *The Freeborn* [MN] *County Standard* in 1890). In 1879 the *Denton* [MD] *Journal* published "A German Detective Story." And "Murdered Himself," which appeared in *The Freeborn County Standard* in 1887, introduced Captain Salegra, a Mexican detective.

The publication of detective stories from far away places in American newspapers and magazines connects to a variety of literary and social motives. It is related to contemporary interest in creating and organizing police and detective forces *ex nihilo*—the same interest that sent Ida Tarbel to France to write up pieces on Bertillon or that led the *Oakland Tribune* in 1891 to run "Japanese Detectives: A Splendid System in Effect in the Land of the Mikado: Instances Showing the Shrewdness of the Almond-Eyed Officials." It reflected a bit of interest in local color—something more prominent in dime novel detectives than in newspaper and magazine fiction. Most importantly, however, the publication of stories about detectives from someplace else reflected the growing belief that the detective story was both a legitimate literary genre and also an international phenomenon. It was this belief that eventually led to Julian Hawthorne's *Lock and Key Library* (1909) with volumes not only containing American, British, and French detective stories, but stories from North Europe, Germany, and the Mediterranean.

Story of a Detective "Expert"
Anonymous
From *The Knickerbocker* for March

The reader of the "Lost Jewels of Achmet Bey," in a late number of *The Knickerbocker*, will need no added inducement to peruse the following, which proceeds from the same pen:

"The circumstances which occurred in Cairo to which I alluded in my account of the recovery of the jewels of Achmet Bey, happened in this wise:

"I had been to Petra and Mount Sinai, and had reached Cairo, *en route* for Upper Egypt. Departing from my regular custom of sleeping at a Khan, I put up at Sheppard's Hotel, determined to atone for past fatigue by a fortnight's rest. Our caravan arrived late in the evening, and when I sat down to tea I found but one companion. He was a large and rather handsome Englishman, whose gigantic frame and ruddy countenance evidently bespoke a traveler for pleasure and not for health. The usual courtesies of strangers passed between us on meeting, and it was not until we were nearly through our meal, that an active conversation commenced.

"Finding our taste somewhat similar, and being much prepossessed in his favor, at my solicitation he accompanied me to my room, where there was a good fire, more for appearance sake than necessity, and soon being involved in a dense cloud of Latakia, (for which my heart now sighs) we unfolded our several histories. He had for some years been the chief 'detective' in a large English city; having grown weary of his calling, and possessing some property, he had determined to travel.—'Not,' as he bluntly and honestly confessed, 'because he was a scholar, and wished to see that of which he had read, but because he simply wished to enlarge his views, and enjoy himself.' He entertained me until long after midnight, with detailed accounts of the adventures and difficulty he had experienced in ferreting out offenders, although he frankly confessed that it was an unpleasant thing to find that what at first was amusement, soon turned into an unpoetical, degraded feeling of spy-like drudgery. About one o'clock we separated, promising to devote the next day to sightseeing: I offering, as an inducement, my knowledge of the language, which would preclude the necessity of other guides than our donkey-boys.

"Two or three days of pleasant companionship had rapidly flown, during which much was accomplished, when the servant who brought fresh water to me in the morning, asked if I had heard of the murder. In answer to my listless inquiries, he told me that Ibrahim, the cobbler, was missing, and that there had been enough blood found on the floor of his room to guarantee the belief that wherever he was, he was not alive. This was all he knew, and I thought little more on the subject until breakfast time.

"Thompson—so I shall call my friend—was already seated when I reached the table, and after bidding me good morning, he asked me the English and American question: 'What news?'

"'It would appear,' I replied, 'that they have had a murder or abduction case during the night, for our old friend of whom you bought your red slippers, has disappeared.'

"'If, instead of murdering him, they had made him wear a pair of his own slippers for an hour or two, I think they would have punished him bad enough,' said Thompson, who the day before had been heroically enduring a pair of Turkish shoes.

"After we had finished our meal I proposed the Pyramids, or the palace of Abbas Pasha, (which latter was not then completed). Thompson said his feet were too much blistered to walk around 'the curiosities,' and proposed we should visit the house where the murder was committed, and, said he, 'Perhaps I can give you a hint or two on circumstantial evidence which will prove useful to you some day.' So saying, he limped out of the hotel, I following, and we were soon cantering gaily toward the bazaars.

"When we reached the house, which was in the thickest part of the Tahan Bazaar, a large crowd had already assembled, and the secretary of the Pasha was loudly vociferating and calling upon them to disperse.

"Thompson seemed to forget his lameness, for dismounting, he plowed a path to the house, I following in his furrow. Watching his chance, when the secretary was engaged in laying down the law to the most persistent, he pushed open the door and walked in, as quietly closing it, leaving none within its walls but ourselves. The sight to me was almost sickening; and, to divert my thoughts, I was about peering into the closets, when my companion called me to stop.

"'Do not touch anything,' he said; 'here is a rare chance to show you that all my adventures were not idle talk. I will guarantee that if you will interpret for me, I can find out who did this deed.'

"I looked at him in astonishment. His keen eye was rapidly scanning the room, and indelibly transferring to his memory all it rested on.

"'We shall not long remain undisturbed here, and therefore don't say anything to me, but note everything, however minute, about the place, and we will talk it up afterward.'

"I obeyed his instructions. In about half an hour the crowd had been dispersed, and the latch was drawn. At the noise we both looked up. It was the secretary who entered, with a broom in his hand; I paid little attention to his looks, however; my friend paid more. The secretary was a little startled at finding two Franks in the dwelling, and he seemed heated and fatigued with his contest with the people outside; he, however, asked us to be seated, and apologized for having no refreshments to offer us. He did not ask us our business, as is the custom among Orientals, although they always couch the inquiry in such terms as to make it appear an act of friendly interest rather than curiosity. Although he did not ask me, it seemed so natural to make some remark about our affairs, that I asked Thompson what excuse we should offer for our intrusion.

"'Tell him,' replied he, 'that we are going to discover the murderer, after the English plan; that we would like him to recommend us to the Pasha, as being excellent diviners.'

"Although I was somewhat troubled to find the requisite words in which to frame this eloquent address, I managed in some manner to convey the idea to him, and with abundant assurances that he would exert his influence with the Pasha on our behalf, we left him.

"After taking a ride for an hour or two longer, we returned and enjoyed a *siesta* before dinner. I took a little walk around the square, which is in front of the hotel, and then went to my friend's room. I found him drawing, at the table, and without looking up, he pushed a piece of paper before me and asked me to draw a plan of the room in which the tragedy took place.

"On comparing them, they were found to agree in general; but in detail his was much more exact than mine.

"He then drew two chairs before the fire, and after clapping his hands in the hall to summon a servant, he ordered some of 'Alsop's East India,' which, though less poetical than sherbet, is far more satisfactory. We lighted our cherry-handled chibouks and drew comfort from their amber mouthpieces.

"'And now,' said Thompson, after we had smoked a while in silence, 'what do you remember about the room, and what things attracted your special attention?'

"I gave him all the observations I had made, without skipping, as I thought, the most trivial thing. When I had ended, he praised my powers of noticing, and said he thought a few lessons would make me an adept. Then, refilling his pipe, he told me his views, as follows. I only omit such things as we talked up and discarded as irrelevant.

"'I noticed that the house was at one end of a small street, although it fronted on the bazaar; there was no occupied house in front of it, and the shops on either side, I remember are closed at night. In the rear there are no houses whose windows command Ibrahim's dwelling. I noticed that the house was composed of the room in which we were and the loft above. Now, that loft has never been opened, within a week at least, as the cobwebs were as thick round it as they are round the mouth of a parish poor box. Now, as the man must have slept somewhere, he slept in that room, and perhaps was sleeping when his assassin entered. I observed in the corner of the room a mat and some pillows, which had not been disturbed, and the only evidence I have that he was sleeping was the evident adjustment of those three ottomans. Now a man is never murdered—at least very seldom—except from covetousness, jealousy, or hatred for an injury done, insanity I look upon as a mere makeshift used by clever counselors to divert the law from its true course; although so popular has the doctrine become that the word murder seems to be defined unpunishable insanity. But that is getting off our subject. In this enlightened country, where it is no object for a man to be insane, we may reduce our inquiries to the three causes of murder before mentioned. And first, let us take up jealousy. Was the man handsome, was he even passably good looking? Was he young? Was he attractive? What think you?'

"'To me,' I replied, 'he appeared to be none of these.'

"'Very well,' continued Thompson, 'at best these are but suppositions; we will find out tomorrow, in a quiet way, a great deal more about him. You think, then, we might dismiss jealousy?'

"'I do.'

"'Then to my mind, he either had something worth coveting, or else he had done someone a real or supposed injury, and this was their revenge. From my experience, I am much inclined to favor this idea, and here are my reasons: he seemed to be a poor man: had he been a Jew, we might have found him working hard, notwithstanding immense, so to speak, latent wealth. Then again the Turks are an extremely jealous people, and from the crafty way this murder was conducted, I am disposed to think the culprit one of that nation. Here again, however, in my mind two ideas clash; I have some reason to think the offender a Bedowee; and if I am correct, I would be willing to bet, from your description of their character, that rapacity was the object; had it been revenge, a less open place would have been selected. To further this opinion, that it was covetousness of treasure, to which we are to ascribe the deed, I would call your attention to the room once more. Do you remember that there was a pile of bedclothing in one corner untouched, although the three ottomans bore marks of a person having reclined on them? Now why were these clothes not used? You know that an inhabitant of these climes, even in the hottest weather, covers himself completely when he sleeps. May we not argue from this circumstance, however slight, that he did not intend to compose himself to sound sleep—what was the motive? We must look for a strong one for this people are not easily caused to forgo rest. What motive stronger than on account of treasure? The blood dashed all around the apartment shows a struggle; the man was not sound asleep; he hears the assassin enter, he mingles the noise first with half-waking dreams the thought of treasure arouses him, and he copes with his adversary. He is at disadvantage, however, and is at length overcome.'

"Thompson stopped; and after sitting, each absorbed in his own thoughts, we separated for the night.

"Early the next morning we went into the bazaar, and found the Pasha's secretary holding forth to the multitude on the probable and improbable manners by which the deceased came to his death. We pushed into the room, not heeding his gestures or vociferations to the contrary. He was too busy to hinder us, for he had his hands full outside. On looking again at the room, we found a mark under the head ottoman, as of a sack or bag drawn across the floor; the mark was almost obliterated but it was there nonetheless. The track was a narrow one. Now as the object had been dragged, it must have been heavy, and as it was a narrow track, the mind caught the idea of a money bag at once. So far, so good. I was looking under the ottoman to see if there was any more treasure of the same sort, when my eye caught a sparkling object. I drew it out and found it a seal, with a piece of guard attached. I showed it to Thompson.

"'Read the name,' he said.

"I did so: 'Ali Ebu Daoud.'

"'Do you know any such person?'

"'Yes, that's our friend the Secretary; I will return it to him now.'

"'Are you a fool?'" said Thompson, stopping me.

"'I beg your pardon for my haste, but I was so excited at seeing that, that I did not know what I said.'

"'Tell me this, was that guard on it when you found it?'

"'It was.'

"'Where do these folks wear their signets?'

"'Round their necks by a guard.'

"'Did you break this guard, or is it as you found it?'

"'As I found it; I was—'

"'Did you get that blood on it, or was it on it?'

"'I had not noticed any, but if there is any, it was on before.'

"'Let us now go.'

"We pushed out, and now the secretary was as anxious to stop our retreat, as before to stop our entrance. With a humble salaam, and pretending not to understand, we rode away. Thompson told me to direct the boys to guide us to the gate which leads to the Tombs of the Mamelukes. I did so; and we soon were standing by the weazen-faced porter. Thompson stopped, and turning to me said:

"'Give the man a piaster, and tell him I lost an ass night before last, pretty late, with a sack on his back.'

"I did so. The porter, whose wit was sharpened by the bribe, asked what color the ass was.

"I interpreted to Thompson.

"'Tell him all beasts are the same color at night, and then ask him over again.'

"I did so. The porter was a little ruffled by the species of answer I gave, and said pettishly:

"'But one beast passed here after night, and that was a horse with two sacks, so I don't know anything about your ass.'

"'Ask if he did not go through without an order?'

"The porter was turning his heel; but the sight of another piaster brought him back, although it did not quite smooth his ruffled dignity; so he only answered: 'By the secretary's own order. Why?'

"Thompson now took his turn at not answering, and rode towards the bazaars. I now began to see what he was driving at.

"When we came to a cobbler's stall, just round the corner from Ibrahim's, Thompson dismounted, and with the blandest manner possible, invited me to come up with him and sit by the cobbler, and traffic for a pair of slippers. After taking pipes, (the cost of which you have included in your bill of shoes) and making his purchase, Thompson proceeded to a systematic but unnoticed pumping. We gleaned from it that the departed Ibrahim was not a man to cause jealousy, and had never for thirty years hurt any man by word or deed; and that on the day of his murder, he had sold the secretary some lands and had been paid for them; and that in the evening, when the secretary had gone to take a receipt, he had found the poor man dead, which fact he did not give out until the next morning, for fear of creating a disturbance. I asked the man why he had not borne witness to these facts. He said his opinion was, that a Bedowee had murdered the man for the money he was known to possess at that time, and 'perhaps the same Bedowee might murder me, who knows?' and with a pious shake of the head he began a new topic.

"Cutting the interview short, we rode to our rooms to consult, and heard on our way thither at one of the Khans, that the Pasha's secretary had offered a reward for the murderer.

"On our arrival at Sheppard's, we retired to my room and discussed the case at large.—Thompson said he would like to bring matters to a better close, but had determined to go with a party of his friends on to Suez that night. On deliberation, we determined to send the secretary a 'notice to call.' I summoned the waiter, and quickly wrote the note.

"To our minds the evidence was complete; it showed that the secretary had bought the lands of Ibrahim, paid for them, and then had gone at night and murdered the victim to get the money back. All we wanted was his own confession. We then arranged that Thompson was to pronounce the sentence. He told me that the facts must be made public, and that as he was to leave Egypt that night, I might take all the honor in the morning. 'For,' said he, 'by that time my sentence will be executed.' He refused to enlighten me further.

"In about an hour the secretary walked in, rubbing his hands and looking flushed (perhaps from rapid riding). Everything I said to him was at Thompson's dictation. Requesting him, therefore, to dismiss his attendants, with which wish he immediately complied, we bid him to be seated. Through me Thompson said: 'You have offered a reward for the discovery of Ibrahim's murderer; am I right?'

"'You are.'

"'If I know who he is, and draw up a contract, will you sign and seal it?'

"'I will sign it.'

"'And seal it, too?'

"'Impossible!'

"'Why so?'

"The man's tact did not fail him; he replied: 'that his seal was worn out, and was now being recut.'

"'Very well; I know who the murderer was and if you will sign the contract, I will seal it with this.' Here Thompson produced the seal.

"The secretary, wretched man, paled and blushed alternately; he was speechless. I interpreted for Thompson here as quickly as I could, (for I dreaded to hear the guilty man speak) as follows:

"'You were paying him his just due; you went to his house; you robbed and murdered him; you placed his body in sacks, and drove them by night into the desert; you thought you were not discovered; you offered a reward; do you see the blood on that signet; blood will not be silent: that betrayed you.'

"I ceased. He was dumb; he did not raise his eyes, nor did he endeavor to recover his ring. We sat in silence some time. At last he raised his head, and said, 'I did not wish to kill him.'

"'I believe you,' responded Thompson, 'and now listen to your sentence. As yet, we three are all who know of the deed.' Here the poor fellow's eye brightened, quickly to be dimmed. 'Send for the money you took, and have it here, in this room, in one short half-hour; if you are here one instant later, all Cairo shall know the author of the deed.'

"He gazed vacantly at us for an instant, and then ran downstairs. We heard his horse's hoofs dash rapidly across the road. I asked not any further explanation from Thompson; he sat in silence; and I knew that a few minutes more would bring the last act of the tragedy on the stage.

"Punctually and panting, Ali Ebu Daoud was back with the blood-stained treasure. But instead of half an hour, an age seemed to have left its withering blight upon his features, as he stood to hear the rest.

"'You have killed a man; one of Allah's beings,' said the judge. 'You have restored the treasure; instead of death, this is your sentence: Before the sun this day sets, you must leave Cairo, never again to return. As the morning gun is fired in the citadel, all Cairo must know the author of this horrid deed.—Go!'

"He gave us one look, a look that will haunt me forever, and then left us, with the mark of Cain upon his forehead; a ruined man. What became of him I know not. Thompson and I parted, perhaps forever, that night; he to go to India by way of Suez; I to go up the Nile in a few days.

"The next day, by Thompson's instructions, I ferreted out the next of kin, and restored to him that to which he was heir, and gave him all the particulars of the sentence of the culprit. Great was the excitement when the secretary was found missing the next day, and great was the feeling manifested when the author of the dark deed was discovered.

"My fame was uncomfortably great, when it was known that I had been in some degree the means of discovering and banishing the offender. So greatly was I inconvenienced, that I hastened my upward Nile voyage. Gardet was not at all pleased at my not having said anything to him till it was all over; but good-natured soul that he was, it did not disturb his equanimity long.

"And thus ends the mystery of Ibrahim the cobbler."

—*Horicon* [WI] *Argus*, May 21, 1858

Vidocq, or the Charcoal Burner of France
Anonymous

A Thrilling Sketch

Not many miles from the city of Rouen, in France, is located a wild and somewhat extensive forest. This wood is chiefly inhabited by charcoal burners; and many are the dark legends in which they figure. Of course, the tales are mostly exaggerated, and in some cases have no foundation at all.—During the year 183-, however, several travelers, whose way lay through this forest, mysteriously disappeared. The whole place was scoured, and the inhabitants rigorously examined, but no clue was obtained: and they were dismissed. For several months after this, no more travelers were missed, and finally the public excitement was allayed. It was at this time that the incident related in this sketch occurred.

It was a fine day in early autumn, and the woods presented a beautiful appearance. The birds were gaily singing, and the rays of an afternoon sun not too warm, were gilding the tree tops. In the very heart of the forest, surrounded by heaps of smoking earth, stood one of these burners. He was a splendid specimen of a man, as far as physical proportions went; fully six feet in height, and stout in proportion. His broad shoulders might have contained the strength of a Hercules. His head was large and covered with a shaggy mass of hair, and his features were decidedly repulsive. His eyes were small and nearly covered with bushy eyebrows. He had altogether a cruel and malevolent appearance.

As we introduce him to the reader he was leaning upon a large axe, apparently in a listening position. The road ran by a place where he was standing but he could not see far along it, on account of a sudden turn a little distance from him. The clatter of a horse's hoofs, however, could be plainly heard, and in a few minutes horse and rider came into sight. The newcomer was a small and active looking man, and from his dress, was a gentleman well off. His eyes were unusually keen and searching and were bent upon the charcoal burner in such a manner that the latter completely quailed before him.

"A fair day, my good man," said the horseman, in the easy manner of one speaking to his inferior.

"Excellent, Monsieur, for one of my trade; I love not the boiling sun of summer, nor the bleak winds of winter."

"Since you are so finely suited, I suppose you must be what so few are in this world—happy."

"You say truly, Monsieur—few, few, indeed, are happy. There is no happiness without contentment."

"And are you content?"

"At times I think I am; but when I see the nobleman riding in his coach and four, rolling in riches, with servants to obey his every wish, and I have to toil hard for my daily bread, I cannot help thinking that God is sometimes unjust."

"And do you never think of appropriating any of the superfluous riches?"

"What does Monsieur mean? I trust no thought of disobeying the laws of God or man alike, ever entered into my mind."

"I meant nothing; it was merely an idle question; but I did not stop to talk thus, but to ask the way to P—. It is getting late, and I must be getting on the move."

"If Monsieur is in a hurry, I can direct him to P—, in about half the time."

"I shall be much obliged to you, my friend."

"This lane begins very near my home; which is about a mile and a half further on.—You had better stop there, as my wife can point it out to you."

"I will do so. Here is a reward," exclaimed the horseman, offering him a piece of gold. The other drew back and refused to take it, alleging that he had done nothing to deserve it. The horseman then put spurs to his horse and rode away, a bend in the road soon hiding him from sight.—Having rode on until he imagined that the sound of his horse's hoofs could not be heard by the coal burner, should the latter be listening, he dismounted and silently retraced his steps. He arrived at the place where he had left his friend, the charcoal burner, but the latter was not to be seen. The stranger hastened back to his horse and remounted.

"It is as I expected," he muttered. "This road makes a large bend here, and by cutting across he can reach his hut before me. I care little, though, as I am 'forearmed.' We shall see who'll come out first. I comprehend why he refused my gold piece; he considers it as his own, and thinks he may as well take all together; but I must hurry on, and finish this business before nightfall."

So saying, he put spurs to his horse and rode away. Ten minutes' sharp riding brought the charcoal burner's cabin in view. As he first caught sight of it, he thought he detected a man's face pressed against the window. Of this, however, he could not be certain, as the face, if such it was, instantly disappeared. At the sound of his horse's hoofs, an old woman appeared in the doorway, and gazing curiously at him, waited till he rode up. The horseman could not help think the woman was a most fitting companion for her husband. The expression of her countenance was even more villainous. The stranger, however, did not stop to criticize her appearance, but courteously saluted her, saying:

"I believe, Madame, that you are the wife of a charcoal burner whom I met up the road."

The woman replied in the affirmative.

"Then I will tell you that I am bound for P—, which I wish to reach before nightfall. He told me of a lane which was much shorter than the regular road, which he said you could point out to me."

"Certainly! If that is all Monsieur wishes, he is easily satisfied. You may see, a little way up, that large tree which towers above the rest. Just beyond that large rock, and the lane enters the road on the other side of it. As it is very narrow and nearly grown up with bushes, you would hardly notice it. But with these directions you can hardly fail."

"Never you fear; I shall not miss the road."

"Is that all Monsieur wishes?"

"I believe so; but stop a minute. I offered your husband a piece of gold, but he refused to take it. Perhaps you may be more sensible."

The old woman greedily took the proffered coin, saying:

"Pierre is too sensitive. We might both starve before he would take a cent."

"I see you differ a little from him," returned the horseman, laughing. He then put spurs to his horse, and rode on. In a few minutes he reached the rock alluded to and could then perceive the entrance to a narrow lane artfully concealed by bushes. He soon made his way through them, and when once in the lane, found it a little wider than he expected. It also became free of bushes, as he proceeded. He stopped a moment to examine the priming of his pistols, muttering:

"My worthy friends are rather sharp.—They do not do their murdering in the open road where spilled blood might lead to their detection, but inveigle the unfortunate traveler into the dark lane, where he may be safely put out of the way and none be the wiser of it. At any rate, I am fully prepared for them, and they will not put me out of the way without a struggle."

Having seen that his arms were ready for use, he rode slowly forward, keeping a careful watch on each side of the road, that he might not be surprised. As long as the woods kept open as they were, he had no fear, as there was no good hiding place for a man. Ere long the woods began to grow thicker and more somber. Little hillocks covered with bushes became frequent, until at last they became a long range skirting each side of the road. The horseman felt that the time which was to try him was near at hand, and he dropped the reins until his hand covered a holster pistol, which he firmly grasped, though in such a manner as a person would not notice, and he then assumed an air of carelessness, though his watch was now keener than ever. At length he came to a place which he felt certain contained his enemy. Nature seemed to [have] adapted this place for the purpose of concealment. The rocks which skirted the road at this place were about breast high, and so perpendicular as to have the appearance of a wall; they were covered with a growth of bushes so thick, as to be nearly impervious. The tall trees on each side of the road, twined their tops together, forming a natural roof of leaves and branches, and rendering the place as dark and dismal as night.

It was indeed a scene sufficient to appall the stoutest heart, but the horseman, although he knew that the next moment might be his last, rode forward with as careless an air as he might have worn had he been traveling the streets of a populous city.—His hand still grasped the butt of a pistol, and his keen eye still searched every covert. Suddenly a pistol shot rang out upon the air, and his hat fell to the ground with a bullet through it, not more than an inch above where his head had been. Instantly turning in the direction of the sound, he beheld a slight wreath of smoke curling up from behind a bush, and without a moment's hesitation he leveled his pistol and fired. The aim was terribly fatal. A wild shriek rang upon the air and the next moment there sprang from behind the bush, not the coal burner, as he had expected, but his wife.—The blood was flowing copiously from her forehead, and she presented a horrible spectacle. She tottered to the edge of the rock and fell into the road a corpse.

"Had I known it to be a woman," the horseman muttered, "I never would have fired. But it is too late to moralize. What can have become of my friend the charcoal burner?"

As he spoke, he turned around quickly and encountered the object of his thoughts. It was lucky for him that he was so quick. The charcoal burner held a gleaming knife in his hand, already uplifted to strike.—While the horseman's attention had been engaged by the tragical end of the woman, he had silently crept up behind him. The would-be assassin sprang forward, making a desperate pass at his breast. The horseman still held the discharged pistol in is hand, and with its long barrel managed to parry the blow.

He then buried his spurs deep into the horse's side, and the goaded beast sprang forward so violently as to dash the charcoal burner to the ground, and sprang completely over him, dashing the knife from his hand, leaving him stunned in the middle of the road. The horseman turned instantly, and drawing his remaining pistol from his holster, waited for the other to rise. The latter struggled to his feet, and leaning against the rocks on the side of the road, gazed sullenly and revengefully on his conqueror. Thus the strange couple regarded each other for some time, until at last the horseman broke the silence:

"So, my friend," he said, "your career is ended at last?"

"Yes! Curse you! I'd rend you asunder too, if—"

"You dared, I presume," put in the stranger.

"I doubt not your good intentions, and can only thank Heaven that you have not a power proportionate to your will, but I am doubly thankful that I have been the means of ridding the earth of such a monster. I presume you can give a pretty good account of those mysterious disappearances of late?"

"Aye, that I can! You are the first richly freighted traveler who has entered this lane and escaped the bullet or the knife."

"Pshaw! Do you take me for one of those simpletons whose purses are better filled than their heads?"

"No!" exclaimed the other with sudden energy. "I know better. From the very first you seemed to have read my intention, and you must have been sent expressly to entrap me. In other words, you are a detective in disguise."

"You are right," was the reply.

"Well, you have come out best, but you have played a desperate game,—and conquered. Few would have escaped as you have, for my wife is a good shot.—But you seemed from the first to be fortune's favorite."

"I certainly had a narrow escape," returned the other, pointing to the bullet hole in his hat.

"But it is not the first time that fortune has proved friendly to me."

"Well, who are you?" at length demanded the other.

"My name is Vidocq!"

"Great heavens! The Parisian detective! I might have known that it would be all up with me when you was pitted against me."

"Yes; business at the metropolis being rather dull, and having heard some rumors of your doings, I thought I would take a trip out here, if only for the good of my health. But it is growing late, and you must be moving."

"Where must I go?"

"To the gallows in the end," was the reply; "but at present to the jail at P—."

"To the gallows!" returned the other fiercely. "Never! Any death but that!"

The detective leveled a pistol at the charcoal burner's head, exclaiming:

"You shall have a bullet through your head, if you prefer it!"

The other ducked his head in expectation of the shot, and then made a desperate spring at the detective. The latter, however, was in no hurry to fire, and calmly awaited the other's attack. The charcoal burner grasped the reins with his left hand, and with his right endeavored to grasp the pistol. The detective, however, caught his right hand with his own left, and holding it up in an iron grasp, passed his right hand under, until his pistol pressed against the other's forehead, when he fired. The other instantly relaxed his hold, and with a terrible cry, fell back a corpse.

The detective having accomplished the object of his visit, did not delay his return to Paris, but having explained the whole affair to the proper authorities at P—, he departed.

—*M'Kean* [PA] *Miner*, November 24, 1860
—Published as "Vidocq; or, the Charcoal Burner of Rouen" in *The Appleton* [WI] *Crescent*, December 29, 1860
—*Oconto* [WI] *Pioneer*, January 12, 1861

In the Cellar
by W.W. Buchanan

If I should ever live to hold my own in the police force for twenty years more, I shall never forget those dreary night patrols which I had to perform in front of the banks at Maryborough, Australia. It was during the very last weeks of my being connected with the ordinary police, and before I was gratified by being at last admitted to the more pleasant duties of a detective.

Many of my readers will recognize the writer of this story; and I may add that my old motto in life—"If anything is worth doing at all it is worth doing well"—so prompted me in my duties while in the police force, that more cases of horror and importance came under my notice, than most of my fellow companions, and taking notes of the worst and most peculiar cases, as I did at the time of their occurrence, enables me, by now referring to my notebook, to place before my readers some of my "police experiences."

Maryborough was at that time in a state of unavoidable dullness; it was just after the police camp had been shifted from the old ground that had served so well when the men had twice as much to do, and when all those grand and useless buildings were standing in a state of new "rawness" on the hill at the back. It used to aggravate me beyond measure to see the police court, the county court and an expansive camp, and nothing to do in one of them; but there was comfort hard by, in the sight of the less aspiring hospital that stood and still stands in good stead to many a poor, penniless fellow in his last extremity.

However, that has nothing to do with my being on guard at the Treasury, nor with the many anathemas I used to favor our martinet of a sergeant with, as on a raw, chilly, moonless night in winter, I paced up and down the dull pavement for four wretched hours.

There were, all told, thirteen members of the force in and about the camp at that time, but I fancied Sergeant B—had got down on me, and gave me that peculiar duty to perform six times oftener than was my share.

I used generally to stand it patiently for the first two hours, while there was slight chance of a passerby, to arouse the echoes of the lonely back street; but after two o'clock, when the cold was at its worst, and perhaps a raw drizzle wetting a fellow into his marrow, the old boy himself could not be expected to take it calmly, so when four o'clock A.M. brought one of my mates to relieve me, he generally found me in too bad a humor to answer the barest words of civility.

It was upon one of these occasions that I took my sulky way up the rise of the hill, on my way to the camp. It was a pitchy dark night, and I had considerable difficulty in finding my way, as there was no decided roadmark. Fixing my eye on what seemed to be a huge, oblong lantern directly on my route, however, I managed to overcome all the obstacles, in the shape of shallow holes and blackened stumps, until I stood parallel with the object which had guided me.

Now, this object had some little interest for me, and had attracted many a glance in my way to and from my duties. It was a calico tent, small in size, and of the most simple construction. There was not a bit of lining to it; and the natural consequence was that, upon a dark night, when a light was burning within, it presented the appearance I have alluded to, and resembled nothing so much as a huge lantern of oil paper.

It must have been very inconvenient to the owners, for every word, save a whisper was audible to the passerby; and every movement was seen, as it was thrown in shadow upon the thin walls of the poor calico.

I used to think, when first I was stationed at this township, that people who lived so entirely in public could have no fear of police supervision, but I am a suspicious fellow, and I soon changed my opinion on the subject.

The tent was inhabited by a digger and his wife. They appeared to be childless, and the woman was the most wretched and miserable being I had ever beheld. She seemed quite young, but ill and brokenhearted, and had a despairing look in her eyes, that used to haunt me for days after I had last seen it. At last I saw it no more for months, and gossip assured me that the poor creature was confined to her bed ill and helpless.

The husband used to work in the Deep Lead, I believe, and I had no reason to doubt that the woman had every necessary comfort, save that of attendance; but *that* she certainly had not, for no doctor was summoned; and no one ever went or came about her, as far as I could see, although I often noticed the man spending his money at the counter of a store, where drink was sold, or carrying home parcels for household use.

This sort of thing had gone on for months; and often when I passed the tent at night, and saw that lonely light burning still and shadowless within, I used to pause and listen, fearing the sick woman lay alone in her sick bed, while the surly-looking man drank his earnings at the Talbot.

It was the case on the particular night I am writing of, and I stopped for a moment to hear if there was any sound audible in the tent. There was none save the flapping of the canvas in the breeze that had sprang up, and I went quietly round to the side of the tent opposite to where I stood; for I guessed it was the unfastened entrance to the place that made the unpleasant noise.

It was. The calico remained untied, and within, sitting at a table, with his arms resting upon it, and his head in dangerous proximity to the flaming candle, was the man himself, fast asleep.

I was just in the humor to inflict upon others some of that officialism under which I myself so often writhed, upon those who could not help submitting to it; and, besides, I was not going out of the strict path of my duty in interfering, and then giving myself an opportunity of learning something more about this strangely-neglected woman. Entering the tent quietly, I laid my hand upon the sleeper's shoulder, and woke him.

He started up in fear, as it were, and such a look of terror in his eyes as he recognized the uniform! But as I spoke, the old sullen look gradually resumed its wont in his features.

"What time of night is this, to be sitting asleep, with the tent door open, and a blazing candle within an inch of the calico?"

"What business is that of yours?" he retorted. "I can burn my own tent, if I like, I suppose—it isn't insured."

"No, you can't," I said; "and neither can you burn your sick wife. And more than that, if I see the door of the tent open again, with a wet southerly wind blowing in upon her all night, I'll report you. What doctor's attending her?"

"None," he replied, with a look that spoke volumes of anger.

"None! She's been laid up—let me see—five months now, and you've had no advice. Come, it's time for me to look after business—I thought Doctor Sartain was attending her."

"No, he wasn't! I've no money to put into Sartain's pocket; and besides, she don't want a doctor, and she won't have one, she says."

"Well, I'll see about it tomorrow; and see you don't set the place on fire in the meantime."

During the conversation, I had kept my eyes fixed upon the end of the little tent, where I knew the invalid must be. Nothing but a rag of a curtain separated the bed from us, and as I spoke those concluding words, it was drawn aside, and a white, death-stricken face peeped out.

"Ned," she said, "give me a drink of water, for the love of Heaven!"

"There isn't a drop in the place," the husband replied, angrily.

"Go and get it, then," I ordered. "A pretty to do, if a dying woman can't get a drink of water in Maryborough! Go at once, and I'll watch till you come back."

With a muttered curse at the pale tenant of the comfortless tent, the man took a billy, and went out. As he did so, the sick woman beckoned me towards her, holding back with the other trembling hand the thin curtain.

"It's no use," she whispered, as I approached to her side; "I'm nearly gone—don't forget. At Amherst, where we lived before—in the cellar—" And as she gasped the last of these weakly-uttered words, she fell back, still clutching the curtain, which even her weight dragged from its weak supports. At this moment, the husband—whom I shall in future call Ned—returned, and advanced towards the bed, with an anger in his eyes that he appeared incapable of controlling.

"What is she bothering about now?" he asked. "Has she been speaking?"

"She'll bother you no more, my man," I replied. "The poor woman is going home."

The sound of her husband's voice appeared to give her one last moment of remembrance; she opened her eyes, and turned them dimly towards him. A spasm passed over her face, and faintly she uttered:

"God forgive you, poor unfortunate—" And she died.

Ned fell into the seat in which he had lately slept, and with the billy of water in his hand still, stared with a bewildered look at the corpse, as if her last words had stupefied him. I doubted much if *his* end would be so quiet; but it was not my business to say so, and so I turned and went onward to the camp, to send some of my mates to take charge of the body, as there having been no medical attendance, an inquest was inevitable.

It was nearly morning when I went to bed and tried to get two or three hours' sleep, but I found it an utter impossibility; turn and twist as I would, I could not forget the strange words of the dying woman. Whatever could they mean? What interest had that cellar for her in such a terrible moment?—or how could I ever discover the secret, now that it rested in a dead bosom, and would soon be buried from the light forever? Sleep was impossible; my thoughts kept revolving in a maze around those singular words—"In the cellar."

Finding rest was not to be won, I arose at eight o'clock, and proceeded to relieve the constable in whose charge the body had been left, hoping thereby to have an opportunity of learning something to throw light on the affair from the lips of Ned himself. In this I was disappointed. As I reached the tent, he intimated that he must go and tell his mate that he could not work that day, and then he went off in the direction of the Deep Lead.

About two hours after, a cheery-looking man, in digger's attire, came to the tent and inquired for Ned.

"I'm his mate," he said. "I thought I might be able to help some way or other, and so I came down."

"Have you not seen him?" I asked. "He said he was going up to you."

"O yes; he came up to the shaft and told me, but he left almost immediately, saying he was coming straight back."

"I dare say he won't be long," was my reply; and the newcomer seated himself beside me upon a piece of wood at the door, and taking out his pipe, commenced smoking.

"It's a sad job," he said. "Ned's had a hard time of it with the poor thing ever since we've been mates."

"Have you been mates long?" I inquired.

"Only since he came to Maryborough; for my own part, I wish I'd never seen the blessed hole."

"No luck, eh?"

"Luck! I've spent every cent I have in that shaft, and now I don't believe I could get five and twenty dollars for my share tomorrow."

"Ned doesn't seem to be hard up, does he?"

"Not he; wherever he gets it, he has lots of cash."

"And yet this poor woman has been lying here for months, without seeing a doctor."

"It was her own fault, I believe; she had a great dislike to doctors; but I never thought she was so bad—only a weakly, useless woman."

"Do you know where Ned was, before he came here?" I once more questioned my companion.

"He once told me he had a store at Amherst, about a year and a half ago; but Ned's a fellow not to tell much of his business. I never asked any questions."

In a short time after this conversation, I left the spot, and during the afternoon the inquest was held. The medical gentlemen found nothing to excite their suspicions in the woman's death. She appeared to have simply died of debility and an utter prostration of energy; and so the thing was over.

I asked a digger's wife, who lived close by the camp, to assist in laying the poor woman out etc., as there appeared to be no single friend to come forward; and then she was buried. Ned requested the woman to take away every article of clothing belonging to his wife, saying at the time, "There's not much, but I've no use for woman's clothes now, and I'd rather, to tell the truth, see them out of the place." And so the woman gathered the few articles of attire together, and carried them home.

The affair seemed to be ended, as far as I was concerned; but I couldn't forget it. I was haunted by the words, "Don't forget—in the cellar."

Turn where I would, on duty or off it, morning, noon and night, I was "in the cellar." In short, there was a secret, and that was quite sufficient for me. I wanted to find it out. At this time I had considerable hopes of gaining my detective card, and I determined, if it should be so, that the very first of my leisure time should be spent in trying to discover that particular cellar at Amherst.

One day, shortly after the inquest, I had just returned from mounted patrol to "Chinaman's," and having stabled and cleaned my horse, was passing towards the boarding room for my supper, when the digger's wife I have spoken of beckoned to me. I was somewhat surprised, to see the air of mystery she assumed as I approached, and how carefully she went inside before she spoke a syllable.

There was a pair of women's scarlet corsets lying on the bed, and lifting them, she came to me, as I stood by the table in wondering expectation.

"I was going to take it over to Ned," she said, "but I thought as it was hided like, perhaps I'd better show it to yourself first, sir."

"What is it?" I asked, looking at the soiled article she held in her hand, and was seemingly alluding to it.

"You know Ned gave me the poor thing's clothes; and as I was having a bit of a wash today, I thought I'd rub them all through, in fear of sickness or anything. The stays wanted a stitch or two in the linin', and I wondered what way she'd fixed the front o' them with a fresh linin' like. There was something rustling, too, and thinking I'd struck a patch, I ripped the rag off. There it is, you see, sir; she sewed that inside, and that was all."

Slipping back a bit of lining, as she spoke, the woman drew out an envelope, and handed it to me. It was torn a little, but had evidently been carefully preserved, and upon it was a crimple address.

"Mrs. Edward Corcoran," I read aloud, "Rush Store, Smyth's Lead, Amherst. Was that her name?"

"I've heard so, sir."

Opening the envelope, which was simply the cover of a posted letter, I drew out the enclosure. It was a *carte de visite*, also carefully folded in a bit of tissue paper. I looked at it and perceived that, although the portrait of a male, it bore no resemblance whatever to Ned, her husband. It represented a much younger man, with strongly marked features; and the strong marks were decidedly Israelitish. An abundance of black hair, a decidedly hooked nose, and the ordinary attire of an office clerk or salesman, and that was all I could see of the portrait.

"There's some writing on the back, sir," observed the woman, as I still gazed, "but I couldn't read it though, not bein' a scholar."

Turning it round hastily, I perceived indeed some writing. First a name—written evidently by the same hand as the address on the envelope; the name was "Reuben Jacobs," and it entirely corresponded with the Israelitish cast of feature I had already recognized in the *carte*; under the name, however, I perceived some ill-defined pencil marks, and holding it more closely to my eyes, the reader must try to guess my feelings, when I traced, in a trembling and ill-written hand, the same words already so productive of interest to me—"*In the cellar.*" Yes, there they were, sure enough, and several other words before and after them; but my efforts were vain to decipher one other syllable.

Giving the good woman strict injunctions to keep silence in the matter for a time at least, I put the precious find in my pocket, and I would not have exchanged it for five and twenty of the best half eagles in

America. How many hours of day and lamplight I spent over those few penciled scrawls I leave you to guess, but more than "In the cellar," I could not make of it, under any influence I brought to bear upon it.

The poor woman had some reason for hiding this little portrait on her person, there could be no possible doubt, and after many guesses, I decided that the most feasible explanation of the pencil marks was, that they had been made by her stealthily during her last illness, and that her hands were incapable of forming the characters, even had she been possessed of more durable material than a wretched, hard lead pencil. At any rate, the marks were almost obliterated, and human ingenuity could make out no more than what I have stated.

About this time I received my coveted appointment to the detective force; but before I had made my arrangements concerning the change, my friend had disappeared from Maryborough, having, as I learned from his last mate, put his tent on his back, and tramped it for some other diggings. This, however, was a matter of very little consequence to me, as I knew that, unless he left the colony, I could easily trace him at any time.

I was not sorry to leave my late quarters, and was appointed to another mining district. At this I was really delighted, as of course Amherst would be within my own especial beat; and for the first month of my sojourn at my new quarters, I enjoyed myself perfectly.

It was pleasant to get up when you liked, and lie down ditto; to wear any clothes you had a mind to; to come and go at any hour of the day, whenever you chose, without consulting in one degree either sergeant or constable in charge, and that is nearly the position an up-country detective holds. There was nothing doing in my line—I had not even the excuse of a hunt for Chinese thieves—and so one morning I saddled my horse and went to Amherst, to look after the "cellar." It was but a pleasant ride of two hours or so, and then I found myself at Amherst, but, of course, as ignorant as the man in the moon of the whereabouts of the object of my search. Recollecting the address upon the envelope, however, I inquired for Smyth's Lead, and soon found myself among the ruins of a line of erections that had evidently bordered the Lead in its palmiest days.

A few scattered places of business still remain at its upper end, but I passed them one by one, in vain search for the "Rush Store" until I stood at the end of the gully, and nothing within sight but one slab hut that stood upon the rise, at the side of the road. This hut appeared to have been longer there than most of the places I had passed, and it was evidently a single man's home, as it was barely enough to accommodate one person.

You will recollect I was in plain clothes, and as I stood looking up and down the road, and examining the appearance of camping-places, and half-tumbled-down chimneys that marked the line of the road, a digger approached the Lead, carrying the inevitable billy in his hand. It was the owner of the lone hut, and as it was near noon I concluded he was making home for dinner.

"Good day to you," I said. "Are there any business places further on?"

"No," he replied, "there's no business now, only what's up at the upper end. Are you in search of anything?"

"I was looking for the 'Rush Store.' It used to be kept somewhere about here by one of the name of Corcoran."

"O, they've gone long ago. Corcoran sold the place, and 'twas shifted before he went. Why, you're standing right on the old site this moment."

The devil I was! I looked around with a start. How did I know that I mightn't tumble into that very cellar, before I knew where I was? I had climbed up from the road, to get a better view from the rise, near which stood the slab hut of the speaker, and sure enough I had unconsciously lit upon the very spot of which I was in search. There were the marks still very distinct, of the corner and partition posts, the rough counter supports, and the fallen down chimney of stones and poles. The floor still bore the evident traces of many feet, and some pipe clay held its own on the rude hearth, but not a sign could I see of cellar or underground excavation of any description.

"Have you lived long here, mate?" I asked the man, who stood looking curiously at me, as I examined the premises, or rather their site.

"I came about the same time as the Corcorans," he answered. "Perhaps I might be able to help you, with my memory some way. Will you walk to my hut, and sit down?"

I gladly accepted the invitation. There was a superiority in the man's appearance, that made me feel like trusting him with my secret. I wouldn't do it now under the circumstances; but I was younger then, and had no cause to regret having done so.

I sat down on a three-legged stool at the door, and when my friend had gathered his fire together and fried some steak, I cheerfully accepted the offer of a share of his humble dinner.

"Now," says he, when our appetites were satisfied, "I see you're anxious in some way about these Corcorans, and I'm no rogue, so, if you'll trust me, I'll help you to the best of my ability."

"Had they a cellar in that store?" I asked, pointing to the site.

"A cellar? What a strange question! But I'm blest if I know, I never heard of one; what the devil are you? You're no digger, one can easily see that!"

"I'm a detective, that's what I am," I said, "and I have very particular reasons for finding a cellar at the 'Rush Store.'"

"A detective! Whew!"

And my friend the digger's astonished whistle rang through the hut.

"Did you ever see a face like that?" I asked, handing him the *carte* so interesting to me.

"Often," he replied, as he examined it. "It is a Jew peddler, who used to come round often, and he always stopped at Corcoran's."

It was now my turn to whistle. The thing was becoming as plain to me as day.

"Tell me all you can about these people," I said, "and then I'll tell you about the cellar."

"Willingly," he answered. "But if you could light on Corcoran's mate he could give you a world of information about their private affairs, about which I know nothing save by guess."

"A mate! Had he a mate?"

"Yes, a mate called Tom, a fair-complexioned man, a German, I think. But I don't think him and the missis hit it somehow; she always looked as black as thunder at him."

Well, we sat half an hour, I dare say, exchanging our stories in this way; and when my friend accompanied me out to examine the ground more closely in search of the cellar, I do believe he was nearly as interested in the matter as myself.

"Now here's where the store stood, you see, fronting the road, of course. Part of the hill had been cut down to make a level foundation, and here in this spot was the counter where they kept the drink. If there was a cellar at all, it might have been a hole under the counter to keep that cool, and has probably tumbled in long ago. But I'll be blowed if it isn't here yet!" he added, pushing a little clay away with his foot. "There are the slabs, only the hill has given way, and pitched some dirt on it, or more likely Corcoran himself covered it up."

It was quite true. In two or three moments, my friend had shoveled away the earth from the top, and laid bare about half a dozen slabs that had lain over the cellar behind the rude counter. We had some difficulty in finding an entrance, but the digger, more accustomed to such work, pushed out a slab and squeezed himself down into the cellar to examine it.

"If anyone comes about," he said, as he disappeared, "tell them you've a notion of camping here."

'Twasn't a bad idea, but no one came, and it was not many minutes ere the man extricated himself from the slabs, and appeared on the surface.

"Well!" I asked impatiently.

"Well, there's nothing in the bit of a hole but the beginning of an old drive. It's very likely, you see, that *it* may lead to something, for I don't see what any man would put a drive in there for. But it's partially fallen in, and will take a little time to clear out. Now, master, I'll give you a bit of advice: just you go to the camp, and get a pair of moleskins on. I've got a little tent under my bunk and I will stick it up right over this hole. It will be a grand shelter, you see, and we can tell any curiosity folk, that you and I are going mates, you see."

"I do see," replied I, "and I think, too; and what I think is, that it's a pity you are not a detective yourself."

I took the digger's advice, then, and procured my disguise at the camp, and it was drawing towards evening as I once more reached Smyth's Lead. Before I gained my friend's hut I perceived that he had already slung the tent, in a temporary manner, over the cellar; and as I approached, he emerged from it, with a look of importance that boded news.

"I have found the cellar, mate," he whispered, leading the way into his own hut, "and something else besides; but as I could almost swear to a pair of eyes watching me at this minute, we'd better take the hut for it."

"Watching!"

"Ay; but let me tell you about the cellar first. After you went I stuck the tent on two forks and a pole I had handy, and then I went down below. I found I could easily clear out the drive without carrying out a bit of stuff, as it was only about three feet long, but opened into a regular bit of a cellar in the side of the hill, propped up with props and caps like a regular underground working. *That's* the place you want.

"Not the least doubt of it, sir. But about the watching?"

"Well, I saw the place was empty, and come up again. As I reached the tent, I saw a man standing in the road looking at the tent strangely. I knew him at once, but I never let on, only commenced tying the well plate to the stick. It was that very chap I told you about, Tom, they used to call him: Corcoran's mate, the German.

"O!"

"I gave him the time of day, and he sneaked up a bit, asking if there was any chance up in the Lead. I told him things were looking pretty blue, and I hadn't much chance. I hoped to do better, now I'd got a mate."

"Is that his place you're putting up?"

"Yes," says I.

"There's been an old place there before," says he.

"Yes, a store," says I, "but it's long since it went. And so he went off as he came; but if things are as I guess, he is not far away."

"You must get into the Force, mate," I replied. "That's the place for you."

And I may mention, par parentheses, that he *did* get into the detective force not long after, in consequence of the part he took in this affair.

I need not weary your patience by reporting every one of our arrangements. It will be sufficient for me to say that, after feigning to go to bed in my mate's hut, my own establishment not having been provided with a "bunk," I stole into the cellar with the assistance of a dark lantern, to do my share of the exploring, while my friend watched above, like a cat on a dark night, all ears, as he lay at full length on the ground behind his hut.

And so I was at last in "the cellar," armed with a pick and shovel, and fully determined to see what was there to fill the last thoughts of a dying woman.

It was an excavation in which a man could not stand upright, and barely seven feet square; and from the rotten straw and pieces of broken cases scattered about, I judged it had served as a hiding place for grog during the notorious raids of the police about that time.

I examined the floor closely, for whatever was there was no doubt buried. It gave me a little clue, being of a dry, gravelly nature, and all rough looking; but choosing the spot farthest from the entrance, where the ground seemed to have been more trampled upon, I commenced to dig. We had agreed to turn every bit of it up to a depth of four feet if necessary; and I was only taking my first spell until relieved by my mate.

Fortune favored me, however. Scarcely had I excavated two feet deep in the spot I had decided upon, when, I being at work with a will, my pick struck right into something that *crashed*, and out of which I had some difficulty in drawing it. Having done so, however, a single minute cleared away the soil from the object, and left exposed a brassbound cedar box, about a foot-and-a-half long and one wide, and upon a brass plate on the lid was engraved in plain Roman letters, "Reuben Jacobs."

You might think the sight gratified me, but it didn't. I dashed my shovel on the ground with an angry exclamation, and knelt down to examine the deposit with a frown on my forehead. O yes! 'twas just a Jew peddler's case of jewelry with a broken lock; and when I raised the lid, the light of my lamp flashed upon a brilliant array of watches and rings, brooches and bracelets, none of them imitations either, but the genuine good colonial gold.

"Audes," I muttered to myself, as I examined them carelessly, "it was of pelf after all that the dead woman was thinking."

Yes, I was disappointed sadly, for I had expected to have discovered a body, the veritable body of Reuben Jacobs. I had made up my mind that the man was murdered, you see, and it seemed that I had simply dropped upon a plant of stolen jewelry. And what about the carte, then, and the similarity of names upon it, and upon this box? Bah! It was a puzzle, and I was disheartened and disappointed.

But there was no use leaving this case for the hider to remove some day, and so before I arose from my knees I lifted it out and laid it on the floor near me. The lamp stood at the edge of the hole, and threw its rays directly into it; and as I turned my eyes back, after resting upon the box, they fell upon a sight that horrified me. It was a man's head—the head of Reuben Jacobs!

The fiend who was guilty of his blood had laid the murdered man's box directly upon the dead face. Surely such heartless brutality was never surpassed; and as I knelt and stared, and saw the discolored features flattened by the weight of the cedar case, I felt nearer swooning than ever I did in the whole course of my police experience.

At this moment the sound of scuffling overhead aroused me from my horror, and I started to my feet and rushed from the cellar and through the tent into the open air. I was in a rage which no words can express, and had the man Corcoran appeared before me at that moment, with only the suspicion of the crime hanging over him, I am sure I should have flown at him, and tried to strangle him; in short I was temporarily bereft of my reason, and it is fortunate I had my cooler mate at hand.

Two bounds brought me to the spot, where I had left him on watch, and from whence the struggling sounds now came.

"What is it?" I cried. "Where are you?"

"It's a man, and I guess who," he answered with an effort, as he knelt upon his opponent with one knee, "but there are no spies coming round my place at night. Here, mate, a brace of your cuffs, if you please."

It was certainly not a very professional act to handcuff a man who was simply prowling about a tent in the dark; but I beg of you to recollect that such things have been done by the force, under order, of course, as handcuffing men for selling a glass of drink, and making them walk three or four miles to the lockup into the bargain besides afterwards.

So I made no difficulty in lending a hand to manacle the stranger, and then we led him into my friend's hut and struck a light.

"Now, mate," I said, turning to the prisoner, who was as white as a sheet, and shaking like a leaf, "I'm a detective officer, and on the lookout for the murderer of the peddler named Reuben Jacobs, whom you and Ned Corcoran buried in the cellar there. If you had no personal hand in the murder, the best thing you can do is to turn queen's evidence, and tell what you know of it."

"I didn't bury him," he answered, firing up, "and if Ned Corcoran said so, he's a liar! I've nothing to hide, but I promised his wife not to tell on him while she was alive."

"She's dead now, so you're clear of that," I said. "Do you remember anything of that?" I added, handing him the portrait of Reuben Jacobs.

"I do well: it was the sight of this that set Corcoran's blood up. He was jealous of the Jew, you see, because he gave the missis some little brooch or other, and a black job was the end of it; well, as she's gone, I'll tell you all I know about it."

I need not give you the man's rambling account; a sketch of the facts will be sufficient.

Corcoran had been madly jealous of the peddler, who was free and jokey in his manner; and that the jewelry had nothing to do with the murder was evident from the fact, that nothing of it was taken save one watch, which we afterwards found on the murderer's person.

One night during one of the Jew's visits, Mrs. Corcoran left her husband and him playing cards, and retired to bed, in a little room behind his shop, and Tom the German shortly after followed her example. She was aroused towards morning by the strokes of a pick, that seemed to come from the cellar; and being a nervous woman, instantly suspected something horrible.

Hastily throwing on a garment, she shook German Tom from his sleep, and they stole down the rude stairs to get a sight of the husband's deed. Upon the floor lay the corpse of the peddler, a tallow candle flaring by its side and Corcoran was working for life and death at a hole in the floor, to hide the terrible evidence of his crime from the light.

The sight was the deathblow to the poor creature. The horror she felt at the vicinity of the murder—which a fear of a similar fate made her conceal—gradually haunted her into her grave; but for her sake German Tom had kept the secret well.

Ned Corcoran never suspected that his midnight deed had been witnessed, and he afterwards confessed that he had allured Jacobs into the cellar for the purpose of helping him to open a fresh case of porter, and that he had driven the pick right into his brain, as he stooped over the case.

I had the satisfaction of arresting the man myself, and of hearing the sentence of death pronounced against him. He was in one of the large mining districts at the time, but I didn't think he ever intended visiting the scene of his crime again.

—Flag of Our Union, August 1, 1868

The Wounded Hand
From a German Detective's Notebook
by Narissa Rosavo

On the 22nd of May, 1875, I stood in our office behind my desk, when our Chief entered the room with a letter in his hand and addressed me with an invitation to undertake the unraveling of a mystery which had baffled the local police at T—. I consented and departed for the scene of the crime which had been committed, much limited, however, as to the time I was allowed for spending on the case.

Two hundred and fifty thousand marks had been stolen from the widow of a well-connected man named Friedow. Her villa stood outside the gates of a small town, and the lost property consisted chiefly in coupons and such value, together with a little coin. Her habit was to keep all papers of importance, as well as money, in a chest of drawers beside her bed. Her sleeping room was situated on the first floor, and had but one window, which looked out upon the yard. Her confidential friends had often advised Frau Friedow to keep her gold at least in some safer place, but she had always resisted such counsel, and put no faith in banks or bankers. As to a safe, she had averred that if robbers did ever molest her, unless her trusty dog and her faithful Frederick, who was her factotum and the only male person upon her property, could protect her, an iron box would avail little beyond, perhaps, delaying the thieves in laying hold of what they wanted.

On the night of the 7th of May the poor lady was suddenly awakened about twelve o'clock. Her room was illuminated. Before her bed stood a small, thin man, with a lantern in his left hand and a hatchet in his right.

In a rough, disguised voice he threatened to knock out her brains if she so much as ventured to utter a sound. The unfortunate Frau was already voiceless from alarm. This speech could scarcely make her more quiet, but she could use her eyes, and did so for the next few seconds while her visitors remained with her. She saw that the speaker wore black hose, a blue blouse and a mask; and that two more men were busy in the background breaking open her chest of drawers. In the farthest back division, covered over by stockings, yarn and flax, lay a round, tin case, in which she kept her movable treasures. She was just recovering herself sufficiently to begin thinking about risking her life by calling for help, when the smothered yelling of a dog was heard without. The thieves had found what they wanted, however, and sprang with it to the window, a sash of which was open. They threw themselves upon a ladder without, and descended to the ground, while the third man still kept guard beside the bed. Frau Friedow cried "Help! Help!" with all her might. "You may scream as long as you like, now," he muttered, turning away and following the others from the room.

Frederick appeared at this instant, having been awakened by the noise. He found the ladder still in its place, and was just in time to save the life of the house dog, which had been almost choked by a cord twisted round his neck, fastening him to his kennel. The manservant roused up the neighbors, but all pursuit, then or later, by friends privately or the police publicly, had been in vain. Not the least clew had hitherto been obtained as to the identity of the housebreakers.

This was how the matter stood when I arrived at T. When I had privately communicated with the Magistrates, my second visit was naturally paid to Frau Friedow. I sought everywhere for any special indications which might put me on the right track, but what I found was desperately little. Like those who had gone before me, I concluded that the robbery had, at any rate, been accomplished by persons well acquainted with the locality, as entrance to the premises had been made by a small door in the yard, of the very existence of which many of the neighbors were unaware. The ladder made use of had been dragged out of a nook in which it had long lain concealed. A pane of glass had been smashed in the window of the bedroom to enable one of the assailants to slip back the bolt. A few footprints had been traced, but there was nothing remarkable about their appearance, and they had been lost at once upon the high road or street upon which the little courtyard opened.

One thing seemed alone certain amid the maze of perplexity; the housebreakers must be sought for from amongst neighbors, servants, friends or relations. Now the neighbor theory, upon investigation, seemed utterly futile, and one glance at old Frederick was enough to dismiss all thoughts connected with the second term in the list. There remained friends and relations in the habit of visiting at the villa. The widow had not the faintest suspicions of foul play in any of these; nevertheless, I made her describe and closely particularize them all to me. I took up half a dozen imaginary scents; I ran hither and thither. I telegraphed in various directions. I worked, in fact, in the sweat of my brow; but, alas! the result was simply nothing, nothing, nothing. I never before had been so utterly puzzled and hopelessly at fault.

On the fourth day of my residence at T., I went again to the villa, where the widow greeted me with eyes full of expectation. "Frau Friedow," I said, "it seems to me hardly possible that you are utterly without suspicion in every quarter. There must surely be some one or other on whom your mind has fixed, if it were but for a second. Confess it is so and confide in me."

"I assure you I have not even a shadowy thought such as you describe," she replied, in a much disappointed tone.

"And has nothing more struck you about those men you saw in your room than you have already mentioned? One remembers things on due consideration which have been often overlooked before. Did you notice no particularity about any of the scoundrels—in the voice, for instance; the way of standing, the hands of him who held the axe? Had he on a ring? Did he look rough like the others?"

"There was one little thing I may not have told you before," she replied slowly. "It was scarce worth telling. When the two fellows ran off down the ladder with my little case the window slapped down as they disappeared. The third man pushed it up again to go after them, but in so doing I think he must have put his hands through the broken pane, and have hurt it with the glass, in his haste. I certainly heard him mutter to himself, as if he were in distress."

"Was there no trace of blood left?" I asked, anxiously.

"None whatever."

I began my investigations anew, and this time with the doctor of the district. We got into a lively dissertation upon wounded hands, and in particular upon hurts inflicted by glass. By degrees I acquired the, to me, very interesting fact that some three weeks since, when the medico was riding home to breakfast after an early call, a strange man had suddenly appeared in the middle of the highway and had implored his help. He complained of having fallen upon a heap of broken glass, and held out his right hand to exhibit its condition. The doctor took out his pocket-case of instruments, and extracted five splinters from the inflamed palm. While he did so the patient whimpered like a woman.

"How was the fellow dressed?" I cried, breathlessly.

"A blue blouse and black underclothes, as far as I can recall."

"Could you identify him again?"

"Perhaps. His face made an impression on me, rather; because it did not seem to match the clothing, and yet, now I think of it, I seem to see only an ordinary brow, nose, and mouth. I fancy it was the set of the head on the shoulders which looked remarkable. Artisans and such folk usually look otherwise. This is all I can say. But what makes this matter interesting to you?"

"I believe your complaining patient to be the principal in the late robbery concerning which I have come down here," I replied, in a low voice. "Can you give me any idea as to what became of the man after you were done with him?"

The doctor looked at me in amazement. "I think he went toward Ems," he replied.

I lost no time going the same direction. An old tree, which forked at the top, and carried a bell in that division, stood on a height near the shore. Here those who wanted to be ferried over the river must stop and ring for the boatman, whose house stood in a sheltered nook at hand. I shirked preliminaries, and made at once for the dwelling. Here I found a gigantic person, who declared herself the daughter of the ferryman, and the customary rower when, as now, her father was absent. I sought to gain the confidence of this damsel. "A friend of mine went over here, I think, not long since," I said. "He was in great haste, being on his way to Holland, in order to escape serving here in the army."

The popular antipathy to the enforced military training loosed her tongue at once. "Yes! Yes!" she replied. "A young man in great haste did surely go over a little time back."

"He wore a blue blouse and black hose?"

"Maybe; but it seems to me that he had others with him or of his party."

"Very probably. Two others, I suppose?"

"This was how it was. One man came to me in the early dawning. I put him across. An hour or so later there came a second, and asked anxiously about the first. When I told him he was beyond he seemed content enough, and followed. The third, your friend with the blouse, asked if he were the first who wanted me that day. He asked me particularly about the two I had already rowed over, and then seemed right gay, and jumped into the boat himself."

"Ah! One of the three carried a tin box?" I said, slipping a coin into my new acquaintance's palm.

"I never noticed," answered the girl. "But I saw that the third man carried a round bundle or parcel wrapped in a red handkerchief under his arm."

"Did he give you a good reward for taking you over?"

"Nothing more than all the world—ten pfennigs."

"With his right hand?"

"Why not?"

"Wasn't his right hand tied up?"

"Not that I saw. I only know he kept one hand in his pocket, whether the right or left I couldn't say now."

I could have embraced the tall ferrywoman, in spite of her forty summers and her uncertainty upon minor points. It was plain, that the three ruffians, for better security, had separated, and that the last comer was the leader in and the chief benefiter by the crime which had been committed. During his confab with the doctor no doubt he had hidden the spoils in some hedge. I was upon his track now.

But I had soon to cry "lost!" It was a grievous disappointment to me. Beyond Ems the clue was nowhere to be followed. I labored in vain in this neighborhood for days. I made friends with all sorts of people, letter-carriers, porters, waiters, and walked many a weary mile in the hot sun, but all to no purpose. I was baffled and wholly at fault as much as though I never had had a hint at all to follow.

Nine days had gone by since I had come to T. I turned into a beer garden in the neighborhood of the town one evening, and sat down near a well-lighted bowling alley, in which about ten gentlemen were busy at a game. My seat was rather in the shade. I paid little attention to the players, but leaned my head upon my hand and reviewed the defeat I had sustained, and the small estimation in which I should be held for the sake of it by my colleagues and Chief at home; feeling altogether extremely out of humor. Suddenly an ill-thrown ball rolled almost to my feet.

"A miss—a miss," shouted several voices together, while one cried: "Why Botteher, is your hand not even yet recovered? You are not complaining of it still?" I felt like a huntsman in a forest who sees the game at his gun's end. I was on the alert that second. I lost no time in finding out all Herr Botteher's antecedents. He was a merchant, one of Frau Friedow's connections, and an occasional visitor at her house. He was a continual guest at this place of entertainment. I brought the doctor here next evening, and set him to work stealthily considering my game. My discomfiture was great when he flatly refused to identify Herr Botteher and his patient as one and the same person. They might be one, he confessed, but then they might not.

If the medico turned rusty, like this, it seemed to me utterly useless to bring hither the ferrywoman on a like errand. I must trust to myself alone. We officials have two methods of doing business of this sort. We use the long or short line, according as either seems most likely to suit. I determined to try one after the other. In order to put Botteher quite off the scent I went now to the host of this house of entertainment, and introduced myself to him as a Hamburg agent for the forbidden lotteries. I begged him to keep this close, but I saw, very plainly by his face, that he intended doing nothing of the sort. Next morning, to my great contentment, I found myself outwardly under the supervision of the town police, and generally regarded by the public as a shabby individual.

I, meantime, was as busy as ever, but it was little I discovered. Herr Botteher was certainly not in good repute among his fellows. Nevertheless, I could hear of no particular difficulty into which he had fallen of late, although I did learn that he had, three weeks since, made a hasty journey. One little fact, however, seemed to me of great worth. Herr Botteher these times slept badly, and was wont to rise often by night and pace up and down through the garden.

I lay lurking for two entire nights under bushes in this same plot; but during all these weary hours whoever did come to the place Herr Botteher unfortunately did not, and in the garden I could find no trace of any hidden treasure or likelihood of such. I fell into greater despair than before. What could I do? Upon one side my absolute certainty of having tracked my man. On the other no earthly means of bringing home his guilt. If I only had even sufficient ground to demand a search through the rascal's house! But I had not. One afternoon I was walking up and down my room considering, when the post brought me a brief but concise and decisive dispatch from my Chief. "Return immediately, unless all matters are in train. Give up. Your presence here is necessary."

This order was like a thunderclap in my ears. My commanding officer was plainly displeased at my long delay. Should I simply throw the cards down and venture all on one trick this same evening, so as to depart tomorrow, at furthest? I decided for the last alternative.

Twelve gentlemen sat in the town clubroom. My friend made one of them. To his great surprise I sat down close to him, and began to talk a little. Presently our nearest neighbor stood up and departed, to my great joy. I bent over Botteher now, and whispered that I had a weighty matter to talk over with him.

"What may it be?" he inquired, calmly.

"You believe I am here as a lottery agent?"

He nodded.

"I am not, however. I have been sent here on detective business by the Prussian Police Office." Herr Botteher took this revelation significantly. On the instant he knew not how to compose his features. He first drew in his face as if wishing to look astonished, and then he tried to smooth away all but supreme indifference. After a second or two, during which I had studied him as a serpent does its prey, he said in a constrained tone:

"How does that concern me, pray, good sir?"

"You have heard of Widow Friedow, from whom a large sum of money has been stolen. I have come here to hunt up the thief. I have got on the right track. You, I know, are related to her, and concerned in the property she possesses as a probable heir."

While I spoke this I looked him straight in the eyes. They sparkled like those of an angry cat making ready to spring.

"And you will arrest me, I suppose?" he gasped angrily.

I should have loved to seize him by the throat then and there, shouting, "In the name of the law." To this day I wonder how I restrained myself, but I did.

"How can you talk so?" I exclaimed calmly. "I only mean that you must help to bring the criminal to justice; being, as you are, interested in the inheritance."

"With all the pleasure in life," he replied heartily. "I will do what I can. But—what is it you want of me?"

"Early tomorrow morning I will come to you to consult over the matter, and we can then decide on our proceedings."

Botteher drew a long breath. "This is most unfortunate," he exclaimed. "I have an urgent summons, and must start from T. before daybreak. Perhaps I may even be obliged to leave this evening. I owe a heavy sum of money, and must appear personally to my creditor to demand further delay. I cannot wait." I could scarce restrain my joy. The game had run his head right into my lasso; only one pull now, and the knot was fast.

"Don't trouble," I said, quietly. "By-and-by will do for me. I shall be in T. for another week; when you come back will answer as well."

"All right. I expect to return in a couple of days," he exclaimed. "But stay, one question! Is Dr. Miding mixed up in this affair?"

"Do you know him?"

"By sight only."

"He will help me to identify the criminal," I said, coolly looking full into my companion's face, which took a horrible tint and expression now.

"Can he do so?"

"Certainly. He saw the man, dressed like a laborer, the morning after the robbery was effected."

"Who was this ruffian?" Botteher asked, breathlessly.

"His name is—Ebbing—I think," I answered at haphazard.

"I don't know him," was the reply to this.

"I dare say," I said; "He only comes here at times." I rose now, broke off our conversation with every appearance of confidence, and departed, having shaken Botteher by the hand. I went stealthily to his house and waited. I had been here but about a quarter of an hour when a trap dashed up to the door. Botteher sprang out of it, went inside for a few minutes, and then reappeared, carrying something under his left arm. As he got upon one side of the vehicle, I jumped upon the other, and seized hold of my game. He made not the least resistance, but sat like one enchanted.

"Are those Frau Friedow's papers you have under your arm?" I inquired.

"Yes, they are," he replied.

I made the coachman take us where I could put the robber in safe keeping.

When a man is suddenly discovered in a crime he is sure to commit some piece of folly. I had reckoned upon this, and was not out in so doing. My game had literally walked into my hand, and I felt rewarded at last for all my trouble and disappointing delays.

Botteher was sentenced to six years in the House of Correction. His coadjutor was not caught.

—*Denton* [MD] *Journal*, April 19, 1879
—*St. Joseph* [MI] *Herald*, April 19, 1879
—*Manitoba* [Canada] *Daily Free Press*, December 13, 1879
—*The* [Syracuse, NY] *Herald*, October 8, 1882

Written in Blood
Anonymous

The Error that Led to the Conviction of a Scoundrel

On the afternoon of June 18, 1870, the Rue Recluse was startled by the report that a murder had been committed at No. 39. At this number a retired hairdresser had been occupying apartments and had lived in a very eccentric manner some eight years. He was reported to be very rich, and to have only one relative, a nephew, who had married and who kept an imitation jewelry shop in the Rue Vivienne.

On the day mentioned the servant on entering the room of the old gentleman found his lifeless form on the floor in a pool of his own blood. The police were immediately notified, and the authorities soon arrived to make the necessary examinations. Shortly after the detective, Guilot, arrived, to whom the Commissioner of Police remarked:

"Your services will be needed, Guilot. The criminal is known, and known in a very positive fashion. The crime having been committed, the assassin fled, believing that his victim had expired. He was mistaken. The unfortunate man still lived. Summoning all his strength, he dipped one of his fingers in the blood that was flowing from his wound, and wrote on the floor his murderer's name. Look!"

On the floor in large scrawling letters was written with blood: "Aguep."

"That," said the Commissary, "is the beginning of the name of the old man's nephew, of whom he was very fond, and who is named Aguepont."

"The devil!" replied the detective.

"I don't suppose he will try to deny it," continued the magistrate. "The five letters are an overwhelming charge against him. Besides, who profits by the crime except the nephew? See, nothing has been disturbed to throw justice on the wrong scent, and the concierge says that he was the only person who visited the apartments of the old man last evening, he having recognized him by the fact that his dog, a great favorite, was with him."

"That's plain," said Guilot. "The fellow is a fool."

While the magistrate turned to give further directions to his clerk, the detective proceeded to make an examination of the surroundings. Everything about the room was in its place; no sign of a scuffle was apparent. Under a chair a cork covered with green wax was found. It had been used, and the wax portion still showed marks of a corkscrew; but on the other end was a deep notch, evidently made by some sharp instrument. This Guilot considered the basis of a clew, and carefully placed it in is pocket.

Approaching the corpse as it lay on the floor, he commenced a minute examination. The instrument of the crime must have been a poniard or a sharp knife. The poor old man had been struck in the throat and the neck cut from ear to ear. Then, looking at the hand, besmeared with blood, the detective, starting back, exclaimed:

"Great heaven! Look! The right hand is perfectly clean—the fingers of the left hand only are stained with blood! It was not the old man who traced these letters."

"And to think I didn't notice it," said the magistrate, mournfully.

"Now," replied Guilot, "can we imagine a murderer stupid enough to denounce himself by writing his name by the side of his victim?"

"It is plain," said the magistrate, "that Aguepont is not the criminal. Who, then, is he? It is your duty, Guilot, to find out."

He paused. An officer entered, who addressing the magistrate, said:

"Your orders are executed, Monsieur. The arrest has been made. Aguepont has confessed everything."

"What!" exclaimed Guilot. "While we are endeavoring to prove Aguepont's innocence he is confessing his guilt."

The Commissary, having gone through the necessary forms required by law, retired.

Then Guilot, calling the concierge before him, elicited from him the following story: The old gentleman's name was Louis Bigot. He was a peculiar old man, of very regular habits. He had very few visitors—in fact, hardly any except his nephew, M. Aguepont, who dined with him every Sunday at a neighboring restaurant. They were never known to have even a dispute, except an occasional squabble about Madame Marie. She being the wife of M. Aguepont, and a very magnificent creature, who, M. Bigot said, led her husband by the nose. Madame Marie and her uncle had been at loggerheads for about a year. She had wanted M. Bigot to lend Aguepont a thousand francs to buy the stock of a jeweler in the Palais Royal, but he had refused, saying that they might do as they pleased with his fortune after his death. She further stated that on the evening before only Aguepont had visited M. Bigot, and had not left till midnight. On every previous occasion M. Aguepont had spoken to her, but last evening he had failed to do so. Although she did not see his face, she knew him from the fact that his dog Bruno was with him.

This was all that could be learned from the concierge.

The detective then left the house and hastened to the Quai des Orfevres, where Aguepont was imprisoned, and he was at once admitted to the prisoner. From him he elicited nothing save a confession of his guilt. Even then he could not dissuade himself but that there was some mystery buried in this strange affair. After several unsuccessful attempts to bewilder the prisoner, the detective asked:

"Where did you buy the revolver you used to commit the crime?"

"I had it in my possession for some time," he answered.

"What did you do with it afterward?"

"Threw it down the outer boulevard."

"Search will be made and it will be found. But why did you let your dog follow you?" asked Guilot.

"What dog?"

"Your dog—Bruno."

Aguepont sank upon his cot and refused to speak further. After vainly trying to draw from the prisoner further information Guilot departed, muttering to himself:

"Who knows! I have seen famous actors in my time."

Leaving the prison the detective turned his steps toward the Rue Vivienne, determined to see Madame Aguepont and obtain from her all she might know concerning the murder. First he determined to find out in what estimation the Agueponts were held by their neighbors. From the neighboring shopkeepers Guilot learned that Aguepont bore an excellent character, and Madame's reputation was above reproach. Not a breath of slander assailed her good name.

"Strange," said the detective to himself, "that such people should be mixed up in such an affair as this."

Having arrived at a shop over whose door hung the sign "Aguepont, Gold and Imitation Jewelry," Guilot entered. He was shown into the back shop, where Madame sat attired in a deep mourning dress. In her hand she held a stamped paper. It was a summons to appear at the Palais de Justice before the examining magistrate.

"Madame," said Guilot, "I am sent there in the service of the law. I am a detective. As you know, your husband has been arrested charged with the murder of M. Bigot."

"Monsieur," she replied, "he is innocent. But see, I have received this summons. What can they want of me?"

"To obtain information which I hope will prove your husband's innocence. Don't look upon me as an enemy, Madame. I wish to ascertain the truth. Will you answer me frankly?"

"Question me, Monsieur."

"You know, Madame," he began, "That last night at 11 o'clock M. Bigot, your husband's uncle, was murdered."

"Alas."

"Where was Monsieur Aguepont at that hour?"

"My God! It is a fatality."

"Where did your husband spend last night?"

"He went to one of our workmen who had broken his word and failed to bring an article which we were to sell today. You know we are poor, and could not afford to lose a sale, no matter how small the profit. About 9 o'clock we went out and I accompanied him to an omnibus, which he entered before my eyes."

"Then your workman will be able to swear he saw M. Aguepont at his house at 11 o'clock?"

"Alas, no."

"And why not?"

"Because he had gone before my husband arrived."

"But the concierge saw him?"

"Our workman lives in a house where there is no concierge."

"At what time did your husband return?"

"A little after midnight."

"You thought he had been absent long?"

"Yes, I scolded him. He said that strolling along he had stopped at a café to drink a glass of beer. That was his excuse."

"Was there nothing peculiar about him?"

"Nothing."

Large tears rolled down her pale cheeks. But Guilot thought behind those tears in the depths of her blue eyes he could detect a gleam of joy.

"Could she be guilty?" he thought.

"But where were you, Madame, during the fatal evening while your husband was on that useless errand?"

"I was here, Monsieur. I have witnesses to prove it."

"Witnesses!"

"Yes, Monsieur. The evening was so warm that I wanted some ice cream, and, not caring to eat it alone, I sent my servant to invite two of my neighbors, Madame Dregot and Madame Caret. They were here till half-past 11. Ask them—they will tell you. My husband is innocent."

"Then how do you explain his confession?"

"He is mad! He is mad!" she exclaimed, sobbing aloud.

After addressing a few words of consolation to the wife, the detective asked permission to examine the house. To this Madame readily assented. Examining everything in both shops, Guilot asked to be shown to the cellar. As he entered his practiced eye scrutinized every object. Fifty full bottles stood in rows. These he closely examined.

"No," he muttered, "not one is sealed with green wax. The cork that protected the weapon did not come from this cellar."

Guilot, expressing himself satisfied, then ascended to the shop. On entering the detective was met by the dog, who, snarling savagely, refused to let him pass. Guilot, to quiet him, called:

"Bruno, Bruno."

The dog, showing his teeth, drew back.

"It is useless to call him," said Madame. "He is not savage: but he obeys only my husband and myself."

"Where was the dog last evening?"

"I don't know," she stammered.

"Perhaps he followed your husband."

"Why, yes; now I seem to recollect."

The detective, looking her straight in the eyes, said:

"Then, Madame, he is trained to follow carriages?"

She was silent.

Not being able to ascertain more, Guilot withdrew. At a neighboring café, over a cup of coffee, he reached the following solution of the problem:

He was sure that Madame had not stirred from the house on the evening of the murder. But it was clear that she was aware of the crime, and acquainted with the assassin. If Aguepont committed the deed it was clear that he would not leave such incontrovertible proofs behind. Who, then, was the assassin? A man whom the dog would follow as it would its owners, since the dog was at the Rue Recluse on the evening of the crime. So it was someone intimate with the Agueponts. He must hate the husband, since he had planned to throw all suspicion on him. On the other hand, he must love the wife, since, knowing him, she would not give him up, at the same time sacrificing her husband. Conclusion: Madame, belying her reputation, undoubtedly had a lover.

"Zounds!" he said to himself. "The dog must be utilized."

The clock struck 3. It was time for Madame to depart for the Palais de Justice. Going to the door of the café, he saw her, after giving a few parting instructions to the little servant, leave her shop. Hastily crossing the street, he entered the shop. The little servant was there, alone.

"Where is Madame Aguepont?" he asked.

"She had gone out, Monsieur."

"How unfortunate. How sorry poor Madame will be. But perhaps you can take your mistress's place, little one. I came back for the address of the gentleman she asked me to visit."

"What gentleman?" the servant asked.

"You know very well; Monsieur—there, now, I have forgotten his name. The gentleman the dog obeys so well."

"Oh, you mean Monsieur Andre?"

"Yes, that's his name. You can certainly tell me where the gentleman lives?"

"Oh, yes; he lives in the Rue du Roi Doré, No. 23."

"Caught," muttered Guilot; then aloud: "Thanks. You have done Madame a great service. She will be delighted. Good-by, little one."

So saying the detective hastened to the Palais de Justice, and, obtaining a warrant, left at breakneck speed for the Rue du Roi Doré. In fifteen minutes he was at the door of No. 23.

"Monsieur André," he said to the concierge.

"Fourth Floor, right-hand door."

"Is he in?"

"Yes."

"I must treat Monsieur André to a bottle of wine. To what shop does he go?"

"The one opposite."

In a second the detective was in the place indicated.

"A bottle of wine, if you please—the green seal."

The wine was brought, and the cork being examined it was found to be a facsimile of the one in the detective's possession.

"Trapped," muttered Guilot.

It did not take him long to leave the shop and reach the fourth floor. He knocked at the right-hand door.

"Come in," said a voice.

The detective entered.

"I arrest you in the name of the law."

The man turned livid.

"Are you playing a trick on me?" he said.

"Don't be childish. You were seen to leave M. Bigot's room, and I have in my pocket the cork you used to prevent the point of the dagger from breaking."

"I am innocent!" exclaimed the man.

"Tell that to the magistrate. He won't believe you. Your accomplice, Madame Aguepont, has confessed all."

"Impossible!" he exclaimed. "She knew nothing—"

"Then you did it alone; so much confessed."

Search disclosed the poniard and letters from Madame Aguepont.

Twenty minutes later, André finding himself in a cell, broke down and confessed all.

He had known M. Bigot a long time. His main object in murdering him was to bring the punishment of the same on Aguepont. This was why he had dressed like him, and was followed by the dog, Bruno. When the old man was assassinated he dipped the finger of the corpse in the blood to trace the final letters Aguep, which had nearly destroyed an innocent man.

"It was cleverly arranged," he said, boastingly. "If I had succeeded I would have killed two birds with one stone—got rid of Aguepont, whom I hate, and of whom I am jealous, and enriched the woman I love."

It was simple and terrible surely.

"Unfortunately, my lad," observed Guilot, "you lost your wits at the last moment. It was the left hand you dipped into the blood."

Andre started, terrified.

"Was it that that betrayed me?"

"Precisely."

Then raising his hands to Heaven he exclaimed:

"That comes of being a real artist."

Then glancing with piteous contempt at the detective, he said, with a sneer:

"Fool, Louis Bigot was left-handed."

Thus an error had brought the scoundrel to justice. Aguepont was set at liberty next day. When questioned he said:

"I love my wife. I wanted to sacrifice myself for her. I believed her guilty."

She was arrested, but acquitted by the same court that sentenced Andre to the galleys for life.

—*The* [Gettysburg, PA] *Star and Sentinel*, March 22, 1882
—*The* [Syracuse, NY] *Herald*, February 5, 1882

The Twisted Ring
Anonymous

Experience of a French Detective in Russia

There was blood on everything in the room. It was on the desk at which the dead man had been seated; it was scattered over the papers; it lay in little crimson pools upon the blotting pad and the carpet; in the last desperate struggle it had spurted from his gaping wounds against the window curtains and walls; the very atmosphere of the chamber seemed imbued with it. A horrible murder had been committed.

Paul Pelaufski, chief of the secret police at St. Petersburg, had paid the penalty of his outspoken hostility to Nihilism.

My name is Alfred Cassagne. I am thirty years of age, and I am a detective.

The following telegram to the Department of Secret Police in Paris had resulted in my taking the next train to the Russian capital:

> "Pelaufski fatally stabbed early morning Nihilists. Send best man at once. Must be stranger to Russia. Ours too well known. Expense no object.
> GURLOFF."

Four days later fashionable St. Petersburg was apprised of the arrival in the capital of a young French gentleman, rich, and, rumor had it, titled, though traveling under the nom de voyage of Mons. Anton Riccard. He was accompanied by a single manservant, a middle-aged person of grave deportment. Pierre Chauffaud was one of the most courageous seconds in the employ of the Parisian secret police. On two occasions he had been known to risk his life to save that of his principal. I had chosen him to accompany me.

On making myself known at police headquarters I was at once taken to the scene of the tragedy. Nothing had been disturbed. I found it as described in the opening paragraph of this story.

The police were entirely at sea in regard to the identity of the murderer. Gurloff placed the case in my hands, and I at once proceeded to make an examination of the material before me.

The assassin had evidently gained admittance to the chief's apartment during the day, and had remained concealed until nightfall, when escape was comparatively easy, and had then sprung upon his victim from behind. Pelaufski had turned to confront his murderer, but not quickly enough to avoid the knife, the first blow from which had struck him in the left breast, the second one lower down, squarely above the region of the heart. The murderer had then caught him by the throat to prevent his crying out, and held him while he slowly bled to death.

Diligent inquiry elicited the fact that a woman had been the last visitor to the dead chief—a woman high in society, the Baroness Woronsko. Suspicion, however, in no way attached to her—in fact, she was one of the most trusted spies in the employ of the Government.

However, I immediately set Pierre Chauffaud to shadow her movements. My impression that she would bear watching was confirmed when I received his report.

The Baroness Woronsko, whilst in the employ of the government, was in reality a Nihilist of the worst description.

Soon the question narrowed itself down to this: Assuming her to be an accessory to the murder of Pelaufski, who was the actual assassin? It was absurd to suppose that a frail, slight woman like the Baroness Woronsko could overcome a strong, courageous man like Paul Pelaufski.

I had one clew, a clew so slight that it had been overlooked by the Russian police, but one which no really first-class detective would have passed unnoticed. On the dead man's throat were the black marks of the fingers which had strangled him. The thumb of the right hand had been pressed violently into the skin of the neck, so as to leave a deep abrasion.

I at once took a careful cast of this thumb-mark with the finest wax, thus reproducing every line exactly.

I knew that the impressions of no two thumbs in the world are alike. It is the prison-mark in China, remember, and there serves the same purpose as the rogues' gallery in America to identify a criminal.

One other clew I had to guide me. A plain twisted ring, worn by the murderer, had left its mark distinctly on the flesh. I caused the impression of the hand, ring and all to be photographed.

Furnished only with these slight clews, I now set out to find the murderer of Paul Pelaufski. Instinct told me, I suppose, to look for him in the best society of the capital. My Parisian letters of introduction easily opened to me the best houses. In particular I sought the society of the Baroness. I soon discovered that she was an abandoned intrigueante. During her husband's absence on his country estates she unscrupulously amused herself with a lover, one Rudolph Pfesh, a Hungarian of handsome appearance and very finely educated. I soon discovered this man to be a red-hot Nihilist. The Baroness for the time was absolutely infatuated with him.

During all this time you may suppose that I kept a sharp lookout for the twisted ring. I did nothing of the kind. Amidst the mass of jewelry nightly displayed in the drawing rooms of St. Petersburg, one might as well have searched for a needle in a bundle of hay. No, I only hoped to use that as confirmatory evidence when I found my man.

And I was fast finding him. Already I had gained the confidence of the Nihilists. During the third month Rudolph Pfesh confided in me the outline of a plot to assassinate the Czar.

Bombs were to cut no figure in this last attempt. A peculiar and singularly treacherous method was to be employed. People would never, perhaps, know how the Emperor met his death. But who was to inflict it?

The circle to which I now belonged, so Pfesh informed me, had drawn lots to decide this, and the choice had fallen on me. I was to become the assassin. But the details would not be confided to me until the night before the day set for the execution of the plot.

That evening I was to attend at the house of the Baroness Woronsko, when I should receive full instructions.

The Baroness' house was in the Nevskoi Prospect. It was a huge mansion surrounded by ornamental grounds. Before noon, completely disguised, Pierre Chauffaud took occasion to thoroughly reconnoiter the place.

Night came. A brilliant ball was in progress. The Baroness had never looked so lovely. In the prime of her womanhood, her figure was displayed to the greatest advantage in evening dress. I looked around me. Pfesh, Dakoutsk, Phloblosh and Chenkamin—all were there. The gathering was honeycombed with the Nihilistic element.

I felt my hand suddenly grasped, and turning around was confronted by—Gurloff. He was without disguise of any kind. I regarded him with wonderment. The second in command of secret police, he must be well known to these people.

Then suddenly it flashed across me. Gurloff is also one of them. Nihilism has penetrated to the police department.

I had the fourth dance with the Baroness Woronsko. It was marked a waltz on my program. She danced superbly. I myself understand the divine art. As to the strains of enchanting music we floated down the long ballroom I could not but wish myself a thousand miles away from St. Petersburg. It went hard with me to betray that splendid creature. I am a Frenchman, and I have to confess that she affected me powerfully.

The music ceased, and she led me into a conservatory. We were hardly seated when she spoke and said:

"I am the one chosen to instruct you by our circle. Tomorrow you will be presented to the Emperor. Being a foreigner, he will extend to you the royal hand, as is his custom."

She paused and glanced nervously around. Quitting my side for a moment, she parted the thick shrubbery and peered out through the glass into the darkness.

"I thought I heard a sound in the garden," she said.

I knew it was the noise occasioned by Pierre Chauffaud and the men with him scaling the wall surrounding the grounds.

"O, it is nothing," I said, but feeling all the time very much like a villain. "Do not be alarmed."

She returned, seated herself by my side, and resumed:

"You have been chosen by our circle to rid the world of this tyrant. Take this ring. No, do not place it on your hand yet. Its touch is death, if you are not extremely careful. Keep it in its case, and just before you are admitted to the audience, place it on your finger. The slightest contraction of your fingers will pierce the hand you hold with a small, hollow needle. Retain the Czar's hand in your own, respectfully, for a moment. During that brief interval you can inject into his palm a deadly poison. Its action is sufficiently slow to afford you ample opportunity to make your escape."

Horror stricken, I gazed upon the deadly ring. To my amazement, it was an exact counterpart of the ring in the photograph.

"Whose ring is this?" I gasped, recoiling from her. Could she be a murderess?

"The ring was Gurloff's," she answered in a low tone. "It was suited to the purpose, and he contributed it to the cause. It was fitted as you see it now by the Hungarian, Rudolph Pfesh."

I saw it all now. Gurloff had himself murdered his chief at the order of the circle, and had sent to Paris for a detective, thinking to thus divert suspicion by apparently taking extraordinary pains to discover the perpetrator of the crime.

A sudden look of terror passed over the face of the Baroness. I saw at once that I had done something or let fall some exclamation to arouse her suspicions, or had Gurloff discovered me to her and was she simply luring me on? If the latter, she had repented early of playing with the fire. With a swift movement she passed me, and standing for a moment in the door of the conservatory, uttered a peculiar cry. In an instant a crowd of desperate men gathered in the doorway, foremost among them Gurloff.

"You thought to learn all our secrets and betray us," hissed Gurloff, pointing his finger at me. "He is a mouchard, gentlemen. Seize him. Your lives depend upon it."

The crowd dashed forward, at their head the murderer of Pelaufski.

"Down with the mouchard!" they yelled, and a dozen hands were on my throat.

"Crash! Bang! Thud!" Pierre Chauffaud and his men were breaking into the conservatory from the outside. The next moment the crowd scattered like chaff, but I never relaxed my hold on Gurloff's throat. He was beaten almost into insensibility and secured.

Two weeks afterwards he was arraigned for the murder of Chief Pelaufski and convicted on purely circumstantial evidence. The twisted ring was proved to be his property, and was in his possession on the night of the commission of the crime. The impression of the thumb of his right hand exactly corresponded with the wax impression taken from the dead man's throat. He suffered death on the scaffold.

The Baroness, Pfesh and many members of the circle were exiled to the gold placer mines of Kara. The ring with which it had been proposed to murder the Czar was sent for by that dignitary. He caused the poison to be injected into the paw of a hound, and the animal died in great agony. Then the ruler of all the Russias sent for me.

"You are a French detective?"

"Yes, sire."

"I am sorry for it. If you had not been a detective I would have made you a noble. I shall instruct my secretary to give you a hundred thousand rubles. The best place on my staff of secret police is yours, if you care to fill it."

"I am a Parisian—"

"I understand," he interrupted good-humouredly. "You cannot live away from Paris. They all say that."

The audience was over. I left his presence and returned to Paris a comparatively rich man. I would not live in Russia if I could, and if I tried to I don't think the Nihilists would let me.—*Chicago Journal*

—*The* [Monroe, WI] *Daily Independent*, October 2, 1890
—*Hornellsville* [NY] *Weekly Tribune*, October 31, 1890

4
Contemporary Reflections

From the beginning detective stories have been about more than simply identifying and capturing criminals. Poe used them to talk about genius, and games, and perception, and a lot more things than orangutans and looking for things where they ought to be. After Poe, however, if the intellectual breadth that was integral to his writing about Dupin didn't entirely disappear, it certainly atrophied. A lot of this was due to the swelling popularity of detective stories in the mid–1800s as well as the virtual proprietorship that story papers and newspapers exercised over most of that particular kind of fiction. The vast majority of detective stories published in America between Poe and the advent of Sherlock Holmes, consequently, contain little in the way of literary sophistication, and most even set aside the technology of suspense. But this does not mean that detective stories of the period reverted to the stripped down Newgate model of being puerile exempla of good versus evil. Individually and collectively they do more than that.

Anthropologically, of course, detective stories reveal things about cultures that other kinds of fiction cannot. A cursory survey of nineteenth-century American fiction, for instance, shows an interest in different kinds of crime from the detective stories of other eras. To be sure there are stories about murder and theft, but there are also a lot of stories which reflect new, nineteenth-century crimes. Counterfeiting, for instance, looms fairly large as subject matter in mid-century fiction because of what was going on in the world of money: until 1865 when Congress established a national currency thousands of state banks issued their own bills and it was easy to make bundles of funny money. Nineteenth-century detective fiction for the first time also displays a lot of attention to jewelry, reflecting the ostentatious upper-middle class folkways of what Mark Twain would call the

Gilded Age. Then, too, a lot of period detective fiction in the U.S. is peripatetic, with detectives traveling from city to city, state to state. And fascination with the means of chasing criminals, the railroad, often became almost an end in itself, witnessed by "Seventy Miles an Hour" in this chapter.

In many ways nineteenth-century detective fiction was caught in the middle. A fair amount of it wallowed in the motives fundamental to sensation fiction. Sensation fiction was the spin-off from the Gothic movement that centered on the travails of and then the ultimate triumph of domestic virtues. It focused mostly on pathos and suffering women—*The Woman in White* being one of the century's blockbusters on both sides of the Atlantic. Sensation fiction was the prevailing literary fashion in Britain with Wilkie Collins and Dickens as its standard bearers. And through them—and lesser writers like Mrs. Henry Wood—sensation fiction had a decisive impact on a lot of American short detective fiction. There are pitiable victims aplenty—witness stories like "The Mute Witness" in *The* [Hagerstown, MD] *Herald and Torch Light* (March 1, 1876) or "The Child Witness" in *The Janesville* [WI] *Gazette* (April 22, 1880). "The Costly Kiss," in this chapter, exhibits the kind of explicit moralizing upon which a fair amount of (but not all) contemporary detective fiction was based. In these kinds of stories the paternal detective hero replaces Poe's cranky, misanthropic genius, and the subject, if not quite sin, becomes morality and the hero helping it prevail. Although the heroes are now detectives doing their jobs, even if they are not God's agents, a whole class of nineteenth-century detectives are pretty clearly working on behalf of Providence. Murder will not quite out unless the detective outs it, but once he does his job, Providence does the cleaning up. Thus in "A Detective Story: The Convict Coachman" (*Indiana* [PA] *Weekly Messenger*, April 28, 1880) what happens to the criminals is that "The young lady is still living a raving maniac in the insane asylum, and the ancient coachman is serving his life term in the state prison." The same sort of thing happens at the end of narratives by Dickens—and Conan Doyle.

But not all nineteenth-century detective fiction yielded to the blandishments of sensation fiction. Space limitations helped: because most period detective fiction is so short (typically under 5,000 words) there is not a lot of time or space to do much more than put forth an articulate account of what happened. But the thing that sets the fiction apart from the news stories of crime on other pages was that narrative's emphasis on cleverness.

Indeed, the term "clever" is ubiquitous in nineteenth-century detective stories and many conclude with a "clever capture." And a general movement toward realism also helped provide distance from sensation fiction. This movement included such things as an interest in historical crimes and the transformation of real detectives like Vidocq, Pinkerton, and then Thomas Byrnes into larger-than-life adventure heroes who move off of the news columns and into the Select Stories column. Sometimes that slight movement toward realism even extended to telling truths about what detectives do besides having adventures, aiding the dispossessed, and solving puzzles and enigmas. Some of these rare stories uncover the fact that police and detectives really exist only to serve and protect entrenched wealth and class. And a few others darken the atmosphere even further by describing the detective doing his job in a world in which the rule of law is at best tenuous.

The Costly Kiss:
A New York Detective Experience
Anonymous

A wholesale hardware store downtown was entered, the safe opened, and sixteen thousand dollars taken, one night last August. Next morning complaint was made, and I was sent to work the case.

On examining the premises everything showed the touch of a professional hand. The lock of the front door had been "tooled" effectually; the bolt was dislodged, and could not be shot. The door of the counting room had been kicked in, the thin partition making this an easy matter. The safe had been opened without violence, a key fitted to the lock having evidently been used. The fall-rope—the stout rope used for hoisting goods to the upper stories—had been cut; one end had been made fast to a handle of the safe; the other end hung out from the window, which opened into an alleyway some fifteen or twenty feet below. It seemed plain that the thief had been unwilling to run the risk of coming out through the front door into the street—it might have been nearly daylight—and had preferred this less exposed exit. Nothing in the store had been taken with the exception of a pair of silver-mounted pistols; the thief had, reasonably, been content with the booty found in the safe.

After concluding this examination I received from the partners a description of the money stolen. It consisted of new bills on a Massachusetts bank—fives and tens—twelve thousand of the amount having a private mark, put on at the bank, for reasons of their own. This mark was a "Co," written in small letters, in red ink, near the right-hand lower corner. Besides, I was shown pistols of the same pattern as the ones taken. Lastly, I took a look at the key of the safe. It was a plain, straight key; the tip screwed on. The make of the key was such that it could not easily be copied; I doubt whether an impression could have been taken from it in wax worth anything. This key had been in the pocket of the senior partner overnight. There was a duplicate tip kept in a drawer of one of the counting room desks very carelessly; but this drawer was found locked, and the tip within. I borrowed this tip, as it might possibly be of use to me.

Before I left, I asked the partners if they suspected anybody on their premises? No: their porter, a respectable black man, had been in their employ for fourteen years; they *knew* him to be honest. Of their clerks, one was a boy, just from the country; next to him was a young man, a nephew of the junior partner, engaged to be married to the adopted daughter of the senior partner, and about to receive an interest in the business; the head clerk was a superintendent of a Sunday school in Brooklyn, and therefore above suspicion; the bookkeeper, an elderly young man, bald, bachelor, quiet, regular, reliable as an interest table. No, again; it was not possible that the work had been done by anyone connected with the establishment. True, the safe had been opened by someone who had used the right key; but if this had been done by one of the employees, he would not have made such a fuss about getting in and out.

The first step I took was to get my cards printed. Here's one of them that I keep as a memento of the case. You see I describe the bills, noting particularly the private mark—the "Co"—and offer a reward to anyone giving information at police headquarters of the person offering such bills; and there is a reward of one hundred dollars for the recovery of the whole amount—a ridiculously small reward, but all they would allow me to offer. These cards I distributed at barrooms, billiard saloons, eating houses, livery stables, lodging houses, including some hotels; shipping offices; the foreign steamers, of course; exchange offices, and other places likely to be patronized by "cracksmen." I also sent some of the cards to the police of other cities. And this was all I could do. I had set my hooks, and now must wait patiently for a bite.

When I first entered the force I was told that I must cultivate my bump of patience, and I have had occasion to learn the value of the advice. It was annoying to have day after day go by with no advance made in my work, but there was no help for it. It was nearly a week before I got even a nibble.

This came in the form of a note left at the office, informing the deputy that something might be learned about the bills marked "Co" by calling at such a number Greenwich Street, a place where I had left one of my cards. I went over there immediately, and found that one of my fives, marked, had been taken there, at the bar, the night before; but it had not been noticed as a marked bill until after the man had gone. The barkeeper, however, remembered the man, and described him. The description answered to no one I knew. All I could do was to circulate the description, and hope that some brother officer might light upon him; I might, myself. Not much, however, from *that* nibble; but as the possessor of the "swag" had begun to spend on his money, I had hopes of having something to do before long.

Next day another call at the office from a livery-stable keeper in East Broadway. I wasn't in when he called, but the sergeant took the man's information, and told him he'd send me up to his place. I went, and found he had taken in a "fineff" ($5), one of my marked bills. It was a man I'd had dealings with before; and when I left one of my cards with him he said, jokingly, that if my man came in his way he'd halter him for me, and put him in a clean stall till called for. Well, what I got from this source was just this: the stable keeper had taken the "V" from a grocer close by; and when the horse man questioned the provision man, *he* said he'd taken it from a widow woman that kept a boardinghouse in that neighborhood. They hadn't questioned the widow but left that for me; so I got her address and went right to the house. It was about eleven o'clock and she was in the heat of getting dinner—came up to see me with a very red face and her sleeves rolled up. However, I won't take time to paint her picture. The amount of my visit there was that she had taken the bill from one of her boarders, a nice little girl, she said, by the name of Jenny Rice; she worked at a bindery downtown, and was the widow's seventh or eleventh cousin, in some way. She gave me an exact account of the relationship, but I never can remember farther than *second* cousin in my own family. Well, I asked the widow how she supposed Jenny came by the bill. I had told her at first that the bill was a bad one, and I had received it in business, and traced it round to her. She said she had no idea; most likely for wages at the bindery.

By this time I had made up my mind that the widow was an honest, reliable kind of little woman, and I gave her some idea of what was in the wind; told her I was an officer, and said something about a reward. I told her I was anxious to know something about Jenny's acquaintances; what young men she knew, etc.

"Now," says she, "Jenny's an honest girl; that I *know*; but I don't like the company she keeps—that's a fact! That is, I don't mean company in general; but there's a young fellow that's walked up home with her, and taken her out to concerts a few times, that I don't like at all. He's got too much money, and is rather too much of a gentleman—not that he's a bit too *good* for her, but he isn't the kind of a young man I want to see paying attentions to my Jenny—she's the same to me as a daughter. Jenny's got his daguerreotype locked up somewhere, the foolish girl! I wish I could get it for you, but it won't do to try to get into her drawer. But *he* couldn't have given her *five dollars*; *that's* out of the question! I'd better ask Jenny where she got it. I'll ask her this noon; and if you'll come here this afternoon I'll tell you what she says."

Now the widow's talk about this young man had interested me, as you may guess. I wanted to *see* him; and I thought I could do it best by being at the house toward night, when he might walk home with Jenny. So I told Mrs. Gould—the widow, that is—that I'd rather she wouldn't say anything to Jenny about the bill at present; that it wasn't best to trouble her, for it was most likely, as she said, that the bill came from the bindery; but that I'd be round that evening, and if the fellow she'd spoken of should happen to come home with her, or come in to invite her to go anywhere with him, why, I could see him, and then find out what kind of person he was. The widow said she wouldn't speak to Jenny if I thought it wasn't best; and if I would make inquiries about this Gregory's character—that was the name Jenny called him by—she'd be very much obliged to me. And we agreed that I should come there that evening, and—if there was any occasion for it—I should pass as a distant relation of hers from Rhode Island, where her husband came from. And so, after fixing on the best time to call, I came away.

At the office again; and there I found a message waiting for me to go to a station house downtown, to see a young woman who had been offered some of my marked bills. You see my hooks were getting nibbles for me in several directions.

On my way downtown I stopped in at the store, and told the partners that I was started at last on several scents, and should drive my man to earth in a few days. The news was acceptable to them, as you may suppose.

Well, at the station house I found a young Irishwoman, who, they said, had been offering some marked bills at a shipping office, in payment for a second-cabin passage to Liverpool. The money was shown me—about seventy-five dollars,—and I recognized it at once. The woman was an unusually pretty Irish girl, well dressed, and having the appearance of being a first-class servant. She gave her name as Margaret—she wouldn't give the other—and she seemed determined to keep her own affairs to herself. I perceived, as I thought, that she was what the French call *enceinte*. Poor thing! I said to myself, it's more than likely that the very rascal I'm after is your deceiver, and has given you this money to get you off to Ireland, out of the way.

I took Margaret into the Captain's sitting room, and tried to talk with her, but I was met at the outset with such a speech as this:

"Mr. Officer," said she, "you may spare your words. My secret is dearer to me—dearer even than the baby that lies near my heart. God bless and preserve it! It will save trouble for me to speak plainly now at the start. I shall never tell who gave me that money."

I was a good deal taken aback by such a speech as that, you know. About all I could say was what I did:

"We must put you in prison until you do," says I.

"Very well," she replied; "I can stand *that* well enough, though I *wouldn't* like to have *his* baby born in a *prison!* But it's a vow I've made, and I'll never be left to break a vow that my conscience and my heart tell me to keep."

"Well, Margaret," I said, "you may think better of this. I'll see you again tomorrow morning"; and I had her put into the room of one of the sergeants, who was absent on leave, for overnight. I thought it possible that a night's confinement might be an argument with her, and, besides, I had a dim hope that my visit at Mrs. Gould's that evening might lead to discoveries which would make the breaking of Margaret's vow unnecessary. I had her safe in hand, at all events, and could afford to wait for something to turn up which should enable me to get hold of her secret. Poor girl! I was sincerely sorry for her. Her real Irish beauty—the most charming beauty, to me, in the world—her dark gray eyes, glistening with tears; her sad situation; her devotion to her betrayer; all these excited my sympathies for her in an alarming degree—for a policeman: a policeman, you know, has no business to *have* such things as sympathies about him.

Well, I was at Mrs. Gould's at the set time, just before tea. Jenny came home alone—a very pretty girl she was, by-the-way, a plump, little bird of a girl, lively as a wren ("Jenny Wren" I called her, to myself)—and as I sat in the sitting room with the widow, I had to be introduced to her as a Mr. Gould, from Rhode Island. She didn't pay me as much attention as I should have liked, but hurried through her tea and went up to her room to dress to go out.

"Tell Sue," says she, "when she comes, to come right up to my room."

"Where are you going?" the widow asked.

"Oh, we're going out to spend the evening; sha'n't be home till late. But you needn't sit up; I've got the key." And so she flitted off.

"That *Sue*," says Mrs. Gould, as soon as Jenny was out of hearing, "*she* goes with Gregory, *too*! He'll be with them girls tonight, sure as rats! If you mean to see him, you'd better follow the girls."

The advice was good, and I soon left the house and got a position across the way from which to watch them when they came out. Sue arrived in a few minutes, and then pretty soon they came out together, and turned into East Broadway, I following at a proper distance behind. They went at a brisk pace down street, and hadn't gone far before they met a young fellow coming up. They had a jolly meeting, laughing and talking at a great rate. I didn't try to get a look at him then; I felt sure they were going together to some place of amusement, and I could follow them in and spot him at my leisure, so I let them go along undisturbed. They went on, each of the girls taking an arm, until they came to the National Theatre, and there they went in. I gave them time to get fairly in, and then I took a pit ticket and went in too. Looking around after I got seated, I soon discovered Jenny by her bonnet—the trimming was rather peculiar—and who do you think, by thunder! was with her? That young clerk, the one that was a relation of one partner, engaged to the daughter of the other, and about to become a member of the firm himself!

"You—blessed young rascal!" says I to myself. "What the—mischief are you up to?"

But I didn't stop to think long there. This Charley, as he was called, might recognize me—for he had seen me at the store—and be on his guard. You see I had at once concluded that he was the burglar. I know that I had no distinct proof of it, but you know we often *feel* sure of some facts before we *are* sure. Well, I got out into the street; and as I wanted to find a quiet place to think, and had plenty of time, I went to a saloon nearby, and sat down over a glass of iced lager.

Now, if you'll think a moment, you'll see I was in something of a quandary. If there had been nothing else to do but the arrest of the man I believed was the guilty party, why I had only to walk back into the theatre and collar Charley Taylor, alias Gregory; for I was sure, I thought, of his being the man. But then, in a case of this kind, in which highly respectable people are mixed up, you know, it's best to be *very* sure and have your proofs before you go to extremities. Now I hadn't *got* any proofs.

And then another thing, *the recovery of the money* was really my main business. Justice is all very well, of course, but I knew that the hardware firm downtown cared considerably more for their sixteen thousand dollars than for the appropriator thereof, especially, mind you, if said appropriator should prove to be *one of themselves*, as I may say. But if I were to go and dash at Charley in a careless way, he might—supposing him guilty—find means to put it out of our reach; or he might—of course he *would*—protest his innocence, and have so arranged matters as to demand our proofs. This would be difficult, perhaps; at all events, I hadn't any at present. I might watch him until he had occasion to pass off some more marked bills, but that might be a long and tedious job; and then again I might trip him up in a few hours. But I had, I thought, a better way. Most likely Jenny had got that five dollar bill from him; that was a pretty fair guess. And most likely, too, poor Margaret's money came from the same hand, though of that I wasn't so sure. A young rascal like him, who would flirt with sewing girls while engaged at the same time to be married to a rich and fashionable young lady, educated, refined, and all that; and more than this, who would steal his own money, so to speak, to the tune of sixteen thousand dollars, was bad enough for anything. If any one of my suspicions was correct, the others were likely to be. Now, according to my theory, both Jenny and Margaret held proofs against him. But Margaret wouldn't expose him, and Jenny, probably, was so much bewitched with the handsome young villain that he could make her believe anything and do anything for him. It was quite unlikely that she would own, for the sake of her own character, that he had given her money. Very well, I could play off the two girls against each other. Make either believe that he was in love with the other, and *then*, you know, jealousy would bring out the truth right away.

By the time I arrived at these results my second glass of lager had disappeared, and I got up, decided on two points at least; one, to let Charley alone for the present—I had him within reach any time I wanted him; and the other to go and see Margaret again, and try the effect of a little honest deception. And I thought I might as well go then as anytime, for it wasn't late. So I went.

When I got to the station house they told me that the poor girl had been sobbing and moaning in a pitiful way, but that for the last hour she was quiet. I knocked at her door, and she came and opened it immediately, and looked just as if she was expecting someone. When she found it was only me, she went back to her chair and sat down, and her face showed, as plain as could be, that she had made up her mind to be faithful to her vow, let what would come. She had taken off her bonnet and arranged her hair—dark, wavy hair, done up plainly and tastily—and she looked prettier than ever. I oughtn't to call her pretty, for that's a *little* word, I think. She was beautiful enough for a queen, but it was that kind of beauty—I declare I can't describe it, but I should like my *sister* to have such a face. It was goodness and liveliness and sweetness and archness, all put together; and her paleness and sad looks rather improved her appearance.

"So you're bound you won't betray Charley?" said I, as I sat down.

She started up like a wild deer at the name Charley; she threw her hands out just as I have seen it done on the stage, and her eyes didn't flash, they *burned*.

"How do you know?—" she began, and then she changed her tone:

"Ah, Mr. Officer, didn't you think you'd caught me that time! His name *isn't* Charley, and it's guess again, Sir, and worse luck to you."

Poor girl! Nature spoke before you did, and betrayed the secret you tried so well to keep.

"No, Margaret," said I, "you can't deceive me. I know all about it."

And I told her enough, and in such a way, as to convince her that I knew everything she feared, and I asked her to trust me and make a clean breast of it.

"Very well, Sir," she said; "you seem to think you know a great deal about our—about my affairs. You know so much you surely can't want to hear any more from me. You'll be an older man than you are, though, before you get me to break my vow."

Then she leaned forward, put her head into her hands, and gave up to her feelings. She hadn't but just controlled her voice while saying what she did. I saw that if I wanted to know anything more from her I must bring all my facts to bear. But did I *want* to know more? Why break the poor thing's heart with the truth?

Well, I sat some time thinking about it. There was no sound in the room but the buzz of the gas, and, once in a while, the saddest of sighs from poor Margaret. I concluded, finally, that it was best to get her statement if possible. I should want to use it to convince the partners of the rascality of Charley; it might, perhaps, save his intended bride from making a life-long mistake; and, lastly, it was best that Margaret herself should know—the sooner the better—the character of the man she was evidently trusting. So, I began:

"Margaret," said I, breaking the stillness and making her start, almost frightened, from her seat, "Margaret, this is a bad business of mine—"

"Sure it is," she interrupted.

"—And I don't like to have it to do; but as I'm in it I must go on, and I want to have it done and over with. Now, listen to me: I shall tell you nothing but the truth, *so help me God!* And I can prove it all to you if you want it. In the first place, you used to live at Mr. Brown's in Tenth Street. Charley boarded there with his uncle, and there he met you. (She was shivering all the time, though it was a hot night; her head was in her hands, so I couldn't see her face.) Charley is engaged to be married to Miss Sarah, the young lady that lives with Mr. Brown's partner—perhaps you know her."

During this last sentence she slowly raised her head and *looked* at me— *such* a look! I declare if some painter could see her as I saw her, he could make a picture that people couldn't look away from.

"Mr. Officer," said Margaret, "if this is a lie you're telling me, may— may God forgive you. But you're—breaking—my heart!"

"Margaret," said I, "it's the sad truth, and nothing more nor less. I have a sister at home, and I couldn't trifle with a woman. And now hear me out. This very night, not more than an hour ago, I saw him making love to a pretty sewing girl at the theatre. He is with her a great deal, takes her to theatres and concerts, and she is in love with him if he isn't with her."

"Oh, my God!" she groaned and rocked herself to and fro. I could hardly stand it. If I hadn't felt so *mad* at Charley, I don't know but I should have had occasion to wipe my eyes too.

"You see, Margaret," I went on, "that this fellow is a thorough *rascal*, and whatever promises he has made you are worth just nothing at all."

"*No*, Sir," she burst in, "he promised me money, and he gave it to me, too, with a free hand, God bless him! He's as generous a man as lives; but the *rest!* Oh the *rest!* I'd be glad to think you'd lied to me, Sir, though I knew 'twould sink you fathoms deep in hell. But something tells me you're speaking the truth with your honest face."

"That money," said I, "Margaret, was *stolen*. He has been living a fast life lately, and he had to rob a store to get money. He broke into his own uncle's store, and took thousands of dollars, and it's that that's bringing everything out. The money was marked."

"And so you're on his track, and I'm fool enough, *curse* my woman's weakness, to help you to more proofs against him!"

She went on now for some time in such a way that I feared her trouble had crazed her. She paced the room, hardly minding me, now cursing herself, now him—"Her *baby*, oh, her *baby*, *his* baby!" And then she fell on her knees at her chair, and uttered one of the wildest, strangest, and yet most beautiful prayers I ever heard. From the tone of the prayer I saw she was thinking of suicide, and I planned how to prevent this. I concluded to take her home with me, and leave her under the care of my mother and sister.

Well, I'm making too long a story of this, but I can hardly help it. I never was so interested for anybody as I was for that poor Irish girl. I pitied the intended bride of Charley, it is true, but I hadn't *seen* her, and besides, I knew that she hadn't suffered wrong from him. But Margaret! There she was, the poor crushed flower, right before me; she's before me *now*, for that matter.

To go on now, and finish up as soon as I can, I took Margaret home with me. She was glad to go, or rather, she went without any objections. I led her along as I would a child. At home I left her in good hands.

And now I had the agreeable little task of undeceiving the simple-hearted Jenny. There wasn't really any *necessity* for it, for I had proofs enough through Margaret; but, as I thought the matter over, I came to the conclusion to use Jenny's proof—if I could get any—and so save Margaret an exposure. In this way, too, I could spare, somewhat, the feelings of Charley's family, especially of the young lady he was engaged to. She was innocent, and it would be too bad to make her suffer more than was necessary; *that* would be enough. So, next day, I found Jenny; met her at noon, and had a talk with her in Mrs. Gould's sitting room. She wouldn't believe what I told her, and said that it was "none of my business" where she got the bill, spiteful and nippy as she could be. I convinced her that it *was* my business and proposed to prove to her that what I told her about Margaret was true. I didn't want to *compel* her to tell me where she got the bill; it was easier and better to get at the truth in a gentler way. And so I asked her to go with me just to *see* Margaret. Well, finally, she consented to go. Now, if I knew how, I should just like to describe the meeting between those two girls; but I *don't* know how; there's no use in my trying. To tell the truth, I left them alone part of the time. When I came in again, in about half an hour, contrary to what I expected—for they began at each other somewhat in the way of cats, to speak plainly—I found them almost in each other's arms, and both crying.

When I took Jenny away, we walked to Mrs. Gould's without a word on either side. As soon as we got seated in the house,

"Now," says I, "Miss Jenny, "Do you want to have Margaret exposed to any more trouble; or shall I have what I want from you?"

"No, no!" she said; "Margaret's had more than her share of trouble. As for me, I've only been flirting, carrying on a little—ha ha! (but it was a hollow kind of laugh, Jenny!) and I can afford to do anything, almost, to spare her. Only I *don't* want to go into court! Must I?"

I told her that it might not be necessary; and then I asked her, plumply, if Charley gave her that bill.

"Yes, he *did!*" she said; "and I'd rather tell the whole story than leave it *part* told. It was this way: Charley tried to snatch a kiss from me one evening, and I told him, in fun, that kisses were worth a dollar apiece. 'I'll give you *five!*' says he. 'Let's see your money,' says I; and then he put the bill in my hand, and I, like a silly girl, gave him the kiss. I tried to make him take back the money, but he wouldn't take it, and finally left it on the floor when he went away. I thought then that, as he cared so little for the money, I could find a better use for it than he was likely to put it to, and so I paid it to Mrs. Gould for board. And *now* he'll find what *such* kisses really cost sometimes, I hope; for, if I *ever* liked him, I'm sure I *hate* him *now*."

So, you see, I had got all the proof I wanted. Perhaps I haven't said, in so many words, that Margaret had admitted that Charley had given her that money which she offered at the shipping office; she did; and, besides this, she had told me that she had seen him have large rolls of bills, which he said he had *inherited*.

Well, my next step was to get hold of Master Charley in such a way that I could secure man and money at the same time. I shall soon come to that now, and the end of the story.

Early next morning I reported progress to the Deputy. He seemed as much interested in the case as I was, and told me to go on and arrest Charley as soon as I could.

From there I went down to the store, and told the partners everything. They were, of course, completely overcome, and didn't know what to say or do. Charley's uncle spoke first, and proposed calling him down to talk with them. I objected to this, and told them why. If they wanted me to recover their money, they must let me do it in my own way; and I told them my reasons for fearing that he would deny the charge, and try to get off himself, and either take the money with him, or get rid of it— put it out of our reach in some way. The sum was a little too large to risk; its loss had straitened them a good deal—for, as you may remember, the hard times were beginning about then—if they could possibly have spared it, I am sure they would have hushed up the matter in some way. They concluded, however, to leave me to finish the case as I chose, making me promise, though, to make nothing public—at least not till I had consulted them.

The way I managed to get the money was this—and I take some credit to myself for the process. If you'll bear in mind that I was to do nothing publicly, you'll understand better why I acted as I did at first:

I found out that Charley was going to the opera that evening with his intended. I went there too. I was dressed in opera style, so as to be ready to play the part of a gentleman of fashion, if necessary. I looked around for some time before I found Charley and his friend; and when I did find them, and saw *her*, I was sorry, I tell you, for what I had got to do. She was not nearly so pretty as Margaret, but she *loved* him; every look and action showed it. I needn't dwell on that, and I don't want to. It's enough to say that here was another heart to be broken, and I was the unfortunate wretch to be the means of it!—Sometimes I think I won't remain in the force another day; but I find I'm getting used to it. I don't want any more cases like this, though.—Between the acts I met Charley in the lobby, and pretending to have something to say to him of importance, asked him to be so kind as to step aside for a moment. He looked at me with surprise, and recognized me as the officer he had seen in the store; but he went with me into a corner a little out of the stream.

"Now," says I, "I suppose you don't want to have the muss of a public arrest here, with your lady to take care of, and acquaintances all around—"

"Arrest for *what!*" says he, putting on the indignant, but taking care to speak low. I almost smiled at the difference between his manner and his tone.

"Well, for taking about sixteen thousand dollars out of a certain safe downtown," says I.

He was excited, of course; but he carried himself with surprising coolness.

"I'm much obliged to you for beginning this so quietly," says he; "but I assure you that you have made a great mistake."

"We won't waste words," says I. "I have only to say to you just this—and if you're a sensible man you'll do what I say, and save yourself a public arrest; *I know Margaret*; *I know Jenny Rice*; *I know*, as perhaps you don't, that almost all of those bills *have a private mark on them*; and I know that *I have got you foul* every way. Now listen to me—you needn't waste time in talking now—I want you to go back and finish the opera with your friend; and you may be sure that I shall be close by you all the time. You mustn't mind it if I claim your acquaintance; and then when you ride home, I'll go too. After you've put your friend inside her door, you are to go with me, quietly. Now, if you fail to obey my directions, in any particular, rely upon it that I shall expose you as publicly as I can. *If* I've made a mistake, you can prove it to me, and nobody need be the wiser for your arrest."

The orchestra began just then, and he knew he must go back to be in his seat when the curtain rose; so he sullenly gave me his word to do as I told him, and left for his place.

I watched him as he played his part with his lady—'twas better than looking at the opera to anyone fond of playing; and when the opera was concluded I walked by his side—I didn't have to speak to him—and saw them into their carriage; then I hurried up onto the box with the driver, making him think I was a friend of the gentleman inside, going to join him after he had seen his lady home, and that I didn't go inside because I didn't want to disturb their tête-à-tête; and so we drove off.

I kept my place, when we got to the house, until he had seen his friend inside her door; I think there was a kiss with their good night—if there was, it was the last—and then he came down the steps, and I joined him. He paid the driver, and then I walked away with him to the nearest station house. On the way he owned that, as for Margaret and Jenny, he had nothing to say; but that it was "too bad to be brought out for a paltry fifteen dollars." And then he told me that he had been one of the first in the counting room the morning after the robbery, and had seen a ten and a five lying on the floor among the loose papers in front of the safe, and had, he admitted, taken them for his own use; but he was sure his uncle and the other partner wouldn't think much of that.

"You forget," said I, "that you gave Margaret at least seventy-five."

He started a little, and then says he,

"Well, I see you're smarter than I am; and I may as well own up. The *porter* did the business, and I caught him at it, and he gave me five hundred to keep mum."

"Why didn't you make a better bargain?" I asked him.

At that he winced a little.

"Now," says I, "you needn't lie any more about this. I know all about you. I haven't followed you for nothing for the past fortnight. *You* opened the safe, and *you've got that money*, and *I want it!*"

With that he trembled and turned pale. We had got inside the station house, and he sat down in the sitting room, and seemed to be entirely overcome. Presently he looked up and began to come the pitiful dodge, and to ask me to help him out of the scrape, to have mercy on him, and all that. He offered me any amount to let him off. I cut him short. Says I,

"I'll show you as much pity as you deserve, you scoundrel! And no more. And the long and the short of it is, that the best thing you can do is to fork out that money and make matters as easy with the firm as you can. What *they'll* do in the mercy line, I don't know."

Then he began sobbing and blubbering, and said that he couldn't restore anything; that he'd got frightened and thrown the greater part of the money into the dock, and had spent nearly all the rest.

"*What* dock?" said I.

"At the foot of Beekman Street," said he.

"Did it sink or float?"

"It sunk—that is—some of it sunk—I believe—and some—floated."

He stammered over this, and I came down on him the moment he got through.

"You *lie*, you rascal!" says I. "You haven't *been* to the foot of Beekman Street! You can't dodge out *that* way, either!"

I said this at a venture, like, for I wasn't sure that he *hadn't* been there, but I suspected him from his stammering; in fact, I had asked him whether it sunk or floated to try him. But I made a good hit; I was right in my suspicions. And he, thinking that I *had* followed him so closely as to know every step he'd taken, saw that there was no use trying to escape me. So he owned up, thoroughly. He told me how he'd planned the robbery, how he'd used the extra tip, putting it back in the drawer after using it—he had found a key that fitted the drawer—and how he had broken the front door lock and left the rope hanging out the window, to make it seem that an ordinary burglar had been in; but he said he hadn't suspected the private mark on the bills.

Well, I kept him at the station over night, and the next morning we went together down to the store. We marched right in—it was early, and no one there but the porter—and upstairs, up to the attic, and there, from behind some old stovepipes, he brought out two rolls of bills, tied up with fishline. Then down to the counting room, where we sat waiting for the firm to come in. As soon as they came there was a *time*.

On counting the money it was found that about a thousand of it was missing. I suppose the firm was content with recovering so much, and to spare the feelings of the family the affair was hushed up. I made the complaint, of course, but the case never came into court, that I know of. Charley walks the streets of New York today, and from the company he keeps I shouldn't be surprised if I had to "cap" him again.

His wife that would have been I don't know anything about. But I know that Margaret is out of his reach. I saw her on board a packet bound for Liverpool on her way home, about three months ago. Her grief brought on a miscarriage, and she was at death's door; but she recovered, and is now at home in Ireland—my sister has heard from her.

If Charley sees this story in print, he may just understand that if he had reformed and tried to live honestly I wouldn't have said a word about him; and one more thing, he had better look out for "shadows," any time of the day or night, and not pay too dear for his kisses.

—*Harper's New Monthly Magazine*, April 1859

"C.S.A."
by George Arnold

Robert Bagley was one of those odd geniuses who seem to have no defined sphere or mission here on this lower earth. He was always engaging in a grand speculation of some sort, which was sure to make a fortune for him; and something was certain to frustrate his plans—some rare and almost impossible combination of circumstances, that nobody could have foreseen—just when the future smiled most brightly upon him.

He began life in a mercantile countinghouse; but found commerce slow in its remuneration, so he took to the stock exchange.—This soon exhausted the small capital he possessed, and a wealthy uncle purchased a share in a newspaper for the young man. Robert wrote the money articles, and used them with some success in his stockjobbing operations, but the newspaper shortly died, and my hero became agent for a patent connected with a printing press. The fortune he had confidently expected did not suddenly accrue to him; so he dropped this patent for another; and falling in with some political people, tried to get a fat berth in the Patent Office at Washington.

He failed, but made a little money out of a contract for illustrating Patent Reports, which he farmed out to some engravers of his acquaintance. The engraving business having been thus brought to his notice, he endeavored to perfect the zincographic process to supersede the use of boxwood, and, in time, made some very interesting discoveries. Among these was the fact that the new process was a total failure.

During one of his "flush" periods, he had lent three hundred dollars to a friend who was about to go to Cuba with a cargo of ice. This friend now returned with a shipload of cigars and oranges, and offered to pay Bagley in trade. He took the amount then in cigars, and opened a neat little store in Broadway for their sale. It was near a theatre, and in time, the actors and managers made it a sort of rendezvous. Robert sold his cigar store next winter, and undertook the management of the theatre.

It was during the season that the great diamond robbery was perpetrated, when Mad'lle de Bavarde lost the splendid jewels given her by Baron von Kowhingen, at Vienna.

The case was a very interesting one, involving much time and research, and Bagley followed it up with the delight of a man who has talent, hitherto undeveloped, for intrigue and diplomacy. He evinced so much skill and perseverance, and outdid even the shrewdest detective officer so cleverly, that his friends advised him to adhere to the business, and he did. The theatrical management was unsuccessful, but the ex-manager soon held a high position in the detective police.

While Bagley was still the lessee and director of the theater, a little episode occurred which has a very material bearing upon this story.

It was just at dusk, and the manager was standing in front of his house, as managers love so, at about the time when the audience begin to gather around the still-closed apertures of the ticket office. He was lost in some dream of the future or some memory of the past, and paid little attention to the external world about him, until recalled by a sudden and unusual request.

A lady, closely veiled, approached him in a hurried manner and begged his protection against the attentions of two men who had been following her and persecuting her with various vulgar flatteries. She seemed in great trepidation and alarm, and had appealed to Bagley, she said, because she knew him by sight, and by name, and had always considered him a polite and worthy gentleman.

The manager placed her in safety in the vestibule of the theatre, and confronted the two persons whose escort she had found so distasteful. They made some show of impertinence at first, but on a threat of the police, and a few vigorous words of reproof, they shrank away.

This was not an emergency to bring forth any astounding degree of heroic chivalry; but the lady, terrified as she was, magnified her deliverance in proportion to her magnitude of alarm, and was disposed to look upon Bagley as the preserver of her life, at the very least.

Her excitement and fear made her quite ill for a brief time, and Robert invited her to sit down in the box office until he could procure a glass of wine and water to overcome her faintness. She accepted, and the half hour's chat that then ensued was as pleasant as possible.

Finally, the clerk entered to open the office and the lady arose to go. Bagley, charmed by her beauty and conversation, gallantly offered her the use of his carriage which stood at the cottage door, and offered to drive her to her home. She consented, with evident gratitude, to this arrangement, and the ride to her residence—a handsome house in Twenty-Third Street, on the East side—was as agreeable as that chat in the box office had been.

On parting from Bagley, his charge gave him a card, and invited him to call upon her when she could thank him in a more composed and tranquil manner for his kindness.

This, he promised both himself and her, he would speedily do; but when he arrived at the theatre again, and examined the card, he was mortified to find that it was blank. Undoubtedly she had given it to him by mistake.

After this, I must confess that the manager's mind was very much haunted by the memory of the bright eyes and pleasant smile of the *inconnue*. He met her, on Broadway, too, just often enough to keep those memories vivid, and always received a very friendly recognition: but did not have an opportunity to speak with her; so he could not learn her address.

He drove through Twenty-Third Street certainly not less than forty times, in the hope of recognizing the house, at the door of which he left her, but there were two consecutive blocks precisely alike, externally, and no sign of the bright eyes that haunted him at any window he passed.

The business of observing persons whose intentions are hostile to the Government of the United States, and of collecting facts which can assure their conviction and imprisonment, is much more widely pursued, just now, than many people imagine.

There are hosts of deputy marshals, secret agents and similar officials, quietly working away in our midst, unknown to any around them; and the man whose belief or practice is disloyal, must be wonderfully shrewd to escape the Argus eyes whose only care is to note his every word and deed.

The reputation that Robert Bagley had gained in connection with the detective service, attracted the attention of those in power, and resulted in his appointment as a deputy marshal entrusted with important secret service in this department. A tough and knotty case was given to him to unravel—as the marshal observed, "to cut his teeth upon"; and he devoted his entire energies to its "working up," as it is technically termed.

The facts were these: A wealthy gentleman, residing in a small town in New York State, had early in the present troubles, hoisted a Confederate flag upon his house, and used very positive language concerning what he was pleased to call "an unjust, unholy, and villainous war of conquest." A little later, he was known to be purchasing arms and ammunition, in considerable quantities; but no one could tell how he disposed of them. Then he bought a light draught, fast-sailing, screw steamer, and sent her off, ostensibly for a Cuban port, in ballast; and a merchant vessel, arriving a few days later, reported having spoken [to] such a steamer off Cape Hatteras under Confederate colors.

All this was very much against the wealthy gentleman aforesaid; and some trustworthy agents were sent to look into his proceedings.—They found, however, that a change had come over the spirit of his dream, apparently. His house now bore the biggest Federal flag in the county, and his conversation was as sound for the Union as that of General Scott himself could be. Not a sign or shadow of disloyalty could be found about him or his premises, and the detectives were sorely puzzled.

Thus the case stood when it came to Bagley's hands, and promised him all the work he could desire.

He employed several agents to keep track of everything that the suspected man did and said; of all his money investments and their results; of the letters he mailed and received; of the visitors he entertained; in a word his whole life, in public and private.

These researches and investigations were crowned with a discovery, at length. Three trunks, large, strongly made, and heavy, arrived at the railroad depot one night, by the late train. They were directed thus:

"C.S.A.
"Grant, Shelby, Esq.,
"R—, N.Y."

Grant Shelby was the name of this suspected gentleman.

Bagley marveled much at the daring recklessness of a man who would openly receive packages marked with the initials of the "Confederate States of America."

"Where are these trunks?" he asked of the agent who brought the intelligence to his hotel.

"At the depot."

"What is in them?"

"I don't know, sir."

The order was well obeyed. One of the trunks contained jewelry, toilet articles, and a thick MS volume, marked with the Confederate initials—"C.S.A."—the others contained ladies' wearing apparel, money, books, music etc.

"Bring me the manuscript volume," commanded Bagley.

It was brought to him unopened, and the trunks were locked again, to be left till Mr. Shelby should remove them. If the MS contained anything to criminate him, he was then to be arrested. If not the destination of the baggage was to be carefully watched, and further development awaited.

The MS was a diary, written in a feminine handwriting. The first entries were dated "New Orleans," and Bagley made sure that he had found a prize, until he saw that the diary commenced in 1857. Turning over the leaves for a later date, he caught sight of his own name and eagerly perused the pages that referred to him.

I do not know that such a course is pardonable to delicate minds: but all governments are essentially Jesuitical in the practice of the theory that "Ends justify Means"; and if we have a government at all we must at times take liberties with private affairs.

The entries that referred to Bagley were not made in New Orleans, but in New York.—The writer of the diary was a woman of cultivation and intelligence, evidently, who had passed her childhood in the South, but had been educated in the North; and her sympathies were plainly Northern, though she had made frequent trips to her early home.

None lately, however. She had returned, according to the diary, from New Orleans to New York, about the first of January (1861) with the design of avoiding the whole of the revolutionary troubles that bid fair to wreck and ruin the entire country below Mason & Dixon's line. Not long after her arrival in the Northern metropolis, she experienced an adventure that she glowingly described in two-and-a-half pages of her journal. It was the little episode I have related; and thus it was that Bagley found his own name mentioned in the volume that had so oddly fallen under his eyes! In a word, the diary was none other than the unknown lady's to whom he had extended his protection that evening in front of the theatre.

I am ashamed to say that my hero read this portion with an absorbing interest, although he must have known that there was nothing whatever that could throw any light upon the treasonable proclivities of Mr. Shelby.

Perhaps he blushed—and perhaps not—to find himself spoken of as "a splendid fellow," "handsome," "chivalrous," and "entertaining." Perhaps he was pleased to learn that his *inconnue* had been "ridiculously anxious for him to call," and "quite *desesperee*," that he did not; how she met him in Broadway and how she exclaimed, mentally with Shakespeare:

"I would that Heaven had sent me such a man."

"By Jove you shall have just such a man, my dear girl!" involuntarily exclaimed Bagley, somewhat excited by the vision that arose before him.

"Mr. Shelby has a visitor today, sir," said one of the secret agents, who soon after entered. "A young lady, sir—very pretty. Came down in the eleven o'clock train today."

"Baggage?"

"Only a guitar case and a little dog, sir."

Bagley was prompt in having the diary returned to the trunk whence it had been taken—an easy proceeding enough, as the railroad baggage master was one of his secret corps.

It was done just in time, too; for Shelby came to the depot for the trunks that same afternoon.

With him came Bagley's friend, the writer of the diary. Of course, Robert was on the spot, and a happy recognition took place. In shaking hands the young lady—who seemed a little trepidated and blushed prettily, dropped her handkerchief. Bagley hastened to pick it up, and saw in one corner the initials, "C.S.A.," neatly embroidered.

The truth flashed upon him. He had suspected before that these letters might represent a personal cognomen, as well as a rebellious government; and now he was sure of it.

He briefly related the fact of her having given him a blank card, and begged her for [her] name.

"Come here Uncle Grant!" she cried, and Mr. Shelby, who had been busying himself with the baggage, approached.

"This is my uncle, Mr. Shelby, Mr. Bagley," she said, "who I am visiting."

The gentlemen expressed themselves proud of each other's acquaintanceship.

"Now, uncle, introduce me to Mr. Bagley," laughed the niece. "We are excellent friends, but he does not know my name."

Mr. Shelby looked puzzled.

"Your niece tells the simple truth, sir" said Bagley. "The mystery can be easily explained, however."

"Then, Mr. Bagley, I am happy to present to you my niece, Miss Arrowsmith," replied Shelby. "And now, Caroline, what does all this mean?"

"Caroline? Is your first name Caroline?—Pardon me, but I have an object in knowing your entire name."

"Caroline Shelby Arrowsmith, at your service."

"C.S.A."

"They are my initials, Mr. Bagley"

"Ha!"

Mr. Bagley was observed to be very thoughtful for some moments.

Now I know very well that the present habit of romance writers is, to finish up their works as if the world were about coming to an end. The readers, for all I know, demand that every character in the story shall be satisfactorily accounted for and settled, so that no earthly interest can adhere to her or him hereafter.—Marriage and death are the means employed to destroy the vitality of our heroes and heroines, and keep the reader from ever inquiring further into their fortunes.

I do not see why this custom should have become so universal with the gentlemen of my cloth; but it has, till the conclusion of a modern novel is hardly more than a catalogue of quietness.

I mean to rebel against the fashion (as rebellion now is the order of the day, and my family name warrants me in such a course) and to refuse my readers any knowledge of the termination of the labors of Mr. Bagley. I am not wantonly cruel, so I will not withhold from you the fact that he married Miss Arrowsmith, but I positively decline to inform you whether Mr. Shelby was proven to be a good and patriotic citizen of the Union, or a dangerous and treasonable enemy, now confined within the gloomy casemented walls of Fort Lafayette.

And the best reason I have for not telling you of his fate is, that I know nothing about it myself.

—The Defiance [OH] *Democrat*, August 16, 1862

Five Thousand Dollars Reward
A Detective Story
by Herbert Lee Standish

The above reward was offered by the United States Government to the person, or persons, who succeeded in bringing to light a gang of counterfeiters supposed to have their headquarters somewhere in the state of Missouri.

My friend, Brompton, of New York, was considered one of the best detectives in the State. He had been very successful, at all events, and had seldom, if ever, failed in a case he had undertaken.

Seeing the above announcement in one of the morning papers, he had made up his mind to take the field at once. His business was soon put in shape, and he left the city the next morning.

He said to me a year later:—

I left home with a full determination not to return until I had succeeded in unearthing the gang. The only thing that troubled me was that some of my brother officers would prove smarter than myself, and be first to find them.

I worked hard, but the end of six months found me at Little Rock, with no more of a clew than I had when I left home. But the idea of giving up had not, for one instant, entered my head. I learned from the papers that others were having no better success than myself; so I was content to work on.

Many times I thought I had found clews; but, on following them up, they had always vanished. I had been over nearly every portion of Missouri, also most of the other states and territories.

After some consideration, I concluded to return to Missouri, and not leave an inch of the ground unsearched, as this still seemed the most likely field for success.

I left Little Rock the next morning, and had been in the State about six weeks, when one night I arrived at an old tavern near the western boundary. It was late when I arrived, and I intended to have retired at once; but, as I passed the barroom door, I heard someone within talking in an excited way, and I caught the words, "haunted house." Wishing to learn the cause of the excitement, I passed into the barroom, and took a seat in the further corner.

There were several men in the room, and one of them was pacing the floor in great excitement. As I entered, he was saying:

"Yes, it was awful! It was the most unearthly sound that I ever heard. I tell you I wouldn't pass that house alone again after dark, for all the gold in California!"

"Did you see the lights?" asked one of the men.

"Yes, I saw everything; but you can bet that I didn't spend any time looking round, after I heard that groan."

I listened for some time, but seeing that I was going to learn nothing in that way, I asked if one of them would not give me the facts of the case, or tell me where the house was situated.

The man stared at me a moment, and then said:

"You must be a stranger in these parts, or you would know where the haunted house is without asking."

Assuring him that I was, he proceeded to give me the history of the haunted house. But he was interrupted so many times by the others, who insisted upon telling their part of the story that I will not attempt to give it in their words. But the main points were that there was an old, stone house a few miles back, that had once stood on the main road, and had been used as a tavern. When the new turnpike was cut through, it was left to one side, and since then it was very seldom that anyone passed that way.

After the place had lost its use as a tavern, it was left unoccupied for some time, but was finally sold to an old German, who lived there very quietly for a short period, when, one morning, he was found murdered in his room. The body lay on the floor near the bed, and the room showed signs of a terrible struggle having taken place.

Since that time the place had been haunted by the old man's ghost; that he could be seen on any night, at twelve o'clock, standing at one of the upper windows, with a lighted candle in his hand; that no one who could possibly help it, ever passed the place now after dark; that several times a huge ghost had been seen to come from a clump of bushes which stood a short distance back from the house, and that the most unearthly sounds had been heard to come from these bushes, and from different parts of the old building.

I waited until each had told his story, for they had all seen the ghost, and then went to my room.

It was too late to do anything that night. But I made up my mind that, on the next night, I would pay the old house a visit, and, if possible, make the acquaintance of his ghostship.

After looking over the paper that I had bought the day before, I retired for the night.

The next day I passed in and about the tavern, and, waiting till about nine o'clock in the evening, I slipped quietly out of the house, and taking my horse, started down the road in the direction I had been told the old stone house lay.

I proceeded at a slow pace, not caring to reach the place much before midnight. The sky was thickly studded with light clouds, which, at times, nearly obscured the new moon, that would set in a few hours. A light wind sighed and moaned in a low, dismal way through the leafless branches of the old trees that lined the roadside. On the whole, I thought it the night, of all others, when spirits would choose to be abroad.

I continued on in this way for more than two hours, and was beginning to think that I must have taken the wrong road, when I suddenly came in sight of the old building. I recognized it at once from the description I had had of it.

Riding my horse into some high bushes, I hitched him, then proceeded on foot to the old house, which stood a short distance back from the road. I passed completely round it, and then made my way to a clump of bushes some distance in the rear. It was from these bushes, I had been told, that the ghost had been seen to come on several occasions.

I concealed myself near the middle of the clump of bushes, and waited. I must have been there more than an hour. The moon had set, and I was beginning to think that I should learn nothing that night. I had watched for the light, but it had not appeared. I was on the point of leaving the bushes and making my way to the house again, when I was nearly taken off my feet by the most unearthly sound that has ever fallen to my lot to hear. It was repeated several times, and seemed to come from the earth directly beneath my feet. And the next instant, a huge, ghostly object, nearly ten feet in height, rose from out the very earth, within a few paces from where I was standing.

It was clothed in a long, white robe, and, as it turned towards me, a strange, phosphorescent light seemed to come from its eyes. It remained perfectly still for some time, then, raising one long arm, slowly turned and pointed towards the house. Looking in that direction, I saw that the upper part of the building was illuminated, and the figure of an old man could be seen slowly passing through the empty rooms.

The object continued to point in that direction while the light lasted, which was but a short time. And then, still keeping its arm extended, it turned slowly round until it pointed directly towards me, and started forward.

At first I thought it had seen me, and quickly raised my revolver, but it kept straight on, passing me with rapid strides, and coming so close that I could have touched it by extending my hand. I followed the object with my eyes until it was lost in the darkness, then rose to my feet.

At first I had thought of following it, but concluded to wait, hoping that it would return. I do not think it was fear that kept me back, for I had always prided myself on fearing nothing in the way of ghosts. Still, I must confess that I had held my breath as it passed me, for it was a horrible-looking monster, and might well have passed for his satanic majesty himself. I was sure that I had seen the horns, if not the tail.

Could I have felt sure that it was nothing more than a spirit, I should have had no fear of it whatever. But I felt sure that it would prove a good substantial one, probably two hundred pounds at least, and should I attack it, the chances were that it would get the better of me. But, after looking an hour for its return, I began to wish that I had hailed it, or had seen what effect a little cold lead would have had upon it.

After waiting some half hour longer, I came to the conclusion that I should see nothing more of the object that night, and would have to return to the tavern not much wiser than I had left it.

But something told me that I had found a clew, at last, which would lead to something to my advantage, could I but succeed in following it up.

I determined, at all events, that I would not leave that part of the country until I had cleared up the mystery of the haunted house. My mind thus made up, I started for where I had left my horse, intending to visit the place again the next night. As I passed close by the side of the building, I noticed a small, narrow door, which opened on a level with the ground. Going up to it, I tried to open it. It was locked. Thinking that I might hear something, I placed my ear to the keyhole, and listened long and intently. At last I thought I detected a faint noise, as of someone hammering. But the sound seemed to come from a great distance, and from below the ground.

I was straining my ear in the hopes of hearing the sound repeated, when I was suddenly seized from behind, and hurled to the ground with such force as to partially stun me; and, before I could regain my senses, or offer any resistance, I was dragged into the building, and bound hand and foot, the door being opened by someone within.

I found myself in a long, narrow hall, in the presence of three rough-looking men, one of whom held a dark lantern, and a large bunch of keys.

After locking and barring the door, two of the men raised me in their arms, and the third leading the way with the lantern, I was taken down a long, narrow flight of stone steps, then through a long, underground passage, which crooked and turned in every direction, and was as damp and musty as an old tomb.

At last they stopped before what appeared to me to be a solid wall. Taking something from his pocket which looked like a small hammer, the guide gave several raps, first fast and then slow. After waiting a few seconds, I heard a low, grating sound, and then a portion of what I had taken to be solid wall was turned noiselessly around, leaving an opening of sufficient size to admit the largest man. Within a moment more I found myself in a large, underground room.

It needed but a glance to show me that I was in the stronghold of one of the largest bands of counterfeiters then in the United States. There were nearly a score of rough-looking men busily at work, and from the amount of coin lying about, I knew they must be doing an extensive business.

Yes, it was true that I had found them at last, but would the knowledge of my discovery ever reach the outside world? I thought the chances were very small indeed.

I had not long to remain in ignorance on this point, for I was taken to the further end of the apartment, and placed on a long bench covered with straw, which I supposed was used for a bed. The cords were removed from my ankles, and I was told that I had better sit up and prepare myself for the next world, as I had just fifteen minutes more to remain in this.

It was as I had supposed. No one, with the secret that I possessed, would ever be allowed to leave the place alive if it could be prevented.

I sat up on the bed and tried to think. Was it true that I was so near the end, that my days were numbered, and that I should never see daylight again?

I had been in many tight places before, but had always got safely out of them. It was the business of my life. Was I to be outwitted at last? It looked like it, certainly; for there was no mistaking that the men meant business. They were already preparing a rope for me, and one said:

"You had better be saying your prayers, if you know any, for you have but ten minutes more to stop with us. We would have you know that when a spy is brought in here, he goes out in a pine box, which is better than he deserves."

This was comforting. Again I tried to think. Could not I pretend to join them? No, I was sure they would never consent to that. The minutes were going, and I was beginning to get confused.

"Five minutes more," I heard someone say.

The rope was ready by this time, and hung from a beam within a few feet of where I was sitting.

"Here comes the cap," said one of the men, at this instant.

Looking up, I saw entering the apartment through the opening in the wall, none other than the huge ghost which had appeared so suddenly before me in the bushes.

Going directly to a large chest that stood at one end of the room, he removed, first, a long, white cloak, and then an immense headgear, nearly three feet in height, from which protruded short horns. Placing these in the chest, he closed the lid, then came towards me.

He was a large, powerfully-built man, standing more than six feet in height, with jet-black hair and beard, apparently about forty-five years of age.

As he closed the chest, something flashed across my mind that I had not thought of before, and in which I imagined I could see a faint ray of hope. It was my only chance, and I determined to try it, at all events.

As he approached me, I broke into a hearty laugh, saying, "I am right glad to see you, captain!" at the same time trying to extend one of my hands, which were still firmly bound.

He drew back, and stared at me in amazement.

"Man alive!" he said, "Do you know you haven't five minutes more to stay in this world?"

"So I have been told by your men," said I, still laughing.

"The man is either a fool, or crazy!" he said, speaking to his men.

"I am neither," I replied.

"Then what can you be laughing at, at such a time as this?"

"I am laughing," I replied, "at the idea of your hanging a pal."

"A pal!"

"Yes. Did you ever hear of Jim Forrest, the counterfeiter?"

"Many times. And I have often wished that I might see him."

"I am your man," I replied. "And if you will remove these confounded cords from my wrists, I will show you some of my coin which, I think, will compare favorably with yours."

He quickly cut the bands, and I drew forth from an inner pocket several gold coins and placed them in his hand.

It was on these coins, which I had come so near forgetting, that I had placed my only hope. They had been given to me, shortly before my leaving home, by the chief of police, and were known to be the work of Jim Forrest, the most skillful counterfeiter in the Union.

He was a perfect workman, and had once been in the employ of the government. The police had been on his track for years, but thus far he had successfully evaded them. He had never done a very extensive business, probably finding but few that he cared to trust.

Taking the coins from my hand, the captain proceeded to examine them carefully by a light which hung from the ceiling; then sounded them on the stone floor, after which he took them to a counter on which were a small pair of scales, and weighed them carefully, one at a time.

As he did so, a smile played over his handsome face, and he said, as if speaking to himself:

"A clever piece of work! A clever piece of work!"

When he had finished weighing them, he came towards me with extended hand, saying:

"Allow me to congratulate you, Captain Forrest, on what I consider a little the neatest job I ever had the pleasure of seeing; and, if it isn't asking too much, I would like you to give me one of these specimens."

Thanking him for his compliment, I told him he was welcome to all of them, as I knew where there were plenty more.

After looking at them once more he placed them carefully in a small safe as if they were a great treasure.

It surprised me to think how well my game was working. The coin seemed to have turned the captain's head. Still I felt uneasy and wished I was well out of the place, for I could see by the looks they gave each other, that the men still suspected me.

Thinking it would alarm them by being too much in a hurry to leave the place, I asked to be shown some of their work. After this I drew the captain aside and pretended to give him an exact description of my place of business,—representing my headquarters as being in the western part of [New] York state, and telling him if he was ever in that part of the country to be sure and give me a call.

After this I told him I supposed I ought to be going as it must be getting near daylight. He asked me to spend a few days with them; but I told him I had already been from home much longer than I had intended and must be getting back.

Seeing that I could not be persuaded to stay, the captain said if I must go he supposed I had better be going now, as it was getting near morning, and no one ever left the place after light for fear of being seen.

Taking a lantern the captain told me to follow him.

We passed through an opening in the wall like the one through which I had entered, but at the opposite end of the apartment, then through a long passage until we came to another wall. An opening was made in this like the others, and taking a ladder from the side of the passage, the captain stepped through, telling me to follow.

I did so, and found myself in an old dry well.

Following him up the ladder I stood in the same clump of bushes in which he had first appeared to me as a ghost in that unearthly manner, as it then seemed, from out the solid earth; but, as I now knew, from the old well.

"What do you think of it?" asked the captain, noticing my look of surprise.

"Oh, it is a capital retreat in case of an attack or raid."

After a few more words we shook hands and were about to part, when he suddenly said, as if it had just occurred to him:

"You have not told me yet how you came to be here at such a time of night."

"It does look a little strange, I confess, but it is very easily explained for all that. You see we jacks of the same trade are apt to know the place most likely to be selected by a brother workman. I accidentally overheard the men at the tavern below here, talking about a haunted house, and I suspected the kind of a place it was at once, and rode out here, hoping to see you. The rest you already know."

"Yes," he replied, and hurriedly shaking hands again, we parted; he returning into the well and I making my way to where I had left my horse.

It was not until I found myself in the saddle that I drew a long breath. And even then I half expected to hear them after me in hot pursuit. But I reached the tavern soon after sunrise without any further trouble, and eating a hasty breakfast, and without waiting for a minute's rest, I mounted my horse and started for the nearest telegraph station some thirty miles distant.

I reached the place about noon, and at once telegraphed to the chief of police at St. Louis to send me a dozen of his best men without a moment's delay.

They arrived that evening, soon after dark, and we started at once, I having already procured horses and laid my plans.

We passed the tavern about ten o'clock, and reached the old house about an hour later. When within half a mile of the place I had halted my men and cut a young hickory about six inches in diameter to be used as a battering ram in forcing an entrance through the wall.

Stationing four of my men at the old well, with instructions to iron all who attempted to escape by that way, I returned to the house where I had left the remainder of my men, and we were soon in the underground passage leading to the stronghold, having no trouble in forcing an entrance into the building.

Placing the men evenly on each side of the ram, and telling them to make as much noise as possible, we started down the passage at a double quick, making as much clatter as a full company of United States troops.

With a terrific crash the ram struck the wall, but it did not give way, probably not having been hit in the right place.

Placing the lantern on the floor where I knew the secret opening to be, we returned for a second charge, and this time was more successful; for striking in the right spot, the slab was knocked completely out of the wall, and so great had been our impetus that we passed through the opening, and the forward man tripping over something, we were piled in a heap on the stone floor within.

I regained my feet in time to see the last counterfeiter leaving the apartment by the passage at the farther end of the room, and whom I easily recognized by his great height, as the captain.

We pressed closely on the heels of the captain; he all the time calling on his men to stand and fight. But they fled like frightened sheep before a pack of hungry wolves.

As he neared the well he comprehended the situation in an instant, and turning, like a lion at bay, he sprang on my party and a terrible struggle ensued in which two of the men were wounded—one by a bullet in his shoulder, and another by a terrible blow from the butt of a heavy revolver, which laid him senseless on the floor. But the captain was finally overpowered and a double pair of irons placed on his wrists.

Stepping into the well, I called to the men above, asking how things had gone up there.

"Lovely," they said. "We have them all; every bird of them, though they came so fast along the last, that we came near losing some."

Telling them to take their prisoners round to the front of the old house and wait for me there, I returned to my men in the passage who were dressing the wounds of their companions. As I passed the captain, who was standing with his back against the side of the passage, the light from a lantern struck on my face. He recognized me instantly, and struggled desperately to free himself; and could he have done so, would have sprang upon me like a panther. But the irons held him, and in a few moments he gave up the struggle and leaned once more against the wall.

"It is a little rough, captain, I will allow, after your generous treatment of last night," I said, going to where he stood. "But you see I am simply doing my duty as an officer of the law."

"Oh, it's all right," he said, after a moment's silence. "There is no one to blame but myself. Had I been any other than the old fool that I was, I would have known as much. I was no more fit for my place than an old woman!" His head dropped on his bosom and nothing could cause him to speak again while under my charge.

The wounded having by this time had everything done that could be to make them comfortable, and the wounds fortunately not proving dangerous, we soon joined the men who were waiting for us in front of the house. And now a new difficulty arose. There were twenty of the counterfeiters, all told, and how was I to get them to the station, which was forty miles away?

After a few minutes' thought I told the men to keep guard over their prisoners until I returned. Then taking my horse, I started for the tavern. Arriving there, I went directly to the landlord and made known my business. After some little trouble we succeeded in hiring a dozen horses. As I was wondering what I would do for the rest, the landlord said:

"I think I have it,—that is if you do not mind waiting a few hours. The mail stage will be down through here a little before noon, and you can probably get passage on that for the remainder."

"Just the thing," I said, "and I will have the men here in time to take it."

Taking the dozen horses that I had hired, I returned to the old house. I found my men awaiting me, having had a good breakfast from provisions found stowed about the place.

We were soon on our way to the tavern, which we reached an hour before the arrival of the stage, having made the counterfeiters take turns in riding the dozen horses.

Having been in the saddle the greater part of the last forty-eight hours, I concluded to go by stage, taking the captain with me.

Seeing the excited individual from whom I had first heard the story of the haunted house, entering the tavern, I went to him and told him that he need have no further fear of going past the old house, as I had captured his ghost, which proved to be a good substantial one, as he could see for himself, pointing to the captain, who was standing at the further end of the room.

"You don't say so!" he began; but ended by thrusting his hands deep in his pockets, and staring at the captain as if he expected every instant to see him disappear through the ceiling. Hearing the rattle of wheels, I left him, and going to the door, opened it just as the stage drove up.

Having no trouble in securing passage for the remainder of the counterfeiters, we were soon on our way to the station.

Looking back, as we were about losing sight of the tavern by a bend in the road, I saw the man standing in the doorway, his hands still in his pockets and the same stare on his face.

We reached the station long before night, and arrived in St. Louis early the next morning.

After seeing the counterfeiters safely lodged in prison, I started for home where I received the congratulations of my many friends and acquaintances, the news having preceded me. It was then that I received the name which still sticks to me of Luck Brompton.

Shortly after this I received from Washington my reward, together with a note of thanks, for the great service I had rendered my country.

—*Ballou's Monthly Magazine*, June 1887
—Originally published as "The Coiners" "by a New York Detective" in *Ballou's Dollar Monthly Magazine*, September 1862
—A much abbreviated version was published in *The Hillsdale* [MI] *Standard*, October 10, 1865

The Detective's Story
Anonymous
From *The Springfield* (Mass.) *Daily Republican*

Late in the Autumn of 1856 I was going home to Vermont for a short visit. Just as I stepped onto the wharf at Buffalo, a gentleman tapped me on the shoulder, and said:

"This way, if you please."

As I did not happen to please, but was turning to look after my baggage, he seized hold of me, and said, "Come along, sir."

I said, "Don't be rude, my man. I am not on duty now, and cannot attend to your case, whatever it may be."

"But I can to yours," retorted he, "so come along without any more ado."

"Claim your baggage! Train leaves here in five minutes!" shouted the porter.

"My trunk! A check for Burlington!" said I.

"Check for the station house," put in my pertinacious, new-made friend.

"What on earth do you mean? You will make me miss the train," said I.

"But not the station," he replied dryly, "so come along."

"Will you please introduce yourself before we proceed with our acquaintance?"

"I am Deputy Crane, of Buffalo," he answered.

"And I am Deputy Wood, of Chicago. But train's off. I will see you on my return to Buffalo."

There was a little confusion. "All aboard!" shouted the conductor. And all aboard they got, excepting Deputy Wood and his trunk, which, to my certain knowledge, were left standing in the depot—the one for a moment about as speechless as the other. Deputy Crane presently remarked that he had never before had the pleasure of meeting Deputy Wood of Chicago; but he thought his friends Smith, Jones & Co., might have been more fortunate, and, if I would have the goodness to walk up to the City Hotel, where they boarded such as me for nothing, he would send for them. I knew there was some mistake; but I thought it would hinder me only one train, and, as the adventure might be worth all it cost, I would go along without further explanation.

We were soon at the iron gate and gratings of the "City Hotel," as Crane facetiously termed it; and, while he was gone for Smith & Co., I had time to reflect. "Great Robbery in Buffalo. The store of Smith, Jones & Co. robbed of some thousand dollars worth of silks, besides notes and drafts for some thousand more. One thousand dollars reward for detection of the thief, &c." This notice had been published so long before, that I should never have thought of it again, had not the present episode refreshed my memory. But I had not long to meditate before Smith, Jones & Co., with half a dozen clerks, were on hand—all identifying me, from Smith down to the errand boy, as being the identical man who was lurking around the premises in a suspicious manner the day before the robbery.

"Well, my man," said Deputy Crane, patting me on the shoulder, "guilty or not guilty?"

"*Hungry*," I replied; "and, if you please, we will go and get some breakfast."

"There is ice in that. But could you feed yourself with your hands tied together? That is according to the rules of the house," answered Crane.

"Now hold on, Crane," I exclaimed, "this joke has gone about far enough. We can telegraph to the chief in Chicago, and get our answer in half an hour, which will put the matter all right; and in the meantime I will eat some breakfast, and be ready for the noon express."

Tearing a leaf from my memorandum book, I wrote:

"Chief Detective Police, Chicago: Describe Deputy Wood, and say where he is."

Crane took the dispatch, signed his own name to it, and sent it forward immediately. Shortly the answer returned:

"Deputy Wood, thirty-five years, red hair, freckled face, five feet eleven, dressed in full suit sheep's gray. On way to Vermont, and probably passed Buffalo this morning. Has any accident happened?"

Signed "————, Chief Detective Police, Chicago."

This was conclusive, and I was straightway escorted, with many apologies, by my new friend, from the "City Hotel" to the American, where I was invited to eat and drink—not at the expense of the city, but of my humble servant. While the chicken was broiling we talked over matters, and came to the conclusion that as I had not been in Buffalo before for more than a year, somebody had who looked wonderfully like me; and a thousand dollars was offered to anyone who would produce him—which reward Deputy Crane almost felt in his pocket when he nabbed me at the station.

After breakfast we walked down to the store of Smith, Jones and Co., and talked over the affair. Jones apologized, and said he supposed they "must have been mistaken in the man, which perhaps was not strange, seeing our attention was not called to you particularly at that time, and several months had intervened; mistakes will happen in very good families, however."

Having delivered himself of this doubtful admission of my honesty, and entirely original joke, Mr. Jones retired into the counting room, looking very unconvinced; and the clerks, as if by common instinct, began to put back all the loose goods on the counter, as though they feared I would grab them on my way out of the store. Crane, I think, was thoroughly convinced, before I bade him good-bye at the depot, that, so far as I was concerned, it was all right; but persisted that it was a very natural mistake—begged my pardon, and hoped I would see him on my return.

For a month or more, while among my friends in Vermont, I thought little of the occurrence. It is true the thousand dollar reward would occasionally come into my mind; but, as I was not employed in the case, the prospect of getting it was exceedingly small. On my return, I spent a few days in New York, visiting old acquaintances, and making new ones, mostly among the detective branch of the police, as the line of business to which I was devoted can best be learned by mingling with adepts.

One day, while passing down West Street, some person slapped me on the shoulder in a familiar manner, saying at the same time:

"How are you, old fellow? When did you get back? Wasn't you going to speak to a fellow 'cause you got a new suit? Made the thing pay, eh?"

Quick as thought, the Buffalo adventure came into my mind, and I resolved at once to follow up the advantage.

"Mum's the word," said I, clapping my lips at the same time to indicate that mum *was* the word; but also more effectually to change my voice.

"Come in, Joe," said my new acquaintance, pointing down the stairs to a drinking saloon. "Nobody here but Bill and the boy. We've had some fine pickings since you left. Didn't expect you back until tomorrow; but come in and get a drink anyway."

Clapping my lips again, I blurted out:

"Business; but I'll be around tomorrow. Have all the boys in at four."

So saying, I dashed on as though I had a thousand stores to rob and several men to murder before I could stop to talk. My friend in utter amazement was still standing where I left him when I turned the corner, thinking no doubt it was very strange, but apparently having no suspicion of identity.

I was certain as I went to my hotel that I had got hold of a string which, followed up, might lead to at least a thousand dollars, and maybe much valuable property and still greater rewards. As the key to the situation was evidently my resemblance to some rascal, I thought it right as I had to bear the resemblance that I should have all the benefit that was to come of it, or at least the lion's share; so I resolved to keep my own counsel, and make up the case as best I could in my own room.

Joe was coming back on the next day; Bill (my new acquaintance) and the boys had been having good pickings, and they would probably be there tomorrow at four, if the real Joe did not come round before and clear up, or add to, the mystery of today. Joe evidently must be headed off, or the other pigeons would scatter before they could be bagged. It was my main interest, having no local responsibility in the matter, to bag the thousand dollars and Joe. But as the street had two ends to it, and the bagging must not be done where it would frighten the other game, I began to see I must have help even in the outset; so I sensibly concluded to lay the whole affair before the chief, and have men enough detailed to ensure success. The case was so plain that there seemed to be but one plan, and in that we were all agreed, namely: to make arrangements that evening to have me stationed in a grocery store on the first corner of the street from the saloon, with two or three assistants, and as many more placed in the corner drugstore down the street, so as to arrest Joe before he met his pals, and by putting him in a close carriage we might take him off so quietly that nobody would hear it. A few men were to be stationed in a private house opposite the saloon, to make a descent if they saw any unnatural commotion about there before the appointed hour. But otherwise all were to concentrate when the hour arrived, and arrest whoever might be present.

One hour before daylight we were in our places, not to attract attention by going there afterward. It was a long, dreary forenoon. We fancied we saw now and then a suspicious person passing; but no more perhaps than we might expect to see on any other street in the city. Noon came. Crackers and raisins had been disposed of at our grocery store, and yet my double had not made his appearance. Whether they had taken him at the drugstore we did not know; but supposed our chance to be much the best.

While we were discussing these probabilities, with eyes all the time directed to the street, my comrades in one voice called out, "There he comes!" and dashed out to arrest him—I meantime persisting it was "not the man—no resemblance—hold on!"

But it was of no use. They had him in the carriage in a twinkling, and all but two were back in the store so soon that our conversation need hardly have been interrupted—only as this episode served to give it a new direction.

"As near alike as twin brothers, except the clothes. Not a doubt of it," they all averred.

But I had still to confess a great many doubts, as I did not see the slightest resemblance. I, who had seen myself for thirty-odd years, ought to know better how I looked than they who had not seen me so many hours. But the sequel will tell who knew best. Four o'clock came, and, as by agreement, we concentrated in front and rear of Hanseomb's saloon. I took my place in the rear, while most of the local stars dashed into the den. We had only a moment to wait before six or eight of the gang came rushing past us in their efforts to escape. Our squad gave instant chase. My friend of yesterday, being the only one I recognized, received my especial attention. Following him around the corner at the top of my speed, I was surprised for the instant to see him slacken his pace, as though waiting for me to come up.

"Bully, Joe! We've dodged them this time anyhow."

The precise state of the case was evident. Without waiting for an answer, he went on hurriedly:

"Jenks saw me, and knows where I live, and this will arouse his suspicions. I'll wager he'll be around to No. 37 before night; and those traps must be moved, or we'll be certain to lose 'em."

"Move 'em tis," said I; and on we went, running where we thought it was safe, and making good time all the way—my companion a little in advance, and wondering what made me so laggard.

We were not long in reaching No. 37 Grove Street. My friend had the latch key in his hand, and was on the point of entering, when I proceeded to dispel his illusion by exhibiting my star and demanding an unconditional surrender. He was belligerent—a tussle ensued, and for a moment it seemed doubtful which would win, Polly or the bear; but the disturbance soon brought several policemen to my aid, and my late associate was taken off to the lock-up.

Hearing a commotion indoors, I thought it best to proceed at once to make an examination. So we turned the key, which was still in the lock, and walked in, without saying, "by your leave madam."

Madam met us in the hall, and demanded our business. We blandly informed her that we knew something of her beautiful mansion by reputation, and were anxious to examine it ourselves by gaslight, if she would be so good as to show us around. She protested that they were honest people, that her husband was out, the hour was late, we were no gentlemen, and finally that she would thank us to leave, just as any honest woman would.

But I cannot go into details. Suffice it to say, we went upstairs, downstairs, and in the lady's chamber: and wherever we went we found more goods than the most thrifty housekeeper could need. Downstairs especially there was a perfect store of valuables—enough to stock two or three variety shops of moderate pretensions, besides one jewelry store. In the morning I sent to Smith & Company, to come and identify their property. In course of the next two days, not only Smith, but the representatives of a dozen other stores which had been robbed, were there. Smith found nearly all his lost silks, many others identified the whole or part of theirs, while much remained that was not claimed by anyone.

There were more than a dozen taken at the saloon, most of whom were known to the police; the matter was vigorously prosecuted, and I believe more than half were duly convicted and sentenced in New York.

But what became of my twin brother Joe, who had unconsciously got these, his particular friends, into trouble?

The conclusion of the whole matter can be told briefly.

Joe was induced to accompany me so far as Buffalo on my return home, where I introduced him to my friend Deputy Crane, who immediately escorted him to the "City Hotel," with which I had once made slight acquaintance. Smith & Co., and the clerks, recognized him at once, and volunteered to see that he had justice. Deputy Crane, Smith, Jones, and all my persistent acquaintances of a month before, begged a thousand pardons for their stupidity in thinking I resembled the thief. But more acceptable was Smith's check for the promised reward, and I was more than willing to forgive Deputy Crane; for it was owing to his blunder that much valuable property was returned to the rightful owners, many rascals made to suffer the penalty of their crimes, and one honest man handsomely paid for looking like a rogue.

—*Janesville* [WI] *Daily Gazette,* February 26, 1864
—*Janesville* [WI] *Weekly Gazette,* March 4, 1864
—Published as "The Detective's Adventure" in *Horrelsville* [NY] *Tribune,* March 3, 1864

Seventy Miles an Hour
James D. M'Cabe, Jr.

M. Eugene Laromie was not a little startled one bright, clear morning, to receive an order commanding him to repair immediately to the Bureau of the Chief of the Secret Police of Paris. I say he was startled, not because such an occurrence was unusual, but because M. Laromie had been, for several days, indulging in what we Americans call "a spree," and his guilty conscience suggested to him that his chief was about to bring him to account for it. Nevertheless, such a summons is something that a French official cannot disregard, and without delay he hastened to the bureau, and was at once admitted to the presence of the chief.

"Good morning, Laromie," said the chief, pleasantly. "You look downcast. No wonder. For three days you have had too much wine in you. Ah, my friend, you see I am quite a good detective! I can tell you how you have spent every moment of those three days."

"Monsieur," said Laromie, bluntly, "one must relax his self-restraint sometimes."

"True, my friend. I have no idea of censuring you. I only wish to warn you to be more careful in the future, as those above me may not think so lightly of your indiscretions as I do. Enough of this, however. I wish to know if your head is clear enough to undertake a most difficult case?"

"I think so," replied Laromie, laughing. "I would not have returned to duty, if it had not been."

"Well, then, my friend, there has been a startling discovery in the last few hours. You know Monsieur Vilele, the banker?"

"Yes."

"What is your opinion of him?"

"I know nothing of him by my own experience," answered Laromie. "He has the reputation of being one of the most upright and reliable bankers in Paris."

"Exactly," said the chief, coolly; "and if he had not fallen into trouble, would, no doubt, have died an honest man. But know, monsieur, that this excellent banker has been terribly imprudent of late. He has speculated heavily in the stocks, and has lost. Two days ago, he received two millions of francs belonging to the government, but, instead of applying them to the purpose indicated in his instructions, he has disappeared, and the government is unable to discover either the man, or any trace of its money."

"You astonish me!" exclaimed Laromie.

"Monsieur Laromie," said the chief, shrugging his shoulders, "I thought you a man of too much experience to be astonished at anything. However, let me resume my story. Monsieur Vilele has disappeared. We have reason to believe that he is still in Paris. The government is extremely anxious to discover him and bring him to justice. I have suggested you as the best person to conduct the search for him, and have received orders to place you upon it at once. Here is a paper signed by the Minister of the Interior, commanding all persons to assist you, in whatsoever way you may desire. You will have a difficult task, I think; but it will bring you a plenty of honor, if you succeed. Do you object to undertaking it?"

"Not at all. It is my duty to obey all orders of this kind; and besides, the more difficult a case is, the better I like it."

"Very good, then, monsieur. I will so inform the minister. You will do well to lose no time, as Monsieur Vilele had already the start of you."

Laromie left the bureau, and, as was his custom when placed in charge of a difficult undertaking, strolled towards the gardens of the Tuilleries, to collect his thoughts and ponder over his plan of operations. There was something about the place, and in the fresh and cheering shrubbery with which it was surrounded, that seemed to inspire him. It was lucky for him that he went there on this occasion, as the sequel will show.

He was sitting on a bench in one of the main avenues, with his head resting on his hands, buried in profound thought. The rustling of a dress aroused him, and looking up half absently, he saw a lady pass by, leisurely. She did not seem to notice him, but walked on, carelessly. He sat for some time, watching her, until she had almost disappeared in the distance, and then, for the first time, noticed a small piece of paper lying on the ground just in front of him. Merely from curiosity, he picked it up and opened it. It was simply a note, and ran as follows:

"DEAR MARIE:—At nine tomorrow night.—V."

He was quite sure that the lady had dropped the paper, and now he remembered that as she passed him she had drawn her handkerchief from her pocket. In this way, no doubt, she had thrown out the paper. Laromie rose from his seat and hurried in the direction the lady had taken, intending to return the note to her; but she had passed out of sight, and, after a fruitless walk of a few minutes, he turned back towards the place he had left. As he did so, he glanced at the note again, and this time the signature attracted his attention.

"V," he exclaimed, suddenly pausing in his walk. "That's the first letter in the name of the man I am looking for. What if this note should have been written by M. Vilele? It's a fortunate thing that I thought of it, as I can settle the matter in a few minutes."

He left the gardens, and proceeded to the house which M. Vilele had occupied for his bank. The head bookkeeper and one or two of the clerks were still there, trying to arrange the accounts of the house in an intelligible form, before surrendering them to the government, which had demanded them, in virtue of its being the principal sufferer. Laromie informed the bookkeeper that he was authorized by the Minister of the Interior to ask for a specimen of M. Vilele's handwriting.

"Anything," he added; "an old letter, or anything that will give me a correct idea of the writing."

The bookkeeper handed him a letter which the banker had left unfinished on his desk, on the day of his disappearance. Placing it by the side of the note he had found, the detective compared the two, closely. There could be no mistake; the same person had written both notes. Turning to the bookkeeper and handing him the note he found, he asked if he recognized the writing. The man glanced at it, and then flushed darkly.

"It is Monsieur Vilele's writing," he said.

"Do you know the person to whom it is addressed?" asked Laromie.

"To my cost, monsieur. She is a very beautiful woman, and but for her this house would have been in a prosperous condition, and I should not have been thrown out of employment. She turned Monsieur Vilele's head, from the first; and now you see the result."

"Do you think Monsieur Vilele and she are in communication with each other?"

"It is likely. This note would seem to indicate it."

"Can you tell me where the lady lives?"

"Not at present. If monsieur will call at eight o'clock tonight, I shall be able to inform him."

"Very well. I will be here precisely at eight."

Laromie was very well satisfied with his morning's work. The note he had found had given him a clue to the mystery, and by following it closely, he might be able to accomplish his task. At eight o'clock he returned to the bank, and found the bookkeeper waiting for him. The latter had succeeded in learning the residence of the woman, and gave Laromie explicit directions how to find it. Without delay, the detective set off for the place. It was in a distant part of the city, and it was after nine o'clock before he reached it. He rang the bell, and the porter appeared. In a sleepy voice, he asked Laromie what he wanted.

"Does Madame R— live here?" asked the official.

"She did live here until this afternoon, monsieur," was the reply. "But she has gone to England, and will not return again."

"I must search the house," said Laromie, sternly. "I am an officer of the law."

"Monsieur is at liberty to do so," said the porter; "but he will find that I speak the truth. Madame left for Calais this afternoon."

It was evident that the man spoke the truth, and Laromie felt that it would be losing time to search the house. With an oath he turned from the door, and hailed a fiacre which chanced to be passing. Springing in, he ordered the man to drive with speed to the railway station. As the vehicle rattled over the paved streets, he settled himself back in his seat, and commenced to think over what had happened. Madame R— had doubt-less escaped him, unless he could telegraph to Calais to have her detained. That seemed hardly probable, as the train left early in the afternoon, and she was now, beyond a doubt, almost safe in England. Still, the effort must be made. Then he thought of the note.

"At nine tomorrow night," he muttered, recalling its contents. "What can that mean? I am certain the note was written yesterday. Perhaps it was for her to meet him at Dover, at nine tonight. That seems a very plausi-ble conjecture."

While he was engaged in these reflections, the carriage drew up to the station. Handing the driver his fare, he passed in, and demanded to see the superintendent. That official appeared, and Laromie stated his busi-ness, which was to learn whether Madame R— had started for Calais that afternoon. The ticket seller was called, and he remembered selling a ticket to London to a lady answering to the description given by Laromie. It was very unfortunate, the superintendent said, but it would be useless to tele-graph to Calais to stop the lady, as she was, by that time, safe in England, and on her way to London, having left Paris at one o'clock in the after-noon.

Laromie was thoroughly vexed, and, in a not very pleasant voice, asked the ticket seller if he had sold a ticket to anyone answering to M. Vilele's description, which he gave him. No such person had purchased a ticket.

"Who is the person, monsieur?" asked the superintendent.

"Monsieur Vilele, the banker."

"What do you want with him? I have a reason for asking this ques-tion."

"I have orders from the government to arrest him."

"*Diable!*" exclaimed the superintendent, starting to his feet. "This explains the whole matter. Monsieur Vilele left here at a little after nine o'clock tonight, in a special train for Calais."

"Who dared allow him to leave Paris?" cried Laromie, furiously.

"I allowed him, monsieur," said the superintendent. "Monsieur Vilele's passport was correct, and I have never heard anything to cause me to think it improper for him to leave Paris."

"True," muttered the detective. "This comes of the government keep-ing the affair secret. What reason did Monsieur Vilele give for wanting a special train?" he asked, turning to the official.

"He said he had a large amount of money at stake in London, and that it was necessary for him to reach there by morning. He paid a thousand francs for a locomotive and one car."

"Monsieur," said Laromie, "my orders are positive to arrest the man. I cannot disregard them. I am authorized by the Minister of the Interior to demand your assistance. I must go in pursuit of this man."

"How can it be done?" asked the superintendent. "I am ready to comply with any demands you may make upon me."

"You have a double track to Calais?"

"Yes."

"How many trains are on their way here by the upper track tonight?"

"Two. One will start from Calais at midnight."

"Telegraph to them to remain over at such stations as you think best, until I pass them. Then give me the best locomotive you have, and I will give chase on the upper track."

"Would it not be well to telegraph them at Calais to arrest him?"

"No. He might escape. I am confident of overhauling him in time to prevent his leaving the country."

"He has a fast train, monsieur."

"Perhaps so, but I shall catch him. How long has it been since he left?"

"The train started at a quarter after nine," said the agent, looking at his watch, "and has been gone an hour and ten minutes, making it now twenty-five minutes after ten. But come, Monsieur Laromie, you have no time to lose."

Laromie followed the agent through the station to where the locomotives were kept. One of the largest and best, which was to take the midnight train from Paris already had steam up, and Laromie at once decided to start with it. Some little arrangements had to be made by the engineer before they could begin their journey, and it was fully eleven o'clock when everything was declared in readiness. As Laromie mounted the platform where the engineer stood awaiting him, he repeated his caution to the superintendent to be sure to have the up trains warned to keep out of the way.

"Fear nothing, monsieur," was the reply. "You will have a clear road. May success attend you."

The next moment the rush of steam through the cylinders, and the creaking of the ponderous driving wheels announced that the chase had begun.

"They are an hour and three quarters ahead of us," said Laromie to the engineer. "We must make good time to catch them."

The engineer smiled.

"They will not travel as fast as we shall," he said, "and, besides, the 'Hercules' is the best locomotive on the line. You were fortunate in securing it, monsieur."

There were only three persons on the locomotive, the detective, the engineer, and the stoker. It was a powerful engine, and being unencumbered with a train of carriages, had nothing to impede its flight. The last barrier was past, the city was left behind, and the speed of the engine was increased. They rattled furiously through the suburban towns, never pausing for a moment, their coming having been already announced by the telegraph all along the road. The railway officials at each station turned out to watch the novel sight of a down train on the upper track, unable to account for the phenomenon. A dash and roar mingled with a shrill scream from the whistle, and the locomotive appeared to their astonished gaze, dashing along at a rate far greater than was permitted to the fastest express train on the line. The next instant it was gone, and when its chattering had died out in the distance, they commenced to speculate at random as to the meaning of this strange affair.

Meanwhile the iron horse was dashing on, on with the speed of the wind. It was a lovely night. The clear starlight made every object distinctly visible, and the air was cool and bracing. Laromie watched the steam gage closely. The indicator rose higher and higher as the pressure of the steam became greater, and the pace of the iron horse grew faster. Here a river flashed for a moment in the starlight, and the iron wheels crashed over the bridge, and the next instant it was lost in the gloom. There the lights of a town glittered brightly, and then seemed to vanish in the unearthly shrieks of the flaming monster as it sped through their midst. On, on they dashed, the engineer standing motionless, with his hand on the lever, and his swarthy face lighted up with an unearthly glare by the red flames of the furnace. On, on, on, and they were steadily gaining on the fugitive. Twice they stopped for water and fuel, and each time heard news that cheered them.

Laromie stood like one entranced. The novelty of the situation, the bewildering speed with which he was whirled through the country, completely bewildered him, so that he took no heed of the flight of time. The cool night breeze swept right by him with such force that it almost took his breath; the trees of the forest seemed to be one unbroken wooden wall; the towns were a confused line of white and flame, and the rivers were but silvery flashes across the dark surface of the pathway of the iron horse. He had never witnessed such a scene before. The locomotive shook like an aspen under the rapid motion of the machinery, and he feared that it might not be able to continue such an exertion, and that the banker might escape him after all.

"Monsieur," said the engineer, to whom he mentioned his fear, "dread nothing. The 'Hercules' is a giant, and will not disappoint you. I am well pleased with its behavior thus far. We shall be in Calais as soon as our friends in the special train."

At A— they stopped again for fuel and water. There, to his great joy, Laromie learned that the special train was only ten minutes ahead of them. They had indeed made good time, and the engineer had not exaggerated the merits of the "Hercules." Now they seemed to fly through the country. In half an hour the engineer touched Laromie, and pointed towards the front of the locomotive. A small red light some distance in advance was all that could be seen.

"It is the special train," said the engineer, quietly, as he opened the valve still wider. The "Hercules" literally jumped forward. The light in the distance grew brighter and larger, and soon the train itself could be seen distinctly. Ten miles more, and they were near enough to distinguish objects on it by the light of the lamps in the carriage and locomotive.

Laromie could see that the compartment nearest the engine was the only one occupied, and in a few minutes he noticed that the attention of the solitary passenger was attracted by the approach of the "Hercules." He could see him throw open the window, and gaze out into the darkness. Then the window at the end which communicated with the locomotive was opened, and he could see the passenger gesticulating vehemently to the engineer. Immediately the train shot forward.

"They will escape us," cried Laromie, furiously. "They are increasing their speed."

"Monsieur," said the engineer, as quietly as ever, "you are on the 'Hercules.' Fear nothing."

He opened the valve to its fullest extent as he spoke, and again stood motionless and silent, with his eyes fixed on the gage, which now clearly indicated that there was danger if this furious speed was kept up. It would not be needed much longer. They were rapidly nearing Calais, and already they could smell the fresh sea breeze as it came over the country from the channel. Laromie now noticed that the special train was slackening its speed. In a moment the "Hercules" flew by it.

"They have reversed their course," he cried. "They are going back, and we shall lose them, after all."

"*Ciel!*" exclaimed the engineer. "They will be ruined. The train we passed an hour ago is coming on right after them, and they will meet it before they can reach a station. What madness! They will be dashed to pieces, for a collision is inevitable."

He turned his attention to checking his own headway, and, upon accomplishing this, hurried back after the special train, whose lights now disappeared in the distance. It was a thrilling moment. Those on the engine knew that the object of their pursuit was doomed, and Laromie felt that the banker would escape him, after all, for it was more than probable that he would be killed in the collision. At that moment the thought flashed across his mind that he was forcing M. Vilele upon his death. But no, he reasoned, he was simply obeying his orders, and the banker had taken upon himself the responsibility of running back upon the wrong track. He could only abide the issues, feeling that he was simply doing his duty.

The lights of the doomed train now came in sight, and the "Hercules" dashed on even faster. The hope of the engineer was to overtake the train and warn it of its danger. They were running through an open plain, at the farther end of which they could distinguish the heavy outlines of a forest. There was not more than a mile between the two locomotives, and it seemed not unlikely that the warning would be given in time.

Vain hope! At this moment a dull red glare shot up from the line of the distant woods. It grew brighter and brighter every second.

"*Mon Dieu!*" cried the engineer, "we are too late. It is the night express. They are lost."

The speed of the "Hercules" was slackened, and the whistle blown violently to warn all parties of their danger. They saw it at last, but not in time to avert it. A minute more, and there was a crash and a shock, which threw the special train entirely off the rails, and broke the locomotive and forward carriage of the express train to pieces, killing and wounding nearly a dozen persons. When the "Hercules" came up, the scene was frightful beyond description.

Laromie's first care was to spring from the engine, and search for M. Vilele. Hastening to where the ruins of the special train were heaped, he saw that his search was ended. The carriage had been entirely demolished, and the banker, who was its only occupant, was lying amid the wreck, dead, and horribly mutilated. The engineer had both his legs broken, and the stoker had been killed. Securing the engineer of the special train, whom he justly regarded as responsible for the catastrophe, Laromie mounted the "Hercules" again, and hastened to the nearest station, from which relief was dispatched to the scene of the accident.

The engineer was brought to trial for the murder of the persons killed by the collision, as by running back on the wrong track he had violated both the laws of the road and the country. He stated that M. Vilele upon seeing the "Hercules" approaching them, had supposed that he was pursued, and had offered him six thousand francs if he would reach the station they had last passed through before the arrival of the night express train. He had tried to do so, tempted by the large reward, and the collision had ensued. The engineer was found guilty, and duly executed.

—*Flag of Our Union*, June 16, 1866

Hunting Rogues
by William Russell
Chambers' Journal

I am not about to reveal the "secrets of the poor house" or the private arrangements of Scotland Yard. The higher positions held by detectives have always been beyond my reach, and I have not therefore been in communication with the legal advisers of the treasury, my occupation being only subordinate to a private detective. In the few years, however, that I was thus employed I was engaged in matters which it may be interesting to record, while the publicity cannot be injurious either to individuals or public security.

I will now proceed to give one or two examples of the kind of business we detectives have to negotiate in the hope that my narrative may prove interesting at least to those whom it may specially concern.

It matters not what my former occupation was; like many others, after dissipating fortune, I found myself alone in the world and without money. For the small amount of twenty-eight shillings a week I became a subordinate to a private detective. My primary value consisted in a perfect knowledge of some of the "gambling hells" in the west of London. For days I was closeted with my superior, giving him information concerning the frequenters of these places, and the amounts won and lost in an evening, the hours of attendance, and the doings of the "bankers."

After describing this gentleman or the other, my superior would say:

"Ah, we know him! Cautious card."

"He's a right to gamble; got plenty of money."

"That fellow wins his money on the race course, and always loses it on the green cloth."

"It's the young swells I want to know about; those that the spiders are getting into their nets; there's something to be made out of them."

At last I described a young gentleman who was evidently new to the game of hazard. He came night after night, I said, and generally left minus a hundred or two, ready cash, but never gave checks or IOUs, so that his name was unknown to the majority, though he went by the cognomen of "The Duke."

"That'll do," said my superior; "we must look after that gent."

"Then," said I, "there is another young gentleman who comes only once a month; he's always supplied at that time with clean bank of England notes, from one hundred to ten, and generally loses something like a thousand in one night. But once I saw him positively break the bank and carry off nearly seven thousand pounds. He came next day, contrary to his usual custom, and he played on that and the two succeeding days, and before he left on the last night he had to borrow a sovereign to take him home. After that, however, he paid his periodical visits, and does so up to the present time."

"Well," said my superior, "he must be looked after. But first you must plant yourself opposite this place where they meet, and follow the young gentleman No. 1, find out where he lives, his occupation etc. There now; that's employment for you the next two days; report to me the third morning. I leave the matter entirely in your hands, and this will be a test of your usefulness to me."

"You are going to make a raid on the place?" said I.

"Oh no," he returned; "that don't suit my purpose. I don't want to kill the goose that lays the golden eggs; let me have my bit out of it, and then perhaps the Scotland Yard folks will spot the den."

That same night I paced during the early hours of night up and down the street where the gamblers' house was situated. Between three and four o'clock in the morning one after another of the habitués of the place turned out, and at last the young gentleman I wanted. There was little difficulty in finding out where he lived, for he gave directions to the cabman in very audible tones. But my next great object was to find out if he had any place of business, and after taking a few hours' rest, I was in sight of his residence by nine o'clock in the morning. A little before ten, the gentleman made his appearance, and, walking some distance, took a seat inside an omnibus. I got outside, and discovered, after a few inquiries judiciously made, that he was the cashier in the establishment where I had traced him, and the nephew of the principal of the firm. My work being completed, I went home and reported to my superior, who was quite satisfied with my first commission.

The following day a "gentleman" (for private detectives can dress like noblemen when it suits them) called at Messrs. —'s, Leadenhall Street. They were foreign merchants. He wished to see the head of the firm.

"Your business, sir?" was the question.

The answer was, "Tell him I must see him; I come on important business."

And he did see him, and communicated to him his belief that something must be wrong, as his nephew, the cashier, was spending lots of money in gambling.

Accounts were examined, and the cashier was seen no more in Leadenhall Street or at the hell. The private detective was satisfied, and so the matter ended.

Now we had to look to gentleman No. 2, and having watched for two days without finding his whereabouts, my superior went with me, and at a comparatively early hour of the night of his usual periodical visit he appeared in the street, and I pointed him out to my superior, who, as the public houses were not closed, dodged him about until he entered a tavern, where we followed. Then there was a quiet and confidential conversation between my employer and the gentleman.

The latter at first indignantly denounced the assumption of anyone daring to catechise him, but upon being told that he was addressing a detective, he quietly pulled out a card stating:

"That's my address; if you have any charge against me, you can make it."

My employer dexterously turned the matter to his own account by asserting that his only wish was to put the gentleman on his guard, as the gambling establishment was being watched, and there would be a raid upon it in a day or two. Upon this, the gentleman was profuse in thanks, and passed over something to my employer, which so satisfied him that he voluntarily offered me a sovereign, which I was nothing loath to accept for the part I had taken in the matter.

My conduct is approved, and I am sworn in a special constable. I have little matters to do which it is not interesting to relate, because they apply to "poor people" who are never worth consideration, and convictions are easily gained against them. But one evening I am walking with my employer down Oxford Street; it is late at night, and when near the Oxford music hall, we notice a young gentleman pulling out his gold at the bar of a tavern and treating liberally those around him. The youth has evidently not been used to the company with whom he is now associated. He blushes at remarks, is dull at comprehending low jokes, yet tries to appear at ease, is profusely liberal, and dashes down his money as if he were a millionaire.

"Hulloa!" whispered my employer, whose experienced eye marks a victim. "There's something wrong here."

And he tries to engage in conversation with the young man, who only responds with:

"What will you have, sir?"

You'd think a detective would refuse to take anything at a suspected person's expense. Not he; that's his opportunity.

"Well, thank you," my employer replied. "There's me and my friend here; suppose we have two drops of brandy, eh? Three penny'orths."

"Better say sixpenny-worth," answered the youth. "Here, Miss; six-penn'orths of brandy."

It is drawn. We drink and talk. Drawing information out of the silly youth as easily as one draws beer from a tap, my employer presently says:

"Let's see, what time was it when you left the office this afternoon?"

"I haven't been there since eleven o'clock in the morning; not at Bishopsgate Street at least."

Here was something important got out of the youth; and the detective following up the idea and taking a bold shot, says:

"But you were expected at the other place?"

"Well, yes."

"Let's see, where is your other place?"

"Oh! In Wallbrook."

"You ought to have been there, you know."

Upon this the youth turned pale, but did not answer.

"What's the number of your place in Bishopsgate?"

The youth gave it.

Then came the more pertinent questions:

"How much money have you got about you? Where did you get it from?" etc.

The boy gave such fencing answers, that at length my employer took him quietly outside, saying:

"You must know that I am a detective officer, and I am not going to part with you till I have communicated with your employer and your friends."

Then came the last stroke of conviction:

"Oh, it will all be put right, my father will satisfy Mr. —."

We took that poor young man under our charge (he was only seventeen); he was placed in a room in my employer's house under my care; and having found who were his parents as well as his employers, the detective officer first went to his parents. Never shall I forget the deep affliction of the mother, who, in the absence of his father abroad, came down immediately on receipt of the news.

"O, my boy," she cried, "what have you done? Tell me all. O, dear! O, dear! And your father away, and your sister ill! What is it? What is it?"

"O, mother, mother!" replied the youth weeping. "I never did such a thing before. But the governor sent me to pay nine pounds all in sovereigns, and I lost one, and then I was afraid to go back."

"And so you got into bad company, and spent the rest. O, you naughty, wicked boy."

"I don't know what to do. By good rights," said the detective, "I should take him off to the police station, instead of keeping him here; but I must see what Mr. — says."

"Yes. Oh, let me go with you to Bishopsgate Street, sir; and I am sure Mr. — will not be hard upon the boy," replied the mother.

To this my employer assented; and in the end the youth was allowed to return home; and the detective was rewarded for saving the youth.

One morning we received a telegram to watch a certain train arriving at Euston Square from Birmingham. A lady described, had left that town by train for the purpose, it was said, of eloping with a man who was to meet her at the London terminus; and the disconsolate husband, too late to stop her, wanted her actions watched by the detectives. I was sent. I saw the lady and gentleman meet; she threw herself into his arms and sobbed. I heard him say: "It will be all right, Millie." A cab was called. I heard the address they were to be driven to, and followed the vehicle, to assure myself this was their destination. I watched until midnight, and they never left the house; and then I called up my employer and told him the address.

"Leave the rest to me," he said. And the next morning he discovered the lady and gentleman were there under different names, and had separate rooms. "This won't do," he said. "We must wait for further evidence before we can make a case." But he telegraphed to the husband that the address was known. My duty was to watch the fugitives; and I found that they went to a lawyer's in Lincoln's Inn Fields, and remained there two hours, and then returned, and so passed the first day; but I had to watch all night. The second day the irate husband came to town and went to the house where his truant wife was domiciled, in company with the detective, thinking he could find out more than had been recorded to him. They were met by an indignant gentleman, who, in reply to the question, "Where is my wife?" said:

"She is with me, under my protection, until she gets rid of a horrible and brutal husband."

"And what right have you sir, to give protection to another man's wife?"

"The right of a brother and guardian! She had written to me previously of your brutal conduct, and then telegraphed that she could bear it no longer. The telegram is here, sir. 'Oh, Sam! What am I to do? My life is in jeopardy. I dare not wait my husband's return.' I had only returned from India a few days, and on receipt of that telegram I telegraphed: 'Come by ten o'clock train: I will meet you at Euston Square. Sam.' This telegram I presume you saw, for it was left behind, I am informed; and you thought there was an elopement."

I never knew all the ins and outs of this affair, which I verily believe was a sell; at least it never came before the court, to my knowledge. My employer I presume, got well paid for it, for he never grumbled about its being time lost. I got a paltry five shillings for night watching, over and above my wages.

As to watching houses and persons, I have had to take a house and record faithfully every person who went in and out of it during the day for three weeks and a month at a stretch, not knowing why or wherefore. Very monotonous work this has been; nothing to come of it but [poor]-wages, an uncomfortable, unprofitable sort of existence. I have had to follow a person from one end of London to the other, and make a record of every call that he made, and have never been used as a witness to prove anything. I began to think that my superiors had all the loaves and fishes, and I only got the crumbs that fell from their table. If there was anything to be done which would bring in something handsome, why, my chief did it himself.

A banker's son, making too free with his father's name, is to be taken into custody by the detective, to be well frightened, and relieved of his ill-gotten spoils; and then returned to his parents without the world knowing of his crime. Yes, sometimes the family plate has been carried off by some hopeless son, and the detective's aid is called to recover it but to hide the crime. And, indeed, if truth were told, nearly one half the cases of robbery of late years have been more or less under the cognizance at least of those closely associated with the family circle.

I once thought that I might make a name for myself as an honest detective. I began to see that there was scarcely a tradesman in London, scarcely a merchant that was not robbed by his underlings, if not by those of a higher grade. I watched carefully and confided my secret information to employers. In some instances the persons were dismissed; that was all.

"We don't care to prosecute," the principal would say, "for trivial matters; it is too much trouble and expense. We would rather submit to small losses than be forced to attend the criminal courts."

I happened to mention to the manager of a large publishing firm not a hundred miles from Paternoster Row, that I knew his employers were robbed and systematically robbed every week. He did not believe me. I then challenged him to give me the name of any book he had in the establishment, and I would get it in three days without its passing through the countinghouse in the ordinary way. He gave me the name of a work of which there were only three in stock, and the selling price was two guineas. I had only to go to a certain rendezvous, talk slang, and say what I required and the price I was prepared to give, and I knew I should have the book. And to the astonishment of the manager I presented it to him on the third day with his trademark still upon it.

"Well," he said, "this must be put a stop to. I must see the principals; and you must call tomorrow and give us full information."

I called as requested, and gave the principals the name of the three who shared in the plunder.

"Ay," they said, "as to the first, that's the porter; we'll prosecute him.

The second is the son of a person who has considerable interest in the business; they are a most respectable family; we cannot prosecute him. The third is a confidential messenger; and he is so exceedingly useful to us, that we don't well see how we could do without him. No; we must not prosecute him. But the porter, we will give him into custody if you like."

I replied that I could not take one without the others; that it was a great pity, after all my time and trouble expended in sifting the matter, they would not make an example of the lot. No; they would not do it; but gave me a five-pound note, and asked me to say no more about it!

I suppose I expressed annoyance at this although I received a larger gratuity than I had hitherto done; and I am afraid that I made no secret of my annoyance, for I wanted this to be my stepping-stone to advancement; but it was not to be. Neither was my conduct admired by my superiors, who told me that I should keep a still tongue, and further that I had no right to take action in any matter on my own responsibility. And as there was no hope of advancement, I retired from the service to enter upon more profitable employment.

—*The Burlington* [IA] *Hawk-Eye,* April 4, 1879

Tracing a Murderer
Anonymous

A man was standing one day, with a kind of unoccupied air, a few steps from the door of the telegraph office, on Second Street, Sacramento. What was remarkable about him was that there was nothing remarkable about him at all—to the casual eyes. He was a man of very ordinary appearance, of ordinary size, of ordinary complexion, with an ordinary face, and especially with an ordinary eye. He stood with his hands idly down in the pockets of a long, loose coat, as though they had dropped there themselves, and he had not taken the trouble to pull them out, and he seemed to be neither thinking of, nor caring about, nor looking at anything.

A boy messenger came tripping out of the telegraph office, taking two or three steps at once, as has been handsomely expressed, and happening to see the uninterested man whom he had seen before, he stopped short, and said:

"Oh, here's one for you; I suppose I might as well give it to you here. You're Mr. Black?"

The man did not say that he was or that he was not, but quietly reached for the dispatch, which the boy handed him and hurried on.

Then Mr. Black with a deliberation that would have been fairly agonizing to anyone looking over his shoulder, unfolded the paper and read:

> MARYVILLE, June 26, 18—.—To Mr. William Black, Police Department, Sacramento. An atrocious murder has just been discovered here. A woman, named Mrs. Wolf, was the victim. Her husband is suspected and in custody, but no evidence against. Hasten to us by the first boat while all is fresh.
>
> L. Morton,
> Sheriff of Yuba County.

William Black was a Sacramento detective, and at that time undoubtedly the most sagacious in California. The boat was to leave in a little over an hour. Mr. Black entered the telegraph office and dispatched to the sheriff of Yuba county the words "All right."

That evening a man with a red shirt on—a man of very ordinary appearance—landed in Marysville. He was a miner, of course, if one may always judge from indications; but he had a lazy look, as if weighed down by a woeful lack of energy; and a person might have wondered if ever such a person did pluck up courage enough to climb the mountains.

The same lazy-looking man later in the evening was in secret communication with the sheriff and several other officials.

"At what hour was the murder discovered?" he asked.

"Nine o'clock this morning—exactly."

"In what way?"

"The news came through her husband. He rushed excitedly into a saloon, on the edge of town, saying that his wife was dead and somebody had killed her. They had come lately from the mines, and were living in a tent of their own, a quarter of a mile out of town. We will conduct you to it by and by."

"A physician has made an examination?"

"Yes; a skilled one. He says it is clear that the woman was murdered—strangled by a pair of coarse hands, the marks of which he found on her throat."

"Did he say how long she had been dead?"

"Yes, many hours."

"What does Wolf say?"

"That he did not sleep at home. He says he was drunk last night, which I have found to be true, and that, being unable to reach home, he lay down under a tree, between here and his home, and slept soundly. When he awoke, according to his story, it was near nine o'clock. Then he got up, hastened to his tent and found his wife dead, and we have some fear that an attempt will be made to lynch him. In fact, there is little doubt of his guilt, but there is no positive proof, and the case needs working up."

"What makes you think he did it?"

"Various suspicious circumstances. His unlikely story of having slept out all night, when within a few yards of his temporary home, and not waking before nine."

"Had they quarreled?"

"It is not known that they had, but—well, they were man and wife, and we might safely presume they had."

"Were there not traces of a struggle left?"

"No."

"Not a thread—a shirt button—a hair?"

"No.

"Tracks?"

"No. The ground is so hard and dry, you know."

"Has any stranger been seen lurking in that neighborhood?"

"No."

"Has any stranger been in town?"

"Well, we have miners down here from the mountain every day—but it was none of them."

Detective Black, who wore a red shirt, was conducted to the scene of the murder. He saw the body at the office of the coroner. He saw the physician; he saw everybody in Marysville, he saw and talked with Wolf three-quarters of an hour. Then he said to the sheriff:

"He didn't do it."

The sheriff was thunderstruck!

"But," said William Black, "keep him in custody till you hear from me. Don't let the people get hold of him, though; for I suppose they would lynch him at a venture."

"We'll take care of him."

"You might arrest and detain any suspicious-looking person found in the neighborhood—always remembering that he's innocent."

"I will."

The conference thus ended.

The next morning a fresh miner made his appearance at Pine Camp, about fifteen miles north of Marysville. He was a lazy-looking man. He lounged about from point to point, talking with the miners, bothering them at their work. Some thought that he was a half idiot. He stopped and talked with groups here and there and asked questions about the best place to locate on. He was green. Then he told them a piece of terrible news—a woman had been foully murdered in Marysville. Her name was Wolf. Her husband had done it, it was thought—in fact there was no doubt of it. The simpleton! That was no news. It had been the talk of the camp for twenty-four hours.

"Oh! Then you knowed it yesterday?"

He went from claim to claim; spoke to everybody; asked particularly about the mining prospects; spoke about the murder.

"That fellow won't do much. He's too lazy looking," was remarked more than once.

The afternoon was wearing away. The man of unsound mind stopped for the twentieth time and talked to a group of four men who were working a claim. He sat on a large stone; he spoke of the murder, actually informed them as news.

"Why, old fellow," said one, "you've been asleep. You're a day behind the age."

The slow creature was a little nettled.

"Wa'al, yes, now," retorted one of the miners, working away.

"A day is twenty-four hours," remarked the stupid man, sarcastically.

"Wa'al suppose it is."

"Then you haven't knowed of it a day."

"You're smart, I admit; but not that smart."

"What'll you bet?"

"Twenty dollars and drinks all around."

"Done."

In those days a bet, if nothing worse, grew out of very slight difference of opinion, no matter how trifling a subject.

The money was staked.

"How is it going to be proved?"

"That's easy."

"Who brought the news?"

"Dave Long—one of our mess. He'd been down to Marysville over Sunday on a bender."

"Where is he?"

"At our cabin. He's cooking this week."

"Well, drop them tools. You're all dry, and so am I. Dave—Smith, is it?"

"No. Dave Long."

All laid down their tools and the party started toward the cabin to have the bet decided and get the drinks.

"Now remember," said the green stranger, "I'm willing to pay if I lose, but a day is twenty-four hours."

"Well?"

He looked at his watch.

"Mark, then, it's just 'leven now."

There were several watches in the party—all were referred to. They varied but a few minutes.

"Let me see," said the miner who had wagered with the newcomer, "let me see. Why of course you'll lose, stranger. 'Twasn't mor'n ten yesterday morning when Dave come, and he took his time getting dinner ready— which was eat at twelve."

"To be sure," said another.

"Oh, wait," said the stranger. "Leave it to him."

"All right. He knows, for he has a watch, and had timed himself coming from Marysville."

They reached the cabin; Dave Long, according to custom, was serving his turn at keeping house for the week.

"Dave!"

"Hello!" replied a gruff voice within.

"Come out."

"What's wantin'?"

"We've got up a bet, drinks included, and it's left for you to decide."

Dave Long came to the door—a big, burly fellow.

"This man here, I don't know his name—"

"Blossom," put in the stranger.

"Well, Blossom, he came round and went to tell us news. 'Twas about that murder, you know. I told him he'd been asleep and was behind the age. Now the bet is that we'd knowed it a day—twenty-four hours—you brought the news and know whether we did or not."

"Now, honor bright," said the self-styled Blossom. "Think first. I know you would not say what isn't true, but you might forget. It's now just eleven. Can you say you got here before this time yesterday? Think now."

Dave Long ruminated.

"Yes, for I looked at my watch to see how long I had been coming. It was only two or three minutes after ten."

"Are you sure?"

"Certain you could swear to it?"

"For you know," put in one of the others, "that you got dinner after you came."

"Yes, durn it, don't I know?"

"But," said the fastidious stranger, "maybe you didn't tell the news right away."

"Yes, I did."

"And brought it straight from Marysville?"

"Yes."

"All right. I've lost. Now for the drinks. Give us your hand, Dave Long."

"Thar it is stranger."

With a movement so quick that the eye could not follow it, the inquisitive stranger snatched both hands of Dave Long and brought them together, and the astonished spectators saw their comrade standing with a pair of handcuffs on his wrists. They also saw the new arrival, the man who lacked the energy, the man who had been asleep for twenty-four hours, the man with the mild name of Blossom, standing at their comrade's elbow with a firm hand on his collar and a revolver at his temple.

"You are my prisoner! Move an inch and you're a dead man. I arrest you for the murder of Mrs. Wolf. I am Detective Black of Sacramento. Neighbors, I've lost the bet."

Long was fairly paralyzed. He could neither move nor speak.

A clamor arose among his comrades.

"Stranger, no nonsense. Dave Long never did such a thing. He's above such a crime. Let him go. We can't stand here—"

"Stand back!" said the fearless officer. "It will go hard with anyone who interferes. This man is guilty, and I can convince you."

"How do you know?"

"Keep cool and I will tell you. He came yesterday morning at ten o'clock and told all about the murder that was not discovered in Marysville till nine o'clock. Did he walk fifteen miles in an hour?"

David Long was as pale as death, and he stood trembling from head to foot—the picture of guilt. His comrades looked on bewildered.

"You see," continued Black, by the way of further explanation, "it was on his guilty mind and he couldn't help blurting it out, considering of course, that the murder would be discovered before daylight or sooner. Luckily it was not discovered till nine o'clock—except to the murderer and he has very kindly volunteered to expose himself."

"Curse my tongue!" exclaimed the culprit, grinding his teeth with rage and fear. "I wish it had been torn out!"

"There's always something," exclaimed the detective quietly. "You left no trace—not a thread nor shred, nor shoestring, not even a hair; but you came right up here and told on yourself."

"Dave Long! Dave Long! Can this be?" exclaimed one of his comrades reproachfully.

The crestfallen wretch hung his head and seemed ready to fall to the earth.

"You poor devil!" said another of his comrades. "Who'd have thought it? If it wasn't for the old times sake we'd string you up. Take him away, Mr. Black, let us see him no more."

"If the camp find it out, they'll lynch him before you can get away with him," suggested another.

Filled with terror at the prospects, Long determined to make one desperate effort for his life. With a sudden spring he released himself from the detective and darted away toward a thicket not far off. He had some hope that his speed might bear him away beyond the immediate reach of Black or miners, where he could work off his manacles. But the agile officer bounded after him and before he had gone thirty yards dragged him down. Maddened at the situation, the prisoner began a fierce and hopeless struggle, attempting with kicks and blows to inflict some injury on his captor; but Black whose strength was extraordinary, clutched him by the throat and soon overpowered him.

"Look here," said he somewhat heated, "if you carry on this way they'll learn what you've done, and hang you up to a tree; and I'll not hinder them. If you will go quietly I can promise you a fair trial, and you may not be hanged for weeks yet."

"Let me up," he faltered, "and I'll go with you."

"And give me no further trouble?"

"No."

The dread of being lynched had a mighty influence on him.

"See that you keep your word, then. And mind, if on the way to Marysville, you make another such a move, I'll shoot you down."

And he allowed him to get up, taking care to maintain his grasp on his arm.

But the scuffle had already attracted attention, and the miners were running up from all directions.

"What's this? What's the matter?" a score of them asked.

They saw by the handcuffs on Long's wrists that one belonging to their camp was in the hands of an officer, and did not like it. They were jealous of the law, and jumping to the conclusion that Long was arrested for merely shooting someone in a little row at Marysville the first thought was to rescue him.

"He shan't go!" shouted one.

"Release him!" added another.

"Don't let him take me," pleaded Dave Long.

The crowd began to close in.

"Stand back!" thundered the detective, flourishing his revolver. "I am Detective Black from Sacramento, and this is my prisoner. If any man dares to interfere I will shoot him down like a dog."

Although threats of bullets were not much in those days, the fearless bearing of the officer, who stood firmly grasping the prisoner, and with a single arm opposing a hundred reckless men, had its effects, and they stood undecided. Taking advantage of the momentary truce, Black hurriedly whispered to the prisoner.

"If you don't tell them not to interfere, I guess I'd better fly. I'll be all right."

"What is it you've done, Long?"

He turned paler than ever.

"We must know what it is. Was it a scrape in Marysville?"

"Yes—yes. Never mind. I'll—I'll be back—" and his heart sank at the thought he never would, "back before long and tell you all about it."

So the detective was allowed to depart with his prisoner.

Two of Long's mess accompanied them, and the culprit was lodged in jail at Marysville that night, while the murdered woman's husband was released.

An effort was made by the authorities to keep the matter quiet for a while; but all the facts leaked out, and the angry population did not wait for the law's slow vengeance.

On the following Friday night, July 20, the miserable wretch was taken from the jail by a party of disguised men and hanged to a tree whose broad boughs overshadowed the scene of the crime.

In his last moments, with the noose around his neck, he confessed his guilt, and died praying for mercy.

—*Palo Alto* [Emmetsburg, IA] *Reporter*, October 9, 1880

5

Vidocqs in Petticoats

In the year in which this robbery took place, very little was yet known of female detectives; still there were only two women in the service,—one an elderly American lady; the other an intelligent young German girl of fine appearance and good address. The name of the last was Lisette Bremer. She was shrewd and reliable, and would be the very person to aid us in this matter [Leopold Davis, "A Detective's Story," *Strange Occurrences,* Boston: published for the author, 1877].

The role of women in late nineteenth-century law enforcement and detection is largely an unexplored field. Contrary to the notion that until the twentieth century women served on police forces exclusively as matrons and female searchers, even a cursory examination of contemporary newspapers yields an impressive, albeit a short, list of women police and private detectives before World War I. Kate Warne, an employee of the Pinkerton Detective Agency from 1856 until her death in 1868 and chief of the Agency's "Female Detective Bureau," tops that list. She helped save Abraham Lincoln from the Baltimore assassination plot on his journey to his first inauguration. Expert with disguises and various accents, Warne first posed as a secessionist from Alabama, infiltrating social gatherings to gain information that helped to verify the plot and then discover its details. She boarded the south-bound train posing as the sister to the disguised president-elect, and, armed with a revolver, she rode in the compartment next to Lincoln's, and he was delivered to Washington unharmed. In addition to the Lincoln adventure, Warne "risked her life many times by donning many disguises from rich society matrons to mystic fortune tellers." Her success prompted Pinkerton to hire several more women detectives and to proclaim, "She succeeded far beyond my utmost expectations. Mrs. Warne never let me down!" (www.pinkertons.com).

Much less is known about other nineteenth-century women detectives.

According to contemporary newspaper reports, women began as part-time operatives used mostly to serve court papers on men on the lookout for process-servers. With the rise of department stores near the end of the century they were widely used as store detectives to stop the seeming epidemic of shoplifting that accompanied that retail innovation. Fannie Leahey and Kittie McNamee ("the young detectives who are employed to keep a vigilant lookout for evildoers at a big concern in Pemberton square") are the focus of a widely reprinted piece from *The Boston Traveler* in 1885 titled "Women Detectives. It Is Said They Surpass Men in Catching Shoplifters." Another widely circulated article from the *New York Sun*, "Female Detectives. What They Are Fitted For and What They Are Not—Useful at Receptions" (1884), determines that women are useful as attendants or hat-check girls at society events because "it is a convenience to have a skilled eye on the property." More seriously, "Vidocqs in Petticoats. Female Detectives and Their Methods of Ferreting Out Crime" (*Washington Post*, December 7, 1890) notes that female detectives are employed in the custom-house looking for smugglers, in private agencies, dry goods stores, and doing "occasional jobs for the police." Like Lisette Bremer in Davis' story, most frequently women originally seem to have gone undercover as domestics to obtain information. With the advent of the Progressive Era, women detectives were sent to purchase quack remedies and to expose physicians willing to perform "criminal operations." Like their male counterparts in the real world, however, some female detectives were less than reputable. A story in the *Miami* [OH] *Leader* in 1892 reports Superintendent Byrnes describing Ellen Peck as "the most skillful female detective he ever knew and on several occasions she has rendered valuable aid to the professional thief-takers," and concludes "she could earn a big salary by turning honest and confining her talent to detective work." Unfortunately, she could make more as a confidence woman than a detective, duping hundreds of marks out of an estimated million dollars.

While women were beginning to establish themselves on both sides of real-world law enforcement, it was not quite the same in the realm of fiction. They could occasionally be crooks—usually partners of male criminals, but sometimes ingenious and worthy opponents of male detectives as in "My Wife's Maid" (1874), "The Diamond Cross" (1876), and "A Clever Capture" (1881). But few women in period fiction act as detectives and those few are very rarely professional detectives but undertake investigations because of personal involvement. In the typical mystery of this era, such as "The Tell-Tale Key" (1875), the heroine takes up detecting in order to clear her innocent husband or fiancé of a crime for which he has been wrongly accused or imprisoned. Once her job is completed, so is her role as a detective. In other period stories, such as "The Detective's Story" (1871), "The Girl Detective" (1877) and Davis' "A Detective Story," (1877), the female goes undercover as a domestic to gain the information needed to clear her fiancé or daughter. In "An Old Offender" (1877), the newlywed wife of a detective must take over the active role of a detective because her husband isn't there to do it himself.

There are, however, several stories in which female characters break out of conventional, supporting roles. In the first, "Personal to Mr. Gimblett" (1885), Martha Chale begins as a criminal's sweetheart and ends with the promise of becoming a detective herself. Wrongly accused of a crime she knows her boyfriend has committed, Chale, the upper housemaid, hires private detective Mr. Gimblett to convince her former employer to write a note persuading the police of her innocence. Once free of police surveillance, she packs the guilty party off to America (without the swag), and as the story ends, the detective Gimblett proposes that they use the reward money "to furnish a cottage for a newly-married couple," proclaiming, "we should run well in double harness, my dear, both in business and domestic life." Another story features one of the most interesting female detectives of the nineteenth century, who may have been based on a real woman. "Clubnose" (1880), originally published in *Chambers' Journal* and then widely reproduced in this country, tells the tale of an English woman who is both a certified nurse and a Scotland Yard detective. In the story, we learn how she began detecting to clear her name and how she received her new name after being pummeled beyond recognition on a subsequent case. In all likelihood this story was based on the English woman eulogized in 1878 in the *Elyria* [OH] *Constitution* who was both a nurse and a female detective and had "features which might be compared with those of a bull-dog."

The Tell-Tale Key; or A Woman as a Detective
Anonymous

"Murder! Murder!" screamed a young girl of about eighteen, as she was running shortly before daybreak on the twelfth of May, 1851, through the streets of Cumberland, Maryland.

A number of persons, attracted by her cries, rushed from their houses, and soon she was surrounded by a crowd, one of whom said to her, as she wrang her hands, and cried piteously:

"What is the matter, Bessie Sheats?"

"My grandmother has been murdered!" she replied, panting and sobbing.

"When, and by whom?" asked the crowd.

"Only fifteen minutes ago," replied the girl. "Thieves had broken into the back room. My grandmother slept in the front room and I in the attic. Half an hour ago I was awakened by a noise downstairs. I listened in terror for a few minutes. Then I heard a door opened, several shots were fired, a loud scream resounded, a heavy fall on the floor. I rushed downstairs; the door between the front and back room was open, and on the floor lay my poor grandmother, with a frightful wound in the forehead—she was dead!"

The crowd, headed by the girl, then hurried to the scene of the horrible murder.

They found the corpse of the old lady, Mrs. Louisa Crowley, as her granddaughter had described. Two bullets had struck her forehead. A part of the skull had been torn off. Death must have been almost instantaneous. While Bessie Sheats was bending over the corpse, moaning and wailing, the citizens who had entered with her examined the condition of the premises. It was easy to see that the burglars had broken into the house for plunder. The windows in the back room, opening upon the garden, had been broken. Undoubtedly the burglars had entered the house in that way.

The drawers of the old lady's bureau in the back room had been opened. Wearing apparel, taken from them had been scattered all over the floor, and a tin box, in which Mrs. Crawley had kept a considerable sum of money in bank bills, stood open and empty.

It had meanwhile become daylight, and the sheriff and the coroner made their appearance. After examining the condition of the premises thoroughly, the coroner impanelled a jury, and began the inquest. Bessie Sheats was the only witness. She repeated her statement as above related. Her grief as she related the painful circumstances became at times uncontrollable. No wonder; the poor girl stood now alone in the world. Her murdered grandmother had been her last surviving relative.

"Did your grandmother have any enemies?" asked the coroner.

"None that I know of," replied the distressed girl, "but—hold on—I remember she had a quarrel day before yesterday with William Stafford, the plasterer. Stafford had an old account against my grandmother, who refused to pay it, because she said the bill was exorbitant. Day before yesterday he called again and demanded payment. Grandmother told him she would give him the money if he would deduct two dollars from the bill. He refused to do so, and became very abusive. 'Mrs. Crowley,' he said to her, 'I know you are well off, and you can pay me. I am poor. My bill is correct, and I won't take a cent less than the full amount. If you don't pay me, I will get the money in a way that won't please you. You are a mean woman, and if you were a man I would break your neck.' So saying he left."

"Now, Miss Sheats," said the coroner, "you know this empty tin box?"

"Yes, grandmother kept her money in it."

"Did you know how much she had in it?"

"About thirteen hundred dollars, mostly in ten dollar bills."

"Would you recognize any of the bills if you should see them?"

"Most assuredly," replied Bessie. "Grandmother made me put a cross on the back of each bill, in the left corner, before she put them in the box."

An order for the arrest of William Stafford, the plasterer, was issued. Stafford was known as a man of violent passions. Rumors that he had been guilty of a murder in Wheeling, where he had formerly lived, were current in Cumberland, and so people in general shunned him. He lived with his wife and two children in a frame building on the outskirts of town.

When the officer whom the coroner had sent after Stafford, knocked at the latter's door, he found Stafford still in bed.

"The coroner wants you," said the officer to him as he jumped out of bed.

"What for?" demanded Stafford.

"Old Mrs. Crowley has been murdered, two hours ago."

"They don't suspect me?" interrupted Stafford.

"Come along," said the officer.

Upon appearing before the coroner's jury, Stafford declared emphatically that he did not know anything about the burglary and murder.

"Where were you last night and this morning?" said the coroner to him.

"I was out in the woods shooting squirrels," he replied. "I did not come home until four o'clock this morning."

The coroner then asked the jury to accompany him to the garden in front of the back room window. There were fresh footprints under the window. One of Stafford's boots was pulled off; it fitted the footprints precisely. Then the prisoner was searched. In his pocketbook were found three ten dollar bills. On the back of each of the bills, in the left corner, was found a cross. They were shown to Bessie Sheats, who immediately identified them as having belonged to her grandmother.

"Of course they did," cried Stafford, upon hearing this, "but the old lady gave me them yesterday morning in payment of my bill. I called at her house, and told her I would consent to a deduction of ten dollars on my bill, which was forty dollars. She took these three ten dollar bills from a tin box in her bureau and gave them to me—"

"Did you give her a receipt?" asked the Coroner.

"Yes, sir; she put it into the tin box."

The tin box was empty. The coroner briefly charged the jury, which found a verdict against Stafford, who was committed to jail. After he had been taken to his cell, the coroner found hanging to the broken shutter of the back room window, a large, peculiar-looking watch key, with a piece of black string attached to it. He went to the jail and showed it to Stafford, but the latter said he did not know it. He was too poor to have a watch. He added:

"Mr. Coroner, this is dreadful for me. I am innocent, as Heaven is my witness. What is to become of my poor wife and children? Oh, they will starve to death!"

The prisoner buried his head in his hands and cried bitterly.

The grand jury happened to be in session, and promptly indicted Stafford for murder in the first degree. Public opinion believed that he was guilty, and even threats to lynch him were uttered. Only his wife stoutly maintained his innocence. She ran to the principal citizens of Cumberland, imploring them to intercede for her husband, whose guiltlessness she frantically protested. But everybody treated her with undisguised coldness.

Stafford himself, on hearing that the grand jury had indicted him for murder, gave way to despair. On the morning of the fourth day of his incarceration he was found hanging to the door of his cell. He had committed suicide.

Everybody in Cumberland took this act of desperation as a confession of guilt. Not so the bereaved wife of the prisoner. Repressing her grief, she went on the day after the funeral of her ill-fated husband to the coroner, to whom she said:

"Did you not find at Mrs. Crowley's house, hanging from the window shutter, a piece of black string with a watch key attached to it?"

The coroner showed it to her, and at her urgent request let her have it.

"What do you want it for?" he asked.

"I want it to prove, with God's help, that my poor William is innocent of the terrible charge that made him take his own life."

The next few days Mrs. Stafford spent in going to every man in Cumberland that had a watch, and asking them to try the watch key the coroner had let her have. They gladly humored her, but, strangely enough, the key was too large for any of the watches worn in Cumberland. The only watchmaker in the place told her that it must be the key to one of the large, heavy old English watches worn many years ago.

The widow did not despair notwithstanding her fruitless search in Cumberland. Close to it is the village of Crawfordston. There she found also a watchmaker. When she showed the watch key to him, he uttered a cry of surprise.

"I know whose key this is," he said. "It belongs to this watch." He took down a thick silver watch.

"Look here," he said, unraveling a piece of black string which had been wound around the stem. This string was torn—the piece to which your watch key is tied belongs to it."

"But how did you get the watch?" asked Mrs. Stafford.

"It belongs to a young fellow from Wheeling. He left the watch with me for repairs, and to make him a new key to it. He said he had lost the old one, and he could not buy any at the stores, as they had none large enough. He will be here tomorrow morning between nine and ten o'clock."

Mrs. Stafford hurried back to Cumberland, where she informed the coroner of her discovery at Crawfordston. Next day the coroner and an officer arrested the owner of the silver watch as soon as he entered the watchmaker's shop at Crawfordston.

"Do you know this watch key?" said the coroner to him.

The young man turned very pale, and stammered a few incoherent words. He was searched, and in his pocket was found a large sum in ten dollar bills, bearing Bessie Sheats' marks. Also a revolver, two of whose chambers were empty.

The prisoner, who gave his name as Barnard Floyd, was taken in irons to Cumberland. The bullets found in Mrs. Crowley's skull were found to fit the prisoner's revolver. His shoe soles were the same size as those of the unfortunate Stafford.

So the latter was innocent after all. Floyd confessed his crime, and was hung for it on the 2nd of November, 1851.

Mrs. Stafford became an object of universal sympathy in Cumberland. The citizens bought her a farm in the neighborhood, and saw to it that her two children were properly educated.

—*The Palo Alto* [Emmetsburg, IA] *Pilot*, May 27, 1875
—*The Freeborn County* [MN] *Standard*, June 3, 1875
—*42 Famous Stories of Detective Adventure*. New York, Excelsior Publishing House, 1896.

The Girl Detective
Anonymous

The door of Rufus Markham's counting room was securely closed, and the proprietor of the large, flourishing cotton factory talked earnestly with a gentlemanly-looking man of middle age, whose face was as impassive as a wax mask.

"Five thousand dollars!" said the individual. "It was a large sum to leave exposed."

"Exposed!" said Mr. Markham. "It was in my private desk, to which no one has access but myself and my nephew, Fred Tyron."

"Would it be possible the young gentleman—"

"Sir," said Mr. Markham, indignantly, "my nephew is not a thief. If he needed ten times that sum he knows I would freely give it to him. He will be my heir, and is as dear to me as a son. It is simply absurd to connect him in any way with the robbery."

"Just state the matter again, briefly as you can, and allow me to take notes, will you, Mr. Markham?"

"Certainly. I drew five thousand dollars out of the bank yesterday, to meet a note that was not presented for payment. Retaining it until after the bank was closed, I concluded to lock it in my desk until this morning, and did so. At nine o'clock this morning the expected note was presented, and I opened the desk. The money was gone, and with it a small memorandum book that was in the same roll."

"The lock was not forced?"

"No, sir; the desk was apparently exactly as I left it."

"And Mr. Tyron has the only duplicate key?"

The gentleman frowned. He was evidently displeased at the turn the detective's suspicions seemed to be taking.

"My nephew certainly has the only duplicate key."

"H'm! Yes. You have the number of the notes?"

"Yes. The roll consisted of ten five hundred dollar notes."

The list of numbers being taken, the detective made a searching examination of the apartment and prepared to take his departure. As he stood near the door, Mr. Markham suddenly said, nervously:

"I think, Mr. Vodges if you make any discoveries, you had better report to me privately before making any arrests."

"Certainly, sir, if you desire it. Will you grant me one favor? Do not mention the robbery to Mr. Tyron, if you have not done so already."

"No one has heard of it but yourself."

"Very good! I will call again when I have any report to make."

"Fred! Fred!" the old gentleman said in a low voice, when he was alone; "Vodges evidently thinks it is Fred! It cannot be! It is impossible that my nephew would rob me! I cannot believe it. And yet he knew the money was there. He was here when I handed Arnold the check, and here when he returned with the money. He knew that Johnson's note was not presented, and Fred alone has a duplicate key. Oh, if it should be! Anna's boy, that I have promised to love as my son. Have I not kept my promise? Where have I failed? And why should he steal from me when all I have is his? I cannot, I will not believe it!"

"May I come in?" asked a bright, pleasant face at the door, and permission being given, Fred Tyron entered the room.

Looking into his handsome young face, bright and frank, with well-opened brown eyes, and curls of nut brown hair, it was hard to connect it with any idea of roguery, ingratitude or theft. His manner toward the uncle who had ever filled a father's place, was the perfection of respectful affection, and before he had been an hour in the counting room, Mr. Markham's uneasy fears were entirely gone.

They were talking of a certain dark-eyed little maiden, who was soon to be Mrs. Tyron, and when Fred left his uncle, it was with the promise that he would call in the evening upon Miss Clarkson, to finally arrange for the wedding day.

The young man, a favorite of fortune apparently, spent the afternoon with his betrothed, received his uncle in the evening beside her, and accompanied the old gentleman to his boardinghouse, receiving an affectionate farewell, when he took up his way to his own rooms in another house. For a week he heard nothing of the robbery.

It was just when summer twilight was fading that, returning from a drive with Maud Clarkson, Fred met his uncle's confidential clerk waiting for him at Maud's house.

"I have a note for you, Mr. Fred," he said, "and as you were not at home, I thought I would wait here for you."

Something in the man's face and manner struck a sudden chill to Maud's heart.

"You have bad news?" she cried.

"Perhaps Mr. Fred had better read the note," was the evasive answer.

But Maud's terror was only increased when Fred, after reading the note, broke into a furious exclamation of rage.

"Who dares say I am a midnight burglar?" he shouted.

"Oh, Fred, what is it?" asked Maud, turning very white.

"My uncle has been robbed of five thousand dollars, and he pays me the compliment of supposing me the thief, because I have a duplicate key to his private desk. I! Great Heaven!" he cried, with a sudden change in his voice. "He cannot mean it! I rob my uncle? I!"

"Mr. Fred," said the clerk, respectfully, "I only waited to see how you took the note, to speak a few words of advice. Mr. Fred, I was with your father when he was killed on a railway train; I was with your uncle when he brought you from your mother's funeral to his home. I took you to boarding school, and brought you home for the holidays, and I've loved you boy and man, since you were ten years old, and that's twelve long years. I know you never took the money, but things look very ugly for you."

"But," said Fred, grasping hard the hand the old clerk held out to him, "I cannot understand it. Listen, and he read aloud the note from his uncle:

Mr. Frederick Tyron: I could not believe, without proof undeniable, positive proof—that you could rob me of five thousand dollars, taken, as you know, from my private desk, on Wednesday last. You are my sister's son, and I never will be the one to imprison or punish you, but you are no longer a nephew of mine. Willingly, I will never look in your face again. Your ill-gotten gains I freely give you to start in some business, trusting you will endeavor to live honestly in the future. Do not try to see me; I will not listen to any explanations I know to be false. Do not write for I will not open your letters.   Rufus Markham

Maud Clarkson grew white as death as she heard the stern edict.

"Oh, Fred!" she cried. "What can you do?"

"Starve, I suppose," was the bitter answer, "as I do not happen to possess the ill-gotten gains so generously presented to me. But I will not ask you to starve with me, Maud. You were betrothed to a millionaire's nephew and heir; the disinherited beggar frees you from your promise."

"Fred," she cried, bursting into tears, "how can you be so cruel?" Then, unheeding the clerk, who was discreetly looking from the window, she came close to Fred's side. "Darling," she said, fixing her large black eyes upon his face, "if all the world believes you guilty, I do not. If all the world casts you off, I will keep my promise."

The young lover had been bewildered, indignant, desperate, but he folded the gentle comforter fast in his arms, and great tears fell on her upturned face.

"God bless you, Maud!" he cried, "I can defy the world if you are true to me. Now, Potter, sit down and tell me what you know of this wretched business."

"Well, Mr. Fred, I never heard of the robbery myself until this morning when Vodges, the detective your uncle employed to work it up, came to make his report. They did not notice me at first, and when your uncle remembered I was in the room, I had heard about all Vodges knew. You remember there was a note coming due last Wednesday?"

"To Johnson?"

"Yes; well, I thought at the time it was curious your uncle gave him a check, when I knew the money was drawn out of the bank the day before to meet that very note. But I never knew till this morning that the money was stolen from Mr. Markham's private desk by false keys, Mr. Fred," said the old man earnestly. "It was all in five hundred dollar notes, and your uncle had the numbers."

"Well?"

"This morning Vodges brought back one of the notes which you gave to T— yesterday in payment for a pearl locket?"

"Stop, Potter? Let me think! Where did I get that note? I have it! Arnold gave it to me to take out a hundred dollars I lent him some time ago. And Arnold—Potter, Arnold borrowed my keys last Wednesday night to open his trunk! Potter, huzza! We know the thief!"

"Not so fast, Mr. Fred—not so fast. It will not be an easy matter to prove this. Were there any witnesses present when Arnold borrowed the keys?"

"No; I was alone in my room, half undressed, when he knocked at my door and said he had lost the keys to his trunk. I lent him a bunch of keys, which he returned before I was out of bed the next day."

"And you were alone when he paid you the money?"

"Yes, I thought he was very flush, for you know as well as I do, Potter, that a note for $500 is not a day visitor in Arnold's pocket."

"He is a cunning scoundrel. He wants to ascertain if the notes can be identified before he tries to get rid of them himself. Mr. Fred, will you leave it to me for a few days—only a few days—and if I do not catch the thief, you may try?"

"But my uncle?"

"Wait till you can prove your innocence before you see him. Only a week. Give me only a week to catch Arnold. And, by-the-way, you will give me an additional chance if you will leave the city. Throw him off his guard by letting him suppose you are banished for his crime."

"Run away," flashed Fred, "like a coward?"

"Only for a week. You see, the probability is that Arnold has the money in his possession yet. He will wait to see the fate of what he has given you before putting any more in circulation; but he has probably hidden it very securely. You he will watch; but if you are willing, I will take your room while you are gone and do a little private detective business on my part."

It was not easy to persuade Fred to consent to Potter's plan, but, Maud's persuasions being added to the old man's, he finally consented to leave the city for a week, and return in that time to vindicate his own innocence in case of Potter's failure.

Before night Fred was on his way to visit another city, and his landlady had agreed to allow Mr. Potter to occupy his place during his absence.

Fred had been gone two days when the old clerk called upon Miss Clarkson to report progress.

"I am completely baffled," he said, in answer to her inquiries. "You see, Arnold knows me, and evidently suspects me. He is so affectionately desirous of keeping me in sight that I cannot get a peep in his room; and whenever he is out he locks the door and gives the key to the landlady. I cannot force his door yet, and by the time Fred returns I am afraid the money will be smuggled away. I am sure it is in his possession now, he is so careful about his room. Nobody gets in there but the landlady. I did think of bribing the chambermaid to let me in when she was at work there, but unfortunately she left today."

A flash of light seemed to pass across Maud's face, but she only said, demurely:

"Your landlady is a German, is she not?"

"Yes; her English is very imperfect. Have you ever seen her?"

"No; but I have heard Fred speak of her. My mother, you know, was German."

"But what has that to do with Fred's case?"

"I will tell you. Vodges has tried to find the thief and failed. You have tried and failed. I mean to try and *succeed!*"

"You! What can you do?"

"Come tomorrow, and I will tell you."

Punctual at the appointed time, Potter made his appearance. With dancing eyes and flushed cheeks, Maud met him.

"Well?" he asked, certain from her looks that she had good news.

"I told you I would succeed."

"And you did! Huzza! I feel as young as Fred himself!"

"To whom I have telegraphed to return. He will be here this evening, and you must bring Mr. Markham, Mr. Vodges, and the proper police authorities, to meet in his room. Then go to Mr. Arnold's room, and remove the pipe of the stove in the elbow. In the joint you will find Mr. Markham's memorandum book and the missing notes."

"You are sure?"

"Listen! This morning, in a calico dress, sunbonnet, and a pair of coarse shoes, for disguise, I applied for the place of chambermaid at the boardinghouse where Mr. Arnold has a room. I braided my hair in two long plaits, and convinced your landlady I was a recent importation from Germany, unable to speak a word of English. She agreed to take me for one week on trial, and before I had been two hours in the house I was sent to tidy Mr. Arnold's room. Never was a room tidied so quickly; and seeing my mistress on her way to market, I shot the bolt and took a survey of the premises. The trunk was locked, the bureau drawers wide open, the closet door ajar. I felt a reluctance to overhaul any private depositories; though I should have done it," she added, resolutely, "if I had been driven to it! I rummaged a little, when, on the closet door, I espied a shirt apparently scarcely soiled, except one sleeve, and that was black with soot. 'What is he doing at the fireplace in summer?' I thought, and went to examine. A few minutes sufficed to convince me that the stove had been moved out, and the elbow of the pipe removed. I repeated the process, to find a roll of five hundred dollar notes and a small notebook with the name Rufus Markham, on the first page. I replaced everything carefully and came home. Now, Mr. Potter, he must be taken by surprise, or he may say Fred put the notes there."

"You are a brave girl!" cried the old man, looking with admiration at the beautiful, animated face. "And Fred will owe you more than life."

"He can repay me by coming to tell me the good news when he is clear."

Eight was striking by the city clocks when Doctor Graham Arnold, dressed in the latest fashion, with a fragrant Havana between his lips, strolled leisurely into his own room.

He had been in the parlor of his boardinghouse for an hour, watching Mr. Potter with some anxiety, but wholly unaware of the little party of four who, in Mr. Potter's temporary apartment, awaited his return to his own room.

Once inside the door, the *nonchalant* look left the handsome face of the young man, and he muttered fiercely:

"I must get out of this! Potter suspects me, and may yet communicate his suspicions to Mr. Markham. I will be off tonight, as soon as the house is quiet."

He opened a small traveling satchel as he spoke, and was rapidly filling it with necessaries for a journey, when he was interrupted by a knock at the door.

Tossing the satchel into the closet, he cried:

"Come in!"

But his face turned livid as his call was obeyed, and a party of five entered the room.

Two policemen stationed themselves on his right and left, while Mr. Markham, Mr. Potter and Fred Tyron followed them.

"Now, Mr. Arnold," said one of the policemen, with a face and voice of the Detective Vodges, "will you tell us where to find those missing notes?"

"What notes?" cried Arnold. "What does this outrage mean?"

"It means," said Mr. Potter, "that your plan to throw the robbery of Mr. Markham's private desk upon his nephew has failed. It means that the $5,000 stolen from that gentleman is now in your possession, excepting only one note given to Mr. Tyron in payment of a debt!"

"It's a lie!" cried the prisoner; but his white face, faltering voice, and shaking limbs were no proof of innocence. "Search my trunks, everything I have."

"No, gentlemen," said Mr. Potter, "draw out the stove, if you please, and look in the elbow of the pipe."

With a cry, Graham Arnold fell senseless to the floor, as Vodges put his hand upon the stove.

Mr. Markham turned to Fred. There was no word spoken. Hand clasped hand, and each read forgiveness in the other's eyes.

Mr. Graham Arnold spent some weeks in jail ere his trial and conviction; but before his sentence was pronounced, Mr. and Mrs. Frederick Tyron were crossing the ocean on a wedding tour to Europe, and only Mr. Potter and Fred ever knew of Maud's first and only appearance as a girl detective.

—*The Allen County* [OH] *Democrat*, July 26, 1877
—*The Edwardsville* [IL] *Intelligencer*, July 4, 1877
—*Spirit Lake* [IA] *Beacon*, July 5, 1877
—*Hagerstown* [MD] *Mail*, July 13,1877
—*Sioux County* [IA] *Herald*, July 26, 1877

An Old Offender
by Capt. Charles Howard

When Carl Binkley, the private detective of the Macacheek airline company, led Courtney Tenney to the altar, he shaved his face until no hirsute appendage, save a fine blond moustache, remained thereon. This whim prevented his recognition by several acquaintances on the day of his wedding, and he and his bride enjoyed more than one outburst of merriment at their expense.

The wedding tour planned by "Bink," as the employees and officers of the road familiarly called him, promised to prove quite extensive, and the directors placed a palace car at his disposal.

But he preferred, and so did his bride, to travel like the rest of the people, and so on the afternoon of the wedding day, they stepped on board of the train amid the good-byes of a host of relatives and friends. They expected to reach their destination at one o'clock on the following morning, and for the sake of Courtney who had a horror of sleeping coaches, the bridegroom refused an offered favor from Scott, the conductor.

As the train rolled westward, the sun sank to rest, and the night stars peeped out again in the sky. It was a beautiful mid-autumn night, and the cool breeze ever and anon blew the yellow leaves against the windows of the coaches.

"Carl, what if an old offender should board the train—I mean a man for whom you have been looking?"

The detective looked down into the smiling face of his newly-made wife and smiled himself.

"Well, I don't know what I would do, Courtney," he answered; "but I suppose I would arrest him, take him to prison, and let you finish your wedding tour alone."

"How jolly that would be!" Courtney laughed. "I really wish such an event would occur. I should be rid of you at least for a time, and I'd have the jolliest wedding tour ever written of."

"I'd like to see you roughing it alone with your three trunks and groomless!" replied Carl, as the brakeman opened the door and shouted "Bloomfield" at the top of his lungs.

At the almost deserted station of the inland town the train stopped long enough to permit two men to board it, and seat themselves in the car that bore the newly wedded.

The new passengers were tolerably well dressed, and passingly good looking. They occupied one seat a short distance behind the detective, and almost directly beneath the lamp that afforded a miserable light.

A detective is constantly watching human faces, and after a while he reads them as he would an open book. Thus it was with Carl Binkley.

When the two men entered the car his eyes were turned upon them, and followed them to their seat.

By and by the conductor collected their fare, and the detective followed him from the car.

"Where are those fellows going?" he asked.

"To Terre Haute," was the reply. "Do they strike you unfavorably?"

"Moderately so," said Bink. "Send a man in to trim the lamp above them."

Then the detective returned to his bride, who thought that something strange was going on, and a minute later a brakeman entered and proceeded to trim the light in the coach.

Binkley did not appear to watch the two men; but nevertheless his eyes were upon them, and before they moved back into a shadier seat he had spotted one, if not both.

"Courtney, I am afraid your wish is about to come true," he whispered to his wife.

She looked up surprised at the solemnity of his manner.

"Why, Carl?"

"An old offender has boarded the train," he replied, "and it is my duty to attend to him. I am certain of my man, though I have not seen him for two years, and his face, smooth then, is bearded now. Jack Hawk has repeatedly committed depredations on our line, and we can send him to the penitentiary with ease. But you see Courtney, you must catch a man before you hang him, and according to this truism, Jack has escaped punishment. I must attend to him, save the company further losses, and put several hundred dollars in my pocket. He suspects nothing yet, I believe. I think he has not recognized me, and I have no doubt that his companion is an old offender, like himself."

The young wife heard her husband through, and then, with wifely fear, asked:

"Is he a dangerous character, Carl?"

"Well, yes," was the reply; "but he's one of those fellows who submit gracefully when they see great odds against them. Of course, I shan't attempt the arrest alone. I'll go forward and see the boys in the express car. Do you watch Jack while I am gone, Courtney. If he has recognized me, which is not likely, as I do not think he has seen me more than twice, he may attempt to play one of his tricks. Here," and Courtney felt a small revolver dropped into her hand. "Do not attempt to use this unless you think he is going to escape. He's up to all kinds of tricks, and I consider him the shrewdest villain outside of prison."

Courtney's hand trembled a little when she hid the weapon in her pocket, and Carl rose and carelessly left the car.

"We're booked for Jeffersonville, if he catches us," said one of the twain in the seat behind the lamp.

"We are, without fail, Jack," replied his companion. "Do you really think he knows us?"

"He's recognized me, sure, and he may have spotted you. But it's all the same thing. If he wants me he'll not let you go. Why, I knew him as soon as I set my eyes on him, and I thought he would not know me, as

I've let my beard grow. He sent that fellow in here to trim the lamps, so he could get a better view of our faces. I saw through the trick when the boy took the first lamp out of its socket. Oh, I tell you, Byrd, it's all day with us if we don't outwit that eagle-eyed chap."

"Of course it is," said the second man, doggedly. "I didn't look for him on the road tonight. And he's going on his wedding trip, I suspect."

"Just so; but that wouldn't stop him if he wanted to catch a man," said Jack Hawk. "And then he's been wanting me for the last two years. Look here! This train doesn't stop again till it runs into Terre Haute. If we're on board then, we're sure to be gobbled. He'll post the men in the express and baggage cars, and they'll proceed to cut off every avenue of escape."

"If they do, there'll be bloody work," grated Hawk's comrade. "I'm not going to be taken. It would be a twenty years' term for me."

"And a life residence at Jeffersonville for Jack Hawk," said the worthy one who boasted that name.

"We must escape," said Byrd McDonaldson. "Ring the bell and when the train slacks, we'll leave it."

"'Twouldn't do, Byrd," he said. "Scott is forward with Bink, and with the first tap of the bell we'd have the posse upon us."

"Then it's all up with us!" said the Scotchman almost ready to despair.

"No; wait here for me."

As he spoke, Jack Hawk left the seat and walked forward.

Courtney Binkley saw him pass her and leave the car by the forward door. She felt that he was up to some trick, but concluded to wait to see what it was.

She soon dismissed the thought of his leaping from the train, which, being as it was the express, was running at terrible speed, and believed that he would not desert his companion in crime.

Jack Hawk stepped upon the platform of the forward car, and drew a rope from his pocket. One end of it he fastened to the knob of the door, and the other end, after making the cord taut, he secured to the strong railing of the car. Satisfied with his work, he next drew a knife, and severed the bell rope, which he prevented from slipping into the cars.

Then he stooped over the coupling, a smile of triumph on his face.

"I can outwit the best detective on the globe," he said to himself above a whisper, and a moment later he arose, having successfully accomplished the work of separating the cars.

Then he sprang to the brake, and presently the speed of the rear coach began to diminish, while the greater part of the train, with newly acquired velocity, darted on.

He re-entered the coach, and sat down beside his partner.

"We're loose," he whispered. "The train is a mile ahead now. We are stopping. Come! Now is the time. Who says I can't beat Bink?"

The men left their seats as Courtney, who had been looking out of the window, dropped back into her seat, and put her hand on Carl's revolver.

The trick which Jack Hawk had played was apparent to her, and the two men had almost reached the rear of the car when she arose and cried:

"Stop where you are, villains! I'll kill the first man who attempts to leave this car without my orders. You two rascals will oblige me dropping into the seats where you now stand, and remaining there until promptly disposed of."

Startled by the unexpected interruption of their plans, Jack Hawk and his companion exchanged pale looks and glanced down the aisle at the little woman clad in bridal robes who pointed the deadly revolver at their breasts.

By this time the car had come to a halt, and the other passengers, comprehending the situation, were rising. Already other pistols were exhibited, and the villains saw that their game was balked.

"Let us be men," said Hawk to McDonaldson, as he dropped into a seat. "When the odds are against me I always submit. That woman would shoot at the drop of a hat. Shoot is in her eye!"

A minute later the two worthies were seated, and two "drummers" guarded them. Of course, all knew that the train would "back" when the absence of the several coaches was discovered, and, in a short time, it was announced as returning.

When the detective came into the car he kissed his brave little wife, and secured the two villains, who submitted like lambs. He acknowledged that Jack Hawk had outwitted him, but said, smilingly, that the best and bravest member of the Binkley family had proved too much for the old offender.

At Terre Haute the villains were handed over to the sheriff, and as Jack had been concerned in several murders, he received a life sentence, while his companion went to Jeffersonville for a long term.

Binkley found himself everywhere congratulated on the coolness of his wife, who still boasts, as well she may, of her capture of Jack Hawk and his criminal associate.

—*The Indiana* [PA] *Progress*, September 27, 1877

"Clubnose"
Anonymous

It was in a hospital in the east end of London that I first made the acquaintance of "Clubnose." An old college friend of mine, who was one of the resident surgeons, was showing me over the wards, and there passed us two or three times a hospital nurse, whose remarkable appearance arrested my attention. She had, I think, the most hideous and repulsive face I ever saw on man or woman. It was not that the features were naturally ugly, for it was simply impossible to tell in what semblance nature had originally molded them; but they had been so completely battered out of shape, that one would have fancied she must have been subjected to much the same treatment as the figurehead on which Daniel Quilp used to vent his impotent fury. The hero of a score of unsuccessful prizefights could not have shown worse facial disfigurement than this tidily-dressed, cleanly-looking woman.

When we had finished our tour of the wards, I turned to my friend, and pointing to the receding figure of the nurse, who had just passed us again, I said: "What a dreadful ill-looking nurse you have there! Why, it must be enough to send a patient into fits to have that face bending over him."

"O!" said he, laughing. "That's 'Clubnose.'" Then lowering his voice, he added: "She's not a nurse really—she's a detective."

"A detective!" I exclaimed. "Why, you don't mean to say that the police dog the steps of a poor wretch even in the hospital?"

"No," he replied: "I don't think she has her eye upon any of the patients—it is the friends who come to visit the patients that she watches. It is her way of doing business. Whenever there has been a crime committed in a neighborhood, she goes out as a nurse to the hospital of the district. I don't exactly know what her *modus operandi* is. She has a proper certificate as a nurse, and performs her duties like any of the rest; but it is understood that every facility for getting the information she requires is to [be] put in her way, without, of course, exciting suspicion. How she picks up her information, I don't know, but I suspect it is by listening to the talk of the patients and their friends, on visiting days. At any rate, I believe she has obtained clues under this disguise when others have failed her; and if the game wasn't worth the candle, I don't suppose she'd try it."

"Do the other nurses know her real character?"

"No. They may have their suspicions; but it is kept a secret from all but the authorities."

"Is 'Clubnose' your nickname for her, or is she generally known by that *sobriquet*?" I asked.

"No; I did not christen her so; it is the name she is known by in the force. Her real name is Margaret Saunders. She has a very queer history, I believe; but she is exceedingly reserved, and I have never had a chance of drawing her out."

And this was all I learned about "Clubnose" on that occasion.

Three or four days later two ladies with whom I was intimately connected were robbed of a considerable quantity of valuable jewelry, and I was entrusted with the investigation of the case. I had paid numberless visits to Scotland Yard, and had no end of interviews with detectives, but still there was no satisfactory clue to the identity of the thieves. One evening I was sitting alone after dinner, when the servant entered and said that "a person" wished to see me.

"Man or woman?" I asked.

"A woman, sir—says she wishes to see you in partickler, sir."

"Well, show her in," I said, inwardly wondering who the strange female might be who wanted to see me at so unreasonable an hour.

The door opened, and a respectable-looking woman wearing a thick veil was shown in. I requested her to take a seat. She did so; and as soon as the servant had retired and the door was closed, she threw back her veil and revealed the distorted features of "Clubnose."

I remembered her in an instant; indeed who that had once seen that face could ever forget it?

"You have come from Scotland Yard?" I said, interrogatively.

"Yes, sir." She answered, quietly. "I am Margaret Saunders, from the detective department."

Her voice was harsh and unpleasant; but there was a firmness and decision about her manner, and a look of intelligence and resolution in her keen gray eyes, which at once inspired confidence. The bonnet she wore concealed to a certain extent the terrible disfigurement of her face; but even then the most reckless flatterer dared not have called her physiognomy prepossessing. It was not a bad face; but one could not look at it without a shudder, so frightfully was it mutilated. The nose in particular I noticed had been knocked into a grotesquely fantastic shape, thereby giving rise to the *sobriquet* by which she was familiarly known. She had come to inform me of a very important piece of evidence which she had discovered, and which, I say at once, led ultimately to the identification and conviction of the thieves. Into the details of the case I need not enter; it was only remarkable because it introduced me personally to "Clubnose," and enabled me eventually to learn from her own lips the story of her life, which I purpose here briefly setting down.

Some five and twenty years ago a crime was perpetrated in London which was marked by such exceptional features of atrocity as to send a thrill of horror through the whole community. A middle-aged gentleman of eccentric habits was attacked in his own house, and not only beaten and left for dead, but mutilated in a peculiarly shocking manner. The miscreants also carried off a considerable quantity of valuable property. The victim of this atrocious crime, strange to say, in spite of the horrible injuries he had sustained, was not killed outright and though for weeks his life was despaired of, he eventually recovered, only, however, to be for the remainder of his days a helpless cripple.

For some time the police could find no clue to the perpetrator of this barbarous outrage; but at last suspicion was attracted to a woman who was known to have been occasionally employed about the house to do odd jobs of cleaning. A person answering her description, it was discovered, had been seen leaving the house in company with a man on the day on which the crime was committed. Some minor circumstances tended to confirm the suspicion that this woman was implicated in the affair, and she was accordingly arrested and charged before a magistrate. After one or two remands, for the purpose of obtaining further proof, the magistrate decided that there was not sufficient evidence to justify him in sending the case for trial and the accused woman was discharged. That woman was Margaret Saunders. She had all along emphatically protested her innocence, and after her discharge, she vowed that she would never rest until she had proved it by bringing the real offenders to justice. The police, baffled by the failure of their charge against herself, were compelled to confess themselves completely at fault; from them, Margaret Saunders could expect no assistance. Alone and unaided she set to work upon her self-imposed task. At the very outset, when it seemed to her that every moment was of value, she had the misfortune to fall down a flight of steps and break her leg. This necessitated her removal to the hospital, and it was as she lay there chafing at the enforced delay and inaction, that there came to her the first ray of light to guide her on her search. In the next bed to her there was a woman who was also suffering from a severe accident. On visiting day she heard this woman say in a low, anxious voice: "Is Robert safe?"

"Yes," was the reply, also in a woman's voice. "He's in Glasgow, ready to bolt, if necessary; but there'll be no need for that, the bobbies have chucked up the game, as they mostly do when they've failed to fix a charge upon the first person they spot—unless there's an extra big reward offered, which there ain't in this case."

How it was suddenly borne home to her that this "Robert" was the man she wanted, "Clubnose" told me she never could quite make out. It flashed upon her all of a minute, she said, and she never had a doubt of the correctness of the instinct that prompted her to the conviction. She lay and listened, but could catch nothing more. She got a good look, however, at the woman who was a visitor, and felt certain she should know her again anywhere. Before leaving the hospital, Margaret Saunders had scraped up a speaking acquaintance with the patient who was so anxious about "Robert," and learned enough to find out in what part of London she must look for information about the character and antecedents of the said "Robert." It was this incident, by the way, that suggested to her afterward the value of assuming the disguise of a hospital nurse.

The ingenuity with which she ferreted out the facts which eventually determined her to track "Robert" to Glasgow, was wonderful. And not less wonderful was her dogged patience. Even when she had run her quarry to earth and was convinced in her own mind that she had her hands upon the real criminal, she had to wait until she could piece the bits of evidence together, and above all, until the victim of the outrage, whose brain had been seriously affected by the injuries he had received, had sufficiently recovered his mind and memory to give some intelligible account of the attack upon him. Even when he could do so, he professed himself exceedingly doubtful of being able to recognize or identify his assailants: he knew, however, there were two of them—a man and a woman.

It was nearly eighteen months after the perpetration of the crime before the patience and perseverance of Margaret Saunders were rewarded with sufficient success to justify her in communicating with the police. The Scotland Yard officials were at first hardly inclined to credit her; but her earnestness convinced them at last that there was "something in it." Perhaps they were helped a little toward that conviction by the fact that she solemnly swore she would never finger a penny of the reward. "She had hunted this man down to clear her own character and set herself right with the world," she said, "and not a farthing of the reward would she touch." It is unnecessary to dwell upon the sequel. Suffice to say that "Robert" was arrested, that his accomplice, who was the niece of the victim's housekeeper, was subsequently taken also; that the pair were tried, convicted, and sentenced, the woman to ten years, the man to penal servitude for life.

Margaret Saunders was highly complimented by the Judge upon the sagacity and acuteness she had displayed, his Lordship observing that she was "a born detective." The press, too, was loud in her praises; and a subscription was set on foot as an expression of the public admiration for the indomitable courage, resolution, and patience, and the extraordinary astuteness which had enabled her to bring two great criminals to justice.

The journal which had suggested and started the subscription deputed a member of its staff, well known as a master of the "picturesque" style, to interview Margaret Saunders and write up a sensational article upon her. He applied to the police for her address, and an inspector from Scotland Yard volunteered to go with him—Sir Richard Mayne, the then Chief Commissioner of Police, having expressed a desire that something should be done for Margaret Saunders to show the official appreciation of her conduct. The journalist and the inspector accordingly proceeded together on their visit to the heroine. They found Margaret Saunders among very unsavory society—in one of the lowest of the filthy dens that swarm about the London docks. Not a very inviting subject for interviewing, and but a sorry heroine for a sensational article. However, they did interview her, and she soon, in language more vigorous than polite, gave them her mind upon the proposed recognition of her services. She wouldn't have anything to do with any subscription or reward—wouldn't touch a farthing.

"Look 'ere," she said, doggedly, "what I done I done for my own sake, and nobody else's. I meant rightin' o' myself, and I have righted myself. That's my business—not yours. I don't want nobody's money nor praise.

Let 'em keep that to themselves. But I'll tell you what," she added, turning sharply to the inspector. "If you mean true by all them fine compliments—"

"Most certainly we do," interposed the inspector.

"Well, then, I'll tell you what you can do to show it."

"What is that?" asked the inspector.

"Why, make me one o' yourselves. If I'm as good as you say, I might be worth something in your line. Make me one o' yourselves—a detective. That's all I ask; and if you won't do that, I don't want to have nothing more to say to ye."

It was a novel and startling proposition, and the inspector was somewhat taken aback by it; however, he faithfully promised to lay the matter before the authorities at Scotland Yard, and let her know the result; with that he and his companion left her. The end of it was that her wish was granted. Margaret Saunders was duly enrolled as a female detective, and a most active and intelligent officer she proved to be.

That is in substance the strange history of "Clubnose's" connection with the police, as she herself told it to me. I questioned her also upon her professional career; but here she was more reticent; still, I gathered that it had been marked by many exciting adventures and hairbreadth escapes from death. I learned, for example, that she owed the horrible disfigurement of her face to the polite attentions of two waterside ruffians whose lady companions she had been instrumental in consigning to the tender care of the jailer of Pentonville.

"They took it out of me werry hot," she said, in her rough, undemonstrative manner. "I reckon they thought they had done for me, but bless ye, I'm tough, and they got their seven years apiece for me—though mind ye, the Scotland Yard folks would never let on as I was one o' them. They was tried and convicted for assaltin' me as a ordinary person. The lawyers tried to make out as I was a policy spy; but they couldn't prove it. But I had to keep clear o' that district for a long while afterwards."

I was curious to know how with such a remarkable physiognomy she was not recognized in a moment wherever she went, and I put the question to her as delicately as I could. I at once found that I had touched her hobby. If there was one thing that she prided herself upon more than another it was her power of disguising herself; and indeed I afterward learned from one of the inspectors that she had good reason for being proud of this accomplishment, for there was no one in the force who could compete with her in the cleverness and variety of her disguises. Twice, however, she admitted that her disguise had been penetrated, and on each occasion she nearly paid the penalty with her life.

On the first occasion, she was pitched out the window and had her leg broken. On the second—which happened not more than a year before my first introduction to her in her professional capacity—she had what she herself called "a precious narrow shave o' bein' sent to kingdom come out-right." She had been for weeks on the trail of a very clever gang of thieves, and had actually been admitted a member of the fraternity, and wormed herself into their secrets, so perfect and artistic was her disguise.

On a certain evening it was agreed that the police were to swoop down upon the gang, acting on "information received" from "Clubnose." On this evening it unfortunately happened that there was present for the first time an old member of the gang who had just got his ticket-of-leave. Whether "Clubnose," through overconfidence in the perfection of her disguise, committed some indiscretion or not, she could not tell; but at any rate in some way the suspicions of the returned convict were roused. He communicated them privately to some of his "pals"—a rush was made at "Clubnose"; she was overpowered, stripped of her disguise, and then "welted," to use her expression, about the head and body with pokers, bars, legs of chairs, and any other available weapon, until she was left "a mass o' jelly." She contrived, however, before they knocked her senseless, to break the window and sound the whistle she carried. The police burst in, too late to save her from the vengeance of the thieves, but in time to make an important capture. They found "Clubnose" with her skull fractured, and with hardly a whole bone in her skin. The injuries to her skull were so severe as to necessitate the operation of trepanning, which was successfully performed; but she said, she had never been herself since, and was constantly troubled with terrible pains in the head.

"Ay," she added, with the rude kind of philosophy which was a curious trait of her character, "that was a gallus bad job, that was. They nigh done for me; but it might ha' been worse. Supposin' now, they'd ha' smashed me up afore I spotted their little game, eh? That would ha' been somethin' to grumble at."

It was a worse "job" for poor "Clubnose" than she imagined. Within six months after my last interview with her she was dead; the cause of her death being an abscess in the brain, produced by the frightful injuries to her head on the occasion when "they nigh done" for her. She must have been missed in the force; for she was—as the Judge described her at the trial which first brought her remarkable qualities into prominence—"a born detective"; and it will be long before the police of this or any other country obtain the services of a woman possessed of the nerve, the astuteness, and the dogged resolution of "Clubnose."—*Chambers' Journal*

—*The Ohio Democrat*, April 29, 1880
—*The Janesville* [WI] *Daily Gazette*, October 16, 1880
—*The Burlington* [IA] *Weekly Hawk Eye*, March 25, 1880

6

Have You Heard the
One about the Detective?

One of the most significant changes to the crime story that occurred in the mid-nineteenth century was the growing capacity for writers and readers to occasionally take its subject matter and its participants both less seriously and less than seriously. Discounting picaresque stories about likeable rogues, most fiction about crime before the mid-eighteen hundreds was mordantly serious, associating crime with sin and identifying detection with making manifest the will of God. Poe moved the detective story into the world of play: it is worth noting that in Poe's Dupin stories no one is actually punished, and the most prominent loser isn't the doer of the crimes but the hapless Prefect of Police. After Poe, other, less-talented nineteenth-century writers also moved the detective story out of the old world of sin and punishment; they did it principally by focusing on the detective as a problem solver, a problem solver who is either a free agent or an agent of the state. What breaking the connection of the crime story with the moral exemplum means is that forward-looking detective story writers of the mid-nineteenth century could choose either to explore crime solving as an illustration of community service and intellectual prowess— as many of them did—or they could choose to see it as an opportunity to relate an amusing instance of ironic circumstance or folly—and that folly could be individual or it could be corporate—since detectives had become part of the governing apparatus of a state with a free press. Many of those who chose the latter path reduced the detective story from a brief short story to an anecdote—or a joke, something implicit in Poe's stories, too. And this, like the detective story itself, fit the needs of contemporary newspapers which often ran columns of jokes and frequently used bizarre or amusing pieces as filler. For narrative devices these detective anecdotes employed the technology of comedy—turning things upside down and springing surprises—versus the sentimental machinery of the sensation story or the other narrative options such as the adventure story, puzzle story etc., that were appearing toward the close of the century.

One of the first things that humorists did was change the nature of the crime story's elemental contest. Traditionally crime stories were contests between good and evil in which good triumphs and evil, once exposed, pretty much just dries up and disappears on its own. Readers knew who was good and who was bad—because bad people were unattractive and anti-social. Poe changed this by making what happens in the narrative into a game: he's quite clear about this in the first section of "Murders in the Rue Morgue." Poe's stories do not focus on the traditional contest between good and evil, but on the match between the detective and the facts, in addition to the one between two detectives. Nineteenth-century wits were quick to pick up on this change. As a result, some of the pieces below bring back the *picaro*, and delight in showing a rogue who is more clever than the detectives—or the narrators. Others center on plots that depend on one-upping the nominal detective hero, not by a rascal but by a newspaper reporter who knows the business better than the boys from headquarters.

In addition to the comic redefinition of the crime story's basic contest, a number of humorists understood Poe's other uses of inversion—of overturning readers' expectations. Thus we find stories appearing that end with something other than naming and catching a criminal and stories that turn out not to be about crimes at all. This technique is fundamental to Poe's surprise ending in "Murder in the Rue Morgue" where the answer to the "who did it" question is "the monkey did it." "The Gramercy Park Mystery," in this chapter, tells an inversion story like Poe's and even has a monkey, but leaves out the gory and gothic accoutrements. And following Poe's motif of surprise coming from finding things where they belong, in "Blown Upon" the comic inversion takes place when the book-keeper of Doowell and Squeelknot finds the "stolen" $15.01 not in the pockets of the usual suspects the police assemble but in the same place where Dupin finds the purloined letter—where it's supposed to be.

And then there's satire. On the personal level, a lot of contemporary writers cast ridicule on detectives' dependence on disguise. But larger social issues occasionally became the object of writers' barbs—the most obvious case in point here being Mark Twain's first excursion into the world of detectives. What got him worked up was reward splitting: until late in the nineteenth century rewards were not offered for the apprehension of criminals but for the return of stolen property, and this, in turn, led unscrupulous detectives to bargain with thieves for the return of stolen goods and into splitting the reward with them. In "Making a Fortune" this became the target of Twain's first look at the faults and foibles of law enforcement and a precursor to his later "The Stolen White Elephant" (1882), *Tom Sawyer Detective* (1896), the Sherlock Holmes pastiche "A Double-Barreled Detective Story" (1902), and perhaps even *Pudd'nhead Wilson* (1894).

The Gramercy Park Mystery
Anonymous

Toward the end of last autumn, Gramercy Park—which, as everybody knows, is one of the most charming localities in the city—has been oppressed with a mystery which no one could fathom. The most daring and inexplicable robberies were constantly taking place. Consternation reigned in the servant's hall. Rings, spoons, brooches, shawl-pins, in short every species of valuables were being daily missed from a number of houses in the Park. No one could tell how they went. Married ladies mourned over their diamonds. Demoiselles wept for lost pledges of affection. The services of a distinguished detective were called in. He watched, examined, catechised the servants, and put on spectacles and false whiskers, but all to no purpose. Intelligence officers reaped a harvest, for everybody was discharging their servants and getting new ones.—One wealthy family had suffered such severe losses that they had almost come to the resolution of doing their own chores. Gramercy Park—usually so tranquil—was in a high state of fever. The very sidewalks could have baked Connecticut pies.

One of the servant sufferers among the many victims was Mrs. Y—, a lady who inhabited one of the handsomest houses in the Park, and who was rather distinguished in society from the fact of her being always accompanied by a very beautiful and intelligent monkey. Other people carried lap dogs—she carried a monkey; and, as to be uncommon is, in nine cases out of ten, to be famous, she had an unblemished reputation for eccentricity. Her distinction did not, however, preserve her from the general calamity. She related, with tears in her eyes, the story of the loss of some family jewels of inestimable value which were stolen from her bedroom. She had the police on the track, but no clue could be obtained to the criminal. The mystery increased in intensity. Barrington and Jack Sheppard faded in significance before the ingenuity of this unknown burglar.

Among the residents of Gramercy Park is a Mr. B—, a middle-aged gentleman, who, having had a long career of success in business, committed some time since the unpardonable folly of marrying a young and pretty wife. As a matter of course, he was jealous. When a man who has gathered all his experiences up to the age when experience ceases to be gathered, as a bachelor, he usually lays it, as a sort of holocaust, on the altar when he marries, and Hymen with his torch soon renders it a complete burnt offering. Mr. B—, therefore, being no longer a sensible man, suspected Mrs. B—; and as Dimes very justly observed the other day, "the man who suspects his wife, converts the sacred gold of the wedding ring into Mosaic metal." Dimes, you will perceive, is sometimes metaphorical.

Well, Mr. B— enters, one fine evening when the windows are open to catch the last sigh of the dying autumn, the apartment sacred to Mrs. B—. Horror! He beholds the dimly-lit figure of a man leap through the open window, and descend by some means unknown to him into the street. He rushes to the casement, but the fiend in human shape has fled. Fortunately, however, he finds that his wife is not there. The next morning, Mrs. B— complains of having missed a diamond ring from her room. The servants' hall is in a turmoil and investigations are instituted. But Mr. B— grinds his teeth, and smiles sardonically, for *he* knows that this is all a blind, to cover the fact of his wife having given said ring to her lover. He lays his plans. The next night, revolver in hand, he watches in his bedroom. The — comes not. But B— is patient. He watches the next night with the same result. On the third night, as the chamber is wrapped in the dusk of twilight, a form appears climbing through the window. B—'s heart almost ceases to beat. He waits. The shape enters; it is that of a very small man, almost a boy. B— raises his revolver, and taking deliberate aim, fires. The intruder staggers, gives one dull moan, and leaping to the window escapes by the same mysterious means as before.—But B— is not to be baffled. Quick as lightening he rushes downstairs into the street, and is just in time to see a dwarfish form flittering along the railings next [to] the Park. He follows. The shape reels along as if mortally wounded, and after a brief chase enters a window on the ground floor of Mrs. Y—'s house. B—, whose curiosity by this time has almost stifled his jealousy, follows. Still led by the dwarfish form, he finds himself on the second story, and beholds his involuntary guide enter a room illuminated by subdued light. He peeps through the half-open door, and beholds a spectacle that transfixes him with astonishment. Mrs. Y— is bending over the form of her pet monkey, who presses one hand on his breast, from which thick drops of blood ooze through his fingers. He moans dolefully, and his mistress seems in the greatest distress. At last, by a supreme effort, the wounded animal drags himself across the carpet to a Japanese casket, opens the lid, and drops into it something that flashes in the lamplight, and then with its great eyes fixed on his mistress with one long look of affection, expires. B— can no longer contain himself. He bursts into the room, and at his appearance, Mrs. Y— turns pale as death. By an irresistible impulse, B— approaches the Japanese casket, and there, almost on the top of a heap of every species of bijouterie, he beholds his wife's lost ring!

An explanation is scarcely needed. Mrs. Y—, it seems, had, by continually placing valuable articles in this casket in the presence of her monkey, so far cultivated his imitative faculty as to induce him to appropriate everything of a similar nature that he saw, and conceal it in the same place.—Accordingly, the lady was accustomed to turn her pet loose in the summer evenings when the windows of neighboring houses were open, and after a short absence he invariably returned laden with precious things which were always deposited in the Japanese casket.

So the mystery was solved. Jocko lost his life. B— was cured of his jealousy. Mrs.—returned the spoil which she had accumulated under an attack of moral insanity. The detective officer took off his false whiskers, and the servant's hall resumed its tranquility. Could any comedy that was not true end more satisfactorily than this anecdote, which is?—*Harper's Weekly*

—*The* [Madison, WI] *Weekly Argus and Democrat*, February 17, 1857

Making a Fortune
by Mark Twain

Samuel McF— was a watchman in a bank. He was poor but honest, and his life was without reproach. The trouble with him was that he felt that he was not appreciated. His salary was only four dollars a week, and when he asked to have it raised the President, the Cashier, and the Board of Directors glared at him through their spectacles, and frowned on him, and told him to go out and stop his insolence; when he knew business was dull and the bank could not meet its expenses now, let alone lavish one dollar a week on such a miserable worm as Samuel McF—. And then Samuel McF— felt depressed and sad, and the haughty scorn of the President and Cashier cut him to the soul. He would often go out to the side yard and bow his venerable twenty-four inch head, and weep gallons of tears over his insignificance, and pray that he might be made worthy of the Cashier's and President's polite attention.

One night a happy thought struck him; a gleam of light burst upon his soul, and gazing down the dim vista of years with his eyes all blinded with joyous tears he saw himself rich, honored and respected. So Samuel McF— fooled around and got a jimmy, a monkey wrench, a crosscut saw, a cold chisel, a drill, and about half a ton of gunpowder and nitroglycerin, and all those things. Then in the dead of the night he went to the fireproof safe, and, after working at it for a while, burst the door and brick into an immortal smash with such perfect success that there was not enough of that safe left to make a carpet tack. McF— then proceeded to load up with coupons, greenbacks, currency, and specie, and to nail all the odd change that was lying anywhere, so that he pranced out of the bank with over one million dollars on him. He then retired to an unassuming residence out of town, and sent word to the detectives where he was.

A detective called on him one day with a soothing note from the Cashier. Mr. McF— treated it with lofty scorn. Detectives called on him every day with humble notes from the President, Cashier and Board of Directors. At last the bank officers got up a magnificent supper, to which McF— was invited. He came, and as the bank officers bowed down to the dust before him, he pondered over the bitter past, and his soul was filled with wild exultation. Before he drove away in his carriage that night it was all fixed that McF— was to keep half a million of the money and to be unmolested if he returned the other half. He fulfilled his contract like an honest man, but refused with haughty disdain, the offer of the Cashier to marry his daughter.

Mac is now honored and respected.—He moves in the best society, he browses around in purple and fine linen and other good clothes, and enjoys himself first-rate. And often now he takes his infant son on his knee and tells him of his early life, and instills holy principles into the child's mind, and shows him how, by industry and perseverance, frugality and nitroglycerin, monkey wrenches, crosscut saws and familiarity with the detective system, even the poor may rise to affluence and respectability.

—*The Indiana* [PA] *Democrat*, November 2, 1871

A Detective's Story
Anonymous

There is a story told of a lady and gentleman traveling together on an English railroad. They were strangers to each other. Suddenly the gentleman said:

"Madam, I will trouble you to look out of the window for a few minutes; I am going to make some changes in my wearing apparel."

"Certainly, sir," she replied with great politeness, rising and turning her back upon him. In a short time he said:

"Now, madam, my change is completed, and you may resume your seat."

When the lady turned she beheld her male companion transformed into a dashing lady with a heavy veil over her face.

"Now, sir, or madam, whichever you are," said the lady, "I must trouble you to look out of the window, for I also have some changes to make in my apparel."

"Certainly madam," and the gentleman in lady's attire immediately complied.

"Now, sir, you may resume your seat."

To his great surprise, on resuming his seat the gentleman in female attire found his lady companion transformed into a man. He laughed and said:

"It appears that we are both anxious to escape recognition. What have you done? I have robbed a bank."

"And I," said the whilom lady, as he dexterously fettered his companion's wrist with a pair of handcuffs, "I am Detective J—, of Scotland Yard, and in female apparel have shadowed you for two days—Now," drawing a revolver, "keep still."

—*The Fort Wayne* [IN] *Sentinel,* December 8, 1880
—*Indiana Weekly* [PA] *Messenger,* September 15, 1880
—*Racine* [WI] *Daily Argus,* October 11, 1880
—Published as "A Detective's Ruse" in the *Chester* [PA] *Daily Times* on August 8, 1880
—Published as "A Good Detective Story" in the *Manitoba* [Canada] *Daily Free Press* on August 28, 1880
—Published as "Trapped" in the *Palo Alto* [Emmetsburg, IA] *Reporter* on January 22, 1881

The Detective
Anonymous

About two years ago Mr. Azariah Boody of Newark, N.J., an enormously rich retired plumber, on returning from Rome where he had been to select a really good cash article of title for himself, was astonished to find the front door of his splendid residence standing open, although he had closed it securely upon his departure. Proceeding further, he at once perceived by the empty wine bottles and costly viands scattered over the magnificent satin furniture, that the house had been burglarized in his absence. (It seems strange that burglars should always scatter costly viands about when they rob a place, but according to the papers, they will do it.) A ponderous hair trunk, in which he kept his valuables, had been opened, and a set of shirt studs and a million dollar package of four percents removed. It was impossible to tell when the robbery had occurred, but the excited millionaire at once started for the office of the "Prefect of Police," as they say in all the French plays.

On the steps of the office he encountered a keen-looking man, with the eagle nose and hawk eye peculiar to detectives, who inquired if he wished to see the chief.

"Immediately!" said the millionaire.

"He is in New York," replied the man on the steps; "but if it is anything of importance I will attend to it in his place."

"I have been robbed," said the victim.

"I knew it," replied the police *attaché*, with the true promptness of the profession. "Let us at once to the spot."

The plumber led the way to the house.

"I trust nothing has been moved since the crime was discovered," said the detective, as they entered the house.

"Absolutely nothing," said the old gentleman, who had read Gaboriau's "M. Lecocq" four times.

"Because," said the detective, "much depends upon careful study of the surroundings," and he again began his investigations by measuring a square inch of the dust-covered lid of the trunk.

He then produced a small pair of scales, and scraping off the inch of dust referred to, carefully weighed the same.

"Let me see," he muttered, making a calculation; "dust settles at the rate of 948-1000ths of an inch per hour. It is therefore certain that the burglary was committed last Thursday, at quarter past 1 A.M."

"Dear me," said the old gentleman; "how wonderful."

The detective now approached the remains of the robbers' repast. "There were three robbers," he said.

"Yes; but here are four glasses used," exclaimed the old gentleman.

"The fourth was merely used to pour the corky top from the bottles," explained the detective, who gave his name as Kickshaw. "One of them was a powerful man of advanced age. See, this bitter cracker wears the marks of six decayed teeth. The second one was a dandy with a long moustache, for you can perceive here he has repeatedly wiped it on this napkin. The third burglar was unmistakably a woman."

"A woman?" gasped the houseowner.

"Precisely. You see she has eaten noting save pickles, and the icing from this cake. In her nervousness she has upset the salt and spilled her wine on the cloth. It was her first affair of the kind."

"Yes, I see," said old Boody, much interested.

"And a pretty woman as well," went on the detective. "You noticed she has brushed the dust from every mirror in the room to look at herself. Next we find that they divided the plunder on the spot. Look! Were not these broken tapes the ones with which your bond-package was tied?"

"They are."

"During the division they quarreled."

"But how do you know that?" said Boody.

"By the overturned chair. Besides, the piano is open and marks of fingers are on the bass keys. Women always sit down and thump on that end of the piano when angry."

"Even when burgling?" said the old party.

"At all times," replied Kickshaw. "It makes no difference whatever. The woman has red hair."

"Had. Eh?"

"Yes—she threw that book in the corner at the old man and made his nose bleed. See this towel stained with blood? No one but a red-haired woman would have done that."

"How do you know it was the old man's nose?"

"Because," replied the detective, using a microscope, "the blood globules are those of an elderly person."

"I suppose they did not remain hereabouts long?" queried the plumber.

"No; they left the next morning for Chicago."

"Great Heavens, what do you mean?" said the old party. "Are you a magician?"

"It is very simple," replied the human "sleuthhound." "On this crumpled scrap of paper you will see some figures. Of course the thieves could not realize on the bonds at once. They, therefore, made a computation to discover how far their immediate cash would take them. Chicago was the result, as the total arrived at is the fare to that city multiplied by three."

"I see—I see," said the plumber.

"I start for Chicago on the next train," continued the thief taker. "Let me see—perhaps you had better let me have five hundred dollars for expenses."

The other instantly passed over the amount.

"Remember," said the detective as he departed, "not a word of what we have discovered. Keep perfectly quiet until you hear from me."

And to this day the defrauded plumber is sitting on his front steps waiting for news from the detective, who, as the high foreheaded reader has already guessed, was the robber himself.

This beautiful and touching episode is to be dramatized for the Adelphi this evening, after office hours.

—*The* [Albert Lea, MN] *Standard*, November 8, 1881
—*The Freeborn County* [MN] *Standard*, November 8, 1881
—*The Stevens Point* [WI] *Journal*, July 21, 1883 (This version credits the *Chicago Tribune* as its source.)

Blown Upon: or The Sagacious Reporter
Anonymous

A Detective Story

A mysterious robbery had been committed, and, for the first time, the police were completely baffled. In broad daylight—for there was no elevated railway structure nor any sky-scraping pile in front of or opposite to the old-fashioned building—the bookkeeper of the firm of Doowell and Squeelknot suddenly missed $15.01 which he had just counted over, while $143.75 which was near his elbow was undisturbed. He could offer no explanation of the disappearance of so small an amount of money when much more was easily accessible. The only conclusion that could be arrived at was that the bookkeeper had been robbed; and the robbery, as has been said, was a mysterious one. The bookkeeper was above suspicion, for his salary was $10 a week.

"Tell me all that you can remember about the robbery," said the Inspector of Police to the bookkeeper.

"I was sitting at my desk, posting up the ledger," said the bookkeeper, "and I opened a drawer to take out a sheet of blottingpaper. As I leaned over, I felt a strong draught on the top of the head—you will observe that I am very bald—and I looked up and saw a man entering the door. I had hardly caught sight of him when my brain reeled and I became unconscious. When I recovered I found myself lying with my head on the desk, and $15.01 were missing. The man seemed to be one of those Polish emigrants who sell three collar buttons for five cents and a pair of suspenders for a quarter of a dollar. I don't remember that he approached my window."

The next day, several persons of Polish appearance who sold three collar buttons for five cents, and a pair of suspenders for a quarter of a dollar, were arrested; but all of them were discharged for lack of evidence, as none of them had $15.01 on his person.

"It is too thin," finally said the Inspector of Police. "How can a man have a cut on his chin if he's struck with a stuffed club on the top of the head?"

"He's bald-headed," said a detective sergeant, who was with the Inspector in the office of the firm.

"Then he had no hair to strike through," said the Inspector.

While the two police officers were consulting as to the advisability of obtaining a photograph resembling a Polish peddler of collar buttons and suspenders, and sending it throughout the country with the offer of $25 reward for information that would lead to the arrest and conviction of the robber, and no questions asked, a reporter of a morning paper entered as usual.

"Phew!" he exclaimed, as the door banged behind him. "What a draught. What's new, Inspector?"

"There are no new developments in the robbery case today," answered the Inspector.

"But we have a clue," said the detective sergeant.

"To tell what it is would defeat the ends of justice," said the Inspector.

"Lemme see the bookkeeper," said the reporter. "I'd like to interview him."

"He's at his desk," said the Inspector and the sergeant, spitting stiffly over their celluloid collars.

But the bookkeeper was not at his desk. In a moment, however, there was a groan, then a faint cry, and, the bookkeeper was seen staggering to his feet, his face pale, but his bald head glowing.

"The robber! The robber!" exclaimed the bookkeeper.

The Inspector and the sergeant were immediately on the alert, and surrounded the reporter, who calmly asked:

"How much money have you lost this time?" The bookkeeper counted his cash and said he had lost nothing.

"Have you had occasion to use a fresh sheet of blotting paper since you were robbed?" asked the reporter.

The bookkeeper confessed that he had not, as business was dull.

"Then look into the drawer now," said the reporter.

The bookkeeper did so, and found there $15 in bills of different denominations, but the odd cent was not to be found.

"Well, I declare!" he exclaimed.

"You see," said the reporter, "that peddler started to come in, and he saw the sign on the door, 'No Peddlers Admitted,' and he backed out, and the draught from the storm doors knocked out the bookkeeper and he struck his chin against the blotting paper drawer in falling, and closed it, and he hasn't looked in it since, and there's your robbery, and your cut on the chin, and your missing $15 that was blown into the drawer and there's your clue."

The Inspector reported that through the energy of the police the greater part of the stolen property had been recovered; and the bookkeeper's employers announced that they had always had the greatest confidence in him, and that they would cheerfully make up the amount of money still missing.

—*Life*, February 15, 1883

A Detective's Story
by H.B.S.

McNab was a detective and the shrewdest of his race.
No rival wight possessed his skill in working up a case.
A crime that baffled the police to him was merely fun,
He often knew the criminal before the crime was done.

Whenever any personage so far forgot himself
And had such vulgar manners as to kill a man for pelf,
They always called McNab, the most sagacious of his breed,
To ascertain the gentleman who did the bloody deed.

So, when a man concocted a most clever plan to steal
By adding strychnine to a fellow-creature's frugal meal,
They called McNab and said: "Go find this erring person, do;
He is a man of middle age, whose optics both are blue."

McNab replied: "With such a clew to find him I'll engage.
If he is, as you say, a blue-eyed man of middle age.
His azure orbs and middle age will be the damning facts
By which I'll bring the gentleman to answer for his acts."

The parson of the parish was a man of most pronounced
Blue eyes and middle age; so on him our detective pounced.
"Ha, ha!" he cried, with proper pride, "the wretched culprit scan!
Behold his eyes—his middle age!" But he was not the man.

McNab, of course, apologized; then, going to the street,
The Bishop—middle-aged—he chanced by accident to meet.
"Those eyes!" cried he, and straightway for the portly Bishop ran,
And brought him into court in chains; but *he* was not the man.

He shadowed next an infant who had optics Prussian blue
And was as middle aged as one could find a child of two.
With circumstantial evidence convincing he began—
The infant proved an alibi; so *it* was not the man.

"Aha!" said he, "I know a maid with eyes ultra marine;
Such striking middle-age, methinks, I ne'er before have seen."
He drove the spinster through the streets within the prison van;
She proved her eyes were gray, and so *she* could not be the man.

At last one day while gazing in the mirror he observed
His own blue eyes and middle age, and he became unnerved.
He said: "Such damning evidence 'twere useless to dispute
And I must be the man, or, maybe I should say, 'the brute.'"

And then he put the handcuffs on his unaccustomed wrists,
And on the law's severest kind of penalty insists.
His reputation thus he saved; his conscience, too, was eased;
They hanged him, as he wished them to, and Justice then was appeased.
—H.B.S. in *Rambler*

—*Chicago Daily Tribune*, February 15, 1886

A Detective's Story
Anonymous

An officer in a reminiscent mood writes to the *Cincinnati Enquirer* the following: You are aware that people who indulge their appetites to excess for strong drink, and who garner the excitement of the gaming table, are apt to form unreasonable and highly erroneous impressions even regarding their best friends. It happened that my young hero, whose name was John O'Brown, obtained the idea that I had something to do with his adoption of the life of a gambler. He imagined that his family had disowned him therefore and that his intended wife had married another man because of his dissolute habits. One evening as I was sitting in my room congratulating myself upon having lived a useful and ornamental life, and planning how I could perform several acts of benevolence without being detected, the door suddenly flew open with a crash in obedience to the mandate of an enthusiastic and industrious foot, and, to my consternation, there stood before me, attired in bloodshot eyes, nobody but John O'Brown.

He held a double-action revolver of uncomfortable caliber in one hand and a Chinese Laundry ticket in the other.

"'I have come to kill you!' he exclaimed, as he stood in front of me rocking to and fro from the effects of a debauch that must have lasted about eight days. As he swayed to and fro like a cobra de capello preparing to strike, his eyes leered at me in a most suggestive way, and I saw that I must act quickly or not at all.

"'I am going to shoot you dead in one minute,' he went on to state, and he began to steady himself to take aim at me. It was a dread moment for me. I had no weapon, and if I had one I could not have brought it to bear upon my young friend ere he had filled me full of holes. All at once I remembered John's penchant for gambling. I concluded to try an experiment that I felt sure would succeed. In fact, so certain was I of the success of my proposed scheme that I regained my composure and was in an instant as cool as ever I was in my life. Said I to John O'Brown:

"'You say you are going to shoot me, John?'

"'That's what I said.'

"'Then, I'll bet you $100 to $10 that you don't shoot me,' said I.

"'I'll go you,' he replied.

"'Put up,' said I.

"'All right,' said he.

"'Let's go and get somebody to hold the stakes,' said I.

"'Come on,' said he.

"He fell into the trap. The odds caught him, and his passion for gambling saved my life, for when we found the men I wanted to hold the stakes they disarmed John and persuaded him to desist."

—*Los Angeles Times*, March 26, 1887

After a Clew
Anonymous

Methods of the Modern Detective Illustrated by a Small Incident

"I'll follow him to the ends of the earth! He shall not escape me!"
The tall, powerfully-built man, attired in a suit of dark blue,

who hissed these words through his set teeth, stood in the shadow of a one-story coal house in a dark, noisome, Philadelphia-like alley, and watched with widely staring eyes a figure moving slowly along down the Hong Kong district of Clark Street.

The watcher was wide awake, and the saloons had not yet closed for the night.

It was evident he was not a policeman.

Emerging from the alley he followed stealthily the object of his pursuit like a sleuthhound on track of its prey. Moving along in the shadow of the buildings and halting now and then, but never relaxing for one instant his eager watchfulness, he kept his man in sight for nearly an hour.

Down Clark Street to Harrison, west on Harrison to the river, across the bridge to Canal, up Canal to Monroe, and westward on that street for many and many a weary block moved this singular—or rather plural—procession.

"He little thinks he is followed," muttered the relentless pursuer. "I'll shadow him to his lair now if it takes till the next centennial!"

At last the man whom he was following halted at a modest dwelling, opened the gate that afforded entrance to the little yard in front, and as he turned to close it his face, plainly visible in the glare of a street lamp close by, was for one brief moment exposed to the hawk-like gaze of the mysterious pursuer in the dark blue suit, who had crouched in the shadow of a friendly Indian cigar sign across the way. The next instant he had disappeared within the house.

With a smothered cry of exultation the eager watcher took out a notebook and pencil and jotted down a memorandum. His fingers trembled with excitement.

"I saw his face!" he said in a hysterical whisper. "I was not mistaken. And now I have his street and number. At last I am on the trail. If he finds out anything about that mysterious disappearance, I'll know just where he goes to get it. Ha! At last! At last!"

He was a high-priced detective shadowing a $15-a-week newspaper reporter to see if he could find some clew to the latest mystery that was baffling the entire force.—*Detroit Free Press*.

—*Marion* [OH] *Star*, May 24, 1889

The Detective from Baltimore
Anonymous

How an Astute Traveler Helped Him Along

I was approaching Washington in the night from Philadelphia, and should have been entirely alone in the smoking car but for a man who got on at Baltimore. He had a bundle as baggage, and he sat down three seats ahead of me and smoked away without a word for twenty miles. Then he turned and asked

"Ever do any detective work?"

"No."

"It's very romantic and exciting. Let me introduce myself as Detective Wadsworth of the Baltimore police."

We shook hands. I gave him my name, and after some general talk he said:

"I hope to catch a crook at the depot in Washington who knows me well by sight. I have to disguise myself to nab him."

He undid the package and took from it a wig, a necktie, and a coat and vest, and from a pocket he drew a pair of blue spectacles. He made the change in three or four minutes, and I had to compliment him on the transformation. I should never have known him to be the same man.

"It's a part of our profession, you know," he explained. "I want you to render me a service when we enter the depot. Go to the back end of the train and work forward. If you meet a fat man wearing a check suit and stovepipe hat whistle so, and I will be there in three seconds."

I agreed to follow his instructions, and I kept my promise. I saw no fat man, however. Neither did I again see my Baltimore detective. I went to a hotel and went to bed, but was aroused from sleep an hour later by a Washington detective, who compared my face with a photograph, and growled:

"Dash it you ain't the man, after all!"

"Who are you looking for?"

"A bad man from Baltimore, who gave us the slip at the depot."

"Describe him."

When he had done so I replied:

"Why that man rode with me in the smoker, and he was a detective. He disguised himself to catch someone here at the depot."

"The dickens he did! And he got you out of the way like the idiot you are! Hang it, man, you had better go and soak your head! Here—I put you under arrest! Come along to the station!"

But they didn't keep me long, and a month later when I ran across the bad man from Baltimore in the city hall in Philadelphia I just exchanged winks with him and passed on. —*New York Sun*

—*The* [Decatur, IL] *Review*, December 6, 1890

7

Finding the
First Anthology

Anthologies lend an air of permanence and legitimacy if not to their contents, then to the subject or genre they represent. So the appearance of an anthology of detective stories should have been a significant event. And it was, but it followed a twisted path.

Detective stories almost made it into the realm of the anthology from the very beginning with William Russell's collected stories in *The Recollections of a Policeman* (1852) and then with the anonymous, neo–Newgate collection of stories titled *Remarkable Convictions* (1865) which presented law cases written up by various hands "intended to demonstrate the effect of circumstantial evidence and to shew how often facts of an apparently trivial nature and wholly unexpected turn up bringing home guilt to an accused party even in the face of an able an ingenious defence [*sic*]." But, although largely fiction and written by various hands, both collections were passed off as detective fact and not detective fiction.

If not into their own anthologies, by the 1870s detective stories began to make their way into anthologies of miscellaneous fiction. There was *The Chamber of Mystery and Other Tales* (1870), a collection of stories originally published in *Chambers' Journal* which included "The Curious Case of Circumstantial Evidence" and three other stories about Russell's officer Waters. Chambers also published twelve volumes of compilations under the series title *Tales from Chambers' Journal*, which reprinted stories involving murder, forgery, theft, bank fraud, highway robbery, and a prison break along with other kinds of fiction. Other miscellaneous anthologies published in Britain that contained detective fiction included *In Australian Wilds, and Other Colonial Tales and Sketches* (1889) and *Strange Doings in*

*Strange Place*s (1890). In 1891 Cassell published *Eleven Possible Cases* featuring stories by Americans Franklin Fyles, Frank R. Stockton, Joaquin Miller, Henry Harland, Maurice Thompson, Ingersoll Lockwood, Edgar Fawcett, Brainard Gardner Smith, Kirke Munroe, Andrew C. Wheeler, and Anna Katharine Green. Occasionally misidentified as a collection of "Detective and Mystery Stories," only "The Girl at the Overlook" by Fyles and "Shall He Marry Her?" by Green barely fall into that category; the rest present a miscellany of gothic, fantastic, comic, and science fiction entertainments. In America, *Suppressed Sensations or Leaves from the Note Book of a Chicago Reporter* (1882) contains several detective pieces, including "A Mysterious Murder" and "The Tell-Tale Skull." In the mid–1880s numerous newspapers advertised the collection "*Sixteen Complete Stories by Popular Authors* embracing love, humorous and detective stories, stories of society life, of adventure, of railway life, etc., all very interesting." And advertisements can also be found in contemporary papers for *Famous Detective Stories: A Collection of Thrilling Narratives of Detective Experience* (1886), but *Famous Stories* is only a sixteen-page magazine-format publication, volume 1, number 117 of the Leisure Hour Library. The most important of the American miscellanies with a detective story connection was Leopold Davis' *Strange Occurrences* (1877), a collection mostly of gothic tales, but containing three detective stories, including the significant piece "A Detective's Story." The first complete American anthology of detective fiction was the 1896 Excelsior House *42 Famous Stories of Detective Adventure*, a 104-page compilation of detective stories drawn from nineteenth-century newspapers, including "The Tell-Tale Key" included in Chapter 5 of this book.

Chapman and Hall published the first real anthology of detective fiction, *The Long Arm and Other Detective Stories* in 1895 containing stories by Mary E. Wilkins [Freeman], George Ira Brett, Roy Tellet, and Brander Matthews. Significantly, while published in Britain two years after the appearance of Sherlock Holmes' "The Final Problem," three of the four writers included in *The Long Arm* were celebrated American authors. Identified by Ellery Queen as "the first legitimate detective story anthology," there was a lot about *The Long Arm* that was scarcely "legitimate." In 1894 the Bacheller syndicate ran what would become the most famous (or infamous) detective story contest of the age: it had an exorbitant prize, it was patently unfair, and today Bacheller would have wound up in court answering charges brought by both the winners and losers. Bacheller's contest offered writers an unheard of prize of $2,000 for the best detective story of from 6,000–12,000 words, and a second prize of $500. Typical prizes of the time were more like those offered by McClure for contests for "Stories of Adventure" or "Dialect Stories" where entrants got $75 for the winning story and $50 for the runner-up. The winning story was "The Long Arm," written by Mary E. Wilkins Freeman (then writing under her birth name, Mary E. Wilkins) in collaboration with Joseph Edgar Chamberlin; "The Twinkling of an Eye" by Brander Matthews won second prize, and purportedly "The Secret of the Treaty" by Roy Tellet (Rev. Albert Eubule Evans) came in third. While entries were not supposed to carry the names of the writers (advertisements for the contest stated that all manuscripts "must be accompanied by a sealed envelope containing the name of its author which will not be opened until a decision is reached"), Bacheller and his editor, Arthur Stedman, actively went after big names in the American literary scene. They spent months persuading the celebrated Freeman to overcome her initial misgivings about writing a submission—even going so far as to visit her personally to extend the invitation—and she finally agreed to write a detective story as "an experiment." And although Freeman split the $2,000 prize with Chamberlin and repeatedly requested that they appear as joint authors, he was never credited, although the announcement of the winning story in *The Critic: A Weekly Review of Literature and the Arts* on June 29, 1895, did acknowledge that the story was a collaborative effort with Chamberlin. And then Bacheller played faster and looser. Ignoring that Freeman had retained copyright to "The Long Arm," after its initial newspapers syndication, "The Long Arm" appeared as the opening story in the inaugural edition of Bacheller's new literary monthly journal *The Pocket Magazine* in December of 1895. According to S. Bradley Shaw, this caused Freeman "to believe that Bacheller's 'contest' was merely a publicity stunt and a deceptive pretense for landing a first-rate story by a famous author in order to assure a successful launching of his new monthly fiction periodical, the *Pocket Magazine*." But he wasn't done yet. After the appearance in *The Pocket Magazine*, Bacheller sold "The Long Arm" as well as the second and third place stories (Matthews' "The Twinkling of an Eye" and Tellet's "The Secret of the Treaty"), to the London publisher Chapman and Hall who added "The Murder at Jex Farm" by George Ira Brett originally published in *Chapman's Magazine of Fiction*, and brought forth the collection without the authors' consent or knowledge as *The Long Arm and Other Detective Stories* (1895).

Bibliography

Kendrick, Brent L., ed. *The Infant Sphinx: Collected Letters of Mary E. Wilkins Freeman*. Metuchen, NJ: Scarecrow, 1985.

Shaw, S. Bradley. "New England Gothic by Light of Common Day: Lizzie Borden and Mary E. Wilkins Freeman's 'The Long Arm.'" *The New England Quarterly* 70.2 (1997): 211–236.

The Long Arm
by Mary E. Wilkins [Freeman] and Joseph Edgar Chamberlin

Chapter I
The Tragedy

(From notes written by Miss Sarah Fairbanks
immediately after the report of the Grand Jury.)

As I take my pen to write this, I have a feeling that I am in the witness-box—for, or against myself, which? The place of the criminal in the dock I will not voluntarily take. I will affirm neither my innocence nor my guilt. I will present the facts of the case as impartially and as coolly as if I had nothing at stake. I will let all who read this judge me as they will.

This I am bound to do, since I am condemned to something infinitely worse than the life-cell or the gallows. I will try my own self in lieu of judge and jury; my guilt or my innocence I will prove to you all, if it be in mortal power. In my despair I am tempted to say, I care not which it may be, so something be proved. Open condemnation could not overwhelm me like universal suspicion.

Now, first, as I have heard is the custom in the courts of law, I will present the case. I am Sarah Fairbanks, a country school teacher, twenty-nine years of age. My mother died when I was twenty-three. Since then, while I have been teaching at Digby, a cousin of my father's, Rufus Bennett, and his wife have lived with my father. During the long summer vacation they returned to their little farm in Vermont, and I kept house for my father.

For five years I have been engaged to be married to Henry Ellis, a young man whom I met in Digby. My father was very much opposed to the match, and has told me repeatedly that if I insisted upon marrying him in his lifetime he would disinherit me. On this account Henry never visited me at my own home; while I could not bring myself to break off my engagement. Finally, I wished to avoid an open rupture with my father. He was quite an old man, and I was the only one he had left of a large family.

I believe that parents should honor their children, as well as children their parents; but I had arrived at this conclusion: in nine-tenths of the cases wherein children marry against their parents' wishes, even when the parents have no just grounds for opposition, the marriages are unhappy.

I sometimes felt that I was unjust to Henry, and resolved that, if ever I suspected that his fancy turned toward any other girl, I would not hinder it, especially as I was getting older and, I thought, losing my good looks.

A little while ago, a young and pretty girl came to Digby to teach the school in the south district. She boarded in the same house with Henry. I heard that he was somewhat attentive to her, and I made up my mind I would not interfere. At the same time it seemed to me that my heart was breaking. I heard her people had money, too, and she was an only child. I had always felt that Henry ought to marry a wife with money, because he had nothing himself, and was not very strong.

School closed five weeks ago, and I came home for the summer vacation. The night before I left, Henry came to see me, and urged me to marry him. I refused again; but I never before had felt that my father was so hard and cruel as I did that night. Henry said that he should certainly see me during the vacation, and when I replied that he must not come, he was angry, and said—but such foolish things are not worth repeating. Henry has really a very sweet temper, and would not hurt a fly.

The very night of my return home Rufus Bennett and my father had words about some maple sugar which Rufus made on his Vermont farm and sold to father, who made a good trade for it to some people in Boston. That was father's business. He had once kept a store, but had given it up, and sold a few articles that he could make a large profit on here and there at wholesale. He used to send to New Hampshire and Vermont for butter, eggs, and cheese. Cousin Rufus thought father did not allow him enough profit on the maple sugar, and in the dispute father lost his temper and said that Rufus had given him under weight. At that, Rufus swore an oath and seized father by the throat. Rufus's wife screamed, "Oh, don't! Don't! Oh, he'll kill him!"

I went up to Rufus and took hold of his arm.

"Rufus Bennett," said I, "you let go my father!"

But Rufus's eyes glared like a madman's and he would not let go. Then I went to the desk drawer where father had kept a pistol since some houses in the village were broken into; I got out the pistol, laid hold of Rufus again, and held the muzzle against his forehead.

"You let go of my father," said I, "or I'll fire!"

Then Rufus let go, and father dropped like a log. He was purple in the face. Rufus's wife and I worked a long time over him to bring him to.

"Rufus Bennett," said I, "go to the well and get a pitcher of water." He went, but when father had revived and got up, Rufus gave him a look that showed he was not over his rage.

"I'll get even with you yet, Martin Fairbanks, old man as you are!" he shouted out, and went into the other room.

We got father to bed soon. He slept in the bedroom downstairs, out of the sitting room. Rufus and his wife had the north chamber, and I had the south one. I left my door open that night, and did not sleep. I listened; no one stirred in the night. Rufus and his wife were up very early in the morning, and before nine o'clock left for Vermont. They had a day's journey, and would reach home about nine in the evening. Rufus's wife bade father good-bye, crying, while Rufus was getting their trunk downstairs, but Rufus did not go near father nor me. He ate no breakfast; his very back looked ugly when he went out of the yard.

That very day about seven in the evening, after tea, I had just washed the dishes and put them away, and went out on the north doorstep, where father was sitting, and sat down on the lowest step. There was a cool breeze there; it had been a very hot day.

"I want to know if that Ellis fellow has been to see you any lately?" said father all at once.

"Not a great deal," I answered.

"Did he come to see you the last night you were there?" said father.

"Yes, sir," said I, "he did come."

"If you ever have another word to say to that fellow while I live, I'll kick you out of the house like a dog, daughter of mine though you be," said he. Then he swore a great oath and called God to witness. "Speak to that fellow again, if you dare, while I live!" said he.

I did not say a word; I just looked up at him as I sat there. Father turned pale and shrank back, and put his hand to his throat, where Rufus had clutched him. There were some purple finger-marks there.

"I suppose you would have been glad if he had killed me," father cried out.

"I saved your life," said I.

"What did you do with that pistol?" he asked.

"I put it back in the desk drawer."

I got up and went around and sat on the west doorstep, which is the front one. As I sat there, the bell rang for the Tuesday evening meeting, and Phœbe Dole and Maria Woods, two old maiden ladies, dressmakers, our next door neighbors, went past on their way to the meeting. Phœbe stopped and asked if Rufus and his wife were gone. Maria went around the house. Very soon they went on, and several other people passed. When they had all gone, it was as still as death.

I sat alone a long time, until I could see by the shadows that the full moon had risen. Then I went to my room and went to bed.

I lay awake a long time, crying. It seemed to me that all hope of marriage between Henry and me was over. I could not expect him to wait for me. I thought of that other girl; I could see her pretty face wherever I looked. But at last I cried myself to sleep.

At about five o'clock I awoke and got up. Father always wanted his breakfast at six o'clock, and I had to prepare it now.

When father and I were alone, he always built the fire in the kitchen stove, but that morning I did not hear him stirring as usual, and I fancied that he must be so out of temper with me, that he would not build the fire.

I went to my closet for a dark blue calico dress which I wore to do housework in. It had hung there during all the school term.

As I took it off the hook, my attention was caught by something strange about the dress I had worn the night before. This dress was made of thin summer silk; it was green in color, sprinkled over with white rings. It had been my best dress for two summers, but now I was wearing it on hot afternoons at home, for it was the coolest dress I had. The night before, too, I had thought of the possibility of Henry's driving over from Digby and passing the house. He had done this sometimes during the last summer vacation, and I wished to look my best if he did.

As I took down the calico dress I saw what seemed to be a stain on the green silk. I threw on the calico hastily, and then took the green silk and carried it over to the window. It was covered with spots—horrible great splashes and streaks down the front. The right sleeve, too, was stained, and all the stains were wet.

"What have I got on my dress?" said I.

It looked like blood. Then I smelled of it, and it was sickening in my nostrils, but I was not sure what the smell of blood was like. I thought I must have got the stains by some accident the night before.

"If that is blood on my dress," I said, "I must do something to get it off at once, or the dress will be ruined."

It came to my mind that I had been told that bloodstains had been removed from cloth by an application of flour paste on the wrong side. I took my green silk, and ran down the back stairs, which lead—having a door at the foot—directly into the kitchen.

There was no fire in the kitchen stove, as I had thought. Everything was very solitary and still, except for the ticking of the clock on the shelf. When I crossed the kitchen to the pantry, however, the cat mewed to be let in from the street. She had a little door of her own by which she could enter or leave the shed at will, an aperture just large enough for her Maltese body to pass at ease beside the shed door. It had a little lid, too, hung upon a leathern hinge. On my way I let the cat in; then I went into the pantry and got a bowl of flour. This I mixed with water into a stiff paste, and applied to the under surface of the stains on my dress. I then hung the dress up to dry in the dark end of a closet leading out of the kitchen, which contained some old clothes of father's.

Then I made up the fire in the kitchen stove. I made coffee, baked biscuits, and poached some eggs for breakfast.

Then I opened the door into the sitting room and called, "Father, breakfast is ready." Suddenly I started. There was a red stain on the inside of the sitting room door. My heart began to beat in my ears. "Father!" I called out—"Father!"

There was no answer.

"Father!" I called again, as loud as I could scream. "Why don't you speak? What is the matter?"

The door of his bedroom stood open. I had a feeling that I saw a red reflection in there. I gathered myself together and went across the sitting room to father's bedroom door. His little looking glass hung over his bureau opposite his bed, which was reflected in it.

That was the first thing I saw, when I reached the door. I could see father in the looking glass and the bed. Father was dead there; he had been murdered in the night.

Chapter II
The Knot of Ribbon

I THINK I must have fainted away, for presently I found myself on the floor, and for a minute I could not remember what had happened. Then I remembered, and an awful, unreasoning terror seized me. "I must lock all the doors quick," I thought; "quick, or the murderer will come back."

I tried to get up, but I could not stand. I sank down again. I had to crawl out of the room on my hands and knees.

I went first to the front door; it was locked with a key and a bolt. I went next to the north door, and that was locked with a key and bolt. I went to the north shed door, and that was bolted. Then I went to the little-used east door in the shed, beside which the cat had her little passageway, and that was fastened with an iron hook. It has no latch.

The whole house was fastened on the inside. The thought struck me like an icy hand, "The murderer is in this house!" I rose to my feet then; I unhooked that door, and ran out of the house, and out of the yard, as for my life.

I took the road to the village. The first house, where Phœbe Dole and Maria Woods live, is across a wide field from ours. I did not intend to stop there, for they were only women, and could do nothing; but seeing Phœbe looking out of the window, I ran into the yard.

She opened the window.

"What is it?" said she. "What is the matter, Sarah Fairbanks?"

Maria Woods came and leaned over her shoulder. Her face looked almost as white as her hair, and her blue eyes were dilated. My face must have frightened her.

"Father—father is murdered in his bed!" I said.

There was a scream, and Maria Woods's face disappeared from over Phœbe Dole's shoulder—she had fainted. I do not know whether Phœbe looked paler—she is always very pale—but I saw in her black eyes a look which I shall never forget. I think she began to suspect me at that moment.

Phœbe glanced back at Maria, but she asked me another question.

"Has he had words with anybody?" said she.

"Only with Rufus," I said; "but Rufus is gone."

Phœbe turned away from the window to attend to Maria, and I ran on to the village.

A hundred people can testify what I did next—can tell how I called for the doctor and the deputy sheriff; how I went back to my own home with the horror-stricken crowd, how they flocked in and looked at poor father; but only the doctor touched him, very carefully, to see if he were quite dead; how the coroner came, and all the rest.

The pistol was in the bed beside father, but it had not been fired; the charge was still in the barrel. It was bloodstained, and there was one bruise on father's head which might have been inflicted by the pistol, used as a club. But the wound which caused his death was in his breast, and made evidently by some cutting instrument, though the cut was not a clean one; the weapon must have been dull.

They searched the house, lest the murderer should be hidden away. I heard Rufus Bennett's name whispered by one and another. Everybody seemed to know that he and father had had words the night before; I could not understand how, because I had told nobody except Phœbe Dole, who had had no time to spread the news, and I was sure that no one else had spoken of it.

They looked in the closet where my green silk dress hung, and pushed it aside to be sure nobody was concealed behind it, but they did not notice anything wrong about it. It was dark in the closet, and besides, they did not look for anything like that until later.

All these people—the deputy sheriff, and afterwards the high sheriff, and other out-of-town officers, for whom they had telegraphed, and the neighbors—all hunted their own suspicion and that was Rufus Bennett. All believed he had come back, and killed my father. They fitted all the facts to that belief. They made him do the deed with a long, slender screwdriver, which he had recently borrowed from one of the neighbors and had not returned. They made his finger-marks, which were still on my father's throat, fit the red prints of the sitting room door. They made sure that he had returned and stolen into the house by the east door shed, while father and I sat on the doorsteps the evening before; that he had hidden himself away, perhaps in that very closet where my dress hung, and afterwards stolen out and killed my father, and then escaped.

They were not shaken when I told them that every door was bolted and barred that morning. They themselves found all the windows fastened down, except a few which were open on account of the heat, and even these last were raised only the width of the sash, and fastened with sticks, so that they could be raised no higher. Father was very cautious about fastening the house, for he sometimes had considerable sums of money by him. The officers saw all these difficulties in the way, but they fitted them somehow to their theory, and two deputy sheriffs were at once sent to apprehend Rufus.

They had not begun to suspect me then, and not the slightest watch was kept on my movements. The neighbors were very kind, and did everything to help me, relieving me altogether of all those last offices—in this case so much sadder than usual.

An inquest was held, and I told freely all I knew, except about the bloodstains on my dress. I hardly knew why I kept that back. I had no feeling then that I might have done the deed myself, and I could not bear to convict myself, if I was innocent.

Two of the neighbors, Mrs. Holmes and Mrs. Adams, remained with me all that day.

Towards evening, when there were very few in the house, they went into the parlor to put it in order for the funeral, and I sat down alone in the kitchen. As I sat there by the window I thought of my green silk dress, and wondered if the stains were out. I went to the closet and brought the dress out to the light. The spots and streaks had almost disappeared. I took the dress out into the shed, and scraped off the flour paste, which was quite dry; I swept up the paste, burned it in the stove, took the dress upstairs to my own closet, and hung it in its old place. Neighbors remained with me all night.

At three o'clock in the afternoon of the next day, which was Thursday, I went over to Phœbe Dole's to see about a black dress to wear at the funeral. The neighbors had urged me to have my black silk dress altered a little, and trimmed with crape.

I found only Maria Woods at home. When she saw me she gave a little scream, and began to cry. She looked as if she had already been weeping for hours. Her blue eyes were bloodshot.

"Phœbe's gone over to—Mrs. Whitney's to—try on her dress," she sobbed.

"I want to get my black silk dress fixed a little," said I.

"She'll be home—pretty soon," said Maria.

I laid my dress on the sofa and sat down. Nobody ever consults Maria about a dress. She sews well, but Phœbe does all the planning.

Maria Woods continued to sob like a child, holding her little soaked handkerchief over her face. Her shoulders heaved. As for me, I felt like a stone; I could not weep.

"Oh," she gasped out finally, "I knew—I knew! I told Phœbe—I knew just how it would be, I—knew!"

I roused myself at that.

"What do you mean?" said I.

"When Phœbe came home Tuesday night and said she heard your father and Rufus Bennett having words, I knew how it would be," she choked out. "I knew he had a dreadful temper."

"Did Phœbe Dole know Tuesday night that father and Rufus Bennett had words?" said I.

"Yes," said Maria Woods.

"How did she know?"

"She was going through your yard, the short cut to Mrs. Ormsby's, to carry her brown alpaca dress home. She came right home and told me; and she overheard them."

"Have you spoken of it to anybody but me?" said I.

Maria said she didn't know; she might have done so. Then she remembered hearing Phœbe herself speak of it to Harriet Sargent when she came in to try on her dress. It was easy to see how people knew about it.

I did not say any more, but I thought it was strange that Phœbe Dole had asked me if father had had words with anybody when she knew it all the time.

Phœbe came in before long. I tried on my dress, and she made her plan about the alterations, and the trimming. I made no suggestions. I did not care how it was done but if I had cared it would have made no difference. Phœbe always does things her own way. All the women in the village are in a manner under Phœbe Dole's thumb. The garments are visible proofs of her force of will.

While she was taking up my black silk on the shoulder seams, Phœbe Dole said, "Let me see—you had a green silk made at Digby three summers ago, didn't you?"

"Yes," I said.

"Well," said she, "why don't you have it dyed black? Those thin silks dye quite nice. It would make you a good dress."

I scarcely replied, and then she offered to dye it for me herself. She had a recipe which she used with great success. I thought it was very kind of her, but did not say whether I would accept her offer or not. I could not fix my mind upon anything but the awful trouble I was in.

"I'll come over and get it tomorrow morning," said Phœbe.

I thanked her. I thought of the stains, and then my mind seemed to wander again to the one subject. All the time Maria Woods sat weeping. Finally Phœbe turned to her with impatience.

"If you can't keep calmer, you'd better go upstairs, Maria," said she. "You'll make Sarah sick. Look at her! She doesn't give way—and think of the reason she's got."

"I've got reason, too," Maria broke out; then, with a piteous shriek, "Oh, I've got reason."

"Maria Woods, go out of the room!" said Phœbe. Her sharpness made me jump, half-dazed as I was.

Maria got up without a word, and went out of the room, bending almost double with convulsive sobs.

"She's been dreadfully worked up over your father's death," said Phœbe calmly, going on with the fitting. "She's terribly nervous. Sometimes I have to be real sharp with her, for her own good."

I nodded. Maria Woods has always been considered a sweet, weakly, dependent woman, and Phœbe Dole is undoubtedly very fond of her. She has seemed to shield her, and take care of her nearly all her life. The two have lived together since they were young girls.

Phœbe is tall, and very pale and thin; but she never had a day's illness. She is plain, yet there is a kind of severe goodness and faithfulness about her colorless face, with the smooth bands of white hair over her ears.

I went home as soon as my dress was fitted. That evening Henry Ellis came over to see me. I do not need to go into details concerning that visit. It seemed enough to say that he tendered the fullest sympathy and protection, and I accepted them. I cried a little, for the first time, and he soothed and comforted me.

Henry had driven over from Digby and tied his horse in the yard. At ten o'clock he bade me good night on the doorstep, and was just turning his buggy around, when Mrs. Adams came running to the door.

"Is this yours?" said she, and she held out a knot of yellow ribbon.

"Why, that's the ribbon you have around your whip, Henry," said I. He looked at it.

"So it is," he said. "I must have dropped it." He put it into his pocket and drove away.

"He didn't drop that ribbon tonight!" said Mrs. Adams. "I found it Wednesday morning out in the yard. I thought I remembered seeing him have a yellow ribbon on his whip."

Chapter III
Suspicion Is Not Proof

When Mrs. Adams told me she had picked up Henry's whip-ribbon Wednesday morning, I said nothing, but thought that Henry must have driven over Tuesday evening after all, and even come up into the yard, although the house was shut up, and I in bed, to get a little nearer to me. I felt conscience-stricken, because I could not help a thrill of happiness, when my father lay dead in the house.

My father was buried as privately and as quietly as we could bring it about. But it was a terrible ordeal. Meantime word came from Vermont that Rufus Bennett had been arrested on his farm. He was perfectly willing to come back with the officers, and indeed, had not the slightest trouble in proving that he was at his home in Vermont when the murder took place. He proved by several witnesses that he was out of the State long before my father and I sat on the steps together that evening, and that he proceeded directly to his home as fast as the train and stagecoach could carry him.

The screwdriver with which the deed was supposed to have been committed was found, by the neighbor from whom it had been borrowed, in his wife's bureau drawer. It had been returned, and she had used it to put a picture hook in her chamber. Bennett was discharged and returned to Vermont.

Then Mrs. Adams told of the finding of the yellow ribbon from Henry Ellis's whip, and he was arrested, since he was held to have a motive for putting my father out of the world. Father's opposition to our marriage was well known, and Henry was suspected also of having had an eye to his money. It was found, indeed, that my father had more money than I had known myself.

Henry owned to having driven into the yard that night, and to having missed the ribbon from his whip on his return; but one of the hostlers in the livery stables in Digby, where he kept his horse and buggy, came forward and testified to finding the yellow ribbon in the carriage room that Tuesday night before Henry returned from his drive. There were two yellow ribbons in evidence, therefore, and the one produced by the hostler seemed to fit Henry's whipstock the more exactly.

Moreover, nearly the exact minute of the murder was claimed to be proved by the postmortem examination; and by the testimony of the stable man as to the hour of Henry's return and the speed of his horse, he was further cleared of suspicion; for, if the opinion of the medical experts was correct, Henry must have returned to the livery stable too soon to have committed the murder.

He was discharged, at any rate, although suspicion still clung to him. Many people believe now in his guilt—those who do not, believe in mine; and some believe we were accomplices.

After Henry's discharge, I was arrested. There was no one else left to accuse. There must be a motive for the murder; I was the only person left with a motive. Unlike the others, who were discharged after preliminary examination, I was held to the grand jury and taken to Dedham, where I spent four weeks in jail, awaiting the meeting of the grand jury.

Neither at the preliminary examination, nor before the grand jury, was I allowed to make the full and frank statement that I am making here. I was told simply to answer the questions that were put to me, and to volunteer nothing, and I obeyed.

I know nothing about law. I wished to do the best I could—to act in the wisest manner, for Henry's sake and my own. I said nothing about the green silk dress. They searched the house for all manner of things, at the time of my arrest, but the dress was not there—it was in Phœbe Dole's dye kettle. She had come over after it one day when I was picking beans in the garden, and had taken it out of the closet. She brought it back herself, and told me this, after I had returned from Dedham.

"I thought I'd get it and surprise you," said she. "It's taken a beautiful black."

She gave me a strange look—half as if she would see into my very soul, in spite of me, half as if she were in terror of what she would see there, as she spoke. I do not know just what Phœbe Dole's look meant. There may have been a stain left on that dress after all, and she may have seen it.

I suppose if it had not been for that flour paste which I had learned to make, I should have hung for the murder of my father. As it was, the grand jury found no bill against me because there was absolutely no evidence to convict me and I came home a free woman. And if people were condemned for their motives, would there be enough hangmen in the world?

They found no weapon with which I could have done the deed. They found no bloodstains on my clothes. The one thing which told against me, aside from my ever-present motive, was the fact that on the morning after the murder the doors and windows were fastened. My volunteering this information had of course weakened its force as against myself.

Then, too, some held that I might have been mistaken in my terror and excitement, and there was a theory, advanced by a few, that the murderer had meditated making me also a victim, and had locked the doors that he might not be frustrated in his designs, but had lost heart at the last, and had allowed me to escape, and then fled himself. Some held that he had intended to force me to reveal the whereabouts of father's money, but his courage had failed him.

Father had quite a sum in a hiding place which only he and I knew. But no search for money had been made, as far as anyone could see—not a bureau drawer had been disturbed, and father's gold watch was ticking peacefully under his pillow; even his wallet in his vest pocket had not been opened. There was a small roll of banknotes in it, and some change; father never carried much money. I suppose if father's wallet and watch had been taken, I should not have been suspected at all.

I was discharged, as I have said, from lack of evidence, and have returned to my home free, indeed, but with this awful burden of suspicion on my shoulders. That brings me up to the present day. I returned yesterday evening. This evening Henry Ellis has been over to see me; he will not come again, for I have forbidden him to do so. This is what I said to him: "I know you are innocent, you know I am innocent. To all the world beside we are under suspicion—I more than you, but we are both under suspicion. If we are known to be together that suspicion is increased for both of us. I do not care for myself, but I do care for you. Separated from me the stigma attached to you will soon fade away, especially if you should marry elsewhere."

Then Henry interrupted me.

"I will never marry elsewhere," said he.

I could not help being glad that he said it, but I was firm.

"If you should see some good woman whom you could love, it will be better for you to marry elsewhere," said I.

"I never will!" he said again. He put his arms around me, but I had strength to push him away.

"You never need, if I succeed in what I undertake before you meet the other," said I. I began to think he had not cared for that pretty girl who boarded in the same house after all.

"What is that?" he said. "What are you going to undertake?"

"To find my father's murderer," said I.

Henry gave me a strange look; then, before I could stop him, he took me fast in his arms and kissed my forehead.

"As God is my witness, Sarah, I believe in your innocence," he said; and from that minute I have felt sustained and fully confident of my power to do what I had undertaken.

My father's murderer I will find. Tomorrow I begin my search. I shall first make an exhaustive examination of the house, such as no officer in the case has yet made, in the hope of finding a clue. Every room I propose to divide into square yards, by line and measure, and every one of these square yards I will study as if it were a problem in algebra.

I have a theory that it is impossible for any human being to enter any house, and commit in it a deed of this kind, and not leave behind traces which are the known quantities in an algebraic equation to those who can use them.

There is a chance that I shall not be quite unaided. Henry has promised not to come again until I bid him but he is to send a detective here from Boston—one whom he knows. In fact, the man is a cousin of his, or else there would be small hope of our securing him, even if I were to offer him a large price.

The man has been remarkably successful in several cases, but his health is not good; the work is a severe strain upon his nerves, and he is not driven to it from any lack of money. The physicians have forbidden him to undertake any new case, for a year at least, but Henry is confident that we may rely upon him for this.

I will now lay aside this and go to bed. Tomorrow is Wednesday; my father will have been dead seven weeks. Tomorrow morning I will commence the work, in which, if it be in human power, aided by a higher wisdom, I shall succeed.

Chapter IV
The Box of Clues

(The pages which follow are from Miss Fairbanks's Journal begun after the conclusion of the notes already given to the reader.)

Wednesday night.—I have resolved to record carefully each day the progress I make in my examination of the house. I began today at the bottom—that is, with the room least likely to contain any clue, the parlor. I took a chalk-line and a yardstick, and divided the floor into square yards, and every one of these squares I examined on my hands and knees. I found in this way literally nothing on the carpet but dust, lint, two common white pins, and three inches of blue sewing silk.

At last I got the dustpan and brush, and yard by yard swept the floor. I took the sweepings in a white pasteboard box out into the yard in the strong sunlight, and examined them. There was nothing but dust and lint and five inches of brown woolen thread—evidently a ravelling of some dress material. The blue silk and the brown thread are the only possible clues which I found today, and they are hardly possible. Rufus's wife can probably account for them.

Nobody has come to the house all day. I went down to the store this afternoon to get some necessary provisions, and people stopped talking when I came in. The clerk took my money as if it were poison.

Thursday night.—Today I have searched the sitting room, out of which my father's bedroom opens. I found two bloody footprints on the carpet which no one had noticed before—perhaps because the carpet itself is red and white. I used a microscope which I had in my schoolwork. The footprints, which are close to the bedroom door, pointing out into the sitting room, are both from the right foot; one is brighter than the other, but both are faint. The foot was evidently either bare or clad only in a stocking—the prints are so widely spread. They are wider than my father's shoes. I tried one in the brightest print.

I found nothing else new in the sitting room. The bloodstains on the doors which have been already noted are still there. They had not been washed away, first by order of the sheriff, and next by mine. These stains are of two kinds; one looks as if made by a bloody garment brushing against it; the other, I should say, was made in the first place by the grasp of a bloody hand, and then brushed over with a cloth. There are none of these marks upon the door leading to the bedroom—they are on the doors leading into the front entry and the china closet. The china closet is really a pantry, although I use it only for my best dishes and preserves.

Friday night.—Today I searched the closet. One of the shelves, which is about as high as my shoulders, was bloodstained. It looked to me as if the murderer might have caught hold of it to steady himself. Did he turn faint after his dreadful deed? Some tumblers of jelly were ranged on that shelf and they had not been disturbed. There was only that bloody clutch on the edge.

I found on this closet floor, under the shelves, as if it had been rolled there by a careless foot, a button, evidently from a man's clothing. It is an ordinary black enamelled metal trousers button; it had evidently been worn off and clumsily sewn on again, for a quantity of stout white thread is still clinging to it. This button must have belonged either to a single man or to one with an idle wife.

If one black button had been sewn on with white thread, another is likely to be. I may be wrong, but I regard this button as a clue.

The pantry was thoroughly swept—cleaned, indeed, by Rufus's wife the day before she left. Neither my father nor Rufus could have dropped it there, and they never had occasion to go to that closet. The murderer dropped the button.

I have a white pasteboard box which I have marked "clues." In it I have put the button.

This afternoon Phœbe Dole came in. She is very kind. She has re-cut the dyed silk, and she fitted it to me. Her great shears clicking in my ears made me nervous. I did not feel like stopping to think about clothes. I hope I did not appear ungrateful, for she is the only soul beside Henry who has treated me as she did before this happened.

Phœbe asked me what I found to busy myself about, and I replied "I am searching for my father's murderer." She asked me if I thought I should find a clue, and I replied, "I think so," I had found the button then, but I did not speak of it. She said Maria was not very well.

I saw her eyeing the stains on the doors, and I said I had not washed them off, for I thought they might yet serve a purpose in detecting the murderer. She looked closely at those on the entry door—the brightest ones—and said she did not see how they could help, for there were no plain finger-marks there, and she should think they would make me nervous.

"I'm beyond being nervous," I replied.

Saturday.—Today I have found something which I cannot understand. I have been at work in the room where my father came to his dreadful end. Of course some of the most startling evidences have been removed. The bed is clean, and the carpet washed, but the worst horror of it all clings to that room. The spirit of murder seemed to haunt it. It seemed to me at first that I could not enter that room, but in it I made a strange discovery.

My father, while he carried little money about his person, was in the habit of keeping considerable sums in the house; there is no bank within ten miles. However he was wary; he had a hiding place which he had revealed to no one but myself. He had a small stand in his room near the end of his bed. Under this stand, or rather under the top of it, he had tacked a large leather wallet. In this he kept all his spare money. I remember how his eyes twinkled when he showed it to me.

"The average mind thinks things have either got to be in or on," said my father. "They don't consider there's ways of getting around gravitation and calculation."

In searching my father's room I called to mind that saying of his, and his peculiar system of concealment, and then I made my discovery. I have argued that in a search of this kind I ought not only to search for hidden traces of the criminal, but for everything which had been for any reason concealed. Something which my father himself had hidden, something from his past history, may furnish a motive for someone else.

The money in the wallet under the table, some five hundred dollars, had been removed and deposited in the bank. Nothing more was to be found there. I examined the bottom of the bureau, and the undersides of the chair seats. There are two chairs in the room, besides the cushioned rocker—green-painted wooden chairs, with flag seats. I found nothing under the seats.

Then I turned each of the green chairs completely over, and examined the bottoms of the legs. My heart leaped when I found a bit of leather tacked over one. I got the tack-hammer and drew the tacks. The chair leg had been hollowed out, and for an inch the hole was packed tight with cotton. I began picking out the cotton, and soon I felt something hard. It proved to be an old-fashioned gold band, quite wide and heavy, like a wedding ring.

I took it over to the window and found this inscription on the inside: "Let love abide forever." There were two dates—one in August, forty years ago, and the other in August of the present year.

I think the ring had never been worn; while the first part of the inscription is perfectly clear, it looks old, and the last is evidently freshly cut.

This could not have been my mother's ring. She had only her wedding ring, and that was buried with her. I think my father must have treasured up this ring for years; but why? What does it mean? This can hardly be a clue; this can hardly lead to the discovery of a motive, but I will put it in the box with the rest.

Sunday night.—Today, of course, I did not pursue my search. I did not go to church. I could not face old friends that could not face me. Sometimes

I think that everybody in my native village believes in my guilt. What must I have been in my general appearance and demeanor all my life? I have studied myself in the glass, and tried to discover the possibilities of evil that they must see in my face.

This afternoon about three o'clock, the hour when people here have just finished their Sunday dinner, there was a knock on the north door. I answered it, and a strange young man stood there with a large book under his arm. He was thin and cleanly shaved, with a clerical air.

"I have a work here to which I would like to call your attention," he began; and I stared at him in astonishment, for why should a book agent be peddling his wares upon the Sabbath?

His mouth twitched a little.

"It's a Biblical Cyclopædia," said he.

"I don't think I care to take it," said I.

"You are Miss Sarah Fairbanks, I believe?"

"That is my name," I replied stiffly.

"Mr. Henry Ellis, of Digby, sent me here," he said next. "My name is Dix—Francis Dix."

Then I knew it was Henry's first cousin from Boston—the detective who had come to help me. I felt the tears coming to my eyes.

"You are very kind to come," I managed to say.

"I am selfish, not kind," he returned, "but you had better let me come in, or any chance of success in my book agency is lost, if the neighbors see me trying to sell it on a Sunday. And Miss Fairbanks, this is a *bona fide* agency. I shall canvass the town."

He came in. I showed him all that I have written and he read it carefully. When he had finished he sat still for a long time, with his face screwed up in a peculiar meditative fashion.

"We'll ferret this out in three days at the most," said he finally, with a sudden clearing of his face and a flash of his eyes at me.

"I had planned for three years, perhaps," said I.

"I tell you, we'll do it in three days," he repeated. "Where can I get board while I canvass for this remarkable and interesting book under my arm? I can't stay here, of course, and there is no hotel. Do you think the two dressmakers next door, Phœbe Dole and the other one, would take me in?"

I said they had never taken boarders.

"Well, I'll go over and inquire," said Mr. Dix; and he had gone, with his book under his arm, almost before I knew it.

Never have I seen anyone act with the strange noiseless soft speed that this man does. Can he prove me innocent in three days? He must have succeeded in getting board at Phœbe Dole's, for I saw him go past to meeting with her this evening. I feel sure he will be over very early tomorrow morning.

Chapter V
The Evidence Points to One

Monday night.—The detective came as I expected. I was up as soon as it was light, and he came across the dewy fields, with his cyclopædia under his arm. He had stolen out from Phœbe Dole's back door.

He had me bring my father's pistol; then he bade me come with him out into the backyard.

"Now, fire it," he said, thrusting the pistol into my hands. As I have said before, the charge was still in the barrel.

"I shall arouse the neighborhood," I said.

"Fire it," he ordered.

I tried; I pulled the trigger as hard as I could.

"I can't do it," I said.

"And you are a reasonably strong woman, too, aren't you?"

I said I had been considered so. Oh, how much I heard about the strength of my poor woman's arms, and their ability to strike that murderous weapon home!

Mr. Dix took the pistol himself, and drew a little at the trigger.

"I could do it," he said, "but I won't. It would arouse the neighborhood."

"This is more evidence against me," I said despairingly. "The murderer had tried to fire the pistol and failed."

"It is more evidence against the murderer," said Mr. Dix.

We went into the house, where he examined my box of clues long and carefully. Looking at the ring, he asked whether there was a jeweller in this village, and I said there was not. I told him that my father oftener went on business to Acton, ten miles away, than elsewhere.

He examined very carefully the button which I had found in the closet, and then asked to see my father's wardrobe. That was soon done. Beside the suit in which father was laid away there was one other complete one in the closet in his room. Besides that, there were in this closet two overcoats, an old black frock coat, a pair of pepper-and-salt trousers, and two black vests. Mr. Dix examined all the buttons; not one was missing.

There was still another old suit in the closet off the kitchen. This was examined, and no button found wanting.

"What did your father do for work the day before he died?" he then asked.

I reflected and said that he had unpacked some stores which had come down from Vermont, and done some work out in the garden.

"What did he wear?"

"I think he wore the pepper-and-salt trousers and the black vest. He wore no coat, while at work."

Mr. Dix went quietly back to father's room and his closet, I following. He took out the grey trousers and the black vest, and examined them closely.

"What did he wear to protect these?" he asked.

"Why, he wore overalls!" I said at once. As I spoke I remembered seeing father go around the path to the yard, with those blue overalls drawn up high under his arms.

"Where are they?"

"Weren't they in the kitchen closet?"

"No."

We looked again, however, in the kitchen closet; we searched the shed thoroughly. The cat came in through her little door, as we stood there, and brushed around our feet. Mr. Dix stooped and stroked her. Then he went quickly to the door, beside which her little entrance was arranged, unhooked it, and stepped out. I was following him, but he motioned me back.

"None of my boarding mistress's windows command us," he said, "but she might come to the back door."

I watched him. He passed slowly around the little winding footpath, which skirted the rear of our house and extended faintly through the grassy fields to the rear of Phœbe Dole's. He stopped, searched a clump of sweetbriar, went on to an old well, and stopped there. The well had been dry many a year, and was choked up with stones and rubbish. Some boards are laid over it, and a big stone or two, to keep them in place.

Mr. Dix, glancing across at Phœbe Dole's back door, went down on his knees, rolled the stones away, then removed the boards and peered down the well. He stretched far over the brink, and reached down. He made many efforts; then he got up and came to me, and asked me to get for him an umbrella with a crooked handle, or something that he could hook into clothing.

I brought my own umbrella, the silver handle of which formed an exact hook. He went back to the well, knelt again, thrust in the umbrella and drew up, easily enough, what he had been fishing for. Then he came bringing it to me.

"Don't faint," he said, and took hold of my arm. I gasped when I saw what he had—my father's blue overalls, all stained and splotched with blood!

I looked at them, then at him.

"Don't faint," he said again. "We're on the right track. This is where the button came from—see, see!" He pointed to one of the straps of the overalls, and the button was gone. Some white thread clung to it. Another black metal button was sewed on roughly with the same white thread that I found on the button in my box of clues.

"What does it mean?" I gasped out. My brain reeled.

"You shall know soon," he said. He looked at his watch. Then he laid down the ghastly bundle he carried. "It has puzzled you to know how the murderer went in and out and yet kept the doors locked, has it not?" he said.

"Yes."

"Well, I am going out now. Hook that door after me."

He went out, still carrying my umbrella. I hooked the door. Presently I saw the lid of the cat's door lifted, and his hand and arm thrust through. He curved his arm up towards the hook, but it came short by half a foot. Then he withdrew his arm, and thrust in my silver-handled umbrella. He reached the door hook easily enough with that.

Then he hooked it again. That was not so easy. He had to work a long time. Finally he accomplished it, unhooked the door again, and came in.

"That was how!" I said.

"No, it was not," he returned. "No human being, fresh from such a deed, could have used such patience as that to fasten the door after him. Please hang your arm down by your side."

I obeyed. He looked at my arm, then at his own.

"Have you a tape measure?" he asked.

I brought one out of my workbasket. He measured his arm, then mine, and then the distance from the cat-door to the hook.

"I have two tasks for you today and tomorrow," he said. "I shall come here very little. Find all your father's old letters, and read them. Find a man or woman in this town whose arm is six inches longer than yours. Now I must go home, or my boarding-mistress will get curious."

He went through the house to the front door, looked all ways to be sure no eyes were upon him, made three strides down the yard, and was pacing soberly up the street, with his cyclopædia under his arm.

I made myself a cup of coffee, then I went about obeying his instructions. I read old letters all the forenoon; I found packages in trunks in the garret; there were quantities in father's desk. I have selected several to submit to Mr. Dix. One of them treats an old episode in father's youth, which must have years since ceased to interest him. It was concealed after his favorite fashion—tacked under the bottom of his desk. It was written forty years ago, by Maria Woods, two years before my father's marriage— and it was a refusal of an offer of his hand. It was written in the stilted fashion of that day; it might have been copied from a "Complete Letter-writer."

My father must have loved Maria Woods as dearly as I love Henry, to keep that letter so carefully all these years. I thought he cared for my mother. He seemed as fond of her as other men of their wives, although I did use to wonder if Henry and I would ever get to be quite so much accustomed to each other.

Maria Woods must have been as beautiful as an angel when she was a girl. Mother was not pretty; she was stout, too, and awkward, and I suppose people would have called her rather slow and dull. But she was a good woman, and tried to do her duty.

Tuesday night.—This evening was my first opportunity to obey the second of Mr. Dix's orders. It seemed to me the best way to compare the average length of arms was to go to the prayer meeting. I could not go about the town with my tape measure, and demand of people that they should hold out their arms. Nobody knows how I dreaded to go to the meeting, but I went, and I looked not at my neighbors' cold altered faces, but at their arms.

I discovered what Mr. Dix wished me to, but the discovery can avail nothing, and it is one he could have made himself. Phœbe Dole's arm is fully seven inches longer than mine. I never noticed it before, but she has an almost abnormally long arm. But why should Phœbe Dole have unhooked that door?

She made a prayer—a beautiful prayer. It comforted even me a little. She spoke of the tenderness of God in all the troubles of life, and how it never failed us.

When we were all going out I heard several persons speak of Mr. Dix and his Biblical Cyclopædia. They decided that he was a theological student, book-canvassing to defray the expenses of his education.

Maria Woods was not at the meeting. Several asked Phœbe how she was, and she replied, "Not very well."

It is very late. I thought Mr. Dix might be over tonight, but he has not been here.

Wednesday.—I can scarcely believe what I am about to write. Our investigations seem to point all to one person, and that person— . It is incredible! I will not believe it.

Mr. Dix came as before, at dawn. He reported, and I reported. I showed Maria Woods's letter. He said he had driven to Acton, and found that the jeweller there had engraved the last date in the ring about six weeks ago.

"I don't want to seem rough, but your father was going to get married again," said Mr. Dix.

"I never knew him to go near any woman since mother died," I protested.

"Nevertheless, he had made arrangements to be married," persisted Mr. Dix.

"Who was the woman?" He pointed at the letter in my hand.

"Maria Woods!"

He nodded.

I stood looking at him—dazed. Such a possibility had never entered my head.

He produced an envelope from his pocket, and took out a little card with blue and brown threads neatly wound upon it.

"Let me see those threads you found," he said.

I got the box and we compared them. He had a number of pieces of blue sewing silk and brown woolen ravellings, and they matched mine exactly.

"Where did you find them?" I asked.

"In my boarding-mistress's piece bag."

I stared at him.

"What does it mean?" I gasped out.

"What do you think?"

"It is impossible!"

Chapter VI
The Revelation

Wednesday, continued.—When Mr. Dix thus suggested to me the absurd possibility that Phœbe Dole had committed the murder, he and I were sitting in the kitchen. He was near the table; he laid a sheet of paper upon it, and began to write. The paper is before me.

"First," said Mr. Dix, and he wrote rapidly as he talked, "whose arm is of such length that it might unlock a certain door of this house from the outside?—Phœbe Dole's.

"Second, who had in her piece bag bits of the same threads and ravellings found upon your parlor floor, where she had not by your knowledge entered?—Phœbe Dole.

"Third, who interested herself most strangely in your bloodstained green silk dress, even to dyeing it?—Phœbe Dole.

"Fourth, who was caught in a lie, while trying to force the guilt of the murder upon an innocent man?—Phœbe Dole."

Mr. Dix looked at me. I had gathered myself together.

"That proves nothing," I said. "There is no motive in her case."

"There is a motive."

"What is it?"

"Maria Woods shall tell you this afternoon."

He then wrote, "Fifth, who was seen to throw a bundle down the old well, in the rear of Martin Fairbanks's house, at one o'clock in the morning?—Phœbe Dole."

"Was she—seen?" I gasped.

Mr. Dix nodded. Then he wrote, "Sixth, who had a strong motive, which had been in existence many years ago?—Phœbe Dole."

Mr. Dix laid down his pen, and looked at me again.

"Well, what have you to say?" he asked.

"It is impossible!"

"Why?"

"She is a woman."

"A man could have fired that pistol, as she tried to do."

"It would have taken a man's strength to kill with the kind of weapon that was used," I said.

"No, it would not. No great strength is required for such a blow."

"But she is a woman!"

"Crime has no sex."

"But she is a good woman—a church member. I heard her pray yesterday afternoon. It is not in character."

"It is not for you, nor for me, nor for any mortal intelligence, to know what is or is not in character," said Mr. Dix.

He arose and went away. I could only stare at him in a half-dazed manner.

Maria Woods came this afternoon, taking advantage of Phœbe's absence on a dressmaking errand. Maria has aged ten years in the last few weeks. Her hair is white, her cheeks are fallen in, her pretty color is gone.

"May I have the ring he gave me forty years ago?" she faltered.

I gave it to her; she kissed it and sobbed like a child.

"Phœbe took it away from me before," she said; "but she shan't this time."

Maria related with piteous sobs the story of her long subordination to Phœbe Dole. This sweet child-like woman had always been completely under the sway of the other's stronger nature. The subordination went back beyond my father's original proposal to her; she had, before he made love to her as a girl, promised Phœbe she would not marry; and it was Phœbe who, by representing to her that she was bound by this solemn promise, had led her to write a letter to my father declining his offer, and sending back the ring.

"And after all, we were going to get married, if he had not died," she said. "He was going to give me this ring again, and he had had the other date put in. I should have been so happy!"

She stopped and stared at me with horror-stricken inquiry.

"What was Phœbe Dole doing in your backyard at one o'clock that night?" she cried.

"What do you mean?" I returned.

"I saw Phœbe come out of your back shed door at one o'clock that very night. She had a bundle in her arms. She went along the path about as far as the old well, then she stooped down, and seemed to be working at something. When she got up she didn't have the bundle. I was watching at our back door. I thought I heard her go out a little while before, and went downstairs, and found that door unlocked. I went in quick, and up to my chamber, and into my bed, when she started home across the fields. Pretty soon I heard her come in, then I heard the pump going. She slept downstairs; she went on to her bedroom. What was she doing in your backyard that night?"

"You must ask her," said I. I felt my blood running cold.

"I've been afraid to," moaned Maria Woods. "She's been dreadful strange lately. I wish that book agent was going to stay at our house."

Maria Woods went home in about an hour. I got a ribbon for her, and she has my poor father's ring concealed in her withered bosom. Again I cannot believe this.

Thursday.—It is all over, Phœbe Dole has confessed! I do not know now in exactly what way Mr. Dix brought it about—how he accused her of her crime. After breakfast I saw them coming across the fields; Phœbe came first, advancing with rapid strides like a man, Mr. Dix followed, and my father's poor old sweetheart tottered behind, with her handkerchief at her eyes. Just as I noticed them the front doorbell rang; I found several people there, headed by the high sheriff. They crowded into the sitting room just as Phœbe Dole came rushing in, with Mr. Dix and Maria Woods.

"I did it!" Phœbe cried out to me. "I am found out, and I have made up my mind to confess. She was going to marry your father—I found it out. I stopped it once before. This time I knew I couldn't unless I killed him. She's lived with me in that house for over forty years. There are other ties as strong as the marriage one, that are just as sacred. What right had he to take her away from me and break up my home?

"I overheard your father and Rufus Bennett having words. I thought folks would think he did it. I reasoned it all out. I had watched your cat go in that little door, I knew the shed door hooked, I knew how long my arm was; I thought I could undo it. I stole over here a little after midnight. I went all around the house to be sure nobody was awake. Out in the front yard I happened to think my shears were tied on my belt with a ribbon, and I untied them. I thought I put the ribbon in my pocket—it was a piece of yellow ribbon—but I suppose I didn't, because they found it afterwards, and thought it came off your young man's whip.

"I went round to the shed door, unhooked it, and went in. The moon was light enough. I got out your father's overalls from the kitchen closet; I knew where they were. I went through the sitting room to the parlor.

"In there I slipped off my dress and skirts and put on the overalls. I put a handkerchief over my face, leaving only my eyes exposed. I crept out then into the sitting room; there I pulled off my shoes and went into the bedroom.

"Your father was fast asleep; it was such a hot night, the clothes were thrown back and his chest was bare. The first thing I saw was that pistol on the stand beside his bed. I suppose he had had some fear of Rufus Bennett coming back, after all. Suddenly I thought I'd better shoot him. It would be surer and quicker; and if you were aroused I knew that I could get away, and everybody would suppose that he had shot himself.

"I took up the pistol and held it close to his head. I had never fired a pistol, but I knew how it was done. I pulled, but it would not go off. Your father stirred a little—I was mad with horror—I struck at his head with the pistol. He opened his eyes and cried out; then I dropped the pistol, and took these"—Phœbe Dole pointed to the great shining shears hanging at her waist—"for I am strong in my wrists. I only struck twice, over his heart.

"Then I went back into the sitting room. I thought I heard a noise in the kitchen—I was full of terror then—and slipped into the sitting room closet. I felt as if I were fainting, and clutched the shelf to keep from falling.

"I felt that I must go upstairs to see if you were asleep, to be sure you had not waked up when your father cried out. I thought if you had I should have to do the same by you. I crept upstairs to your chamber. You seemed sound asleep, but, as I watched, you stirred a little; but instead of striking at you I slipped into your closet. I heard nothing more from you. I felt myself wet with blood. I caught something hanging in your closet, and wiped myself over with it. I knew by the feeling it was your green silk. You kept quiet, and I saw you were asleep, so crept out of the closet, and down the stairs, got my clothes and shoes, and, out in the shed, took off the overalls and dressed myself. I rolled up the overalls, and took a board away from the old well and threw them in as I went home. I thought if they were found it would be no clue to me. The handkerchief, which was not much stained, I put to soak that night, and washed it out next morning, before Maria was up. I washed my hands and arms carefully that night, and also my shears.

"I expected Rufus Bennett would be accused of the murder, and, maybe, hung. I was prepared for that, but I did not like to think I had thrown suspicion upon you by staining your dress. I had nothing against you. I made up my mind I'd get hold of that dress—before anybody suspected you—and dye it black. I came in and got it, as you know. I was astonished not to see any more stains on it. I only found two or three little streaks that scarcely anybody would have noticed. I didn't know what to think. I suspected, of course, that you had found the stains and got them off, thinking they might bring suspicion upon you.

"I did not see how you could possibly suspect me in any case. I was glad when your young man was cleared. I had nothing against him. That is all I have to say."

I think I must have fainted away then. I cannot describe the dreadful calmness with which that woman told this—that woman with the good face, whom I had last heard praying like a saint in meeting. I believe in demoniacal possession after this.

When I came to, the neighbors were around me, putting camphor on my head, and saying soothing things to me, and the old friendly faces had returned. But I wish I could forget!

They have taken Phœbe Dole away—I only know that. I cannot bear to talk any more about it when I think there must be a trial, and I must go!

Henry has been over this evening. I suppose we shall be happy after all, when I have had a little time to get over this. He says I have nothing more to worry about. Mr. Dix has gone home. I hope Henry and I may be able to repay his kindness some day.

A month later. I have just heard that Phœbe Dole has died in prison. This is my last entry. May God help all other innocent women in hard straits as He has helped me!

—From *The Long Arm and Other Detective Stories*. London: Chapman & Hall, 1895.

The Twinkling of an Eye
by Professor Brander Matthews

Chapter I

The telegraph messenger looked again at the address on the envelope in his hand, and then scanned the house before which he was standing. It was an old-fashioned building of brick, two stories high, with an attic above; and it stood in an old-fashioned part of lower New York, not far from the East River. Over the wide archway there was a small weather-worn sign,

"Ramapo Steel and Iron Works"; and over the smaller door alongside was a still smaller sign, "Whittier, Wheatcroft & Co."

When the messenger boy had made out the name, he opened this smaller door and entered the long narrow store. Its sides and walls were covered with bins and racks containing sample steel rails and iron beams, and coils of wire of various sizes. Down at the end of the store were desks where several clerks and bookkeepers were at work.

As the messenger drew near, a redheaded office boy blocked the passage, saying, somewhat aggressively, "Well?"

"Got a telegram for Whittier, Wheatcroft & Co.," the messenger explained, pugnaciously thrusting himself forward.

"In there!" the office boy returned, jerking his thumb over his shoulder towards the extreme end of the building, an extension, roofed with glass and separated by a glass screen from the space where the clerks were at work.

The messenger pushed open the glazed door of this private office, a bell jingled over his head, and the three occupants of the room looked up.

"Whittier, Wheatcroft & Co.?" said the messenger, interrogatively, holding out the yellow envelope.

"Yes," responded Mr. Whittier, a tall, handsome old gentleman, taking the telegram. "You sign, Paul."

The youngest of the three, looking like his father, took the messenger's book, and, glancing at an old-fashioned clock which stood in the corner, he wrote the name of the firm and the hour of delivery. He was watching the messenger go out. His attention was suddenly called to subjects of more importance by a sharp exclamation from his father.

"Well, well, well," said the elder Whittier, with his eyes fixed on the telegram he had just read. "This is very strange—very strange indeed!"

"What's strange?" asked the third occupant of the office, Mr. Wheatcroft, a short, stout, irascible-looking man with a shock of grizzly hair.

For an answer Mr. Whittier handed to Mr. Wheatcroft the thin slip of paper.

No sooner had the junior partner read the paper than he seemed angrier than ever.

"Strange!" he cried. "I should think it was strange! confoundedly strange—and deuced unpleasant too."

"May I see what it is that's so very strange?" asked Paul, picking up the despatch.

"Of course you may see it," growled Mr. Wheatcroft; "And let us see what you can make of it."

The young man read the message aloud: "Deal off. Can get quarter cent better terms. Carkendale."

Then he read it again to himself. At last he said, "I confess I don't see anything so very mysterious in that. We've lost a contract, I suppose; but that must have happened lots of times before, hasn't it?"

"It's happened twice before, this fall," returned Mr. Wheatcroft fiercely, "after our bid had been practically accepted and just before the signing of the final contract!"

"Let me explain, Wheatcroft," interrupted the elder Whittier gently. "You must not expect my son to understand the ins and outs of this business as we do. Besides, he has only been in the office ten days."

"I don't expect him to understand," growled Wheatcroft. "How could he? I don't understand it myself!"

"Close that door, Paul," said Mr. Whittier. "I don't want any of the clerks to know what we are talking about. Here are the facts in the case, Paul, and I think you will admit that they are certainly curious," began Mr. Whittier. "Twice this fall, and now a third time, we have been the lowest bidders for important orders, and yet, just before our bid was formally accepted, somebody has cut under us by a fraction of a cent and got the job. First we thought we were going to get the building of the Barataria Central's bridge over the Little Makintosh River, but in the end it was the Tuxedo Steel Company that got the contract. Then there was the order for the fifty thousand miles of wire for the Transcontinental Telegraph; we made an extraordinarily low estimate on that. We wanted the contract, and we threw off, not only our profit, but even allowances for office expenses, and yet five minutes before the last bid had to be in, the Tuxedo Company put in an offer only a hundred and twenty-five dollars less than ours. Now comes the telegram today. The Methusalah Life Insurance Company is going to put up a big building; we were asked to estimate on the steel framework. We wanted that work—times are hard, and there is little doing as you know, and we must get work for our men if we can. We meant to have this contract if we could. We offered to do it at what was really actual cost of manufacture—without profit, first of all, and then without any charge at all for office expenses, for interest on capital, for depreciation of plant. The vice president of the Methusalah, the one who attends to all their real estate, is Mr. Carkendale. He told me yesterday that our bid was very low, and that we were certain to get the contract. And now he sends me this," and Mr. Whittier picked up the telegram again.

"But if we were going to do it at actual cost of manufacture," said the young man, "and somebody else underbids us, isn't somebody else losing money on the job?"

"That's no sort of satisfaction to our men," retorted Mr. Wheatcroft, cooking himself before the fire. "Somebody else—confound him!—will be able to keep his men together and to give them the wages we want for our men. Do you think 'somebody else' is the Tuxedo Company again?"

"What of it?" asked Mr. Whittier. "Surely you don't suppose—"

"Yes I do," interrupted Mr. Wheatcroft swiftly. "I do, indeed. I haven't been in this business thirty years for nothing. I know how hungry we get at all times for a big fat contract; and I know we would any of us give a hundred dollars to the man who could tell us what our chief rival has bid. It would be the cheapest purchase of the year, too."

"Come, come, Wheatcroft," said the elder Whittier, "you know we've never done anything of that sort yet, and I think you and I are too old to be tempted now."

"Nothing of the sort," snorted the fiery little man; "I'm open to temptation this very moment. If I could know what the Tuxedo people are going to bid on the new steel rails of the Springfield and Athens, I'd give a thousand dollars."

"If I understand you, Mr. Wheatcroft," Paul Whittier asked, "you are suggesting that there has been something done that is not fair?"

"That's just what I mean," Mr. Wheatcroft declared vehemently.

"Do you mean to say that the Tuxedo people have somehow been made acquainted with our bids?" asked the young man.

"That's what I'm thinking now," was the sharp answer. "I can't think of anything else. For two months we haven't been successful in getting a single one of the big contracts. We've had our share of the little things, of course, but they don't amount to much. The big things that we really wanted have slipped through our fingers. We've lost them by the skin of our teeth every time. That isn't accident, is it? Of course not! Then there's only one explanation—there's a leak in this office somewhere."

"You don't suspect any of the clerks, do you, Mr. Wheatcroft?" asked the elder Whittier sadly.

"I don't suspect anybody in particular," returned the junior partner, brushing his hair up the wrong way. "And I suspect everybody in general. I haven't an idea who it is, but it's somebody! It must be somebody—and if it is somebody, I'll do my best to get that somebody into the clutches of the law."

"Who makes up the bids on these important contracts?" asked Paul.

"Wheatcroft and I," answered his father. "The specifications are forwarded to the works, and the engineers make their estimates of the actual cost of labor and material. These estimates are sent to us here, and we add whatever we think best for interest and for expenses, and for wear and tear and for profit."

"Who writes the letters making the offer—the one with actual figures, I mean?" the son continued.

"I do," the elder Whittier explained; "I have always done it."

"You don't dictate them to a typewriter?" Paul pursued.

"Certainly not," the father responded; "I write them with my own hand, and what's more, I take the press copy myself, and there is a special letter-book for such things. This letter-book is always kept in the safe in this office; in fact, I can say that this particular letter-book never leaves my hands except to go into that safe. And, as you know, nobody has access to that safe except Wheatcroft and me."

"And the major," corrected the junior partner.

"No," Mr. Whittier explained, "Van Zandt has no need to go there now."

"But he used to," Mr. Wheatcroft persisted.

"He did once," the senior partner returned, "but when we bought those new safes outside there in the main office, there was no longer any need for the chief bookkeeper to go to this smaller safe; and so last month—it was while you were away, Wheatcroft—Van Zandt came in here one afternoon, and said that, as he never had occasion to go to this safe, he would rather not have the responsibility of knowing the combination. I told him we had perfect confidence in him."

"I should think so!" broke in the explosive Wheatcroft. "The major has been with us for thirty years now. I'd suspect myself of petty larceny as soon as him."

"As I said," continued the elder Whittier, "I told him that we trusted him perfectly, of course. But he urged me, and to please him I changed the combination of this safe that afternoon. You will remember, Wheatcroft, that I gave you the new word the day you came back."

"Yes, I remember," said Mr. Wheatcroft. "But I don't see why the major did not want to know how to open that safe. Perhaps he is beginning to feel his years now. He must be sixty, the major; and I've been thinking for some time that he looks worn."

"I noticed the change in him," Paul remarked, "the first day I came into the office. He seemed ten years older than he was last winter."

"Perhaps his wound troubles him again," suggested Mr. Whittier. "Whatever the reason, it is at his own request that he is now ignorant of the combination. No one knows that but Wheatcroft and I. The letters themselves I wrote myself, and copied myself, and put them myself in the envelopes I directed myself. I don't recall mailing them myself, but I may have done that too. So you see that there can't be any foundation for your belief, Wheatcroft, that somebody had access to our bids."

"I can't believe anything else!" cried Wheatcroft impulsively. "I don't know how it was done, I'm not a detective—but it was done somehow. And if it was done, it was done by somebody! And what I'd like to do is to catch that somebody in the act! That's all! I'd make it hot for him!"

"You would like to have him out at the Ramapo Works," said Paul, smiling at the little man's violence, "and put him under the steam hammer?"

"Yes, I would," responded Mr. Wheatcroft. "I would indeed! Putting a man under a steam hammer may seem a cruel punishment, but I think it would cure the fellow of any taste for prying into our business in the future."

"I think it would get him out of the habit of living," the elder Whittier said, as the tall clock in the corner struck one. "But don't let's be so brutal. Let's go to lunch and talk the matter over quietly. I don't agree with your suspicion, Wheatcroft, but there may be something in it."

Five minutes later, Mr. Whittier, Mr. Wheatcroft, and the only son of the senior partner left the glass-framed private office and, walking leisurely through the long store, passed into the street.

They did not notice that the old bookkeeper, Major Van Zandt, whose high desk was so placed that he could overlook the private office, had been watching them ever since the messenger had delivered the despatch. He could not read the telegram; he could not hear the comments; but he could see every movement and every gesture and every expression. He gazed from one speaker to the other, almost as though he was able to follow the course of the discussion; and when the three members of the firm walked past his desk he found himself staring at them as if in a vain effort to read on their faces the secret of the course of action they had resolved upon.

Chapter II

After luncheon, as it happened, both the senior and the junior partner of Whittier, Wheatcroft and Co. had to attend meetings, and they went their several ways, leaving Paul to return to the office alone.

When he came opposite to the house which bore the weather-beaten sign of the firm, he stood still for a moment and looked across with mingled pride and affection. The building was old-fashioned, so old-fashioned, indeed, that only a long-established firm could afford to occupy it. It was Paul Whittier's great-grandfather who had founded the Ramapo Works. There had been cast the cannon for many of the ships of the little American navy that gave such a good account of itself in the war of 1812. Again, in 1848, had the house of Whittier, Wheatcroft and Co.—the present Mr. Wheatcroft's father having been taken into partnership by Paul's grandfather—been able to be of service to the government of the United States. All through the four years that followed the firing on the flag in 1861, the Ramapo Works had been run day and night. When peace came at last, and the people had leisure to expand, a large share of the rails needed by the new overland roads, which were to bind the East and West together in iron bonds, had been rolled by Whittier, Wheatcroft and Co. Of late years, as Paul knew, the old firm seemed to have lost some of its early energy, and, having young and vigorous competitors, it had barely held its own.

That the Ramapo Works should once more take the lead was Paul Whittier's solemn purpose, and to this end he had been carefully trained. He was now a young man of twenty-five, a tall handsome fellow, with a full moustache over his firm mouth, and with clear quick eyes below his curly brown hair. He had spent four years in college, carrying off honors in mathematics, was popular with his classmates, who made him class poet, and in his senior year he was elected president of the college photographic society. He had gone to a technological institute, where he had made himself master of the theory and practice of metallurgy. After a year of travel in Europe, where he had investigated every important steel and iron works he could get into, he had come home to take a desk in the office.

It was only for a moment that he stood on the sidewalk opposite, looking at the old building. Then he threw away his cigarette and went over.

Instead of entering the long store, he walked down the alleyway left open for the heavy wagons. When he came opposite to the private office in the rear of the store, he examined the doors and the windows carefully, to see if he could detect any means of ingress other than those open to everybody.

There was no door from the private office into the alleyway or into the yard. There was a door from the alleyway into the store, opposite to the desks of the clerks, and within a few feet of the door leading from the street into the private office.

Paul passed through this entrance, and found himself face to face with the old bookkeeper, Van Zandt, who was following all his movements with a questioning gaze.

"Good afternoon, major," said Paul pleasantly. "Have you been out for your lunch yet?"

"I always get my dinner at noon," the bookkeeper gruffly answered, returning to his books.

As Paul walked on, he could not but think that the major's manner was ungracious. And the young man remembered how cheerful the old man had been, and how courteous always, when the son of the senior partner, while still a schoolboy, used to come to the office on Saturdays.

Paul had always delighted in the office, and the store, and the yard behind, and he had spent many a holiday there, and Major Van Zandt had always been glad to see him, and had willingly answered his myriad questions.

Paul wondered why the bookkeeper's manner was now so different. Van Zandt was older, but he was not so very old, not more than sixty, and old age in itself is not sufficient to make a man surly, and to sour his temper. That the major had had trouble in his family was well known. His wife had been flighty and foolish, and it was believed that she had run away from him; and his only son was a wild lad, who had been employed by Whittier, Wheatcroft and Co., out of regard for the father, and who disgraced himself beyond forgiveness. Paul recalled vaguely that the young fellow had gone west somewhere, and had been shot in a mining camp, after a drunken brawl in a gambling house.

As Paul entered the private office he found the porter there, putting coal on the fire.

Stepping back to close the glass door behind him, that they might be alone, he said, "Mike, who shuts up the office at night?"

"Sure I do, Mr. Paul," was the prompt reply.

"And you open it in the morning?" the young man asked.

"I do that!" Mike responded.

"Do you see that these windows are always fastened on the inside?" was the next query.

"Yes, Mr. Paul," the porter replied.

"Well," and the inquirer, hesitated briefly before putting this question, "have you found any of these windows unfastened any morning lately when you came here?"

"And how did you know that?" Mike returned in surprise.

"What morning was it?" asked Paul, pushing his advantage.

"It was last Monday mornin', Mr. Paul," the porter explained, "an' how it was I dunno, for I had every wan of them windows tight on Saturday night—an' Monday mornin' one of them was unfastened whin I wint to open it to let a bit of air into the office here."

"You sleep here always, don't you?" Paul proceeded.

"I've slept here ivery night for three years now come Thanksgivin'," Mike replied. "I've the whole top of the house to myself. It's an illigant apartment I have there, Mr. Paul."

"Who was here Sunday?" was the next question.

"Sure nobody was here at all," responded the porter, "barrin' they came while I took me a bit of a walk after dinner. An' they couldn't have got in anyway, for I lock up always, and I wasn't gone for an hour, or maybe an hour an' a half."

"I hope you will be very careful hereafter," said Paul.

"I will that," promised Mike, "an' I am careful now, always."

The porter took up the coal scuttle, and then he turned to Paul.

"How was it ye knew that the winder was not fastened that mornin'?" he asked.

"How did I know?" repeated the young man. "Oh, a little bird told me."

When Mike had left the office, Paul took a chair before the fire, and lighted a cigar. For half an hour he sat silently thinking.

He came to the conclusion that Mr. Wheatcroft was right in his suspicion. Whittier, Wheatcroft and Co. had lost important contracts because of underbidding due to knowledge surreptitiously obtained. He believed that someone had got into the store on Sunday while Mike was taking a walk, and that this somebody had somehow opened the safe. There never was any money in that private safe; it was intended to contain only important papers. It did contain the letter-book of the firm's bids, and this is what was wanted by the man who had got into the office, and who had let himself in by the window, leaving it unfastened behind him. How this man had got in, and why he did not get out by the way he entered, how he came to be able to open the private safe, the combination of which was known only to the two partners—these were questions for which Paul Whittier had no answers.

What grieved him when he had come to this conclusion was that the thief—for such the housebreaker was in reality—was probably one of the men in the employ of the firm. It seemed to him almost certain that the man who had broken in knew all the ins and outs of the office. And how could this knowledge have been obtained except by an employee? Paul was well acquainted with the clerks in the outer office. There were five of them, including the old bookkeeper, and although none of them had been with the firm as long as the major, no one of them had been there less than ten years. Paul did not know which one to suspect. There was in fact no reason to suspect any particular clerk. And yet that one of the five men in the main office on the other side of the glass partition within twenty feet of him—that one of these was the guilty man Paul did not doubt.

And therefore it seemed to him not so important to prevent the thing from happening as it was to catch the man who had done it. The thief once caught, it would be easy thereafter for the firm to take unusual precautions. But the first thing to do was to catch the thief. He had come and gone and left no trail. But he must have visited the office at least three times in the past few weeks, since the firm had lost three important contracts. Probably he had been there oftener than three times. Certainly he would come again. Sooner or later he would come once too often. All that needed to be done was to set a trap for him.

While Paul was sitting quietly in the private office, smoking a cigar with all his mental faculties at their highest tension, the clock in the corner suddenly struck three.

Paul swiftly swung around in his chair and looked at it. An old eight-day clock it was, which not only told the time of day, but pretended also to supply miscellaneous astronomical information. It stood by itself in the corner.

For a moment after it struck Paul stared at it with a fixed gaze, as though he did not see what he was looking at. Then a light came into his eyes and a smile flittered across his lips.

He turned around slowly and measured with his eye the proportions of the room, the distance between the desks and the safe and the clock. He glanced up at the sloping glass roof above him. Then he smiled again, and again sat silent for a minute. He rose to his feet and stood with his back to the fire. Almost in front of him was the clock in the corner.

He took out his watch and compared its time with that of the clock. Apparently he found that the clock was too fast, for he walked over to it and turned the minute hand back. It seemed that this was a more difficult feat than he supposed, or that he went about it carelessly, for the minute hand broke off short in his fingers. A spasmodic movement of his, as the thin metal snapped, pulled the chain off its cylinder, and the weight fell with a crash.

All the clerks looked up; and the redheaded office boy was prompt in answer to the bell Paul rang a moment after.

"Bobby," said the young man to the boy, as he took his hat and overcoat, "I've just broken the clock. I know a shop where they make a speciality of repairing timepieces like that. I'm going to tell them to send for it at once. Give it to the man who will come this afternoon with my card. Do you understand?"

"Cert," the boy answered. "If he ain't got your card, he don't get the clock."

"That's what I mean," Paul responded, as he left the office.

Before he reached the door he met Mr. Wheatcroft.

"Paul," cried the junior partner explosively, "I've been thinking about that—about that—you know what I mean! And I have decided that we had better put a detective on this thing at once!"

"Yes," said Paul, "that's a good idea. In fact, I had just come to the same conclusion. I—"

Then he checked himself. He had turned slightly to speak to Mr. Wheatcroft, and now he saw that Major Van Zandt was standing within ten feet of them, and he noticed that the old bookkeeper's face was strangely pale.

Chapter III

During the next week the office of Whittier, Wheatcroft and Co. had its usual aspect of prosperous placidity. The routine work was done in the routine way; the porter opened the office every morning, and the office boy arrived a few minutes after it was opened; the clerks came at nine and a little later the partners were to be seen in the inner office reading the morning's correspondence.

The Whittiers, father and son, had had a discussion with Mr. Wheatcroft as to the most advisable course to adopt to prevent the future leakage of the trade secrets of the firm. The senior partner had succeeded in dissuading the junior partner from the employing of detectives.

"Not yet," he said, "not yet. These clerks have all served us faithfully for years, and I don't want to submit them to the indignity of being shadowed—that's what they call it, isn't it?—of being shadowed by some cheap hireling, who may try to distort the most innocent acts into evidence of guilt, so that he can show us how smart he is."

"But this sort of thing can't go on forever," ejaculated Mr. Wheatcroft. "If we are to be underbid on every contract worth having, we might as well go out of the business!"

"That's true, of course," Mr. Whittier admitted; "but we are not sure that we are being underbid unfairly."

"The Tuxedo Co. have taken away three contracts from us in the past two months," cried the junior partner; "we can be sure of that, can't we?"

"We have lost three contracts, of course," returned Mr. Whittier, in his most conciliatory manner, "and the Tuxedo people have captured them. But that may be only a coincidence, after all."

"It is a pretty expensive coincidence for us," snorted Mr. Wheatcroft.

"But because we have lost money," the senior partner rejoined gently, laying his hand on Mr. Wheatcroft's arm, "that's no reason why we should also lose our heads. It is no reason why we should depart from our old custom of treating every man fairly. If there is anyone in our employ here who is selling us, why, if we give him enough rope, he will hang himself, sooner or later."

"And before he suspends himself that way," cried Mr. Wheatcroft, "we may be forced to suspend ourselves."

"Come, come, Wheatcroft," said the senior partner, "I think we can afford to stand the loss a little longer. What we can't afford to do is to lose our self-respect by doing something irreparable. It may be that we shall have to employ detectives, but I don't think the time has come yet."

"Very well," the junior partner declared, yielding an unwilling consent. "I don't insist on it. I still think it would be best not to waste any more time—but I don't insist. What will happen is that we shall lose the rolling of those steel rails for the Springfield and Athens road—that's all."

Paul Whittier had taken no part in this discussion. He agreed with his father, and saw he had no need to urge any further argument.

Now he looked up and asked when they intended to put in the bid for the rails. His father then explained that they were expecting a special estimate from the engineers at the Ramapo Works, and that it probably would be Saturday before this could be discussed by the partners and the exact figures of the proposed contract determined.

"And if we don't want to lose that contract for sure," insisted Mr. Wheatcroft, "I think we had better change the combination on that safe."

"May I suggest," said Paul, "that it seems to me to be better to leave the combination as it is. What we want to do is not to get this Springfield and Athens contract so much as to find out whether someone really is getting at the letter-book. Therefore we mustn't make it any harder for the someone to get at the letter-book."

"Oh, very well," Mr. Wheatcroft assented, a little ungraciously, "have it your own way. But I want you to understand, now, that I think you are only postponing the inevitable!"

And with that the subject was dropped. For several days the three men who were together for hours in the office of the Ramapo Iron and Steel Works refrained from any discussion of the question which was most prominent in their minds.

It was on Wednesday that the tall clock that Paul Whittier had broken returned from the repairers. Paul himself helped the men to set it in its old place in the corner of the office, facing the safe, which occupied the corner diagonally opposite.

It so chanced that Paul came down late on Thursday morning, and perhaps this was the reason that a pressure of delayed work kept him in the office that evening long after everyone else. The clerks had all gone, even Major Van Zandt, always the last to leave—and the porter had come in twice before the son of the senior partner was ready to go for the night. The gas was lighted here and there in the long, narrow, deserted store, as Paul walked through it from the office to the street. Opposite, the swift twilight of a New York November had already settled down on the city.

"Can't I carry yer bag for ye, Mister Paul?" asked the porter, who was showing him out.

"No, thank you, Mike," was the young man's answer. "That bag has very little in it. And besides, I haven't got to carry it far."

The next morning Paul was the first of the three to arrive. The clerks were in their places already, but neither the senior nor the junior partner had yet come. The porter happened to be standing under the wagon archway as Paul Whittier was about to enter the store.

The young man saw the porter, and a mischievous smile hovered about the corners of his mouth.

"Mike," he said, pausing on the doorstep, "do you think you ought to smoke while you are cleaning out our office in the morning?"

"Sure I haven't had me pipe in me mouth this mornin' at all," the porter answered, taken by surprise.

"But yesterday morning?" Paul pursued.

"Yesterday mornin'!" Mike echoed, not a little bit puzzled.

"Yesterday morning, at ten minutes before eight, you were in the private office smoking a pipe."

"But how did you see me, Mr. Paul?" cried Mike in amaze. "Ye was late in comin' down yesterday, wasn't ye?"

Paul smiled pleasantly.

"A little bird told me," he said.

"If I had the bird I'd wring his neck for tellin' tales!"

"I don't mind your smoking, Mike," the young man went on, "that's your own affair; but I'd rather you didn't smoke a pipe while you are tidying up the private office."

"Well, Mister Paul, I won't do it again," the porter promised.

"And I wouldn't encourage Bob to smoke, either," Paul continued.

"I encourage him?" inquired Mike.

"Yes," Paul explained, "yesterday morning you let him light his cigarette from your pipe—didn't you?"

"Were you peekin' in thro' the winder, Mister Paul?" the porter asked eagerly. "Ye saw me, an' I never saw ye at all."

"No," the young man answered; "I can't say that I saw you myself. A little bird told me."

And with that he left the wondering porter, and entered the store. Just inside the door was the office boy, who hastily hid an unlighted cigarette as he caught sight of the senior partner's son.

When Paul saw the redheaded boy, he smiled again mischievously.

"Bob," he began, "when you want to see who can stand on his head the longest, you or Danny the bootblack, don't you think you could choose a better place than the private office?"

The office boy was quite as much taken by surprise as the porter had been, but he was younger and quicker witted.

"And when did I have Danny in the office?" he asked defiantly.

"Yesterday morning," Paul answered, still smiling, "a little before half past eight."

"Yesterday mornin'?" repeated Bob, as though trying hard to recall all the events of the day before. "Maybe Danny did come in for a minute."

"He played leapfrog with you all the way into the private office," Paul went on, while Bob looked at him with increasing wonder.

"How did you know?" the office boy asked frankly. "Were you lookin' through the window?"

"How do I know that you and Danny stood on your heads in the corner of the office with your heels against the safe, scratching off the paint! Next time I'd try the yard, if I were you. Sports of that sort are more fun in the open air."

And with that parting shot Paul went on his way to his own desk, leaving the office boy greatly puzzled.

Later in the day Bob and Mike exchanged confidences, and neither was ready with an explanation.

"At school," Bob declared, "we used to think teacher had eyes in the back of her head. She was everlastingly catchin' me when I did things behind her back. But Mr. Paul beats that, for he see me doin' things when he isn't here."

"Mister Paul wasn't here, for sure, yesterday mornin'," Mike asserted; "I'd take me oath o' that. An' if he wasn't here, how could he see me givin' ye a light from me pipe? Answer me that! He says it's a little bird told him—but that's not it, I'm thinkin'. Not but that they have clocks with birds into 'em, that come out and tell the time o' day, 'cuckoo! cuckoo! cuckoo!' An' if that big clock he broke last week had a bird that could tell time that way, I'd break the thing quick—so I would."

"It ain't no bird," said Bob. "You can bet your life on that. No birds can't tell him nothin', more'n you can catch 'em by putting salt on their tails. I know what it is Mr. Paul does—at least, I know how he does it. It's second sight that's what it is! I see a man onct at the theayter an' he—"

But perhaps it is not necessary to set down here the office boy's recollection of the trick of an ingenious magician.

About half an hour after Paul had arrived at the office Mr. Wheatcroft appeared. The junior partner hesitated in the doorway for a second, and then entered.

Paul was watching him, and the same mischievous smile flashed over the face of the young man.

"You need not be alarmed today, Mr. Wheatcroft," he said. "There is no fascinating female waiting for you this morning."

"Confound the woman!" ejaculated Mr. Wheatcroft testily. "I couldn't get rid of her."

"But you subscribed for the book at last," asserted Paul, "and she went away happy."

"I believe I did agree to take one copy of the work she showed me," admitted Mr. Wheatcroft a little sheepishly. Then he looked up suddenly. "Why, bless my soul," he cried, "that was yesterday morning—"

"Allowing for differences of clocks," Paul returned, "it was about ten minutes to ten yesterday morning."

"Then how do you come to know anything about it? I should like to be told that!" the junior partner inquired. "You did not get down till nearly twelve."

"I had an eye on you," Paul answered as the smile again flitted across his face.

"But I thought you were detained all the morning by a sick friend," insisted Mr. Wheatcroft.

"So I was," Paul responded. "And if you won't believe I have an eye on you, all I can say then is that a little bird told me."

"Stuff and nonsense," cried Mr. Wheatcroft. "Your little bird has two legs, hasn't it?"

"Most birds have," laughed Paul.

"I mean two legs in a pair of trousers," explained the junior partner, rumpling his grizzled hair with an impatient gesture.

"You see how uncomfortable it is to be shadowed," said Paul, turning the topic, as his father entered the office.

That Saturday afternoon Mr. Whittier and Mr. Wheatcroft agreed on the bid to be made on the steel rails needed by the Springfield and Athens road. While the elder Mr. Whittier wrote the letter to the railroad with his own hand, his son maneuvered the junior partner into the outer office where all the clerks happened to be at work, including the old book-keeper. Then Paul managed his conversation with Mr. Wheatcroft so that any one of the five employees who chose to listen to the apparently careless talk should know that the firm had just made a bid on another important contract. Paul also spoke as though his father and himself would probably go out of town that Saturday night to remain away till Monday morning.

Just before the store was closed for the night, Paul Whittier wound up the eight-day clock that stood in the corner opposite the private safe.

Chapter IV

Although the Whittiers, father and son, spent Sunday out of town, Paul made an excuse to the friends whom they were visiting, and returned to the city by a midnight train. Thus he was enabled to present himself at the office of the Ramapo Works very early on Monday morning.

It was so early, indeed, that no one of the employees had arrived when the son of the senior partner, bag in hand, pushed open the street door and entered the long store, at the far end of which the porter was still tidying up for the day's work.

"An' is that you, Mister Paul?" Mike asked in surprise, as he came out of the private office to see who the early visitor might be. "An' what brought ye out o' your bed before breakfast like this?"

"I always get out of bed before breakfast," Paul answered. "Don't you?"

"Would I get up if I hadn't got to get up to get my livin'?" the porter replied.

Paul entered the office, followed by Mike, still wondering why the young man was there at that hour.

After a swift glance round the office, Paul put down his bag on the table and turned suddenly to the porter with a question.

"When does Bob get down here?"

Mike looked at the clock in the corner before answering.

"It'll be ten minutes," he said, "or maybe twenty before the boy does be here today seein' it's Monday mornin' an he'll be tired with not working of Sunday."

"Ten minutes," repeated Paul slowly. After a moment's thought he continued, "Then I'll have to ask you to go out for me, Mike."

"I can go anywhere ye want, Mister Paul," the porter responded.

"I want you to go—" began Paul, "I want you to go—" and he hesitated, as though he was not quite sure what it was he wished the porter to do, "I want you to go to the office of the *Gotham Gazette* and get me two copies of yesterday's paper. Do you understand?"

"Maybe they won't be open so early in the mornin'," said the Irishman.

"That's no matter," said Paul, hastily correcting himself. "I mean that I want you to go there now, and get the papers if you can. Of course, if the office isn't open, I shall have to send again later."

"I'll be goin' now, Mister Paul," and Mike took his hat from a chair and started off at once.

Paul walked through the store with the porter. When Mike had gone, the young man locked the front door and returned at once to the private office in the rear. He shut himself in, and lowered all the shades, so that whatever he might do inside could not be seen by anyone on the outside.

Whatever it was he wished to do, he was able to do it swiftly, for in less than a minute after he had closed the door of the office he opened it again, and came out into the main store with his bag in his hand. He walked leisurely to the front of the store, arriving just in time to unlock the door as the office boy came around the corner, smoking a cigarette.

When Bob, still puffing steadily, was about to open the door and enter the store, he looked up and discovered that Paul was gazing at him. The boy pinched the cigarette out of his mouth and dropped it outside, and then came in, his eyes expressing his surprise at the presence of the senior partner's son downtown at that early hour in the morning.

Paul greeted the boy pleasantly, but Bob got away from him as soon as possible. Ever since the young man had told what had gone on in the office when Bob was its only occupant, the office boy was a little afraid of the young man, as though someway mysterious, not to say uncanny.

Paul thought it best to wait for the porter's return, and he stood outside under the archway for five minutes, smoking a cigar, with his bag at his feet.

When Mike came back with the two copies of the Sunday newspaper he had been sent to get, Paul gave him the money for them, and an extra quarter for himself. Then the young man picked up his bag again.

"When my father comes down, Mike," he said, "tell him I may be a little late in getting back this morning."

"An' are ye goin' away now, Mister Paul?" the porter asked. "What good was it that ye got out o' bed before breakfast and come down here so early in the mornin'?"

Paul laughed a little.

"I had a reason for coming here this morning," he answered briefly; and with that he walked away, his bag in one hand, and the two bulky and gaudy papers in the other.

Mike watched him turn the corner, and then went into the store again, where Bob greeted him promptly with a request why the old man's son had been getting up by the bright light.

"If I was the boss or the boss's son either," said Bob, "I wouldn't get up till I was good and ready. I'd have my breakfast in bed if I had a mind to, an' my dinner too, an' my supper. An' I wouldn't do no work, an' I'd go to the theayter every night, and twice on Saturdays."

"I dunno why Mister Paul was down," Mike explained. "All he wanted was two o' thim Sunday papers with pictures in thim. What did he want two o' thim for I dunno. There's reading enough in one o' thim to last me a month of Sundays."

It may be surmised that Mike would have been still more in the dark as to Paul Whittier's reasons for coming downtown so early that Monday morning, if he could have seen the young man throw the copies of the *Gotham Gazette* into the first ash cart he passed after he was out of range of the porter's vision.

Paul was not the only member of Whittier, Wheatcroft & Co. to arrive at the office early that morning. Mr. Wheatcroft was usually punctual, taking his seat at his desk just as the clock struck half past nine. On that Monday morning he entered the store a little before nine.

As he walked back to the office, he looked over at the desks of the clerks as though he was seeking someone.

At the door of the office he met Bob.

"Hasn't the major come down yet?" he asked shortly.

"No sir," the boy answered. "He don't never get here till nine."

"H'm," grunted the junior partner. "When he does come, tell him I want to see him at once—at once, do you understand?"

"I ain't deaf and dumb and blind," Bob responded. "I'll steer him in to you as soon as ever he shows up."

But, for a wonder, the old bookkeeper was late that morning. Ordinarily, he was a model of exactitude. Yet the clock struck nine and, half past, and ten, before he appeared in the store.

Before he changed his coat Bob was at his side.

"Mr. Wheatcroft, he wants to see you now in a hurry," said the boy.

Major Van Zandt paled swiftly, and steadied himself by a grasp of the railing.

"Does Mr. Wheatcroft wish to see me?" he asked faintly.

"You bet he does," the boy answered, "an' in a hurry, too. He came bright and early this morning a purpose to see you, an' he's been awaiting for two hours. An' I guess he's got his mad up now."

When the old bookkeeper, with his blanched face and his faltering step, entered the private office, Mr. Wheatcroft wheeled around in his chair.

"Oh, it's you, is it?" he cried. "At last!"

"I regret that I was late this morning, Mr. Wheatcroft," Van Zandt began.

"That's no matter!" said the employer. "At least I want to talk about something else."

"About something else?" echoed the old man feebly.

"Yes," responded Mr. Wheatcroft. "Shut the door behind you, please, so that that redheaded cub out there can't hear what I am going to say; and take a chair. Yes; there is something else I've got to say to you, and I want you to be frank with me."

Whatever it was that Mr. Wheatcroft had to say to Major Van Zandt, it had to be said under the eyes of the clerks on the other side of the glass partition. And it took a long time saying, for it was evident to any observer of the two men, as they sat in the private office, that Mr. Wheatcroft was trying to force an explanation of some sort from the old bookkeeper, and that the major was resisting his employer's entreaties as best he could. Apparently the matter under discussion was of an importance as grave as to make Mr. Wheatcroft resolutely retain his self-control; and not once did he let his voice break out explosively as was his custom.

Major Van Zandt was still closeted with Mr. Wheatcroft when Mr. Whittier arrived. The senior partner stopped near the street door to speak to a clerk; and he was joined almost immediately by his son.

"Well, Paul," said the father, "have I got down here before you, after all, and in spite of your running away last night?"

"No," the son responded, "I was the first to arrive this morning—luckily."

"Luckily?" echoed his father. "I suppose that means that you have been able to accomplish your purpose—whatever it was. You didn't tell me, you know."

"I'm ready to tell you now, father," said Paul, "since I have succeeded."

Walking down the store together, they came to the private office.

As the old bookkeeper saw them, he started up, and made as if to leave the office.

"Keep your seat, major," cried Mr. Wheatcroft, sternly but not unkindly. "Keep your seat, please." Then he turned to Mr. Whittier.

"I have something to tell you both," he said, "and I want the major here while I tell you. Paul, may I trouble you to see that the door is closed so that we are out of hearing?"

"Certainly," Paul responded, as he closed the door.

"Well, Wheatcroft," Mr. Whittier said, "what is all this mystery of yours now?"

The junior partner swung around in his chair and faced Mr. Whittier.

"My mystery!" he cried. "It's the mystery that puzzled us all, and I've solved it."

"What do you mean?" asked the senior partner.

"What I mean is, that somebody has been opening that safe there in the corner, and reading our private letter-book, and finding out what we were bidding on important contracts. What I mean is, that this man has taken this information, filched from us, and sold it to our competitors, who were not too scrupulous as to be unwilling to buy stolen goods!"

"We all suspected this, as you know," the elder Whittier said. "Have you anything new now?"

"Haven't I?" returned Mr. Wheatcroft.

"I've found the man! That's all!"

"You, too?" ejaculated Paul.

"Who is he?" asked the senior partner.

"Wait a minute," Mr. Wheatcroft begged. "Don't be in a hurry, and I'll tell you. Yesterday afternoon, I don't know what possessed me, but I felt drawn downtown for some reason. I wanted to see if anything was going on down here. I knew we had made that bid, Saturday, and I wondered if anybody would try to get it on Sunday. So I came down about four o'clock, and I saw a man sneak out of the front door of this office. I followed him as swiftly as I could, and as quietly, for I didn't want to give the alarm until I knew more. The man did not see me, as he turned to go up the steps of the elevated railroad station. At the corner I saw his face."

"Did you recognize him?" asked Mr. Whittier.

"Yes," was the answer. "And he did not see me. There were tears rolling down his cheeks, perhaps that's the reason. This morning I called him in here, and he has finally confessed the whole thing."

"Who—who is it?" asked Mr. Whittier, dreading to look at the old bookkeeper, who had been in the employ of the firm for thirty years and more.

"It is Major Van Zandt!" Mr. Wheatcroft declared.

There was a moment of silence; then the voice of Paul Whittier was heard saying, "I think there is some mistake!"

"A mistake?" cried Mr. Wheatcroft. "What kind of a mistake?"

"A mistake as to the guilty man," responded Paul.

"Do you mean that the major isn't guilty!" asked Mr. Wheatcroft.

"That's what I mean," Paul returned.

"But he has confessed," Mr. Wheatcroft retorted.

"I can't help that," was the response. "He isn't the man who opened that safe yesterday afternoon at half past three, and took out the letter-book."

The old bookkeeper looked at the young man in frightened amazement.

"I have confessed it," he said piteously. "I have confessed it."

"I know you do, major," Paul declared not unkindly. "And I don't know why you do, for you were not the man."

"And if the man who confesses is not the man who did it, who is?"

"I don't know who is—although I have my suspicions," said Paul; "but I have his photograph—taken in the act!"

Chapter V

When Paul Whittier said he had photographs of the man who had been injuring the Ramapo Steel and Iron Works, showing him in the act of opening the safe, Mr. Whittier and Mr. Wheatcroft looked at each other in amazement. Major Van Zandt stared at the young man with fear and shame struggling together in his face.

Without waiting to enjoy his triumph, Paul put his hand in his pocket and took out two squares of bluish paper.

"There," he said, as he handed one to his father, "there is a blue print of the man taken in this office at ten minutes past three yesterday afternoon, just as he was about to open the safe in the corner. You see he is kneeling with his hand on the lock, but apparently just then something alarmed him, and he cast a hasty glance over his shoulder. At that second the photograph was taken, and so we have a full-face portrait of the man."

Mr. Whittier had looked at the photograph, and he now passed it to the impatient hand of the junior partner.

"You see, Mr. Wheatcroft," Paul continued, "that although the face in the photograph bears a certain family likeness to Major Van Zandt's, all the same that is not a portrait of the major. The man who was here yesterday was a young man, a man young enough to be the major's son!"

The old bookkeeper looked at the speaker.

"Mr. Paul," he began, "you won't be hard on the—" Then he paused abruptly.

"I confess I don't understand this at all!" declared Mr. Wheatcroft irascibly.

"I am afraid that I do understand it," Mr. Whittier said, with a glance of compassion at the major.

"There," Paul continued, handing his father a second azure square, "there is a photograph taken here ten minutes after the first, at 3:20 yesterday afternoon. That shows the safe open, and the young man standing before it with the private letter-book in his hand. As his head is bent over the pages of the book, the view of the face is not so good. But there can be no doubt that it is the same man. You see that, don't you, Mr. Wheatcroft?"

"I see that, of course," returned Mr. Wheatcroft forcibly. "What I don't see is why the Major here should confess if he isn't guilty!"

"I think I know the reason for that," said Mr. Whittier gently.

"There haven't been two men at our books, have there?" asked Mr. Wheatcroft. "The major and also the fellow who has been photographed?"

Mr. Whittier looked at the bookkeeper for a moment.

"Major," he said, with compassion in his voice, "you won't tell me that it was you who sold our secrets to our rivals? And you might confess it again and again, I should never believe it. I know you better. I have known you too long to believe any charge against your honesty, even if you bring it yourself. The real culprit, the man who is photographed here, is your son, isn't he? There is no use in your trying to conceal the truth now, and there is no need to attempt it, because we shall be lenient with him for your sake, major."

There was a moment's silence, broken by Mr. Wheatcroft suddenly saying, "The major's son? Why, he's dead, isn't he? He was shot in a brawl after a spree somewhere out West two or three years ago. At least that's what I understood at the time."

"It is what I wanted everybody to understand at the time," said the bookkeeper, breaking silence at last. "But it wasn't so. The boy was shot, but he wasn't killed. I hoped that it would be a warning to him, and he would make a fresh start. Friends of mine got him a place in Mexico, but luck was against him, so he wrote me, and he lost that. Then an old comrade of mine gave him another chance out in Denver, and for a while he kept straight and did his work well. Then he broke down once more and he was discharged. For six months I did not know what had become of him. I've found out since that he was a tramp for weeks, and that he walked most of the way from Colorado to New York. This fall he turned up in the city, ragged, worn out, sick. I wanted to order him away, but I couldn't. I took him back and got him decent clothes and told him to look for a place, for I knew that hard work was the only thing that would keep him out of mischief. He did not find a place, perhaps he did not look for one. But all at once I discovered that he had money. He would not tell me how he got it. I knew he could not have come by it honestly; and so I watched him. I spied after him, and at last I found that he was selling you to the Tuxedo Company."

"But how could he open the safe?" cried Mr. Wheatcroft. "You didn't know the new combination."

"I did not tell him the combination I did know," said the old bookkeeper with pathetic dignity. "And I didn't have to tell him. He can open almost any safe without knowing the combination. How he does it I don't know; it is his gift. He listens to the wheels as they turn, and he sets first one and then the other; and in ten minutes the safe is open."

"How could he get into the store?" Mr. Whittier inquired.

"He knew I had a key," responded the old bookkeeper, "and he stole it from me. He used to watch on Sunday afternoons till Mike went for a walk, and then he unlocked the store, and slipped in and opened the safe. Two weeks ago Mike came back unexpectedly, and he had just time to get out of one of the rear windows of this office."

"Yes," Paul remarked as the major paused, "Mike told me that he found a window unfastened."

"I heard you asking about it," Major Van Zandt explained, "and I knew that if you were suspicious he was sure to be caught sooner or later. So I begged him not try to injure you again. I offered him money to go away. But he refused my money; he said he could get it for himself now, and I might keep mine until he needed it. He gave me the slip yesterday afternoon. When I found he was gone I came here straight. The front door was unlocked; I walked in and found him just closing the safe here. I talked to him, and he refused to listen to me. I tried to get to him give up his idea, and he struck me. Then I left him, and I went out, seeing no one as I hurried home. That's when Mr. Wheatcroft followed me, I suppose. The boy never came back all night. I haven't seen him since, I don't know where he is, but he is my son, after all, my only son. And when Mr. Wheatcroft accused me, I confessed at last, thinking you might be easier on me than you would be on the boy."

"My poor friend!" said Mr. Whittier sympathetically, holding out his hand, which the major clasped gratefully for a moment.

"Now we know who was selling us to the Tuxedo people we can protect ourselves hereafter," declared Mr. Wheatcroft. "And in spite of your trying to humbug me into believing you guilty, major, I'm willing to let your son off easy."

"I think I can get him a place where he will be out of temptation, because he will be kept hard at work always," said Paul.

The old bookkeeper looked up as though about to thank the young man, but there seemed to be a lump in his throat which prevented him from speaking.

Suddenly Mr. Wheatcroft began explosively, "That's all very well! But what I still don't understand is how Paul got those photographs!"

Mr. Whittier looked at his son and smiled.

"That is a little mysterious, Paul," he said; "and I confess I'd like to know how you did it."

"Were you concealed here yourself?" asked Mr. Wheatcroft.

"No," Paul answered. "If you will look around this room you will see that there isn't a dark corner in which anybody could tuck himself."

"Then where was the photographer hidden?" Mr. Wheatcroft inquired with increasing curiosity.

"In the clock," responded Paul.

"In the clock?" echoed Mr. Wheatcroft, greatly amazed. "Why, there isn't room in the case of that clock for a thin midget, let alone a man."

Paul enjoyed puzzling his father's partner.

"I didn't say I had a man there, or a midget either," he explained. "I said that the photographer was in the clock—and I might have said that the clock itself was the photographer."

Mr. Wheatcroft threw up his hands in disgust.

"Well," he cried, "if you want to go on mystifying us in this absurd way, go on as long as you like! But your father and I are entitled to some consideration, I think."

"I'm not mystifying you at all; the clock took the pictures automatically. I'll show you how," Paul returned, getting up from his chair and going to the corner of the office.

Taking a key from his pocket, he opened the case of the clock and revealed a small photographic apparatus inside with the tube of the objective opposite the round glass panel in the door of the case. At the bottom of the case was a small electrical battery, and on a small shelf over this was an electromagnet.

"I begin to see how you did it," Mr. Whittier remarked. "I am not an expert in photography, Paul, and I'd like a full explanation. And make it as simple as you can."

"It's a simple thing indeed," said the son. "One day while I was wondering how we could best catch the man who was getting at the books, that clock happened to strike, and somehow it reminded me that in our photographic society at college we had once suggested that it would be amusing to attach a detective camera to a timepiece, and take snapshots every few minutes all through the day. I saw that this clock of ours faced the safe, and that it couldn't be better placed for the purpose. So when I had thought out my plan, I came over here and pretended that the clock was wrong, and in setting it right I broke off the minute hand. Then I had a man I know sent for it for repairs; he is both an electrician and an expert photographer. Together we worked out this device. Here is a small snapshot camera, loaded with a hundred and fifty films; and here is the electrical attachment which connects with the clock, so as to take a photograph every ten minutes from six in the morning to seven at night. We arranged that the magnet should turn the spool of film after every snapshot."

"Well," cried Mr. Wheatcroft, "I don't know much about these things, but I read the papers, and I suppose you mean that the clock 'pressed the button,' and the electricity pulled the string."

"That's it precisely," the young man responded. "Of course I wasn't quite sure how it would work, so I thought I would try it first on a weekday when we were all here. It did work all right, and I made several interesting discoveries. I found that Mike smoked a pipe in this office and that Bob played leapfrog in the store and stood on his head in the corner there up against the safe."

"The confounded young rascal!" interrupted Mr. Wheatcroft.

Paul smiled as he continued.

"I found also that Mr. Wheatcroft was captivated by a pretty book agent, and bought two bulky volumes he didn't want."

Mr. Wheatcroft looked sheepish for a moment.

"Oh, that's how you knew, is it?" he growled, running his hands impatiently through his shock of hair.

"That's how I knew," Paul replied. "I told you I had an eye on you. It was the lone eye of the camera. And on Sunday it kept watch for us here, winking every ten minutes. From six o'clock in the morning to three in the afternoon it winked ninety times, and all it saw was the same scene, the empty corner of the room here, with the safe in the shadow at first and at last in the full light that poured down from the glass roof over us. But a little after three a man came into the office and made ready to open the safe. At ten minutes past three the clock and the camera took his photograph—in the twinkling of an eye. At twenty minutes past three a second record was made. Before half past three the man was gone, and the camera winked every ten minutes until seven o'clock quite in vain. I came down early this morning and got the roll of negatives. One after another I developed them, disappointed that I had almost counted a hundred of them without reward. But the ninety-second and the ninety-third paid for all my trouble."

Mr. Whittier gave his son a look of pride.

"That was very ingeniously worked out, Paul; very ingeniously indeed," he said. "If it had not been for your clock here I might have found it difficult to prove that the major was innocent—especially since he declared himself guilty."

Mr. Wheatcroft rose to his feet, to close the conversation.

"I'm glad we know the truth anyhow," he asserted emphatically. And then, as though to relieve the strain on the old bookkeeper, he added, with a loud laugh at his own joke, "That clock had its hands before its face all the time—but it kept its eyes open for all that!"

"Don't forget that it had only one eye," said Whittier, joining in the laugh. "It had an eye single to its duty."

"You know the French saying, father," added Paul. "'In the realm of the blind the one-eyed man is king.'"

—From *The Long Arm and Other Detective Stories*. London: Chapman & Hall, 1895.

Index